PRAISE FOR
THE SHELL HOUSE DETECTIVES

"Emylia was born to write detective fiction."
—Veronica Henry, author of *The Impulse Purchase*

"An expertly plotted and hugely compelling murder mystery.... Crime fans are in for a treat."
—Lucy Clarke, author of *One of the Girls*

"A big-hearted page-turner with twists you won't see coming and the best pair of amateur sleuths I've read in a long time. I loved it!"
—Lucy Diamond, author of *Anything Could Happen*

"My favourite new crime series."
—Ginny Bell, author of *The Dover Café* series

"Irresistible, beautifully written, and hugely compelling....Kept me turning the pages for one more delicious chapter well into the night."
—Rosie Walsh, author of *The Man Who Didn't Call*

"Gorgeous writing and a plot crammed with suspense, this is your perfect new crime series for 2023."
—Kate Riordan, author of *The Heatwave*

"Beautifully written, gripping, and so atmospheric....One for fans of Richard Osman!"
—Emily Koch, author of *What July Knew*

THE
SHELL HOUSE
DETECTIVES

ALSO BY EMYLIA HALL

Women's Fiction

The Book of Summers
A Heart Bent Out of Shape
The Sea Between Us
The Thousand Lights Hotel

For my mum and dad

Prologue

Helena stands on the balcony, her hands gripping the cool metal railing. There's nothing but dunes between her and the sea, and on a day like today the waves in the bay are white horses. She closes her eyes and hears their thundering gallop; it's as if they're getting closer and closer – and it's only a matter of time before they run straight on over her.

Sea Dream – that's the name she's given the house. When Roland said she could pick it, she felt like a child being indulged. But the truth is he doesn't care about names – or not the poetry attached to them, anyway.

Truth. A word that delivers a sharp and precise cut, every time she thinks of it – so mostly she tries not to. But ever since they moved to Cornwall her mind has been surging and pounding, just like those relentless waves. And what's brought in on this angry tide?

Lies.

The lie she told five years ago. And the lie they've both lived ever since.

She turns away from the water and peers through the glass back into their home. A vast painting on the wall brings the only colour to the all-white, minimalist interior. *Why do you want a picture of the sea when you've got all this?* he'd said, sweeping his arm at the view. *You're never happy, that's your problem.* But there was laughter in his voice, and she enjoyed her role of princess. She commissioned the painting of just the same aspect – on a still day, though, a mill-pond day – as if to share the joke.

As a little girl she dreamt of living by the sea. For nearly a year she went to sleep with a seashell under her pillow, until one morning she woke to find it snapped clean in two. She thought it terrible luck – and a sign that her sea dream would never happen.

Yet here she is. Standing on the balcony of a house – their house, and that was only possible because of Roland – that sticks out among the dunes like a beacon, all gleaming glass and chrome and brickwork. Sea Dream makes the few scattered wooden beach houses around it look like broken-down shacks. It's a luxurious haven with a blue horizon, and at night the island lighthouse winks in her direction. Storybook stuff, and she's the heroine.

People would kill for your life, Helena, she tells herself. As if that's any kind of a comfort.

She turns, hearing Roland in the house behind her. He's on the phone, his feet pacing the newly laid boards as he speaks to his brother. *Oh God, not a visit.* Her stomach clenches at the thought. She quickly turns back to face the ocean and fills her lungs with crystalline air. A pair of seagulls fly screaming overhead.

She's got everything she's ever wanted. She can't ruin it now.

But the fear swirling inside Helena says something different – and ever since they moved to Sea Dream, it's been building and building. At what point will she break? Maybe when that raging tide finally gallops all the way in. She wonders if she'll prove herself to be a match for it. Or if, instead, it'll sweep her away entirely. As if she were nothing. As if she'd never been here at all.

1

Ally has always loved the beach at night. The sea seems louder, its pull stronger, and on a clear evening like this the sky is loaded with stars. A giant moon has drawn the spring tide all the way out, and the sand is a vast and silvered mirror. As Fox darts across it, quick as a fish, his brush tail waves for joy.

She can't help but feel alive in these moments.

Up ahead, Ally can see the light of home – a warm glow in the dunes – and she heads towards it. The path she takes through the marram grass is one she's followed for nearly forty years.

Once inside The Shell House, she'll do the things that have become her habit: pour a glass of crisp white wine or make up some tea with garden mint. Then she'll sink on to the sofa with a book, Fox stretched out across her feet. It's then that the absence of Bill will settle around her, and she'll sit with it – because what else is there to do?

They've become gentle things, these nights. A little empty, perhaps, but not unhappy. She couldn't be called unhappy.

Ally climbs the three wooden steps to the door. Once she's opened up, Fox skitters ahead, his paws leaving a delicate trail of saltwater prints on the white-painted boards. She shrugs off her old wax jacket and hangs it on the peg, then unlaces her hiking boots, her back creaking as she bends. Next, she goes to the fridge. It's definitely a wine night tonight. She'd hoped the walk would clear her head, but it hasn't really worked.

You're never alone by the sea, Ally tells herself as she pours a glass. And it's true, the ocean is energy and company in a way that other landscapes can't match. But her daughter, Evie, over on the other side of the world, doesn't see it that way. And earlier today, on the phone, she made her point more forcefully than ever before.

'It's time to decide, Mum.' Then she lowered her voice – a little theatrically, Ally thought – and said, 'Scott reckons we could be letting it as an Airbnb, but I'd rather you were in there.'

Granny flat. It was Evie's husband, Scott, never the most tactful, who first called it that. While Ally can't argue with the name – and with grandsons like hers, why would she want to? – it suggests a diminishment that she isn't quite ready to accept: tacking what's left of her own life on to somebody else's. Besides, she's only sixty-four.

'It's been a year now,' her daughter went on. Then, 'You think it's what Dad would have wanted? You all on your own?'

While the concern was real enough, Ally knows it's also partly about control: as she gets older, no matter what comes her way, Ally has less chance of suddenly derailing her daughter's carefully ordered life if she's under Evie's watchful gaze in the Sydney suburbs. And there have been enough hints about childcare too. The proposal was born out of love, but it also has practical benefits for Evie.

'But I'm not on my own,' Ally said.

At that, Fox lifted his pointed little nose – just as if he knew. Bill had brought him home as a puppy nearly a decade ago, curled in the pocket of his coat; a fire-red, wire-haired mongrel. He was a thank-you from an elderly man who had a farm out on the cliff road. Ally can't even remember why now. Seeing off vandals? Not doling out a speeding ticket?

'Plus, I'm busy with my art,' she added, though the truth is she's hardly done a thing with it in the last twelve months. But she knew her daughter wouldn't be able to help herself, and sure enough there it came: a noise that fell between despair and derision. *Why don't you do some pretty seascapes instead?* Evie has said often enough. *Or painted pebbles? Tourists love that stuff.* Ally's giant collages, made of plastics litter-picked from the shore, have never made sense to her daughter.

'I don't want to put the pressure on,' Evie went on, her voice switching notes to one Ally imagined her using in the boardroom, 'but I think we need to know your plans, Mum. Otherwise, you know, we could be getting the rental bookings in. How about you take a week to decide once and for all?'

Ally murmured assent.

Then, in a softer voice, one that – had they been together – would probably have been accompanied by a well-intentioned squeeze of the arm: 'I just don't think there's anything left for you in Porthpella, Mum.'

They ended the call soon after. And Ally stayed sitting, turning her phone in her hand.

What if Evie was right?

It's a pocket paradise, Porthpella, a place of golden sands and turquoise sea and candy-coloured wooden houses popping up from the dunes. Come summer it's ablaze with parasols and beach mats, the scents of coconut surf wax and sizzling sausages filling the salty air, but now, in early springtime, it belongs mostly to the locals and a handful of day trippers. It has always been Ally's favourite time of year, the calm before the Easter holidaymaker storm, with new-washed skies and white-tipped waves and carpets of flowers on the clifftops. But this year is different; instead of a sense of anticipation, the days ahead feel emptier than the beach at low tide.

It was Bill who was stitched into the fabric of the community, not Ally. When he retired from the force, the house was full of cards, boxes of chocolates, and personalised beer mugs; even an expensive-looking putter, though Bill was never one for golf. At least he died knowing how important he was to people round here. It isn't like that for Ally; it never has been. She's always kept herself to herself. Perhaps when someone does that for long enough, people stop asking anything of them. Which is probably what they want, isn't it?

On that thought, she makes for bed.

The sea is loudest in the bedroom, and it has always surprised Ally how, after all these years, she's never stopped noticing the sound of it. Perhaps it's because the sea is never the same: sometimes it's a faraway murmur, like holding a conch to her ear; other times it's a thrashing and crashing that shakes everything in its path – nature's version of stadium rock.

It's probably, too, because the bedroom is the quietest room. Here, there's no burble of the radio, no sounds of cooking or washing, just the Atlantic pounding the shore, a few metres beyond the white-painted wooden walls.

Tonight, despite it being low tide, Ally can hear the ocean's roar, and she's pretty sure it's got something to do with the conversation with her daughter: as if everything around her is reasserting itself to remind her just where she is and – by definition – where she is not.

She goes over to draw the curtains. She and Bill used to sleep with the window open whatever the weather – flung wide in summer, just ajar in winter – but these days she always shuts it fast. It's one of those numerous small adjustments she's made since his death. What is it, a precaution? Or maybe it's just because she doesn't feel very expansive: the outside world isn't invited into The Shell House.

Out to sea, the island lighthouse is shining as usual; the moon is high and Ally stands taking it in for just a second – the perfect button of it; the metallic light it casts over the water – before snapping the curtains shut.

She undresses methodically then climbs into bed and reaches for the lamp. It's gone ten o'clock and she's tired tonight. She's just clicked the light off when she hears a short, sharp bark from the living room.

'Shh, Fox,' she murmurs.

He barks again. A volley this time.

'Foxy, what is it?'

She switches the light back on and swings her legs from the bed. It'll be nothing. Just the sight of a mouse zipping across the boards. Or something outside – a car looking for a place to turn on the bumpy track, or late-arriving tourists hunting for their weekend cottage. Fox seems more skittish these days, as if he feels the house is out of balance.

She opens her bedroom door and stops dead. From here she can see across the sitting room to the front door, where the frosted pane perfectly frames a silhouetted figure. There's a head and shoulders – but no accompanying knock.

Now that Ally's there too, Fox sits neatly; almost expectantly.

Who goes to a door and then just stands there? She casts around for something, then feels ridiculous – just what exactly is she looking for, a rolling pin or a baseball bat? For goodness' sake. Instead, she turns the overhead light on, and the sudden illumination temporarily blinds her. She squints.

The figure in the doorway shifts. Fades. Then crowds the pane.

There's a loud knocking.

Fox barks again, his tail whacking the floor in excitement.

'Who is it?' she says, stepping closer, her voice higher than she'd like.

'I need help.'

It's a man's voice, one that's young, and rough at the edges. And cut with a desperation that speaks to something deep inside of Ally.

'Do you need me to call the police?' she says.

'It's Sergeant Bright I'm looking for. It's him I need.'

She takes a breath. There isn't anybody who doesn't know what happened to Bill, not in a place as small as this.

'He's not here,' she says.

'When's he back?'

At her feet, Fox gives a small whine. Her hand goes to the neck of her nightdress.

'He can't help,' she says, 'I'm sorry. Let me phone—'

'But he said he would. He promised. He said to come if I ever . . .'

And it's the emotion in his voice that gets her: that word – *promised* – is bursting with it. She feels a burning in her throat, as if in reply. Her hand reaches for the door – then she stops. If Bill were here, he'd have opened up straight away. Nothing to do with his job; just because it was what you did.

Ally reaches again for the catch. She can hear her daughter's voice, taut with disapproval: *You did what?* She hesitates, then unlocks the door.

The figure's already turning away as she opens up. He spins back around, and his arms flail as if he's drowning.

She takes him in. Dirty white trainers, grey jogging bottoms that are baggy at the knee, a too-big hoody, and a knitted hat pulled low. A young man; hardly more than a boy, really.

Ally's heart thunders in her chest. His eyes fix on hers and need leaches from them. This man, this boy, a random piece of salvage, brought in on the tide.

'I'll wait for Bill to come,' he says.

8

2

Bill. Not Sergeant Bright this time, but Bill. Ally thinks of the kickboxing club her husband set up a couple of years ago, where a stream of unlikely lads flowed into the community centre on a Thursday night: kick, punch, kick, punch – an artful dance that had some of the stiffer villagers tutting, *Isn't it just encouraging them?* Bill turned up to watch every week without fail, while Kaz, the burly coach from Penzance, put them through their paces. Could he be one of those boys?

Ally realises her arms are folded tightly around her body.

'How do you know Bill?'

'He said she died,' he says, his voice shaking. 'But that's not true, because they'd have told me. They'd have had to.'

She can't follow. 'What – Bill said that?'

'No, that man. About Nan.'

Something about the way he says it: *Nan.* The tenderness. She was right to open the door.

'I lost my phone, didn't I? But a thing like that, they find a way to tell you. Even if you've got out. Don't they? He's lying, that man. And he's sitting there . . . where her house is. This massive posh house where Nan's is. *Was.*' He smacks his hand to his head, in a gesture of desperation. Two bright pink spots of colour have appeared on his pallid cheeks. 'I don't . . . it's not . . .'

None of it makes sense to Ally. But he doesn't look drunk. Bill would have been able to tell if he'd taken something, and probably made a decent guess at what it was, but what does she know? The young man looks so pained she can feel the weight of it in the middle of her chest. He needs someone, that much is clear. But doesn't he know that she's not that someone?

'It was like I was dreaming. Turning up. Where's the gate? Where's the fence? Nothing. Gone. Just this massive block. All glass. Then he comes out, tells me to . . . clear off. Your nan sold up then died, he said. Sold then died! As if.'

He's treading the boards of the decking, trainers clumping; up and down, up and down.

'Let me phone the police for you . . .' she begins.

'Hunter. Roland Hunter. That's the name for Bill. I didn't touch him. But he got right up in my face. I wasn't going to take that, was I? Sergeant Bright will know what to do. Won't he? Please. He said to come if I needed anything.'

Ally suddenly feels extraordinarily tired.

'Bill died,' she says. 'A year ago. He's not here anymore.'

He stops; stares at her, aghast. Then tucks his arms around himself, squats like a mollusc. He looks like a little boy in that moment.

'But he promised.'

Ally gives a low laugh; she thinks she probably sounds as disturbed as him. 'Even so.'

He blinks back at her.

'How did you know my husband?'

'He put me away. Eighteen months in Dartmoor.' He rubs at his nose with the back of his hand. 'I've just got out. And it's . . . all this. This . . . *madness*.'

The sea roars, upping its tenor. A cold breeze drives in, and Ally's nightdress flaps at her knees. She shivers.

Getting to his feet, he peers past her into the house, and she sees it through his eyes. The wicker sofa with her sea-blue cushions. Shelves lined with beach finds: the shark teeth, the jars full of sea glass, the perfect starfish. One of her pictures, a blaze of colour, on the far wall. Then he looks directly at her, his eyes full of appeal.

Have you got somewhere to go? That's the question Bill would have asked.

But instead she says, 'I'm sorry but I'd like you to leave now. It's the police you need to talk to. If you want me to ring them I will, but I—'

He mutters something that she can't catch. Then abruptly turns and starts off down the path.

'What's your name?' she calls after him.

But he doesn't answer. The gate bangs on its hinges – then he's gone.

3

Jayden sits in his car, staring straight ahead, watching the early morning waves come rolling in. It's impossible to tell at this distance what size they are, but by the look of the few vehicles in the clifftop car park – an old camper van, a couple of stickered-up Transporters – other people have had the same idea: it's on.

That's what Cat's cousin would say: *on*.

Pumping.

Surf's up, dude.

Something like that anyway; Jayden hasn't learnt to speak Surfer yet.

He reaches for his thermos and twists the lid; a cup of tea before he gets out there. Though that's probably breaking all kinds of rules: Waves before Brews – not a sticker he's seen anywhere, but still. Even a geriatric rambler would probably get a mile or two under their belt before they cracked open the thermos. The sea, though, is *ice*: springtime might have come to Cornwall, but the water temperature is stuck in winter. Jayden knows he's going to need all the warming-up he can get.

He's about to pour when his attention is caught by a movement on the coast path. It's a jogger – though more of a runner, the pace they're going at. As the figure flashes past he sees it's a woman. He's too far away to see her face but there's something about the way she's moving – elbows out, head dipped – that almost makes her seem as if she's running away from something, rather than just running: that's the thought that immediately flits into his head. He scans behind her, but the cliffs, the dunes, are empty. When he looks again, she's gone.

It's muscle memory, that's all; he's been trained to anticipate peril. Seeing it unnecessarily, though? Yeah, he's pretty sure his counsellor back in Leeds would have something to say about that.

Jayden pours his tea and settles back in his seat. The waves keep on coming. He watches a handful of people out on the water. He sees one catch something and perform a zigzagging dance that ends in a disappearing act.

He takes a sip of tea.

Not even eight o'clock in the morning. What is he doing?

This was Cat's back garden once. And if she wasn't eight months pregnant, no doubt she'd be the one dusting off this old surfboard of hers that they salvaged from her dad's barn. And she wouldn't be stalling with a plastic-tasting cup of Assam; she'd be out there, bossing those waves. He's never seen his wife surf, but he imagines her doing it with effortless brilliance, just like she does everything else.

The thought of falling short is what gets Jayden up and out, hefting the board from the roof and pulling on the borrowed wet-suit that's too big in the shoulders. Cat likes the idea of him surfing – and he likes that she likes it. It fits with her picture of the kind of family they'll now that they're in Cornwall; one where he works regular hours, stays away from bad news and, above all, is there for their child.

Not like Kieran.

Kieran, who's always at the edge of his thoughts, ready to press in. And who will never be there for anyone again. Two small girls growing up without their dad, and a wife who Jayden still doesn't have the words for when she texts.

He kicks the door shut; tucks the board under his arm.

After what happened, after the gentle-voiced people in quiet rooms, after the long stretch at home doing nothing, Cat had wanted him to get out of the police altogether.

Leave it to other people to make the world a better place, Jay. Because you know it could have been you. Then where would we be? And her hand went to her bump – unconsciously, probably, but he hated the thought of it. How fragile life was; how easily snapped out.

Could have been him? Should have been him. Because why not?

But as his mum said last week, he's got different responsibilities now – and anyway, if he changed his mind, didn't Cornwall need police officers too? He didn't have the heart to tell her that when he handed in his badge, it was for good – though *good* feels nothing like the right word. Plus, his wife has other ideas for them. Cat's been working on her dad, persuading him to turn those far fields into some kind of upmarket camping outfit. Yurts and firepits. It isn't exactly what he imagined himself doing after all those years of training – not even thirty yet and already out to pasture – but she's excited about it. And he likes seeing Cat excited. He just doesn't have the backbone to tell her it's more her dream than his.

With neither heart nor spine, what does that make him then? He's into ocean-creature territory, surely; the deep holds all kinds of creepy things that defy the logic of existence. Two days ago, he almost trod on a totally transparent jellyfish washed up on the sand; it was dead, as far as he could see, though he tried sloshing sea water over it to stir it back to life.

Jayden starts heading down to the beach, cutting over the dunes. Further along, there are the colourful beach houses that remind him a bit of where they used to go in Trinidad when he was a kid. Those sun-soaked holiday memories: his silver-haired great-grandfather rocking in his chair on the veranda, bursting into spontaneous laughter just as some people burst into song; his grandmother taking over the kitchen, serving up her legendary macaroni pie; the garden hammock Jayden used to swing in, gobbling up all his holiday reading way too soon. His dad, kicking back with a bottle of Carib, saying, *Couldn't we all just move here? Maracas has definitely got the edge on Whitby*, despite the fact his dad's white skin turned red with sunburn and he gave the mosquitoes a full-course dinner every night.

He and Cat will have to take the baby there when she comes along. Get some sunshine in her – and show her what beaches can really be.

Though he has to admit, when the light is right, Porthpella has it going on. In some ways, anyway. With just one pub, one shop and a chippie in the village centre, it isn't exactly what he's used to. But compared to where they are out at Upper Hendra, Cat's family farm, Porthpella is a thriving metropolis. *Don't forget the gallery tea room too*, his mum-in-law said, *they do a decent cheese scone in there, Jayden. Not too salty.*

The sea is bone-shakingly cold, despite the wetsuit. The surfers he saw from the car park are scattered far out in deep water, which is all good with Jayden. He wants his own space to get it wrong in – a whole lot closer to shore. He settles himself on the board and paddles, which is the one part he's actually alright at. There's something satisfying about self-propulsion, feeling his muscles working. He's hardly been in any time – five minutes max – when a tall-as-a-house wave comes out of nowhere and smacks him right on the side of the head. How his face then hits the board he doesn't know: logic doesn't seem to apply on a breaking wave. The burn goes all the way to the back of his throat, his eyes sting, and there's blood in the water as if there's been a shark attack. As he bursts back through the surface, he makes a sound like a strangled seabird. Eventually, he stumbles through the shallows, his hand pressed to his gushing nose as he casts round for the board. He snatches at the frayed end of the leash that's still attached to his ankle.

Cat's board has gone.

Jayden sinks down into the sand, feeling like a kid who's just had his lunch money taken by the school bully. Meanwhile the waves keep rolling on in. He wipes his bloody hands in the sand.

It's moments like this when he calls the whole thing into question. Him, a Leeds boy, a city boy, adrift in the back of beyond – a very white back of beyond, at that. What's he even doing? Catastrophising, Cat calls it. He can hear her now: *You get knocked off your surfboard one time and you want to call the whole thing off?*

He hears a shout from behind and, at first, he thinks it's some-one taking a pop. He readies himself to laugh it off. No one should try to learn to surf without a sense of humour, should they?

'Hey, help!'

He springs to his feet. Sees a figure further down the beach, by the cliffs. Arms waving.

Another yell: 'Get help!'

At that, Jayden starts to run. He doesn't even think about it. And that's something he'll definitely come back to later: *He doesn't even think about it.*

4

It's one of those early mornings when the combination of sea and sky, no matter how many times she's seen it before, strikes Ally as implausibly blue. She has to stop and breathe it in; observe a moment's gratitude. Sometimes it feels like it's this place keeping her going – the air her only sustenance, the tide the only movement she can bear to be around.

You know, we've got a beach or two in Sydney, Mum, her daughter said when she first suggested – and Ally protested – the move. *You're acting like you'd be locked up inland or something.*

Ally cuts over the dunes, Fox trotting beside her, his nose high in the air. Sunlight catches the white tops of the waves and she heads towards them. Just as she steps down into the sand, a faint sound catches her ears: the far-off bleat of sirens. It isn't exactly common in Porthpella. She immediately thinks of her night-time visitor, and the fact that, afterwards, she didn't call the police. Should she have?

The events of the night are still turning in her mind as she moves on down the beach, walking as she always does, eyes on the strandline. Miles can pass easily, every step measured out in everyday treasures: drapes of oarweed, the denim blue of mussels, the pearlescent shimmer of top shells. And, more often than not, a litter-picker in the hand for the trash. *This is your beat*, Bill used to say, gently teasing her. *You patrol that strandline like nobody else.*

It's past eight o'clock, later than when she normally goes out, but last night took something from her that she still hasn't quite got back. She lay in bed after the young man had gone, her body thrumming with adrenalin, thoughts racing, his visit twining in her mind with Evie's entreaties: it was the small hours before she finally fell into an uneasy sleep.

Bill had promised he'd help him. Whoever *he* was.

She thinks of Bill all the time, but now, a year on, her thoughts are mostly – *mostly* – peaceful. It seems like every day the tide brings in a new memory and she stoops to pluck it from the wet sand; she keeps hold of these glinting treasures – feels lucky to have them at all. A dozen times a day she thinks of things she wants to say to him, but they're mostly the minutiae of a life shared; rarely does a question come along where Ally *needs* an answer from Bill. But last night the fact that she couldn't talk to him sucked the breath from her, and made her miss his warm bulk beside her in a way that she didn't know what to do with.

The visitor has shaken everything up.

So, she does what she's always done – come rain or shine, she combs the shore. It has always calmed her: the concentration, the sense of possibility, the world within a world. The riches she finds would be trampled by others, most people seeing nothing special in a pristine variegated scallop, or the bobble-like seeds she gathers. But Ally knows better. Her garden blooms with tropical flowers, carried over the sea from faraway places, the seed cases miraculously surviving the lashing to sprout through on Cornish soil. And every so often she comes across something a little extraordinary: a Bristol blue glass bottle, nicked and chipped but intact; the tiny stone kitten, one ear missing, that Evie kept on her bedside table for years; blunted triangles of willow-pattern pottery.

They've always called it wrecking, not beachcombing, down here. Maybe because when a storm brings the wreck of a ship in, there are rich pickings to be had. Once, further along the coast, a container ship went down and motorcycles and washing machines were brought in on the tide; people stumbled through the shallows, carrying them off – a rightful claiming, they said, because once something is lost to the sea it's anybody's for the taking.

The art Ally's made as long as she's been in Cornwall is almost entirely created from what she finds along the shore – specifically, the things that shouldn't be there. It started as litter-picking: untangling ribbons of plastic from driftwood, gathering Smarties lids and broken flip-flop straps and pop bottles. Man-made detritus washing in from who knows where and who knows when. Of course, she collects the obviously beautiful things too – the Venus shells and smooth-as-toffee sea glass – but it's the plastics that become her pictures. What she can't use, she bags and sends to be properly disposed of, but the vivid finds, the unusual shapes and rainbow colours, she sorts and keeps, slowly building vast and delicate collages of landscapes. From a distance, her pictures show beauty spots and coastal views, but if you look closer, you can see that every piece is plastic. Maybe not the kind of thing most of the galleries around here want, but that has never mattered to her; she's never looked for outside approval.

In their early days in Porthpella, the long beach walks she took with Evie at her chest lifted her up, when so much was pulling her down. Baby Blues was the only name for it back then, and even that was spoken in a whisper – and with a look that said, *Do you have to make such a fuss though?* The beachcombing, the sketches in her journal, the litter-picking; these were the ways she coaxed herself back by increments. Bill was her rock and her daughter the star in her sky, but it was the sea that saved her.

All the way back then – and now.

Ally breathes deeply – in and out, in and out – steady as the tide. She feels the sand beneath her feet, the pull of the ocean to her right. She follows the trail. When it comes to treasures, the sea shows what it wants to show: no more, no less. She can never force a find, but by the act of looking, it's possible to discover a kind of peace.

She walks on, eyes down, and as soon as the object reveals itself, it's as if it was specifically waiting for her. As if to say, *Life has changed now, you'd better move with it.*

It's not quite on the strandline, rather a few feet up. It's the flash of pastel pink in the sand that catches her eye, then the glint of metal. It's caught in a tangle of seaweed that's strayed higher up the beach: bladder wrack, the rubbery children's favourite, the one they gather and hurl at one another. She hurries towards it, as if it might disappear, snatched by a long-tongued wave or an eager gull. She bends down and carefully extracts the object. It's a watch, and an expensive one at that. Its face is cracked but it ticks on. She turns it over and squints at the engraving: *Roland & Helena. 17/09/2018.*

Ally only sees the blue lights as she's further down the beach, with the watch safe in the pocket of her jacket. It's an ambulance, and from the looks of it, it's parked on the very tip of the cliff. She can see a handful of people gathered beneath the overhang. As she moves closer, she sees a police officer, although she can't recognise him at this distance. She probably wouldn't even recognise him up close, for she was never one of the 'wives' in that way, and there's no one pounding the streets of Porthpella anymore. She takes in the green coats of paramedics, the hefting of a gurney.

She goes cold. *God, no.*

Twenty years ago – or about that – Bill came home one night and took her in his arms and held her so long and hard she felt all of his sorrow passing into her. She knew without asking, then, that someone had died. At this same cliff.

A young dad, Bill said. *Paul Pascoe. Couldn't see how he could go on, his note said.*

Now, Ally's chest fills with dread; her heart beats fast as a bird's. She walks towards the scene as if she's pulled by something. With every step, her mind sorts through the fragments of the night before, the things the visitor said – the big glass house where his nan's had been.

It couldn't be. Could it?

She sees a small gathering of wetsuited surfers, and Fox pelts on without trepidation. The officer is nodding, writing in a notebook, while the sound of his radio carries on the breeze. They start to disperse just before she gets there, the gurney carried up the cliff path. The officer looks up as she approaches. He waves at her – too jauntily, Ally thinks. He's young, pink-cheeked, round as an apple.

'Morning. It's Mrs Bright, isn't it?'

Perhaps he saw her at Bill's funeral; the church was packed, standing room only, and at one point she felt like she couldn't breathe at all. In as level a voice as she can muster, Ally asks what's happened.

'Young bloke. Attempted suicide, by the looks. Still breathing – just. Bloody miracle. Don't s'pose you saw anything, did you?'

'No, I . . . I heard the ambulance just as we were setting out. My dog and I.' She gestures to Fox, who's currently getting his head petted by one of the surfers. She hesitates. She doesn't want to ask the next question, but she has to. 'Who is it, do you know?'

'He's carrying a wallet but there's not much in it.'

'Is there a name?'

The officer doesn't detect the urgency in her voice. Or, if he does, maybe he squares it away as no more than that of a concerned citizen.

21

'Lewis Pascoe.'

And there's no extra weight as he says the name. Probably because this constable is too young to understand the connection; twenty years ago, he'd have been in nappies.

He goes on. 'Touch and go, the boys said there. They've taken him to Truro.' His phone rings then, and he nods to her; wanders up the beach to take the call.

Ally watches him go. He trudges heavily in the sand, nudges at a rock with the toe of his boot, before making his way up the rough-cut stone steps.

Lewis Pascoe.

She feels someone watching her. She turns to see a young man in a red and grey wetsuit, with brown skin and close-shaven black hair. The concern in his face makes her eyes fill. She exhales in one ragged breath.

5

'You okay?' Jayden asks Ally.

He heard the way she asked the question about the man's identity, and he saw the stricken look on her face as it was answered too. There was something there. Not that the PC twigged.

The arrival of this woman has given Jayden something to focus on – and he's glad of it. Because he looked so dead, the young man, with his body heaped, and blood clotted in the sand. Blood that Jayden could hardly look at. The surfer who found him at the foot of the cliffs was shocked initially but Jayden got the feeling it'd be an anecdote for his mates later; he saw him sauntering back towards the water, once he'd answered the few questions from the police.

As Jayden faced his own questions – *It's just from a nosebleed . . . No, I didn't get in a fight . . . No, I've never seen him in my life* – it felt like a good job that the other guy, the sort-of-nonchalant body-finder, had vouched for him. And he felt a small flare go off inside of him.

Now Jayden's head spins; he feels dizzy suddenly. The woman's little red dog is still twining round his legs, and he reaches down to pat him. The action roots him.

He asks again: 'Are you okay?'

She starts. Blinks. Her short grey hair is blown across her face. She wears a kind of fisherman's blue tunic, jeans and old hiking boots. She's older than his mum, younger than his nan. She looks at him first distractedly, then questioningly.

He puts his hand to his face. 'Surfboard,' he says. 'We had a disagreement; the board made its point with a bit more, er, force.'

'Did you . . . see anything?' she asks.

Jayden jerks his head. The cliff rises up behind them, twenty-five feet or more of sheer rock. You'd think it'd be the end, if you stepped off there. It still might be, for the kid. How bad did it have to be, to do a thing like that?

They moved fast, the medics. And Jayden made himself stay in the moment – the sand beneath his feet, the gulls drifting overhead, the feel of his wetsuit against his skin – but he was pulled back to that night in Leeds anyway: to the flashing lights, the radio crackling, him saying his friend's name over and over and over; to everything he'd tried to do and failed at anyway.

He feels the dizziness threaten again and makes himself focus back on the woman.

'I didn't see anything,' he says. 'The guy who found him thought . . . well, he thought he was dead. No idea how long he's been unconscious. Did you . . . you know him, do you?'

She widens her eyes. They're sea green, and Jayden sees something in them that he can't quite read.

'Because, if you wanted to go to the hospital, I could drive you?' he offers.

'What? No. No, I don't know him.'

She clicks for her dog. The dog responds by licking Jayden's hand. The raspy little tongue is centring, and he breathes slowly.

'Sorry, I just thought you did. When they said his name.'

And as he says it, the persistence takes him aback. What business is it of his? Any of it?

'I briefly met him yesterday,' she says carefully, and this time her voice has an obvious tremor in it.

24

'But you didn't mention that to the police just now?'

What is this, Jayden, an interview?

She gives a brief shake of her head, and he feels a spark of intrigue.

'Someone wants to do a thing like that, you can't stop them,' he says, carefully.

He knows it's just one of the things that people say when finding words is too difficult. And he's not even sure he means it, because there are plenty of stories where people are stopped. The commuter on the Tube platform, the passer-by on the bridge; sometimes all it takes is for someone to interrupt the runaway train of thought.

She shakes her head again. 'No. But . . .'

The woman looks completely stranded, he thinks, standing there. And Jayden knows there's more to this than she's saying – and he realises that he wants to know what. Maybe because he's still reeling from the shock of it and he doesn't want to be alone. Maybe because he doesn't want to walk straight back in and say to Cat, *So yeah, your board . . .* Maybe because he wants one thing down here in Porthpella that feels like it's his. Whatever it is, it suddenly feels like his job to find out what's going on with this woman.

He can see that she's trying to collect herself, to seem okay for the sake of other people – and he knows that move so well; the effort it takes.

'I need a drink,' he says. 'The hard stuff. I've only got tea in the car. Coffee? There's that place just down from the car park.'

Her eyes still look faraway, so he goes on.

'It's a shock. And it's good not to be alone. I'm Jayden by the way. Jayden Weston. You're Mrs Bright, right?'

He overheard her telling the PC, but she doesn't look surprised that he might know her name. He figures her for a local, on this run of coast where everyone knows everyone.

'Ally, yes. And okay, yes. Coffee.' She gives the smallest smile. 'Thank you.'

'And this guy?' He nods to the dog, who's now busying himself with Jayden's bare toes.

'That's Fox.' She looks down, says, 'He seems to have taken to you. That's not his usual style.'

As they walk away together, Jayden forgets to glance at the shoreline, in case Cat's board has washed in. All he can think of is the question he's now determined to find the answer to: what has Ally Bright got to do with the man who jumped?

6

Saffron traces a cresting wave in the microfoam of the flat white she's just made herself. She's still working on it: from the wrong angle it can look like somebody's ear, and that isn't very appetising. Not that most people notice. Hang Ten is a takeaway place a lot of the time, her creations hidden under lids. It's only on rainy days, when people push inside to the dinky interior and mist up the windows, that the cups and saucers come out.

She takes her coffee and looks out on to the beach. The flurry of activity on the clifftop has passed — what was the ambulance for, an early hiker with a twisted ankle? — and it's back to watching breaking waves and the dots of surfers out on the water; the purposeful strides of dog walkers. At Hang Ten it's too early yet for the post-school drop-off crew — Fridays are always popular with them — but a windblown mum came in just now, and something inside of Saffron twanged as she saw the babe's rounded cheeks, their whorl of hair.

Is this broodiness? She's twenty-three, way too young for all that.

She's snapped out of it by the appearance of the police officer shouldering his way in. PC Tim Mullins, who she knows from school; she can picture him now in Mrs Oswald's pottery class, sitting at the back, laughing like a drain and flicking clay balls.

She never would have had Mullins down as a future upholder of the peace.

'We've had a jumper, Saff,' he says, with way too much relish. 'Kid called Lewis Pascoe. You see anything?'

Saffron's hand goes to her mouth. 'Oh no, really? Someone jumped?'

Lewis Pascoe. The name rings a bell, and how she wishes it didn't.

'He botched it, mind. He's on his way to Truro, to the ICU – if he's lucky.'

Pascoe. The penny drops. It's his nan she knows, not Lewis himself. And not really his nan either, because to say that old Mrs Pascoe – Maggie – kept herself to herself would be an understatement. Saffron couldn't blame her, because the story goes that her son – Paul, was it? Paul Pascoe? – was in and out of trouble for as long as anyone round here could remember (which was way back, because people in this community are elephants, apparently). Then one day he went and stepped off the cliff and ended his life. Poor Maggie never recovered from it, and people said that she never stopped looking to blame someone for it, either. Mostly it was the police who got it from her. She said it'd been harassment, plain and simple: that Paul was driven to it, because no one round here believed in second chances, and the police were always on his back about this, that and the other. And Saffron sees where Maggie was coming from. People seemed to forget that someone like Paul Pascoe had once been a little darling, just like the one strapped to that mum's chest just now, and old Mrs Pascoe had been a doting young mother, holding nothing but possibility and love and hope in her arms.

Hippy-Dippy, that's what Mullins called her at school. Because she laced her hair with tiny plaits and had a beaded anklet. Because, from time to time, she liked a smoke – and who didn't, on a summer's night with a sky full of stars and the crackle of a fire and the sea pounding like a bass note. And she used words like *love* and *hope* in everyday conversation. Hippy-Dippy, obviously.

'Nice big white coffee, cheers, Saff.'

Ah, that's why he's really come. And of course, he'll expect it for free: on account of the uniform, apparently.

She sets the machine going.

Poor Lewis Pascoe. So he's out of prison, then. It was Maggie who told her about that, in a rare moment where she opened up, as if for a minute she'd forgotten herself, the words spilling out: *He's a good boy, Lewis. He was only with me a couple of weeks when the police were on his case, see.* Saffron can just picture her as she said it, in her scuffed leather shoes and shapeless skirt and the kind of saggy knitted hat that even Broady would struggle to pull off. (Broady being the finest beanie-wearer and wave-catcher – and, if she were putting all her cards on the table, owner of the finest six-pack – she knows.)

I've told him I'll have nothing to do with him until he's back out, Maggie said. *It's the only way I can go through this again.* She used to come in for a cup of tea from time to time, and when she did Saffron always gave her a little something extra – a fresh-baked almond biscuit, or a wedge of flapjack. Nothing really, a small gesture like that, but when someone like old Mrs Pascoe, practically a recluse, chose Hang Ten, it felt like an honour. And for Maggie it was probably an unlikely spot in every way, with the reggae soundtrack and the Hawaii posters and skate decks on the walls – except for Saffron's smile, which she hopes welcomes everybody. When she heard a few months ago that old Mrs Pascoe had sold up and moved away, Saffron felt a little hurt that she hadn't popped in to say goodbye.

'What happened?' she says now. But it doesn't feel right, Lewis's last moments being narrated by Mullins, and she immediately regrets the question.

'Bugger knows.'

'I did see a young guy this morning,' she says, 'just as I was heading down here.'

'Was it Pascoe?'

'I don't know. He was . . . early twenties? Maybe. If that. Grey tracksuit.' She wrinkles her nose. 'I think it was grey.'

'Bingo. That's got to be Pascoe. Buzz cut?'

'Yeah. He was by that new place, down in the dunes.'

He'd looked kind of lost; standing at the side of the path as she cycled past, his shoulders hunched like he was a craggy sort of seabird.

'It was early,' she says, passing Mullins his coffee. 'Before seven.'

'Good job it wasn't attempted murder,' he says, raising it in a *cheers!* gesture, grinning, 'because you'd be the prime suspect. Last to see him!'

Saffron ignores him, and instead says, 'What was he even doing out here, now that his nan's moved?'

'Moved? Moved to the big house in the sky, more like. He's got no next of kin, has Lewis.'

Then he taps his walkie-talkie at his shoulder – the walkie-talkie that's displayed in a way that Saffron can't help thinking is way too showy.

'Before I came in here, I got intel that he's fresh out of Dartmoor prison,' he says grandly. 'Probably couldn't adjust, could he?'

He takes a slurp. Smacks his lips.

It isn't that Saffron doesn't believe that people can change. But Mullins was a lunk at school and he's pretty much a lunk now. He was the kid who put chewing gum in girls' hair. Who bellowed in the corridors just to hear the sound of his own voice, and kicked his sports bag along instead of picking it up and carrying it. And now, when he's out of his police uniform, he tosses back pints and throws his weight around in The Wreckers on a Friday night. Not someone she'd ever give a badge to, personally. And she can't help feeling that the last sergeant, Bill Bright, would have agreed with her.

'I'd best be off – no rest for the wicked,' says Mullins, winking at her. He pauses at the door and laughs. 'Someone should have told Pascoe that one before he jumped.'

He's gone before Saffron can tell him that you can't go around talking like that. Especially not in a uniform.

Saffron looks to the sea again, picks up her coffee, tries to re-find her vibe. But all she can see is old Mrs Pascoe. *He's a good boy, my Lewis.* What if Saffron had stopped her bike when she passed him this morning? Asked him if he was alright?

And had Maggie really gone and died?

The door opens, a gust of wind coming in with it, and she thinks it's Mullins back for more – to blag a brownie and offer some more tone-deaf jokes – and she's ready to tell him that it's not cool, Mullins, not cool at all. But instead it's a pair of new customers.

She recognises the older grey-haired woman as Bill Bright's wife, Ally, Porthpella's resident beachcomber. Saffron's not sure she's ever been in Hang Ten before, though she's seen her often enough, walking the shoreline, bending to pick up who knows what. And she recognises the tall, mixed-race guy with her too, because he came in last week and they joked about something. The weather? The waves? He's not smiling now though, and nor is Ally Bright, and Saffron wonders if they saw what happened down on the beach. She blinks rapidly, pushes the heel of her hand into her eye, smearing her mascara with it.

'Morning!' she says brightly. 'What can I get you?'

'Is it alright to bring the dog in?' asks Ally, tentatively. Her face is small, pale, worried.

'I prefer dogs to some people.' Saffron grins, brightening at the sight of the little red-furred mongrel. 'Does he want a biscuit?'

31

7

They go inside, because in true Porthpella form a light drizzle – a mizzle – has blown in from the sea. The clear blue skies Ally woke up to are now scudded with cloud.

She shivers, wraps her jacket around her instead of taking it off.

At some point in the last couple of years, this place – Hang Ten – sprang up, but she's never been inside before. The coffee shop is small, and she's self-conscious, but Jayden gestures to the one and only corner table. Ally takes a seat in a yellow-painted wicker chair, leaning back against a colourful tie-dye cushion. A voracious Swiss cheese plant clambers up towards the ceiling, fairy lights looping round its stem. The ceiling is a mosaic of stickers: peace signs and *Aloha!* and Sex Wax surf wax. The floorboards are painted sky blue and the counter is loaded with cakes. She must have seen the bright painted shack hundreds of times, but never thought it was a place for her.

Ally folds her hands in her lap and closes her eyes for a second. Fox settles at her feet, crunching a bone-shaped biscuit. He yaps excitedly and she reaches down, lays a hand on his bristled back to quieten him.

The young woman with the pink hair – Saffron, a Porthpella girl that Ally remembers Bill saying was making a go of the place – is temporarily obscured by a puff of steam from the coffee machine.

What's she – Ally – doing here?

'So,' says Jayden, sliding into the seat across from her, stretching out his long legs, 'I probably don't have many of these morning surfs left. My wife's eight months pregnant.'

Ally can feel herself smiling on autopilot. She says congratulations.

She and Bill were both so young when Evie was born; Ally had just graduated from art school, Bill was a newly minted PC. The flat in Falmouth was tiny, and Ally, far away from any family, felt like the walls were pressing in. Like her perfect little daughter – so unexpected, so treasured – was taking the actual breath from her. Some days she'd stand over her daughter's cradle, feel her chest splitting, gasp for air like a fish on land. Bill found her like that more than once, and even his strong hands on her shoulders didn't feel as if they were reaching her. Then he took the job down here, in the far, far west, where the skies were wide and the sea wild.

There's a place, he said. *It's called The Shell House. I think the three of us could be happy there.*

The young woman sets down their coffees, her bangles jangling, and Jayden thanks her. She hovers, as if she's about to say something more, then she appears to think better of it.

'I suck at it, by the way,' Jayden says to Ally. 'The surfing.'

Ally takes a sip of coffee. It's velvety and strong and tastes even better than the stuff she makes at home. She resets the cup carefully, but it still clatters in the saucer. She sees Jayden pretend not to notice.

'Why are we here?' she asks suddenly.

'Because when something like that happens, I don't think we should all just go on like it's nothing.'

'But people do,' says Ally. 'It's all they ever do.'

She can hear the tang in her voice, and she stops.

'And I thought you might want to talk.'

Jayden says it as if talking is easy. Doesn't he realise she's tight as a clam?

She imagines trying to tell Evie what's happened. Where could she possibly start? Not with opening the door to a desperate young man after dark, that's for sure. The problem with saying anything to her daughter is that Ally always has to create space for her reaction – and it is so hard not to be knocked off course in the face of it. Pragmatic Evie wouldn't understand a guilt like this.

Of course, Ally will have to tell the police about Lewis coming to her house – she just didn't quite feel ready for it down on the beach. She'll phone and tell them straight away, after this.

How did she not realise who he was at the time? She can't stop replaying what Lewis said – that Bill promised he'd help him – and the look on his face, like he was no more than a little boy lost. Is she so wrapped up in her own world that she couldn't step outside of it to help someone else?

Jayden's right: she does want to talk. But she knows she won't like the sound of her own words when she does.

She watches him as he drops a sugar cube into his coffee. Stirs. He smiles at her – a smile that's somehow apologetic and reassuring, like a nurse's before they give you a jab.

'He came looking for my husband,' she begins.

Because all her stories seem to start with Bill.

'Lewis Pascoe?'

'Lewis Pascoe. Only I had no idea who he was.'

And on she goes. By the time she's finished – almost finished – her coffee is cold. As she tells Jayden what Lewis said, about Bill apparently promising to look out for him, she hears her voice creak.

'It's alright,' says Jayden. 'I get it.'

And without knowing this young man who sits across from her at all, she can see that he does. He understands. Encouraged, she goes on, telling him as much as she can remember.

'You see,' she says, 'Bill took it hard, what happened with Lewis's dad. He was first to the scene. This exact same cliff. And then there was Maggie's reaction afterwards, the way she turned against people around here, and especially the local police. She wouldn't so much as look at Bill if she passed him. That was twenty years ago. She wouldn't look at any of us for twenty years.'

'And you said her grandson, Lewis, came to live with her a while back?'

Ally nods. 'Lewis would have been just a baby when his dad killed himself, living with his mum on the other side of the country, I think. But then at some point Lewis actually came down here and moved in with his nan, must have been two or three years ago. And I remember Bill saying he'd had to arrest him, that he'd hardly been here five minutes and he'd got into trouble. I know Bill didn't feel very good about that, not on top of the history with Maggie.'

Ally presses her hands to her eyes. It's coming back now – fragmented, but none the less. Bill had retired not long after.

'I remember Bill saying he felt sorry for Lewis. Said he didn't have anyone anymore, apart from his nan. I think Lewis's mother must have passed away too. But I was in Australia with Evie at the time, she'd just had her new baby . . . I suppose I didn't pay much attention to what was going on back here.'

'What had Lewis done?'

'I think it was burglary,' says Ally. 'The thing is, last night, I only spoke to Lewis for all of five minutes – and I didn't even realise who he was. I can't pretend to know anything about his life now. But . . .'

How could she put it?

'Last night, he didn't look like someone who was ready to give up,' she continues. 'Not to me, he didn't. He looked like he was only just getting started.'

Jayden's listening intently. So too, she's sure, is the girl behind the counter. And she knows how she must sound: like someone desperately trying to convince themselves that there were no signs; that there was nothing they could have done. But it isn't that. Or at least not entirely.

'But if it's the same cliff his dad jumped off?' asks Jayden, gently.

'I know,' says Ally. 'I know.'

She picks up her cup and puts it down again. Jayden leans back in his chair, his brow creased.

'He was there again this morning.' The girl is beside them, her hands thrust into the pocket of her denim apron. 'I saw him. Lewis. Right outside Sea Dream, that new place with all the gin-palace vibes. I thought he was just passing it. Are you seriously saying he didn't know anything about his nan until he turned up there last night? Not about her selling the place, her dying, nothing?'

'Nothing,' says Ally. 'He says he knew nothing at all.'

'All that glass,' she says, 'I'm amazed he didn't at least break a window. I think I would've, given the circumstances . . . Well, wouldn't you?'

The girl heads back to the counter and Ally and Jayden sit quietly for a moment. The café's music – something with an incongruously happy beat – fills the space between.

All at once, Jayden leans forward.

'I just thought of something,' he says, with animation; his soft northern accent suddenly more pronounced. 'Something I saw this morning. And you know what, I reckon it could be connected.'

8

Jayden makes the call from back inside his car, using the number that the girl in the café gave him. *Don't ask me why I've got Mullins's mobile number*, she said, rolling her eyes.

His fingers tap the steering wheel. Further down the beach he sees a paddleboarder take to the water with smooth and even strokes; maybe that could be more his thing. His nose still stings, and he's gingerly pressing at it when the phone's answered.

'Timothy Mullins's phone,' says a voice that's older and deeper than that of the officer he spoke to on the beach. 'Which shouldn't be ringing while he's on duty, by the way.' Followed by a gruff laugh.

Jayden hesitates, then says, 'It's connected to a case. I wanted to offer some potential information. Who am I speaking to?'

'Who are you speaking to, sir? You're speaking to DS Skinner. Devon and Cornwall Police. The best way to contact us is via an online query form, or at the following number, 0—'

'I'm in Porthpella. It's to do with Lewis Pascoe. I was talking to Officer Mullins earlier, and—'

'Name?'

'Jayden Weston.'

'Address, Jayden?'

'Er, Upper Hendra. Just outside of Porthpella. I can't remember the postcode, we've only just moved and are staying—'

'Cliff Thomas's place?'

'That's it. Do you know him?'

'Know him? Man and boy. Ah, okay, got it. You're his son-in-law, are you? From up north.'

And at that, Jayden hears something in the officer's voice change: the penny must have dropped. Though he notices the sergeant doesn't mention West Yorkshire Police.

He sucks in his breath. 'That's me. Jayden. Cat's husband.'

'Go on then, Jayden.'

There's a creak in the background, as if the speaker has just settled back in a chair.

'I was at the beach car park early this morning. I didn't think much of it before, but I saw a woman running in the dunes.'

'Jogging?'

'Well, yeah. She was in jogging gear. But she was running, not jogging. Honestly? It looked like was running away from something. If you know what I mean.'

It's a delicate distinction, and she was at a distance, but it struck him then; and now – after what happened with Lewis – it's struck him again. Something about it just hadn't looked right.

'What was it about her that made you think she was running away and not just . . . running, sir?'

'Just an impression, I guess. There's a difference, I think. She wasn't running steadily, or with a rhythm, it was more . . . I don't know, charged. Messy. You know?'

'And this connects to Lewis Pascoe's attempted suicide, how . . . ?'

Jayden rubs the back of his head. 'I don't know. But it was about 7.45 this morning. The timing of it feels a bit relevant. I think she'd be worth tracking down and talking to. In case she saw something that affects how you look at things. She was white,

38

tall, long dark hair tied back in a ponytail. Blue Lycra bottoms, I think . . . dark blue, maybe black. A grey top.'

'Milk and two sugars.'

'What?'

'Sorry, that was Lynn. Just moved down here, haven't you, Jayden?'

'That's right,' he says, caution in his voice.

'He's a good bloke, Cliff. He told me about you. Half thought he was going to ask me for a job for you, but he said you're done with it all. Couldn't cope. Well, fair enough, it's not for everyone, police work. Not at all. Especially after what you experienced.'

Jayden grits his teeth. Breathes through his nose. All he can hear is the words *couldn't cope*. Is that how Cat's dad really sees it? Jayden had the support and did the work. He processed the experience, reset his stress responses. Professionally, he was fit to get back out there – he just didn't want to. Not anymore.

'Terrible business, all that,' says Skinner. Then seems to wait.

'Yeah.' Because what else can he say?

Skinner coughs; moves on quickly. 'And here, well, it's about the community, the people, people we know by name, every one of them. Not like big-city policing. Couldn't be more different. But I expect you've seen that for yourself. I don't blame you, feeling like a fish out of water down here.'

Jayden waits for the next blow: here it surely comes, the reminder that there aren't many people who look like him in this particular part of the world. *We're not all that multicultural down here, lad*, his father-in-law said the first time he visited, as if that wasn't something he could see for himself.

But Sergeant Skinner goes somewhere else instead.

'Just don't go trying to make up for sitting on the sidelines, son. Looking for problems where there aren't any. I've seen that before.

The worst is when coppers retire, but they want to keep playing detective, when—'

'I'm not playing detective,' says Jayden. 'I'm just saying what I saw. It could be relevant.'

He tries to keep the irritation out of his voice – not least because that'd probably get back to Cliff too: *A bit chippy, that son-in-law of yours* – but he's not sure he's successful. There's a pause before the sergeant speaks again. This time, formality is resumed.

'Well it's noted, and thank you, Jayden. Woman running in the dunes. Sports gear. Give my best to Cliff.'

'I think it's worth checking out,' he says again, but somehow the air goes out of him at the last minute.

As he hangs up, Jayden drops his head on the steering wheel, as frustrated with himself as with Skinner. Frustrated with Cat's dad too. Frustrated? No, hurt. Properly hurt, if he let himself be – although he isn't sure much good can come of that feeling. Not now that they're in Porthpella – and here to stay, for better or for worse.

9

Ally wanders slowly along the sand. The mizzle has cleared to bring streaked blue skies and a choppy sea. A stiff breeze tugs at the collar of her jacket and she dips her head; keeps her eyes on the shoreline.

She didn't wait for Jayden to finish his call with the police. She felt drained, suddenly, the need to be near people replaced by the far more familiar desire to be alone. She waved at him as she left the café, but inside his car, deep in his phone call, Jayden didn't notice.

Ally doubts that she'll see him again, but, nevertheless, she appreciates his kindness. And she does wonder what the police said to him about the running woman. If Bill had got a call about someone in the area when a person jumped from the cliff, he'd have made it his business to find them. Jumped or fallen. She hopes fallen. Pathetic, really, the desperate need for personal absolution, when the fact of Lewis can't be changed. But even so, Jayden said the woman had looked . . . what exactly? Not distressed – he didn't use that word – but as if she were running away from something.

Is there a chance she was running away from Lewis Pascoe? Or that she saw something else?

When Lewis turned up at Ally's door last night, he didn't look threatening. He just looked sad; confused. And she knows now that she was too shuttered; she wasn't able to place herself in his shoes. Would she have acted differently, if she knew who he was? The truth is, she can't say. And now look what's happened.

You can't just carry on after something like that.

Ally pulls her jacket around her. Chews at her lip.

When Maggie Pascoe left Porthpella, there was no kind of farewell in the community, but even if there had been, Ally knows she wouldn't have noticed it. She was still in the depths of grief when the diggers came rolling in on Maggie's little old bungalow. Ally saw the big glass house go up in its place, quick as a mirage, and just didn't have the space in her heart to care. She stooped her head and kept on walking, Fox at her side.

Just as she's doing now.

But if Bill were alive, he'd have made sure he'd known where Maggie was moving to. He'd have wished her well, even if she didn't want to hear it, not from him or his sort. And when the time came, he'd have heard news of her death too, you could count on it – and his first thoughts would have gone to her grandson.

Because that's who Bill was.

But none of those things happened. And now a man who's hardly more than a boy is hanging on to life by the thinnest of threads. And when – if – he wakes up, he'll be, if the girl in the café is to be believed, all alone in the world.

Whatever kind of reception Lewis received at the new house – Sea Dream, it's called – it hindered the situation, not helped. Ally has seen the occupants in passing and taken them for second-homers; not to judge on appearances, but they don't look like they'd have welcomed finding Lewis on their doorstep, demanding answers.

Just as she didn't either.

Shame curdles in her stomach.

I'm sorry, she murmurs. Sorry to Lewis, sorry to Maggie, and sorry to Bill too.

Fox dances on his hind legs and pats her thigh with his paws. She half-heartedly throws a length of seaweed. He eyes it, unimpressed: *That the best you can do?*

Ally makes a series of quiet resolutions, one with every step.

She'll find out what happened to Maggie after she moved, and then, when Lewis wakes up – and she has to believe it's *when* and not *if* – she'll be the one to tell him: gently, kindly, as anyone deserves to be told. Death brings substantial administration along with it, and perhaps she can help him navigate it. If Maggie sold her house, maybe there's money that Lewis stands to inherit? And she can find out what provisions there are for helping people who are just out of prison, and make sure that he accesses the services.

These thoughts occupy her as she walks. They give her determination. She can feel the push of the bigger question: why did Lewis Pascoe fall off the cliff at all? She voiced it in the café and instantly regretted it. She knows that if she lets it in, she's not sure she'll be able to let it out again. And she's hardly equipped to answer it, is she?

Instead of carrying on along the beach, she takes the path over the back of the dunes.

Fox looks at her quizzically. He knows this route, but he rarely goes this way with Ally. She's never been one for the village.

They cut across the lane, over a stile, then skirt the edge of a cauliflower crop. The fields stretch out like patchwork, the sea a hem of blue. Less than fifteen minutes on foot and they're in Porthpella proper. Even after forty years it always surprises her how close it is. It feels like a world away, most of the time.

The Wreckers Arms has the commanding spot on the small square, picnic tables arranged outside, sun umbrellas flapping in the wind. A chalkboard advertises home-cooked food. Bill used to like a pint of Doom Bar in the sunshine, and he'd draw conversation from even the grouchiest of old-timers hunkered down at the bar. Years ago, they won a ham in the Christmas raffle, and came third in the Grand National sweepstakes, Bill bringing home a crisp £20 note that he promptly gave to Evie to buy new jeans. And every so often they'd walk across the dunes on a summer's evening and sit outside at the sticky tables, Evie blowing bubbles in her lemonade. If Ally went in now, she's not sure the landlord would recognise her.

Narrow lanes skirt off from the square, terraces of grey-stone cottages and converted net lofts. There are holiday cottages of course, but unlike some villages in their part of the world, where on a winter's evening you can sadly count on a single hand the homes with lights on, Porthpella has remained a place for locals too. They'd both hoped Evie might stay, but London called; London then Sydney. And what could you do about that?

On the other side of the square is the brightly painted facade of the Bluebird gallery and tea room. Sunita left a message for Ally the other day, asking if ahead of the summer season she'd want to swap out the picture of hers that's displayed on the back wall and put something new in instead. Ally suspected it was a kind way of saying *your work isn't selling* but she's yet to phone her back, because that'll mean saying aloud that she hasn't done anything new in months.

She dips her head and hurries over to White Wave Stores. Wenna knows everything, and everyone. It's early, only March, but the summer displays are out: a rack of postcards flutters in the breeze; a rainbow palette of buckets and spades and beach balls. Inside, the shop smells of freshly baked bread.

'Ally, love, how are you?'

Ally smiles gratefully at the welcome, then feels a tinge of guilt that she doesn't come in more often. Her weekly order box is left on the veranda of The Shell House, and most of the time she hardly swaps more than a wave as Wenna's husband, Gerren, drives on.

Wenna takes off her glasses, and they hang on a string around her neck. When she turned fifty, she got a tattoo of a starfish on her wrist, and it was the talk of the village by all accounts. Ally's eyes go to it now: a spark in an otherwise-conventional appearance.

'You heard what's happened to Maggie Pascoe's grandson?'

News spreads fast in Porthpella.

Ally nods. She doesn't say anything about Lewis coming to her house last night. She simply tells Wenna what she's heard about Maggie.

'Oh dear, has she really? Funny old fish, she was. She came to me for milk, bread and Garibaldi biscuits. The rest she got at the superstore out of town. Passed on, eh? Well, that I didn't know. Course, I knew she moved away. Not that she'd tell me herself, but she wanted some mail sent on. Sheltered housing, up near St Austell. Fair enough too, she was getting on. And she was glad to get out of that creaky old house in the dunes, I reckon. No offence, love. Course, the new lot I never see. But what I have seen is the Waitrose van heading out that way. I'd say they'll miss us when we're gone but is that true?'

She shrugs. Unscrews the lid of a jar and offers Ally a toffee.

Ally briefly shakes her head. Says, 'Wenna, did you have any idea that Maggie's grandson was in prison?'

'Put there by your Bill, wasn't he?' says Wenna, through the sucking of her sweet. 'Oh, I remember hearing when he went down for it. Burglary, wasn't it? Silly lad, he'd hardly been here. Gerren reckons he fell in with some blokes down from Plymouth. Not that you could breathe a word about it to Maggie. She'd come in for her Garibaldis and that was it.' A slurp; jaws working now. 'But course we all knew about what happened with Paul. Sad business. I remember it like it was yesterday.'

After her son's death, Maggie retreated so far in on herself that even the likes of Wenna stopped trying at some point.

'I couldn't have the address, could I? Where Maggie went?'

As Wenna disappears out the back, Ally picks a few bits off the shelves. The first things she sees, really. A box of fudge, with a sun-faded cover. A couple of tins of tomatoes. Then she takes a basket and fills it; it was the mention of Waitrose that did it.

'Here,' says Wenna, handing Ally a folded piece of paper. 'Paradiso Heights, it's called. Let's hope it was, eh? Poor old boot.' She leans closer. 'You doing alright are you, Ally love? We never see you very much. And how's that daughter of yours? She planning a visit any time soon? Dear lord, there isn't a day that passes when I don't think of your Bill. Now, anything else for you?'

Ally suddenly thinks of telling her about the Sydney proposal. But she hasn't sorted it out in her own mind yet, and it isn't like it would be earth-shattering news to anyone here. Wenna is only being friendly to pass the time of day.

Some people could disappear in a place like Porthpella, and never be missed. Maggie Pascoe was one, and Ally's pretty sure she's another. That's just how it is.

'Thank you,' she says, tucking the piece of paper with the address into her pocket, 'but that's everything. What do I owe you?'

It's only when Ally's left the store and is halfway across the square that it strikes her as strange that Wenna didn't ask her why she, of all people, wanted that information about Maggie. It would have been hard to explain if she had: the duty, the guilt, and what about the nagging feeling that there's more to this? Because Ally Bright isn't one to get caught up in other people's business.

10

Jayden finds Cat at the lookout. It's her favourite place, a wooden bench perched on the very top of the farm's highest hill. It's where she and her friends used to play at sentry duty, their binoculars trained on boats coming into the bay. One time she slept out here – a tiny Cat, curled up in a sleeping bag, cushions softening the bench; she woke up beneath a film of dew, a spider's web strung between her fingers.

Hearing stories like these, Jayden thinks of his wife as almost another species altogether. How was she ever happy in the city? He pictures her striding to work down The Headrow, buses thundering past. Or dancing in Potternewton Park, with glittered cheeks and a can in hand, Carnival whirling around them, beats, bodies, smoke, concrete. He wonders if the longing for the coast was in her, even then?

Now she sits with a notebook resting on her perfect dome of a stomach, and Jayden clocks a list. Cat loves a list. A stiff breeze crackles an open bag of Haribo beside her and blows her honey-blond hair across her face.

Her natural habitat. And as much as Cat said the move was about him, about them, she knew it was about her too.

'How was it?' she says with a smile.

And he knows now he won't mention that phrase *couldn't cope*. Cat would get upset – or worse, she wouldn't. And Cliff would deny it – or worse, he wouldn't. And what would be the point of all that?

He drops down beside her. 'Babe, I lost your board. Sorry. I'll replace it.'

She raises an eyebrow. Maybe she sees something in his face because she just shrugs. 'Don't worry about it, it was pretty shot out. Probably holding you back.'

He wonders if there will ever come a time when she stops tiptoeing around him.

She gently rubs at his cheek with her thumbnail. Holds up a trace of dried blood.

'CSI Porthpella. Get into a fight with a local?'

Her eyes are electric blue, and when he first met her – at a friend's barbecue in Chapeltown – they were the first thing he noticed about her. He couldn't stop staring. *I was born by the sea*, she said, as if that explained it; as if it were the most important thing about her.

He's never been able to lie to those eyes.

'There was an accident at the beach,' he says. 'A young guy went off the cliff. Lewis Pascoe.'

He tells her how it went: the shout, the running, how he squatted and felt for a pulse.

'His blood was still wet on the sand. He hadn't been there long.'

'God, Jay.'

But what Jayden does hold back is how his own heart was thumping in double time, sweat breaking out on his brow. How, when the medics came, he rocked back on his heels and felt a swell of nausea and had to gulp in air. Then did that thing, the naming of objects: wetsuit, egg-shaped pebble, horizon line, kiteboarder, little red dog.

It was the dog who did it; the dog who brought him back.

'Jay,' she says softly. 'Was it alright?'

'I'll find out. I'll call the hospital.'

'I mean with you.'

'Me? Oh yeah. Yeah.'

'Well, that's good. Isn't it?'

He gives a brief shake of his head. 'The saddest thing is, his dad died at the same spot. Years ago. So, the police reckon it's attempted suicide.'

'Oh no.'

They're quiet for a beat. He shifts in his seat, leans down towards her bump.

'Morning, little one,' he says, his lips grazing her stretched-tight t-shirt.

It's so easy to change the subject, now that there's a baby on the way.

'Wait,' she says, lifting her shirt, her bare skin instantly pricking with goosebumps.

'Woah,' says Jayden. 'That's it, babe, you go. She's turning somersaults in there.'

'Glad to see her dad.'

'No rush for that though. You cook all the way through, you hear me?' He plants another kiss.

'I think she's going to be early,' says Cat. 'She wants to bust out. Get in on the fun.'

And who is he to argue? Cat's the one doing something magical, the ordinary miracle of making another person out of her body. If anyone were to know, it's her.

'Okay. I get that. Not too early though, alright? We want all the bits in the right place.'

'What, ten little fingers and ten little toes? Jay, she's ready. She could come now and be perfect.'

Jayden blows out. 'Don't say that. She'll hear. Start to get ideas.'

'Too late for that.' She taps her bump. 'These walls have ears.'

'Out in four weeks. No early release.'

The thought of Lewis wipes the smile from his face.

'He'd been in prison,' he says. 'The guy who went over.'

'Was he from round here then?'

'His nan used to live down in the dunes. Maggie Pascoe? Bit of a recluse, apparently, blamed a lot of people for her son's death. And this kid Lewis didn't know she'd moved away, didn't even know she'd died. It must have happened just after he was released, and the message hadn't gotten to him. They'd—'

'Jay, don't let it stress you.'

'Don't worry. Do you know Ally Bright? She's in the dunes too.'

'Ally Bright?' She wrinkles her nose. 'Sounds familiar. But I don't think so. Mum and Dad probably will.'

'She was married to the sergeant around here.'

Cat's watching him carefully, as if even using the word *sergeant* could be some kind of trigger, but he goes on.

'So, this guy pitches up at Ally's house the night before. He's all upset, looking for Ally's husband. He'd gone to his nan's house, and she's not there. Her house isn't even there. Just this massive new-build in its place.'

'No way. He didn't even know? But, what, so then he . . . tried to kill himself?'

Jayden gets up. He stands with his hands on his hips, and his loose shirt flutters in the breeze. He gets why Cat likes to come here, to the brow of this hill. It makes you feel stronger. Or he can see how it might, anyway.

'That's what the cop who turned up reckoned. Jumping to conclusions. Ally's feeling guilty. She was really shaken up, you know? I actually think there could be more to it. And Saffron, the girl at the café, thinks—'

'What was this, a community meeting? Jay, you don't need to care about this stuff anymore.'

'Somebody nearly dying right in front of us? That's not something to care about?'

He realises what he's said.

'You know I don't mean that,' she says carefully. 'I just don't want to see you getting . . . stressed out.'

She fixes him with those blue eyes, and the love in them makes his heart stutter. But there's a quiet command there too. He can't blame her. Back in Leeds, she was right there with him through everything that he was feeling, and that took its own toll. She did her best to help, but there was a time when no one could reach him.

He won't let anything take them back there.

Jayden kneels beside her. He already knows there's no point telling her about his call with DS Skinner. He takes hold of both of her hands. 'No stress,' he says. 'You're right, it's not my business. You're my business. Both of you.'

The creases in her cheeks soften.

'This field is going to be our business. Can't you just see it?' she says.

'Tent city?'

'An idyll. Halcyon Camping.'

'Halcyon. You know my dad's going to get his Greek myth vibe on. Once you start him . . .'

'I love your dad, Jay. And I love your mum. And I love what we're going to build here together.'

He squeezes her fingers. He doesn't know how to tell her that he felt a spark of something back in Hang Ten; an old, familiar feeling. Even before that, on the beach: the call and response; how he'd run towards the scene as if he were hard-wired. As if it was his duty.

He'd been planning on going for detective – that's what he's never told Cat about. He told Kieran, but no one else. It was the

51

day it happened, and Kieran thought it a desertion, he could tell, but he clapped his shoulder anyway, said, *You'll smash it, bro.* Instead, Jayden left the force, losing the job he loved, his home city and his best friend – all in one hit.

And now he's relegated to someone who simply can't cope, apparently. Standing on the sidelines but sticking their nose in through force of habit.

He can feel himself getting revved up again.

'What are you thinking?' she says. 'You've got that look.'

'No look,' he says.

But he's thinking this: surely the running woman is worth finding. Even if DS Skinner doesn't agree. Old Jayden would have really enjoyed proving someone like that wrong, but this new Jayden? He's still working out what he would do.

11

Roland Hunter closes the door on the chub-faced Officer Mullins and lets out a deep breath.

So, the little convict tried to top himself. Not that Roland will use those words when he tells Helena; she's already shaken up enough.

He was clearly confused, he'll say to her. Then lay it on thick, add: *Probably taken something. Poor kid. It's tough on the outside.*

Something like that anyway.

Roland goes to the kitchen and picks himself a pod; fires up the coffee machine. He chews on his thumbnail while he waits.

It was a shock last night: he can admit that now. And, sure, his temper enjoyed a run-out, but who wouldn't react like that, when a no-hoper like Pascoe turned up yelling blue murder at their door? And he'd had to show Nathan that he was the man of his own house. Not that he particularly wants to show his brother anything – this whole visit is a copycat exercise, Nathan's favourite game. So, Roland has built himself a decent gaff in Cornwall? Well, obviously Nathan is going to be down at the first opportunity for a long weekend, lining up a bunch of viewings, houses with price tags that'll make even Roland's eyes water. He's like a dog that always has to eat out of another mutt's bowl – just to show he can. It was the same when they were kids: Nathan always wanted what Roland had – and even as a butterball toddler, would stop at nothing to get it.

Still, Pascoe at his door gave Roland a chance to flex his muscles and prove himself top dog. It worked too. *Atta boy!* Nathan trilled afterwards, smacking the table with his hand. *That's what I'm talking about!*

Pascoe must have thought it a sick kind of magic trick. Looking for his nan's shack – all fibreboard, asbestos and sticking plasters – and seeing Sea Dream in its place instead. But she'd done well for herself from it: the old crone didn't have two coins to rub together until Roland came along, and she got herself a nice spot in a retirement home inland. So she hadn't told her jailbird grandson? Well, if Lewis hadn't bothered to write her sorry little letters, or drop his 10p into a prison payphone to say *Hey Nanny* every once in a while, whose fault was that? Not Roland's. Nor was it his fault that Lewis had no clue she'd died. Roland had thought they'd really been scraping the barrel when the home called him: did he know how Maggie Pascoe's grandson could be contacted? Well, hardly. *We don't move in the same circles*, he'd said, with a sarcasm that tasted like syrup.

Who knew where the reprobate had been? And more to the point, who cared. Standing on Roland's doorstep last night, eyes as wide as Bambi's and fists bunched like onions. Blathering about a job and a lost phone and *she can't be, she can't be.*

But Lewis isn't dead, then: he's in Intensive Care.

The decidedly unvenerable PC Mullins was all ears just now, as Roland set him right about what happened last night.

'My wife was distinctly unsettled,' he said. 'Well, you would be, wouldn't you? Deranged kid like that comes around spitting blood. She didn't sleep a wink. Not much of a welcome to Porthpella for my brother either, was it? *Enjoy your weekend by the sea – watch out for the rampaging youth.*'

He looks at his watch. Helena should be back by now. Well back. As should Nathan.

'And did Pascoe come again this morning?' Mullins asked.

Roland hesitated.

'Matter of fact, he did. But he was in a very different state of mind.'

'Depressed?' Mullins offered, brightly.

'I'd say,' said Roland. 'It was like he'd slept on it. And didn't much care for the reality he'd woken up to.'

Just as Mullins was leaving, something occurred to Roland: how did anyone even know that he and Pascoe had crossed paths?

'I didn't want to make a fuss last night,' he said, 'but I'm beginning to think I should have reported it. Might have saved the kid from himself. How did you hear of his visit to us?'

'Ally Bright,' Mullins declared with a smile. 'The old sarge's widow. Pascoe paid her a visit too.'

Now, Roland leans against the counter, and sips at his coffee meditatively. Ally Bright, eh?

It was supposed to be a quiet life, out here in the dunes. Not this sort of thing laid at his door. He wanders to the window, stares out down the beach. She loves this place, Helena, but he can't say he feels the same. Salt water doesn't have that much over ditch water as far as he can see; just another type of dull. And the gulls are a headache: rats with wings. But when the sun decides to show its face and the sky dredges up some sort of blue and the sea gets in on it too – yeah, then he can see it. And old Nana Pascoe used to have, through dumb luck or canny forebears, one of the sweetest spots in all the dunes. But it's his now – fair and square – his and Helena's. Tough luck, Lewis boy.

Where *is* Helena?

And exactly how long did it take Nathan to run his car into the garage? Though it's quietly pleased him that Nathan's house viewings have been temporarily derailed by a broken brake light. Knowing his brother, he'll be distracted, trying to chat up some surfer girls – and failing spectacularly. Back in the day, he used to try it on with Helena too. And Roland always quite enjoyed the spectacle; of all the things his wife is, susceptible to a short-arse trader with halitosis is not one of them.

Roland cracks his cup back in its saucer and slips his phone out of his pocket. He hits Helena's number. It rings. He holds his phone away from his ear and listens: it's coming from upstairs. He walks up the floating staircase, following the sound. And there's her phone, on the bedside table, bleating at him. He sees his name and a picture of the two of them in Barbados – or the Maldives? Somewhere like that – faces pushed together, synchronised smiles. He hangs up and it flashes 'Missed Call': three in a row.

Helena, you dozy moo.

He can't imagine going anywhere without his phone, least of all out for a run. To be fair, he can't imagine going for a run at all. For most of his adult life, Roland had an unearned strength and athleticism, then all of a sudden, he hit fifty and the paunch came with it. From some angles it looks like he's tucked a bowling ball under his t-shirt. Not that Helena seems to care. But doesn't Nathan like to have a go. Last night, the first thing his brother said when he turned up wasn't *Hello* or *Thanks for having me*, but, with a pat on his belly, *When are you due, mate?*

Roland tosses his own phone on to the bed, where it skids off and clatters to the floor. He swears, feels frustration burning in his throat. His wife was scared last night after Lewis's visit, genuinely scared. And who wouldn't be? Hammering at the door. Lunging towards them. Spittle and tears. After he'd gone, Roland held her tight and he felt her shaking all the way to her bones.

And now Pascoe is considered the victim. It beggars belief.

He was surprised this morning when Helena went out running anyway. For all she knew, Pascoe could have been waiting for her, looking to exact some kind of petty revenge. Roland wouldn't have expected her to have that kind of pluck. Or be that stupid.

He checks his watch again. It's coming up on half ten. Where the hell is she?

Through the window, the beach is empty as a plain.

An hour later, when Helena still hasn't returned, Roland pulls on his jacket to go and look for her. There's a knock at the door just as his hand is on the handle. *About bloody time!* he thinks, his worry flicking instantly to anger. But it's his brother on the doorstep, holding a cardboard box.

Nathan's face is set to his usual combative expression. He has a theory, does Nathan, and it's one he's held his whole life: Roland lives on Easy Street. Roland's view, in turn, is that Nathan likes to make life hard for himself, positively revels in it. Sure, he works all hours in the city, has two broken marriages and a killer combo of high blood pressure and low self-esteem, but just because Nathan has made poor choices doesn't mean that he, Roland, has it easy in comparison.

This place, Nathan said on arriving at Sea Dream yesterday, *it must be worth, what, a mill? One-point-five?* His lip curled in envy, his eyes going to Helena's svelte figure, taking her in just as he took in the other luxury fittings, the other exquisite views.

I think you'll find it's priceless actually, Roland said.

But, Nathan being Nathan, the properties he brought up on his phone last night, outright flaunting, far exceeded Sea Dream.

'Where have you been?' Roland says now. 'You've been gone ages.'

'Garages round here,' Nathan replies with a roll of his eyes, 'I'm not sure they've seen a Lexus before. Still, cheapest I've ever paid to replace a light. Then I saw a sign for a vineyard on the way back, took me a few miles out the way but I picked up a couple of bottles that may or may not be awful.'

'Helena's still not back,' says Roland. 'I'm going to look for her.'

'What, from this morning? Oh, hallelujah, she's finally seen the light and left you. I expect I'll get the call any minute now.' He pantomimes taking his phone out of his pocket. 'See, there it is now: message from her. *Oh Nathan, it's you, it's always been you!*

Roland glowers. They're kids again, circling like junior silverbacks.

'Piss off, Nathan,' he says. 'She's been gone over three hours. You stay here in case she comes back. Ring me. No pratting about either.' A thought occurs to him. 'Hang on, what time's your first viewing?'

'Viewing?'

'Houses. Hello? Why you're here?'

'Oh, sure,' says Nathan. 'Timing's flexible. When you're spending as much as me, it's flexible, baby.'

Roland's pretty sure that's not true – an appointment is an appointment – but he's got bigger things on his mind right now. He moves past his brother, then stops in the doorway. 'By the way,' he says, 'that no-hoper who came here last night and again this morning. He tried to kill himself. Couldn't even succeed at that though, apparently.'

'What?' says Nathan.

But Roland's already on his way out. Eying the sky, he sees that clouds have scudded in and he zips up his jacket.

'Kill himself?' shouts Nathan from the house. 'What are you talking about?'

As Roland strikes off across the dunes, he thinks of cupping his hand to his mouth and yelling, *Helena!* But that would look desperate. And if Nathan heard, he'd only laugh at him later, when she was home and safe. Almost immediately, his foot sinks into a hole and sand fills his shoe. A vast gull sails down and watches him shake it out; fixes him with its beady eye.

'You piss off too,' he hisses. Then, louder, flapping his arms, 'I said, piss off!'

The gull doesn't bat a feather.

Roland has the sensation, suddenly, that he's being watched, and not just by the damn seabird, or his damn brother. He spins round, but there's no one there, just an ocean of spiked grass and the sagging roof of a holiday cottage, set back from the path. His nearest neighbour. He thinks about knocking on the door. *Have you seen my wife?* But he'd feel stupid doing that too. Like a man who can't keep his house in order. And he's already been snubbed by the guy once, when he asked him in for a glass of malt.

He hovers uncertainly, then circles back towards his own place. It's pointless, wandering about like this.

He lets himself in. When he calls out Nathan's name there's no answer. Then he calls Helena's. He takes out his phone and turns it in his hand.

He can't be sure of what time she left, but it was before eight o'clock. A four-hour jog? Helena is out for forty minutes most days – if that.

He dials the number on the card Mullins left him. He'll demand to speak to someone more important; that overgrown schoolboy in polyester won't be any use to him. And this time he'll tell them about Lewis Pascoe's parting shot that morning. After all, he has a witness: Nathan heard Pascoe say it too. That'll make those useless coppers sit up and listen, won't it?

Why he didn't think to mention it before, he doesn't know. Probably because it was wrapped up in that pathetic, plaintive little voice that Lewis had decided to assume this morning: the verbal equivalent of a wolf in sheep's clothing. Maybe because it didn't seem to matter before. But with Helena still not back? Well, it was a threat, plain and simple, and the more Roland thinks about it, the more obvious that is. Something like anger, like fear – or like a toxic mix of the two – swirls in his gut.

As his call's answered, he clears his throat.

'Roland Hunter here,' he says. 'Put me through to whoever's in charge.'

12

Gus Munro shifts and stretches in his chair. The chair creaks along with him.

His laptop is balanced on a stack of books, all that he could find in this little beach house: an RSPB guide to British seabirds; a history of lighthouses; an ancient copy of the Yellow Pages.

If he were doing this properly, he would invest in a decent seat – one on wheels, with a tilting back. But he isn't doing this properly, is he? Not by a long chalk.

Stop with the self-deprecation.

He is doing this pretty properly, in fact. He's bought the books on creative writing. And he's given himself this time – this lavish, indulgent, eight-week stretch of time – to get a story down. Find his flow. Find *himself*.

Because that's what this is all about really, isn't it?

Sixty-six years old and he's totally unmoored. Flailing in open water. A novel is something to hang on to. Something solid. Even if it's terrible – and it will undoubtedly be terrible – you wouldn't be able to argue with the fact of its existence.

His friends back home in Oxfordshire suppressed their smiles as they wished him well in Cornwall. They didn't use the words *midlife crisis* but that's what it is, isn't it? Or *later-life*, to be more exact. They also knew that, if Gus had his way, he'd still be blundering on, turning a consciously blind eye to Mona's dissatisfaction.

It's the right thing for both of us had been Mona's line, which was a straight-up lie. And another favourite: *All we had keeping us together was force of habit.*

Surely there were worse things than habit though. Weren't they a couple of old shoes that had still, essentially, fitted? Gus was no kind of a boat-rocker. And it'd seemed so cruel on the cats.

The truth is, divorce has diminished him, fractured what he considered the very structures of his life. The home they'd shared for thirty years, sold to a family with more kids than he could count. Finally, those extra bedrooms getting used, and so perhaps it was the natural way of things – they hadn't filled the space enough. Mona had a pair of arms to walk straight into, and a new-build riverside flat that he can't picture her in in a million years, but still: there she is.

This holiday let is an interim measure. A temporary fix. But won't everything be temporary from here on in? He can't imagine putting down roots all over again.

He thinks of his potting shed. The ground he enriched year on year. The cherry tree that flung confetti petals every spring. The birds that came. Were they the same birds, all those seasons? They might as well have been; a puff-chested robin, a pair of blackbirds, once a woodpecker that he called for Mona to come and see but it'd taken flight long before she got there. *What, Angus? What?* Always such exasperation. As if his very presence was an inconvenience to her.

He gets up; stretches out his back. He put in a late session last night, hunched at this table, on what might have been deemed a roll had what he'd produced been any good. He read it this morning and cringed, then deleted the whole damn lot. But he can't consider it time wasted, not when the evening passed without him noticing. Evenings are the hardest. He misses Mona's company, if not actually her. Last night he turned Paul Simon all the way up, so he couldn't even hear the sea. And wrote out his nonsense.

Now he strolls to the window, a flash of movement catching his eye.

It's only the man from the big house – Roland, that's his name. He's striding in chinos, his thick hair lifting in the breeze. Gus finds it quite difficult to look at him, knowing what he knows about the man's wife; he can almost feel the colour rising in his cheeks simply at the thought of it. He turns abruptly away.

Writing a novel is the perfect excuse for reclusiveness. Not that that is Gus's way – he was quite loquacious once, but it feels like a long time ago; here, he wants to crawl into his shell. Let the waves crash over him.

And Roland isn't his cup of tea – nor his dram of whisky. They got talking one day, without Gus realising he was from Sea Dream, but he soon regretted saying he was here to write, because Roland held forth on the topic for some minutes: how he thought Gus looked like an arty-farty type, how personally he didn't see the point of novels, and was there any sex in it? Gus turned down the offer of a drink and then skedaddled back to his hermitage.

He turns back to the room.

Mona wouldn't be seen dead in a place like this – which is a large part of its appeal, to be honest. Pine-clad walls. Red, white and blue nautical-striped bunting looping the empty bookcase. A cushion stitched with the words *Vitamin Sea*. The pegs he hangs his coat and hat on are little wooden sailing boats, and the bathroom light pull is a pilchard. In the kitchen there's a chalkboard with *Happy Hollibobs* written on it.

God awful, she'd have said.

But Gus thinks it quite jolly; harmlessly nostalgic. And he didn't choose it for its interior styling. Plus, it was a snap decision.

One that he would probably have hesitated over forever if he hadn't just hit Book Now and had done with it.

All Swell – that's the name of it. He'd imagined himself penning faintly witty letters to his friends and signing off *All Swell!* Only, Gus has lately realised that there is life as it sounds, and life as it actually is. Moving to Cornwall to write a novel; a bachelor pad, Robinson Crusoe-style. Six months ago, if Rich or Clive told him they were doing such a thing he'd have thought it sounded marvellous. Uncomplicated. Enviable.

The truth is, it is all and none of these things. At its best, it feels like a long-overdue awakening. At worst, it feels lonely as all hell. Most of the time, it's somewhere in the middle.

He wanders through to the miniscule kitchen and fills the kettle. It's a flimsily built lean-to, and on gusty nights the glass rattles in the window frames. He imagines in high summer it'd be a hot house. He'll be gone by then, of course; the lease only running through until the end of the Easter holidays. He decides to take a thermos and bring his tea out on to the beach. After all, these are the sorts of moments he's come for; not just the hours spent gazing into white space, watching a flashing cursor, but when he steps outside of himself and leaves the contents of his head behind. He hasn't gone in the sea yet, but he's told himself he will, just as soon as it warms up a bit. He doesn't want to drop dead in freezing waters; it's a long time since his body had any sort of a shock.

Even as he's thinking this, he knows it's not quite true. But you can't call what happened a body shock. It was less visceral than that. And too complicated by other emotions.

It was just by chance, the first time. Looking from his window at dusk – because that's what you're supposed to do, isn't it, when you have a sea view? – he noticed a light flick on in the top floor of Sea Dream. And then a perfectly silhouetted woman standing there, looking out. She was almost comically beautiful, the kind of woman he might have drawn in his sketchbook as a shy but hopeful teenager. And she was entirely naked. He pulled back sharply – nobody wants to be a peeping Tom – but then he couldn't stop himself edging forward again. And she was still there.

She was there the next night too.

And the next.

He had a conversation with himself after that. Took to closing the curtains before dusk crept in. And staying away from that window altogether.

But then yesterday evening he was so drawn into his work that he forgot, and as he went upstairs to get a jumper, he saw the light from Sea Dream and then the woman stepping into it.

Gus was in the world of his novel – and then, suddenly, he wasn't.

He stared, and as if she could feel his eyes on her from twenty metres across the dunes, she turned from whatever she was looking at – the sea, he supposed, because what else was there out there? – and directly faced him.

She waved. Or it seemed like she did. Maybe she was just lifting her arm.

But he fell over himself stepping backwards, heart thumping. Sixty-six, and feeling like a schoolboy.

She couldn't possibly have seen him, because his room was in near-enough darkness. But he grabbed his jumper and settled back at his desk; turned his music all the way up. But then 'Graceland' came on, which always makes him think of Mona even if he doesn't want it to. And yes, okay: he's lonely.

Gus is just stepping outside of the hut when he hears the grumble of an engine on the track. Then the incongruous bleat of a police siren – just two short, sharp sounds – as it stops.

Strange, but he dreamt of sirens last night; or at least he thought he did. He woke late, feeling like he'd gone ten rounds

65

after his night with the book, the aftershock of a dream ringing in his ears. Now he's not so sure. He doesn't believe in premonitions. But he doesn't quite not believe, either.

He rounds the corner to see the police car is parked up outside Sea Dream, fifty yards away, looking as out-of-place here as the house itself does. The vast windows of the upper floor reflect the watery sunlight, and from this angle, the whole thing appears to gleam. He sees Roland come out and stand with his arms folded, watching as the officer clambers from the car. Then the two of them go inside.

Here Gus is, penning a detective novel, and something's afoot on his very doorstep? Perhaps luck is with him on this venture, after all. Then he realises what a callous thought that is and checks himself immediately. Something actually bad could have happened. Though didn't the look on Roland's face seem more triumphant than worried? And what about his wife? Where is she in all of this?

Gus shakes his head at the thought and turns away from Sea Dream, from the police car, the shut door. Being a curtain-twitcher – being any kind of watcher from windows – is never a good look.

13

Ally rocks back on her heels and slips off her gardening gloves. Every weed has been pulled, the underside of every leaf checked for snails and slugs. She's been out here since after lunch and her job is more or less done. Being occupied was good as long as it lasted.

The beachside garden is small, but abundant. Jungle-like kale and purple sprouting broccoli grow alongside azaleas, wise-faced pansies and bursts of daffodils. Terracotta pots house fat spiked succulents, and a couple of head-turning fan palms complete the picture. Ally's garden is where she brings the gifts she finds along the strandline. There are seashells pressed into the soil. A clay pot holds a clutch of cuttlebones and razor clams and a particularly plump mermaid's purse. The grass glints with sea glass and, when the wind's blowing onshore, it's scattered with sand: the line between beach and garden blurred. Here she is, living in paradise, with her own private patch of it out back.

She goes and sits on the turquoise-painted wooden bench, outside the lean-to that serves as her studio. The hours that she and Evie used to spend here on those lazy pre-school days; watching the chasing waves, tracking the clouds, picture books open in their laps. Ally would draw a treat from the pocket of her apron, a silver-wrapped toffee or a couple of squares of chocolate, and they'd lean into one another. Bill on this same bench with a beer in his hand, sun on his shoulders, laughing more easily than anyone she'd ever met or would ever meet again. They were days that, when you were living them, felt as if they'd last forever.

What a fallacy that was.

She phoned Paradiso Heights as soon as she returned from the village earlier. Heard from a soft-voiced girl called Naomi that Maggie Pascoe had indeed been a resident in one of their flats. And that she'd passed away from a stroke just ten days ago. While she'd listed her next of kin as her grandson Lewis Pascoe, apparently the mobile number that they had for him hadn't worked.

'We did try to trace him,' Naomi said. 'We found out from the local police that he was in prison, but when we spoke to the governor there, they said he'd just been released. He hadn't checked in with his probation officer yet, but they said that when he did, they'd inform him. Sounds like he slipped through the cracks a bit, if you ask me. So sad. We even spoke to the man who bought her house, in case he knew anything; total longshot but we figured it was worth it. Plus, he knows the owners here. But he couldn't help either. She's at the funeral home though, Maggie – she's safe there. Her grandson can still give her the send-off she deserves. He can say his goodbyes.'

When Ally told Naomi what had happened to Lewis – and how he hadn't known anything about his nan's death – she sounded genuinely upset and asked if she could do anything.

But what was there to be done?

Now Ally wonders whether the young man she met this morning, Jayden, would want to know this information. After all, he gave her his number, and said to call without hesitation. And she's interested in hearing what the police said about the jogger. He seemed almost as shocked about Lewis as she was, and she couldn't help but think of Bill, finding Paul Pascoe all those years ago. Jayden's reaction to Lewis aside, there was something about his manner that reminded her of her husband as a young man.

But he wouldn't really want her phoning him, would he?

The sound of a car driving too fast along the track interrupts Ally's thoughts, and something stirs in her. This is a place where people are supposed to be able to lose themselves: children spilling happily from the beach into the dunes; dogs tearing along without a care. It's a bulky white Range Rover, and it slams to a stop right outside her gate. The fluorescent buoys hanging from her fence – pretty as cherries – are pressed right up against the fender.

She gets to her feet, her brow creased in irritation.

'Ally Bright?'

She doesn't recognise the man. As he comes closer, pushing into her garden, he adjusts his face to show her a smile, but it doesn't quite stick. His eyes are small and angry. His beard is fastidiously trimmed, as neat as an Elizabethan's.

Her thoughts go immediately to Lewis, and it must be the guilt that makes Ally think he's connected to him. She can almost hear the words – *why didn't you help when Lewis asked for help?* She braces herself.

'My wife jogs along this way most mornings,' he says, by way of introduction. 'And I'm told by the local coppers that you're down on the beach a lot. Long black hair. Blue leggings. Very tall.'

He's so curt that Ally can feel herself recoiling; a crab disappearing into its shell.

'You've seen her before, yes?' he says.

'I'm sure I must have.'

'What about this morning, did you see her this morning?'

She gives a brief shake of her head. 'I don't think so. No.'

'Which is it? You don't think so, or no?'

Ally fixes him with a look. 'I said I don't think so. This morning . . . there was an accident down at the cliffs. It's rather occupying my mind. I can't—'

She thinks then of the jogger Jayden saw. She's about to mention it when he cuts in.

'Don't I know it,' he snaps. 'Some delinquent hurls himself over and my wife goes missing, and you're telling me they're not connected?'

Ally starts. It's as if a switch has been flicked, and this man makes no attempt to hide his anger.

'I'm not telling you anything of the sort,' she says, levelly. 'I honestly don't know. But I do know a woman was seen early this morning, jogging on the coast path. The police have been told.'

Not jogging, Jayden had said, *running*. Running fast. And what's the difference between running fast and running *away*?

'What? On the coast path? Going in which direction?'

'That's as much as I know. You'll have to ask the police.'

He puts a hand to his face and rubs it vigorously. 'I've just come from talking to the police – or the excuse for an officer that seems to serve around here. Pug-faced schoolboy.' He blinks. Something flashes across his features, a suddenly remembered thought. 'They don't make 'em like they used to, eh? Or so I'm told.' He shows her all of his teeth in an approximation of a smile. 'Sorry. I haven't introduced myself. I'm Roland. From Sea Dream. The big glass house, mile or so that way,' he says, jerking his thumb over his shoulder.

Ally nods slowly, as unease flickers in her chest. She thinks of the watch on the table just inside the door. The engraving. It feels sinister now, this shoreline picking.

'Your wife is missing, you said?'

'She went out this morning and hasn't come back. Even PC Mullins didn't like the sound of that, given the circumstances. That convict turning up, making threats, and then—'

'Lewis is terribly injured. He's in hospital.'

'You think I care about him right now?'

He starts to pace the small patch of lawn. She hears a crunch as his foot comes down on one of her seashells: a sunset scallop.

'I'm sorry for your worry,' she says. 'I'm sure there'll be an explanation, that she'll turn up. In the meantime, the police will be doing everything—'

'Yes, yes, okay,' he says, dismissively.

She realises her heart is thrumming in her chest. Surreal, to have two intrusions in two days after so many months of quiet. Maybe it's because of what happened afterwards, but compared to this man turning up at her door, Lewis was just a boy; a heartbroken boy. And she turned him away.

'That PC Mullins said you're always out on the beach. That you see everything that happens around here.'

His small eyes are looking directly at her.

'I don't think many people are interested in the things I look for,' she says. She reaches down to the razor-clam pot, plucks out a Lego octopus. Holds it up. 'Spilled from a container ship in 1997. Pieces still wash up occasionally.'

She doesn't know why she says this; perhaps a deliberate effort to appear unfazed. But then Roland lifts his finger; jabs the air in front of her chest. And she suspects this is why; his ugly temper is clear to see.

'And you welcome unexpected visitors into your home too, I hear,' he says. 'Then cast aspersions about your neighbours.'

'I've cast no aspersions. I just told the police what I know. Which is what Lewis told me. He was distressed when he came here.'

'Couldn't you see he was off his rocker?'

He spits the words – Ally actually sees spittle fly – and she feels herself recoil.

'The news that his grandmother had died was a terrible shock,' she says. 'When you told him . . . that was the first he'd heard. And

71

then on top of that, her house gone, he must have thought he was in the worst kind of dream . . .'

'God knows why that lot bothered phoning and telling me about the Pascoe woman. I'd done some consulting for them, that was all. Happened to have one of their brochures with me when I saw Maggie in that tatty old shack of hers. She liked the look of Paradiso Heights – and liked the sound of the offer I made her even more. But that's where the connection ended. As if I'd be in touch with her delinquent grandson.' He gives a snort of amusement. 'I'm not wasting my time talking about this. These sorts of people don't matter. Helena matters.'

Ally sucks in her breath.

Bill stuck up for the little people. That was how he put it. That was his politics. Ally is proud of everything he did, but just as he was happiest out on the streets or in the town hall or the pub, deep down she's always preferred open space to community. Too much human company seems to drain her of essential energies, whereas Bill thrived on it. God, she misses him. And he made Lewis a promise.

'My husband knew Lewis Pascoe,' she says. 'That was why Lewis came to me.'

'All I care about is the fact that my wife's missing. And that kid has got something to do with it – or one of his cronies has. I can get him on assault charges alone. Turning up at my door like that. Making threats. He'll be back inside as soon as he's woken up. If he wakes up. Let's hope he doesn't, frankly.'

'I'd like you to go now, please,' she says, her voice as level as she can make it. 'If I hear anything at all about your wife, I'll be sure to tell the police.'

It's as if Roland draws himself up to his full height, chest puffing out. Somehow it feels as if he fills the whole garden. He stares down at her for one beat, two – and Ally's body tenses, on high alert. Then he turns, about as slowly as a person can, and saunters off down her path.

She waits until he's back in his car, and finally lets out a deep breath. Then she crouches down and gathers the broken shards of the scallop shell; cups them in her hand. She lets stillness envelope her again. She closes her eyes, as the sound of the sea pushes back in.

For most of Ally's adult life, she's followed the strandline. It's the place that holds the secrets of the ocean. It's what's left behind, after the tide's been in and out: the dark tangle of seaweed and driftwood, shells and man-made rubbish. It's where, once the noisy water retreats, you see things revealed – if you care to look closely enough. The police, the ambulance, Roland Hunter; they're all gone. Lights, radios, bulbous white Range Rovers: gone.

And here she stands, now, on the strandline: looking at what remains.

There's a phone call she needs to make, to an old friend of Bill's. And at least one question she needs to ask.

14

Jayden's washing up the lunch dishes – his mum-in-law always cooks a sit-down lunch on Fridays – when his phone rings. It vibrates in the back pocket of his jeans as he's up to his elbows in soapy water.

Sue raises her eyebrows and grins. 'Please don't ask me to get that.'

He laughs. Cat's mum is one of the most good-humoured people he knows. Or maybe it's just in comparison to Cat's dad, who so rarely cracks a smile you'd think he disliked life and everything in it. The first time Jayden met him, he was pretty sure Cat's dad didn't like him. But Cat – the doted-upon only daughter – laughingly reassured him that it was the opposite of that, and Jayden just had to get used to her dad and his ways. Which he has. Mostly. Maybe that's why Skinner's words threw him: *couldn't cope.* Jayden's decided he's really got to get over that one.

'Oh, for goodness' sake,' Sue says, plucking the phone from his pocket and holding it up to him. 'Not your mum? I thought it'd be your mum.'

Jayden doesn't recognise the number. He wipes his hands on a tea towel, takes it from her.

'I'll be back. Don't you go finishing these, alright?'

'Get on with you,' she says.

Jayden wanders out into the hallway, the slate floor cold beneath his socks.

'Is that Jayden? It's Ally Bright. We met this morning at . . .' Her voice trails off.

'Ally, hi. Everything okay?'

He's intrigued – intrigued and pleased – and as he makes for the door there's energy in his stride. The yard is bright with sunshine after the dark interior of the farmhouse. Daffodils flash from cracks in the paving, and a round ginger cat sleeps in an old tractor tyre. Weird to think that this is his world now, though he wonders if he'll ever really see it like that.

In Hang Ten he told Ally that he used to be a constable back in Leeds. He said it was a lifestyle change that brought them down here, that with the baby on the way new ventures beckoned. Not quite a lie. But afterwards, he wondered why he even went there – because Ally hadn't asked. He doesn't usually go around telling people he's ex-police. Maybe because he's still getting used to the 'ex' part; or because it opens up too many questions – or really just one; or maybe because, here in Porthpella, the story has already travelled ahead of him.

'Have the police been in touch with you?' she asks.

'No, they haven't.'

'Jayden, this morning, the runner you saw, the one you called them about . . . A woman's gone missing. She was last seen leaving her house in the dunes early this morning and she's still not back. I can't help wondering if it's the same person.'

Jayden's hand tightens around the phone.

'She's called Helena Hunter,' Ally goes on. 'Roland Hunter's wife. They're the owners of the same house that Lewis went to last night. And the same house that he was seen outside of again this morning.'

Jayden quickly exhales. With that connection, the police will definitely want to be speaking to Lewis. Only they can't.

He's leaning against the gate to the top field, and he pulls back from it now, agitation sparking inside him.

'I knew something was up with her. I mean, she was gone before I'd really processed it, but I could have shouted after her, or . . .'

He didn't trust himself, that's the truth of it. And it was just an impression, and you can't act on every single impression, can you?

'I spoke to a DS Skinner this morning.' He feels his chest tighten at the memory. 'You know him?'

'I know of him.'

'He wasn't a whole lot interested in what I had to say. But this changes things, right? Are the police taking it seriously? Because it's only been a few hours but . . .'

'Her husband says they're taking it seriously. Because of what happened with Lewis.'

'You've spoken to her husband?'

On the other end of the line, Ally hesitates.

'Roland Hunter came to see me an hour or so ago. My house is on one of his wife's jogging routes apparently, and he'd been told that I'm often down on the beach. I suppose he thought I might have seen something.'

Jayden hears a different note in her voice. He's never met the Hunters, but he's seen their white Range Rover barrelling through the village from time to time.

'It was the first time I've met him, to be honest. I know the circumstances were unfortunate but . . . he's rather a forceful character.'

'Are you okay, Ally?' Jayden asks.

Again, she hesitates.

'He was anxious about his wife,' she says, carefully. 'And he was probably feeling helpless, and instead that was coming through as anger, but . . . the way he talked about Lewis . . . he didn't have an ounce of pity for that boy's situation. And he was hell-bent on connecting the two events.'

'Go on.'

'Well, he was blaming Lewis. No question about it. He said he could already get him on charges of verbal assault . . . He said he was aggressive but, Jayden, Lewis wasn't that way with me. In fact, as far as I can see the only person who was being aggressive was Roland Hunter in my garden.'

'What did Roland do, Ally?' says Jayden, gently. 'Do you want to report him? Because I can—'

'No, no. It was nothing. But I'll have my eye on him from now on.'

And there's a steel in her voice that makes him smile. Ally Bright is not a person to underestimate.

'Anyway, that's more or less it,' she says, in sudden wrap-up mode. 'I just thought you'd want to know. About the missing woman, I mean, because I think you were quite right there. It's a rotten mess. Sorry to bother you, Jayden. Thank you. Bye now.'

And she ends the call.

Jayden stares at his screen, surprised by the abrupt finish. Then he looks up, breathes deeply, as overhead a bird of prey floats lazily. He feels, categorically, as if something has shifted. This isn't just a sad story anymore. This is a case. Isn't it? The missing woman is too much of a coincidence. And Jayden doesn't believe in coincidences. Not when it comes to police work. And maybe Ally Bright doesn't either – though she might not like the shape of the dots that Roland Hunter is joining up. Jayden watches as the bird swoops and dives towards an invisible target.

He makes up his mind and hits redial.

The phone rings on and on, and he imagines her moving from another room in her house. Or maybe turning it over in her hand, wondering whether to answer, all the time still blaming herself for something that wasn't in any way her fault.

'Hey, it's me again,' he says. 'Jayden.'

As if he was the one to call her the first time.

'Hello, Jayden.'

And he can't tell what's in her voice – relief? Surprise?

'Ally, I'm just thinking,' he says. 'About the possible connections here. And what Roland was saying. Maybe Lewis was different at their place, you know? Maybe he'd run out of steam by the time he got to yours.' Then, carefully, 'I mean, how much do you really know about Lewis Pascoe? If Roland was antagonistic, pressed Lewis's buttons, then it wouldn't be a surprise if Lewis lost it. Not under the circumstances. It's a pretty natural assumption for Roland to then link that incident and his wife going missing. Don't you think? Or . . . are you thinking something else?'

There's quiet at the other end of the line. Maybe she really wanted to end it there before, and he's got the callback wrong.

'Jayden . . . this isn't like me. To ask these questions, to get involved. To be here, phoning you. Someone I hardly know. Asking for . . . I don't know what.'

'Ally, it's cool. I want to help. We were both there with Lewis. We're both in this, alright?'

She's quiet, but he doesn't rush to fill the space. He waits.

'At school I had a nickname,' she says, 'and it stuck all the way through. It's still with me now, in one way or another. The other girls used to call me Ally All Alone. I suppose I found fitting in hard – and, well, a lot of the time it was simpler not to try.'

Her voice is low, and her words don't sound well practised; they sound, in fact, like she doesn't often put them together this way at all.

78

'And then I met Bill, and he made everything so . . . easy. And now here I am. Doing this – whatever this is.' She stops. Starts again. 'I don't know what people round here would think of me asking all these questions. This now, with you. I'm just not sure if . . .'

Her voice runs out. And Jayden knows, without question, that he was right to ring back. He thinks of his mum, and what she would say in this moment. What she *did* say.

'Other people don't get to decide who you are, Ally. Only you do that.'

'But what if the only reason I'm getting involved is because it's the kind of thing that Bill would have done? What if, now that he's gone, I'm . . . Well, I'm sure that's what anyone round here would think. That I'm trying to . . . fill the hole. As if that's even possible. But do you see what I mean?'

'Ally, who cares? The only person who gets a say in this is you.'

'I know,' says Ally, uncertainly. 'It's just . . . oh, I don't know.'

Jayden leans back against the gate.

'Listen, I get it,' he says. 'Some people like to put other people in boxes. Why that is I don't know, but they do.'

He feels it down here sometimes, the way some people look at him. Porthpella isn't exactly Leeds. But it isn't just here; he grew up with it too.

'My mum and dad, they always said that you can't let other people decide who you are – and that goes for anything, for everything, you know? You just have to be who *you* want to be.'

Jayden feels a surge of emotion. Just mentioning his parents makes him miss their easy company, makes him miss his home city, his friends; makes him miss pretty much everything about his old life.

'And you can't let other people decide what you're capable of either. Ally, what you're talking about now, getting involved in this case . . . well, if you want to do it, then that's all good – that's all you need to worry about. Not what anyone else says or thinks.'

He didn't expect to say so much, but Ally makes a small sound of acknowledgement; of thanks. 'I think that's very good advice, Jayden,' she says. 'I'm grateful.'

'You know what,' he says, 'DS Skinner pretty much accused me of "playing detective" earlier, and I let it bother me, you know. I let it bother me when I shouldn't have. Because if I feel like there are questions not being asked . . . well, I'm going to care enough to ask them. Just like you are, right?'

'*Playing detective?*' she says, and her quick outrage makes him smile. 'He really said that to you? Right, okay, in that case . . . perhaps we should give him something to really talk about. Jayden, I did some digging earlier. Can I tell you about it?'

'Definitely yes.'

He hears her take a breath. And he feels a fizzle of anticipation.

'You remember me telling you about how Bill arrested Lewis? And how he wished it hadn't happened like that for Paul Pascoe's son? Well, I spoke to Stewart, an old colleague of my husband's. He's retired now, but he always had a head for detail. It was a long shot, but I knew he and Bill talked about everything that mattered.'

'Okay,' says Jayden.

'You're sure you don't mind me telling you all this?'

'I want you to.'

And as he says it, Jayden realises how true it is. He wants to be talking about this case – not about tent pitches or crop rotation or whether Cliff can stomach having tourists wandering all over his land all summer long, *playing football with my damn cauliflowers.*

This case. There he goes again.

'Well, Stewart remembered Lewis straight away. He said that Bill confided in him that Paul's suicide had hit him hard, and that when Bill met his son, Lewis, it all just came back to him. What happened was Lewis was caught breaking into a big house just past Carbis Bay, after he'd only been in Porthpella a matter of weeks.'

'He was living here then?'

'That was the plan. His mum had recently passed away and Lewis had nowhere else to go, so he moved in with Maggie. They'd been somewhere in the south-east before, him and his mum. Anyway, his head can't have been straight at all, that's what Stewart said, and it was Bill's theory that Lewis had been used by someone who used to know his dad, someone who took advantage of his vulnerability. Stewart called Lewis the fall guy – said he took the blame for the crime, out of some kind of misguided loyalty to the dad he never knew, and then was sentenced by a judge who took offence to his . . . petulance. That was the word Stewart used.'

Reasons. There are always reasons. And some of them, a lot of them, can break your heart. His mum and dad come into Jayden's head again, in the way that they've kept doing since he took up residence with Cat's family. *Don't ever go thinking you're better than anyone*, his mum always said, back when he was a kid. *Ah, but Gracie, Jay's left foot is categorically better than Simon Morris's goalkeeping*, his dad would add, *so what's he supposed to do with that?* He knows how blessed he is to have so-solid parents. And what is that? Pure luck.

'Petulance . . .' says Jayden. 'Not a crime, but if you team it with breaking and entering . . . Did Stewart say if it was a first offence?'

'A first serious one, certainly. But the homeowner was something of a celebrity – an actress, with a lot of fine jewellery, apparently – so that probably didn't help matters. Lewis was sent to Dartmoor prison for eighteen months. So, after Stewart, I phoned the prison.'

Jayden can feel himself smiling. If this is Ally in hesitant mode, he wonders what she's like when she's certain.

'And what did they say there?'

'I eventually spoke to the governor. That was an adventure in itself, getting through to the right person, but he turned out to be quite forthcoming. When I asked what Lewis had been like, he said that he'd struggled inside, was perhaps even bullied. But he said he was a good lad, and that he'd kept his head down. And that he'd been looking forward to starting anew.'

Perhaps even bullied. In Jayden's experience, if an institution admitted that much, then there was no 'perhaps' about it. Back in the beginning, if he'd had to say what made him choose the police, it was bullies. Plain and simple. Bullies – and people getting away with it.

'You found all this out today?' he says.

'After Roland Hunter left me, I was . . . I don't know. I had to do something.'

Jayden nods to himself, quietly impressed.

'And so, your husband's promise,' he says, 'you think it was that he'd help Lewis get back on his feet when he got out of prison?'

'I think so,' says Ally. 'Knowing Bill, he'd have wanted to make sure Lewis stayed on the straight and narrow. People mattered to him; he didn't just let them flit in and out of his life like nothing. And especially because of Paul . . .'

Jayden hears her voice break, and he feels his own eyes fill in response. It didn't matter if you were in Leeds city centre or deepest Cornwall, being in the police meant having to deal with the kind of challenging events, day in day out, that a lot of people probably wouldn't have to face in their whole lifetime.

'Bill sounds like a good man, Ally. And a good police officer.'

'He was both. Can I tell you something else, Jayden?'

'Yeah. Please keep going.'

'I asked Stewart a bit more about what happened with Paul Pascoe,' says Ally. 'It was a long time ago, but I knew he'd remember. He said Paul had always been in and out of jail, but they only looked at what Paul was doing, not why he might be doing it. They didn't think so much about mental health or other factors, then. After Paul killed himself, it was Bill who took the brunt of the verbal beating from Maggie. That's what Stewart said.' Ally pauses. 'Bill never told me that part. He only ever said *we*.'

'But Bill couldn't blame himself.'

Even as he says it, he knows it doesn't work like that. It's never worked like that. Twenty years ago, would the support have been there for Bill at work?

'It didn't stop him feeling bad. It sounds like Lewis didn't have that many stand-up people in his life. And yesterday, Lewis came looking for Bill for help. That means something, because asking for help? That's the opposite of what Maggie Pascoe ever did. Poor woman.' She sighs. 'And now Helena Hunter is missing. You know, I think I found her watch down on the beach. It's engraved with her and Roland's names. I put it in my pocket, and then, with everything, I forgot about it. I've told the police and they're sending someone to collect it.'

Jayden lets this new piece of information settle. Finding Helena's watch on the beach doesn't sound good.

'You didn't give it to Roland when he came?'

Ally hesitates. 'I didn't . . . trust him.'

Jayden raises his eyebrows. 'Then, good work. The police will fingerprint it. They'll probably fingerprint you too.'

There's a wash of quiet.

'Ally, you still there?'

'I know I have little to base not trusting Roland Hunter on, but . . . I can't shake the feeling that there's more to it all.'

'What – with Helena Hunter? Or Lewis?'

'Perhaps both. Jayden, what if Roland Hunter was involved in Lewis falling? And what if Helena was running away from something. That was what you said, wasn't it? Running away, not just running. What if she was running away from *someone*? Or something she'd seen?'

'I hear you, Ally. And I think these are important questions.'

'Roland Hunter is so sure that there's a connection between Lewis and Helena. And what if there is, but what if it's Roland who's the link?'

The third point of that triangle.

'The police will be looking at all the angles,' he says.

'I'm sure.' Then, her voice dropping, 'Do you think Lewis will pull through?'

'I don't know,' he admits.

His hand smooths the top rung of the gate as he thinks again of Lewis lying in the sand. When Jayden first saw him, he looked gone. Departed. Lewis had had to face so much loss in the hours before that, maybe his own life had seemed like the least of it.

'Ally, you want me to call the hospital? Get an update on Lewis?'

'I can do that,' says Ally. 'I've already taken up too much of your time.'

'I've nothing much else to do right now,' he says, with a quick laugh.

There's nothing else I want to do right now. That's more it, isn't it?

Jayden can see Cat framed in the doorway of the farmhouse. She's holding her hand to her eyes, shading them, looking for him. He leans back against the gate, just out of view – and immediately feels guilty.

'Just one more thing,' says Ally. 'What do you think I should do next? If anything? And if it's not an imposition, me asking. It's just, I'm not sure who else . . .'

'What are you leaning towards?'

'I want to help Lewis,' says Ally. 'I should have last night, and I need to make up for it. Any way I can. Finding out what happened to Maggie, I thought that would feel like . . . something. But it's not enough. Lewis is lying in Intensive Care and I think the man who hurt him – perhaps not physically, but certainly emotionally – is the one who's now pointing the finger at him. Meanwhile there's a woman missing, and—'

Cat's spotted him. She's walking across the yard. Blond hair flying, her stomach huge beneath her denim dungarees.

'I think,' says Jayden, 'that you should give Roland Hunter a wide berth. If he comes again . . . you call me, Ally, right? And talk to the police, tell them what you told me. If they're not very . . . responsive . . . just don't let it derail you, okay? Say what you need to say. Even if it sounds vague, you know.'

'Okay. And I'll be giving them Helena's watch. And I hope to God she turns up soon.'

'Exactly,' he says. 'And you know what, I'm going to do some digging too. I'm going to see what I can find out about Roland Hunter. I want to fill in his background.'

'You mean you're going to play detective, Jayden?' she says with a smile in her voice.

He laughs. 'Ally, if we wake up tomorrow and decide we want to be Porthpella's answer to Holmes and Watson . . . well, guess what? That's up to us.'

Ally gives a low laugh. 'Does that make me Watson? I'd have thought I was more of a Miss Marple.'

'I was kind of, like, trying not to stereotype.' He sees Cat coming closer and knows he needs to wrap things up. 'Look, Ally, I've got to go, but . . . we'll stay in radio contact, right?'

'If you're really sure.'

'Surer than sure,' he says.

And the surprising part is that he actually is.

15

Saffron is just closing up when the customer comes in. An early-season holidaymaker, but one who's sticking around for a while; a couple of months, he told her. He's become one of her favourites, stopping by every few days. He looks more like a St Ives artist than the retired teacher he said he is, with his shaved head, tanned and stubbled face, and rotation of fisherman's jumpers.

'Hey,' she says, 'how are you doing?'

'Not bad, not bad. Oh, are you about to shut?'

She hesitates. It's gone 5 p.m. The till is emptied. She's wiped down all the tables. Turned off the coffee machine at the wall. The last of the afternoon sun is looking like the best of the day, and she has plans to paddle out on the way home, see what the waves have to offer.

'Course I can serve you,' she says. 'You can't stand between a man and his . . . flat white, is it?'

'Please. I don't know where they've been all my life.'

She laughs. 'Something sweet with it?'

'I shouldn't. Wandering down here is the only exercise I'm getting.'

'What place are you renting?'

'All Swell. The little blue house, with the anchor on the front porch.'

'I know it,' says Saffron.

'There's commitment to the nautical theme,' he says, his mouth twitching with a smile, 'and there's heaving an almighty iron anchor up your front steps. Still . . .' He reaches his hand to his head, as if once there was hair there to run his fingers through; an old habit, dying hard. 'It suits me. I'm Gus, by the way. Gus Munro. I don't think I've said that before.'

'Saffron. Pleased to meet you. What are you doing down here? On holiday, right?'

'Oh yes, I can't pretend it's work. But I am working, in a way. But for pleasure, if you see what I mean.'

'Now I'm intrigued,' she says.

'Oh, it's not very intriguing. I'm just another old man trying to write his novel before he dies.'

'A novel? Cool.' She pours his milk; wonders what pattern to make and settles for a classic leaf.

'Now that's a work of art,' he says, watching. 'Something my novel is very definitely not.'

'What kind of thing is it?'

'Crime. I've a surly detective, who is currently a very poor imitation of Morse and . . . someone a lot less effective and compelling than Morse.'

'Cool,' says Saffron again, without being entirely sure of who Morse is.

As if on cue, Mullins walks in, one hand riding high on his police radio, podgy elbow cocked. Saffron doubts anyone has ever laid *effective and compelling* at his door. But maybe that's just the difference between fact and fiction.

'You're back,' she says.

'Missing persons case, Saff.'

Mullins's eyes flick to Gus; his lips pout at the company. But then he always did like an audience. She realises he's got something in his hand, and he holds it up: a photo.

A glamorous dark-haired woman smiles enigmatically from the picture. Her sunglasses are pushed up on her head and she wears a crisp white shirt. Even in this two-dimensional picture it's easy to see she has the shimmer of wealth. And it's easy to recognise her too.

'This is Helena,' he says, his voice grave. 'Helena went for a run early this morning. Left her phone, wallet, keys at home. And, ten hours later, she still hasn't come home.' Then he breaks back into his normal tone, 'Doesn't sound good, does it, eh?'

Saffron feels a thud of shock.

'I know her,' she says. 'I mean, I don't *know* her. But she's been in.'

She has a good head for customers. When the holiday season is running at full tilt then it's harder to mark people out, but between seasons, faces stick. Particularly the ones that are especially friendly – or especially not. Helena is in the latter camp.

'She said the lemon drizzle was dry,' says Saffron. 'And it's so not.'

'Which gives you motive,' says Mullins, followed by a burp of laughter.

Saffron glances to Gus, who raises his eyebrows. She gives a brief shake of her head. 'Please tell me you're not the only person looking for this poor woman.'

'Her husband's out pounding the dunes. And you wouldn't want to cross him, I can tell you.' Mullins shuffles on his feet. 'And then, course, the sarge is all over it. Probably send CID in soon enough.'

'May I see the picture?' asks Gus.

Mullins swivels and holds it up. And Saffron sees recognition flash across Gus's face – plus something else she can't quite put her finger on. She gets a queasy feeling in her stomach. Is a woman really missing?

'That's my nearest neighbour,' he says. 'The Hunters. I couldn't remember her name . . .'

'Helena,' says Mullins.

'Helena.' Gus rubs at his chin. 'Ah, yes. That's it. I've seen her out running.'

'Have you, yeah? Like to watch?'

Gus gives him a long look. 'But I didn't see her this morning. I slept in for once.'

'You ever spoken to her?'

Mullins's feet are planted wide. From the look on his face, he thinks he's on to something.

'We've said hello a couple of times,' says Gus, his hand going to his head. 'If that. I had a longer conversation with her husband once, when I first got here. But that's it. I haven't been very social.'

'Yet you're in here. When it's coming up on closing.' He looks to Saffron, back to Gus. 'Eh?'

Saffron knows Mullins is grandstanding. Asserting his authority in that way petty officials do: a little bit of power is a dangerous thing and all that. And yet. She looks at Gus more closely. What does she actually know about this man, other than the fact he likes chunky jumpers and has a nice voice and is way older than her dad would be – probably, possibly, but who knows anything about her dad? Strange that thought should drop in.

'And no one's seen her at all since she went out this morning?' she says, picking up a tea towel, putting it down again.

'That,' says Mullins, his eyes still on Gus, 'is what I'm trying to establish. I'm talking to *neighbours*.'

Then she puts it together. All Swell is the house near the big glass one. The Lewis Pascoe one. How did she not realise that before? Gus's talk of giant anchors threw her off.

'Helena Hunter,' she says. 'She lives in the glass house?'

'Sea Dream, yep. That's the one.'

'The one I said I saw Lewis Pascoe outside of.'

'Yep.'

'And the one that was built on Maggie Pascoe's land. That Ally Bright said Lewis went to last night.'

'Yep again.'

She leans back against the wall.

This morning she was Team Lewis. Who wouldn't be? Ally, who seemed about as sensible as a person could be, was definitely Team Lewis. And Jayden, who was one of the first to find him at the cliffs, seemed like he was Team Lewis too; his eyes had swum as he talked about it, and she can't remember the last time she saw a man looking like he might cry.

'Exactly,' says Mullins. 'It doesn't look very good for Lewis Pascoe.'

'No, it doesn't. He's still in Intensive Care, isn't he?'

'Yep. And he's had two run-ins with the Hunters in as many days. Making threats. Threats serious enough to be classified as assault.' Mullins rubs his brow. 'That's what Hunter reckons any-way. Verbal assault.' He turns to Gus again. 'You hear any of that going on, neighbour?'

Gus puts down his coffee. His face is full of bewilderment. Like everyone, he probably came here because he thought he was stepping into a picture book, not a real place with real people. Or unreal people: these aren't exactly everyday things – disappearances and cliff falls.

'No. When was this?'

'Last night, around nine, and then this morning around seven, seven thirty.'

'I was working,' says Gus, 'then sleeping. Like I say, an unchar-acteristic lie-in. What's this about a Lewis Pascoe?'

'There was an incident at the cliffs early today,' says Mullins, tight-lipped for once.

'It's all online,' says Saffron.

Her gaze moves to the window. The beach is full of golden light, the waves pulling in perfectly. She wants to be down there, paddling out. But a woman is missing. A woman who left footprints on this very beach this morning, a jog like any other day: only she hasn't come back. And Lewis, falling from the cliff: it should have killed him, and maybe that was the point. You can't just wash those things off.

'Most people who go missing are found within twenty-four hours,' says Mullins. And Saffron's listening to him, wanting to believe that he's got this. 'And it's not that unusual, to leave your stuff at home when you go out running – your phone and that. Not many pockets in those Lycra get-ups, is there? No, it's the Pascoe factor. That's what changes things.'

'The Pascoe factor,' repeats Gus quietly. His eyes are on the window too, as if the truth is out there somewhere, traced on the sand with a stick.

'Lewis needs to wake up,' says Saffron.

'And I need to find Helena Hunter,' says Mullins. And he almost sounds like a hero, until he adds, ''Ere, Saff, is there a bit of that brownie going?'

16

Fox dances at the edge of the incoming tide, yapping excitedly, as if this great mystery called the sea is a new one to him. Ally hurls a piece of driftwood and he darts after it. Returns it with glee. She throws it again.

The best thing about owning a dog is the reminder to take pleasure in the simple things – and a lot of the time it works. There's nothing like seeing him tear out the door, up and over the dunes, sand flying at his paws; it makes her tip her head back, take the good of it all in. But after a day like this, when her mind is full of unrest, Ally knows she's going through the motions. And her canny little dog knows it too.

Lewis is clinging to life in Truro hospital.

Helena Hunter is missing.

Is there a connection? It feels like there has to be. But what?

The angry face of Roland looms in her thoughts. His hair falling across his forehead, his spiked little beard. The way he spat his words.

She crouches down as Fox returns the stick. As she fondles his ears, his black eyes, always so soulful, glimmer at her.

'What are we going to do?' she says.

Bill had never not known what to do. The only time she really saw his confidence knocked was after what happened to Paul Pascoe. And all this time, Ally had no idea that Maggie had delivered her grief-stricken tirade to him. When Stewart told Ally that, a small well of sadness opened up inside of her: what else had Bill kept from her? He'd always wanted to be the strong one for them all, and so no matter how biting Maggie's words had been, he hadn't shared the load. Ally knows that, twenty years on, when he arrested Lewis, Bill would have gone to speak to Maggie – and likely faced more of the same then too. That time was such a blur, that was the problem. Ally was away in Sydney helping Evie with her newborn, and Bill wouldn't have bothered her with it, not while she was out there. But perhaps it stirred something up for Bill, meeting Lewis, who'd just been a baby when his dad killed himself. Whatever it was, the meeting had mattered to both of them.

And, so, it matters to Ally.

When she called Jayden, Ally hadn't even been sure of what she was trying to say. But his response made her feel purposeful. *He* sounded purposeful. So she phoned the police straight after, was patched through to the new sergeant, Skinner. He talked about her husband's legacy. *Life and soul, the guys all say here, life and soul.* She appreciated his words, but it still felt strange, as if there'd been a whispered briefing before he spoke to her. And she didn't like the double standards: this same man dismissing Jayden one minute, and now gushing to her. But when she tried to talk about Roland Hunter, Skinner's tone changed. She felt her contribution was awkward and unsolicited; it seemed the notion of 'playing detective' was a broad church indeed.

'We're taking it seriously,' Sergeant Skinner said, with a puff of self-importance. 'Helena Hunter is classified as high risk, on account of the threats made by Pascoe.'

Ally knows a little about how missing persons are handled by the police. Bill dealt with a fair few in his time: the teenage girl from Hayle who'd fled from internet bullies; the elderly man who'd simply forgotten where he lived and lain down in the churchyard, as if giving up altogether. Bill talked and she listened, and she always thought *if someone I loved was missing, I'd want this caring man to find them*. What Ally doesn't know is anything about Helena Hunter. Whether she has a habit of spontaneous trips or unscheduled plans. Or the state of her mental health, her physical health. The quality of the Hunters' marriage. But these are things that the police will be working on. They'll be interviewing Roland. Searching the home. Analysing phone records and bank statements. While Lewis Pascoe is in Intensive Care, oblivious to it all.

If he is oblivious, that is.

She met Lewis for all of five minutes. A long five minutes, where for almost every second of it she was wanting him to leave, but even so, she felt no real threat from him, not once her imagination calmed down and she saw him for what he was: a confused, upset young man. What threats did he make to the Hunters? If Helena Hunter has been classified as high risk, that means the police fear for her safety.

Ally stands back up and Fox circles her, barking. The incoming tide runs over her shoes.

She felt petty describing Roland's visit to Skinner; vulnerable in a way she didn't like to admit. 'He was agitated,' she said. 'I couldn't help feeling he was spoiling for a fight. And it was as if he had a personal vendetta against Lewis.'

The response from Skinner was that Roland was undoubtedly under a lot of stress. 'We can ask him not to bother you again,' Skinner said, in such a tone that made Ally see herself through his eyes: someone living on their own, anxious. When it wasn't that at all.

'I didn't quite trust Roland Hunter,' she said. 'I think that's what I'm trying to say.'

At that she detected a noise of impatience from Skinner. It wasn't like with Jayden, where she felt like she could say anything.

Ally's found herself turning her and Jayden's conversation over in her mind ever since; it's been a long time since she talked with anyone like that. Knowing what to say to someone to make them feel at ease, that's a gift. Bill had it too.

Skinner had another call come in not long after that, and she was ushered off the line; courteously, but definitively.

Then her next call. To the hospital. Where she had to admit that no, she wasn't family. That Lewis had no family. Where, eventually, she extracted the following: *No change in his condition.*

And after that? All these phone calls, these encounters? She felt like she'd temporarily stepped from her own world into a different and unfamiliar one. Re-entering her own left her with something like the bends. There was nothing she could do except come out here, to the back garden beyond her back garden. And keep on walking. With the buffeting winds and calling gulls. Throw a stick and make a small dog happy.

They've walked a good mile along the beach, past Hang Ten, and further on still is the stretch of beach in front of Sea Dream. Ally looks to the cliffs where Lewis fell, and they shine golden, inappropriately beautiful in the late light.

'Gorgeous out here, isn't it?'

At the voice Ally turns and sees a man she half recognises, standing with his hands planted in his pockets. He's her age, or thereabouts. An open smile on his face.

'God, sorry, I didn't mean to make you jump.'

'You didn't,' she says.

He did, of course. But it isn't like with Roland, or Lewis. This third man is like her: that's the thought that passes through her mind, *someone like me.* Which in the next instant she bats away as a silly thought.

He nods again. Points at the sky. 'Sorry. I'm still getting used to it. Total grockle.'

And it is beautiful, the sky. Somehow, in the last few minutes, it's gone from common or garden blue-grey to silver-streaked azure. Sunset is nigh. How did she not notice?

'Emmet,' she says. 'That's what you are down here. An emmet, not a grockle.'

'Is that better then, to be an emmet?' he asks. 'I'm not sure it sounds better.'

'I think it's probably worse,' says Ally, a smile twitching her lips. And she doesn't even feel like smiling; but if she's not careful it'll break through.

'Well,' he says, throwing out an arm – taking in the abstracted sky, the white-capped waves, all of it – 'enjoy your walk.'

'You too.'

He turns. 'There's a woman missing. My neighbour actually. I just talked to the police. It feels strange not to mention it. But then it feels strange to mention it, as well. Just . . .' He rubs at his head. 'Keep an eye out. For yourself. And for her. I mean . . .'

'I know,' she says. 'Thank you.'

He furrows his brow. 'You don't sound worried. I mean, not that I think you should be worried. But, it is worrying, isn't it, it's always worrying . . . And I can't imagine round here you have very much to worry about normally. Crime-wise, I mean.'

'I was married to the local sergeant. You'd be surprised.'

'What, the young chap? Mullins, is it?'

And she laughs, the sound escaping from her like a cork from a bottle; so unfamiliar that she wants to clap a hand across her mouth – or do it again.

'The former sergeant,' she says. 'Before that lad's time. And what I mean is . . .'

But he's laughing too. 'A cast-aside toy boy. Glamorous divorcee. Not beyond the bounds of possibility.' He stops abruptly.

'Sorry, that's disrespectful. I've been too much in my own company. Keep getting it wrong.'

He waves a hand, as if dismissing himself.

'Gus Munro,' he says, already turning to go, as if he's thought better of the whole conversation. 'Clueless, er, emmet. It was good to meet you . . .'

'Good to meet you, Gus.'

He's walking away as she looks down at the stick in her hand and feels Fox's insistent paws against her leg.

Glamorous?

'The name's Ally,' she says quietly, to herself. Then she turns in the other direction and hurls the stick towards the sky, which still blazes with uncomplicated beauty.

17

Roland stands in front of Helena's double wardrobe, the doors thrown wide. *Is anything missing?* Mullins asked earlier, and how on earth is he supposed to know a thing like that, because what man really pays attention to the comings and goings of his wife's closet? With Helena, it would be an impossible task. He pulls at the silk hem of a dress, one of dozens like it. A skimpy leather jacket slithers off its hanger without him even touching it.

He slams the doors shut.

It was an insult for Mullins to even suggest it, as if Helena had neatly packed a bag and strolled off. *Standard procedure*, the wet-eared lad protested, but it was farcical. Especially given Pascoe's threat.

How would you feel if you lost the only person you loved?

That was Pascoe's parting shot early this morning, and what could be clearer than that? Even the police agreed it didn't look good. Roland should have told that one to the Bright woman, no doubt a bleeding-heart leftie who thought Lewis was special just because he'd been dealt some hard knocks in life.

So, Roland could hardly be blamed for losing his cool a little bit, when the police bleated on about Helena's passport, her suitcase, her knicker drawer. Bloody Nathan stepping in, as if he were suddenly a man of the people, with: *Cool it, Roland, the officer's just doing his job.* And the extra weight Nathan gave to the name *Roland* too, the amused curl to his lip. *This is what women do, brother, they create problems. But leave the hysterical reactions to them, okay?*

His brother is downstairs now in the pool room, knocking balls in without a care in the world, chewing nuts and drinking up his Chablis. Nathan has been lurking at Sea Dream all day and has clearly decided he'd rather play the big man in Roland's drama than go and actually view the properties he drove down from London to see. He even said he enjoyed his own chat with the police earlier; said it was like being in a TV drama, as if it were all just a game. Then he asked where they'd be going out for dinner. As if.

Roland takes out his phone again and sits down on the edge of the bed. He stares at it just as dumbly as before. Mullins wanted him to contact all of Helena's friends. Like, what, she decided to jog on off the beach and settle in with a mate for a ten-hour chat? It was another way of insinuating that she left of her own accord. And, although that's impossible, he hates that he's turning it over in his brain anyway. It's coming on for nightfall, so how can he not?

He's already told the police everything he knows about that morning, which isn't much. Pascoe came back early, wanting to go another round, waking them both up. Nathan stayed sleeping. Pascoe eventually blew himself out and left. Helena then appeared in her Lycra and took herself off for a run. The last thing Roland said to her was *see you later, love*. In fact, when he stops and thinks about it, that's probably the only thing he said to her after they woke, what with the Pascoe business.

Is there anyone out there he should be ringing? Helena doesn't have a gaggle of girlfriends that she goes about with. In fact, he can't think of a single significant acquaintance down here. There's the other stuff, he supposes – a woman's basic upkeep, hair and nails and all that – but he's never paid attention there. Her hairdresser, whoever the hell she is, might be privy to all her secrets, for all he knows.

Roland brings up Helena's number. He handed over her phone to the police earlier, but he has an overwhelming urge to call her anyway. He closes his eyes tightly as rage sparks behind his lids. He's not sure he's ever felt this powerless.

He's a fixer. That's what he is and that's what he does. No matter the job, he's always reacted, adapted, improvised. An old teacher once said to him, *The trouble with you, Hunter, is you think you've got all the answers*. He took it as a compliment.

Right now, though, he's got nothing. And the one person who must know what's happened to his wife is being mollycoddled in hospital.

Unless Pascoe has cronies – and Roland suggested this to Mullins. The kid tried playing the 'all alone in the world' card when he pitched up on the doorstep, but he could have acted with a mate, couldn't he? Any minute now, Roland's phone could trill with a ransom demand.

That's the only problem with wealth; it makes you a target.

Helena could be gagged and bound, Pascoe's plummet nothing more than a falling-out among thieves. It's a damn sight more plausible than his wife packing a bag and taking a spontaneous weekend trip without telling him.

And you know what makes him really sure of this? It isn't the watch. The Rolex he bought her, engraved with the date he proposed. Helena doesn't normally wear it to go running, but the police found it down on the shore. With a cracked face. He was triumphant at first, *I bloody told you!* Then, what it meant, the violence of it, settled with him; made him want to puke.

They're checking it for fingerprints, but if it was dunked in the ocean it's hardly likely to offer much of a clue.

The police said they'll be looking into acquaintances of Pascoe's, but if he's been inside for the last eighteen months, and has no next of kin, they reckoned they won't have a lot to go on there, either. But it's basic, isn't it? All of it is basic. You watch the hospital. See who comes to leave a sad little bouquet of garage flowers; a bunch of grapes.

Roland focuses in on this thought; it's an action, and he needs to do *something*. He always does something. But he isn't stupid enough to try to pay the kid a visit himself; he knows how that would look. Send Nathan instead? He'd never agree to it though – and asking him would be more trouble than it's worth. No, the smart move is to conduct a little surveillance operation. See who comes and goes at the ICU.

And try not to think of the hours ticking past, all the time that Helena is still not found. If he closes his eyes, he imagines he can hear her scream. She's always had a good scream on her, his wife.

Roland jumps, then, as he sees the flashing image of a stick in the doorway. A man's shadow moves on the wall. *Pascoe*, he thinks, *Pascoe back for vengeance*. But Pascoe is lying in a coma.

'Brother,' says Nathan, stepping into the room. He twirls the pool cue. Grins. 'You're a bit jumpy, aren't you?'

Roland grits his teeth. Nathan's been acting as cool as a cucumber, maintaining that Roland has nothing to worry about. Roland wants to wring his neck – or, at the very least, run him out of the house. Instead, he says, 'Shouldn't you have been out today? Looking at properties?'

'I thought I was better off here with you. Moral support and all that.' Nathan waggles the pool cue. 'You look like you need to smash a few balls. Come on, I've racked them. And we need dinner. Show me how you do Friday nights round here.'

Roland looks his brother up and down, eyes narrowed. It isn't like Nathan to set aside his own plans for the day. In fact, any kind of flexibility is not his brother's style at all. But maybe this is an unprecedented situation. Perhaps this whole thing might bring the two of them closer together? But then Roland brushes that idea away; it's an even stupider thought than Helena having left of her own accord.

'I've lost my appetite,' he says gruffly. 'You do what you want.'

18

Jayden's phone is a rectangle of light. Beside him in bed, Cat is fast asleep, one arm thrown up behind her head as if sunbathing. This is what she does these days – sleeps early, wakes late. She's blessed in pregnancy; Jayden's sister had insomnia and anxiety in the last months. She phoned him once in the small hours, the week before her due date, saying, *I don't think I can have this baby*. But she did, and his niece Charmaine was about the sweetest thing he'd ever laid eyes on. Women are just stronger than men; that's Jayden's theory. And it's as if, deep down, men know it, so they make out they're more at every turn. Some of them do, anyway.

And maybe Roland Hunter is one of them.

Jayden was troubled by Ally's description of her encounter with Roland. He doesn't like the thought of her feeling vulnerable – of anyone feeling vulnerable – for even a second.

They were both shaken this morning at the beach. And he knows Ally feels emotionally involved because she turned Lewis away rather than took him in; which is pretty much what anyone would have done if there was a pounding at their door late at night. But Jayden knows a thing or two about guilt. Logic, rationality – they don't much apply once your head is set on a certain course.

But as Ally talked about Roland coming to her garden, it was clear there was something else at play too. Back in Leeds, Jayden had been involved with a few missing persons cases. It's the not knowing – worry as a physical thing, gnawing at everything, until all people can do is think the worst. They handle it in different ways: close in on themselves, crumpling like balled paper, or shoot out arrows at anyone who comes close. It's tough to be Roland Hunter right now. No question.

Jayden helped Cliff clear out the big barn that afternoon, and he kept his thoughts well away from DS Skinner. He didn't want to get into what Cliff may or may not have said; what Cliff may or may not, deep down, really think of his decision to leave the police. So instead, as he hauled sacks of grain and swept up rat droppings – who even is he now? – he thought squarely about Ally and their conversation. He kept coming back to this one thought: for all Ally's connection to Lewis, she didn't strike him as a person who would usually be blinded by emotion. Whatever she thought about the way Roland treated Lewis, it wouldn't stop her pitying a man who was going out of his mind with worry. But there hadn't been much sympathy for Roland in Ally's voice. Concern for Helena, of course – but not for Roland.

Was it instinct? Kieran used to talk about instinct, like it was something you either had or hadn't. *It's what separates good cops from great cops*, he'd say. *I'll only ever be a good cop, Jay. Because I only trust the facts. A damn good cop. But you, you could be a great cop. That's the difference.*

But the truth is, the only difference between them that matters is that Kieran is dead, and Jayden isn't.

Jayden feels a push of sadness in his chest. He doesn't fight it; he's no match for it anyway – even now. Then he makes himself, forcibly, turn his thoughts back to Ally.

Is Ally trusting her gut when it comes to Roland and Lewis? Or does Jayden have her wrong altogether, his own instincts shot to pieces?

You were right about the woman running, Jay.

And it's Kieran's voice he hears – the easy lilt of it, nearly always a smile chasing his words. Jayden sucks in his breath. Okay, he *was* right about the woman running – not that any part of him wants to revel in that.

Beside him, Cat murmurs, and he watches her; she looks like a little girl when she sleeps, with her thick lashes and rounded cheeks, as innocent as a babe. He drops a kiss on her forehead, and as she shifts slightly, he holds his breath. He's only just got started on his desk research – bed research – and he doesn't want to stop it now. He knows that if his wife suspects he's getting involved in whatever went on in the dunes this morning, he'll have to let her exercise her divine right as an expectant mother: if she doesn't like it, she can shut it down.

He goes back to his phone and scrolls through the search results for *Roland Hunter*. A solicitor in Tunbridge Wells. A sports physio in Edinburgh. A freshman at Iowa State.

He adds *Cornwall* to his search. Roly Hunter is a jewellery maker based in Perranporth, but as he clicks on the website, he sees a blond-haired woman. He goes back. Then, at last, he finds someone who could be him, but it's no more than a name on a list: a charity golf tournament at a health club in Saltash, two years ago.

So, Roland keeps a low profile, does he? Jayden types in *Helena Hunter*, but nothing jumps out at him. He gives up, goes back to Roland.

If you type Jayden's name into Google, it won't take long to find the news reports from the night Kieran died. He did it once, just once – and he instantly regretted it. The worst night of his life, documented in black and white. **Police officer dies in tragic stabbing in Leeds.**

Cat caught him at it then. *See, nobody blames you, Jay. And the internet loves blame, it lives for it. And nobody could ever blame you. You did everything you could. You did more.*

Jayden types in *Roland Hunter* again. Then his finger hovers over what word to put next. The internet loves blame. Well, Cat was right. He types in *crime*. It's a long shot. The screen is flooded with the self-published works of a crime writer living in Wisconsin. Roland Hunter of Wisconsin is an active blogger, and Jayden thumbs past entry after entry. He tweaks the search: *Roland Hunter UK crime*. The American writer features again. *The London Loner* has seventy reviews on Amazon, and Jayden could download it right now for $3.99. Then something else catches his eye. He clicks the link to Surrey Live.

Tragic Godalming burglary unresolved.

Then: John Hunter, husband of the murdered victim of a bungled break-in, appeals for witnesses to come forward.

Jayden's about to leave the page when he stops; scrolls down. There's a picture of John Hunter, gazing directly at the camera. And although he's only seen Roland once or twice in the village, Jayden recognises this man straight away. His eyes go to the caption: John Roland Hunter, forty-six, of Godalming, was out of town on the night of the break-in.

John Roland Hunter?

He quickly screenshots the page. Then he types *John Hunter burglary* into Google.

As entries flood the screen, his mouth drops. Third one down. Husband in tragic burglary case admits he was playing away the night his wife was killed by intruders.

The name Helena Cavendish blares from the article as if it has a siren attached to it. He glances across at Cat; he can't believe she's sleeping through it.

It has to be the same Helena. And Roland Hunter is definitely John Hunter.

105

19

Ally wakes early on Saturday. She's a lark by nature, but this morning her thoughts yank her from sleep like a riptide. It's 5.40 a.m. She lies restless, trying to find sleep again, but then gives up. Sunrise is around 6.30 a.m. this time of year, and after last night's sky, it'll likely be a beauty; front-row seat on the veranda, a cup of coffee, Fox at her feet. It's a good way to start the day.

At the thought of sky, the man from the beach pops into her head: Gus Munro. And perhaps just because it's an unexpected diversion from thoughts of Lewis and Helena, she finds herself wondering if he's an early riser; any appreciator of skies should be, by rights. Then she dismisses him as quickly as he came. She has no business.

She's not sure she has business with any of it.

After her shower she makes coffee. She sets the pot on the stove and before long it's spitting. Fox twines round her legs. She fills her mug and opens up the door. The air that greets her is soft, mild, and it wraps itself around her as she takes her seat on the veranda. She can hear skylarks singing up above the dunes, a whistling melody. Rabbits bounce from burrow to burrow, just-visible bobtails flashing white among the marram grass. Silver-dark water, sky heading towards fire.

How could she leave all this behind?

She remembers sunrise in Sydney being a hard cut from dark to light – none of this delectable ebbing. She also suspects this is a corrupted memory. That whole month she was immersed with her newborn grandson, rocking him with one arm – oh, she does miss holding those boys; that would be one thing about moving, and a big one at that – while she made tea for Evie with the other. And all that time, Bill was here, and Lewis was getting himself into trouble.

From back inside the house she hears her phone buzz.

She and Evie have set days and times for their conversations, which is how her daughter likes it. And Ally can understand that, when your life is busy. Her own life is a clear expanse of beach, but the last two days have been exceptional: cluttered and tumultuous; debris after a storm. The way she wittered on to Jayden, she was sure he'd think her mad. Only, he didn't seem to. Now she's on her feet, heeding the buzz of the phone. Jayden's on her mind, so when she sees his name on the screen it doesn't even seem that strange.

Morning! I know it's well early but my surf slot (as was) is coming up. I've got something on Roland. Want to meet at Hang Ten? Not sure when it opens though!

Such a breezy message, as though they're friends. Or colleagues. Or something.

Ally reads it again, hesitating. Then, before she can change her mind, she taps out a reply:

Would you like to come here? The Shell House. From Hang Ten head towards the lighthouse, last in the dunes at the beach's end.

When did she last invite someone to the house? She's about to reconsider when her finger accidentally pushes Send. Before she can react, his reply buzzes in.

Great. Get the kettle on!

❧

As Jayden lopes down the track he raises his hand and waves. Fox rushes to the gate with exuberance and Ally watches as Jayden squats to pet him.

'Good morning,' he says, looking up with a grin.

'Good morning to you too,' she says.

He stands and looks at the house. 'I can see why it's called The Shell House.'

The house itself has timber walls, like all the old places in the dunes, and there's a winding stone path, with a decorative edge of seashells. It leads all the way to the veranda, where Ally sits now; there the shells continue, set into the lower wall.

'It was like this when we first came here,' says Ally. 'It goes on inside too, little shell details, where you least expect it.'

'I bet your grandkids love it,' he says.

Did she tell him about Evie? She must have. She talked so much yesterday.

'They're all the way in Australia. They've only been a handful of times.' When she says it like that, isn't moving to Sydney the reasonable thing to do? She adds brightly, 'But they did love it, yes. Of course, Zak, the oldest, tried to count them. I think he made it to one hundred and then gave up. Coffee? Or do you prefer tea?'

'If there's one going, I'll take a coffee,' Jayden says, skipping up the steps, his feet light on the rickety wooden boards.

She gestures to the bench. 'Out here? Or in?'

'Can I see inside?' he says. 'These houses down here, they make me think of where my grandmother was born in Trinidad. Takes me right back to holidays when I was a kid.' He glances at her sideways. 'Man, I love a beach house.'

'Be my guest,' says Ally. She stands aside and he follows Fox inside. 'Do you still have family in Trinidad?'

'My grandmother's brother's there, and all of his lot. So yeah. But they're mostly in London, my mum's family, since the sixties anyway. Dad's side have been in Yorkshire since the Vikings, I reckon. The story goes he wanted Thor for my middle name but my mum ruled it out. I still need to thank her for that.' He slowly turns around, taking the room in. 'I always pictured a village sergeant living in a house by the church or something. Right in the middle of it, you know? Or is that just my mum watching too many *Heartbeat* reruns?'

'Oh, Bill would have liked that in some ways, I think. To be so easily found. But I suppose I've always preferred to be more at the edge of things. It was a gift to me really, this house – that's what he always said.' She glances at him. What is it about Jayden that makes her want to keep talking? He's a good listener; maybe it's that simple. 'I was a new mother when we moved down here,' she goes on, 'and I was struggling in every way, but here I just felt immediately at home. The wild space was just what I needed. What I still need. And the funny thing is it's not that remote; the village is only fifteen minutes on foot from here.'

'And you've got your own beachside community going on?'

Ally nods to the window, where a triangle of roof – another weatherboard house – is just visible.

'Well, most of these are holiday lets or second homes these days. In fact, they almost all are now.'

'Except for the Hunters'.'

'Except for the Hunters'.'

The coffee pot spits and hisses and Ally clicks off the gas. She pours two mugs and takes the lid off a tin of biscuits. 'Ginger nut?'

Jayden scoops out two. Grins. Then he's looking around the open-plan interior. His eyes settle on the piece on the back wall. It's massive, she knows that, and she feels a bit self-conscious of the fact – but where else can she put it? And Bill always liked it.

'Woah,' he says. 'Now that's cool. That's the view from the beach here, right?' He moves closer, then exclaims, 'It's all plastics? Man, some of these pieces are *tiny*.'

Ally nods. 'Everything found on this stretch of coast, I'm sad to say. Over several years though. I save a lot, sort a lot. Recycle a lot too, of course. It certainly makes litter picking more interesting.'

'You made it? But it's really cool.'

She laughs. 'Don't sound so surprised.'

'I mean, *really* cool. Why aren't you like a world-famous artist or something? Or . . . are you? And now I feel really stupid?'

'It's just something I like doing,' she says. 'Very much amateur.'

'But you do sell them, right?'

It's as if Jayden can't take his eyes from it, and she feels absurdly flattered.

'One or two, over the years. I tend to give them away, if anything.' She laughs again. 'Whoever'll take one. I'm not sure they're all that easy to live with. I think people like art that's easy to live with. A lot of the galleries down here do, anyway. Who wants a constant reminder of the way we're destroying the planet hanging over their mantelpiece?'

'I would,' says Jayden. 'My mates would. You should be famous, Ally Bright. Are you working on one now?'

How can she explain it? That since Bill's death, she just hasn't felt like being creative. She still litter-picks, and of course she beach-combs along the shore, but it's been a year since she did anything new. She finds herself telling him this, more or less.

'I get it,' he says.

And there's something in his look that shows he genuinely does.

'My friend died. We were officers together. The police changed for me, after that, you know? Nothing felt right.'

She wants to ask why he died, but she doesn't. Instead she says, 'Is that part of why you left?'

'Something had to change. And Cat thinks Cornwall is the answer to everything. Hey, this place,' he says, switching the subject, 'it's making me envious. Cat's parents have had this holiday cottage for years, kind of like a barn conversion before they got cool. It's pretty small, and very basic, but it was going free, so . . . that's where we are. We're lucky to have it.'

'Is that where you'll live with the baby?'

Jayden makes a non-committal noise. 'That's the plan.' He rubs at his chin. 'And it's great, right. Fresh air, all that. Tell you what, though, one day I'd love to be somewhere like here, right on the beach. But I bet it's crazy money.'

'These days, yes, I think it is. Not back when we moved here though.'

They've wandered on to the veranda. Jayden stands cradling his mug, steam rising. He looks out to the water.

'I drove past Sea Dream on the way down here,' he says.

'That was out of your way, if you came in through the village.'

'Yeah. I just wanted to see what was going on. And the answer's not much. Roland Hunter's not an early riser. Or if he is, he's lying low. Full house, though. There's a Range Rover, a Lexus, and one of those new Minis outside. I figure he's got friends with him? Or is that how he rolls?'

Ally shakes her head. 'I've only seen him in the Range Rover.' She knots her hands in her lap. 'I'm not a snooper,' she says. 'I've never even done Neighbourhood Watch. I'm starting to wonder if this all feels . . .'

'You're a concerned citizen,' he says. 'A good Samaritan.'

'So not Holmes and Watson anymore?'

But his face is serious. 'Ally, look, I've got to show you something. That's why I had to see you this morning. I think it changes

111

things. Big time.' He puts down his coffee and takes out his phone. He taps and scrolls. 'Now, look. Who's that?'

It's Roland Hunter. Looking very slightly younger perhaps, certainly less grey in his hair, but unmistakeably Roland.

'Roland is his middle name,' says Jayden. 'He's really John Hunter. Or he was five years ago, when he hit the headlines because his wife was killed in a burglary that went wrong. Hunter wasn't in the house at the time. He was out of town. Staying with his lover, Helena Cavendish.'

Ally can feel her eyes widen like a cartoon character's.

'The police will know all this already,' says Jayden. 'It won't be news to them.'

He passes Ally his phone, and she reads over the article.

'So, after his wife died, they married and moved down here,' she says.

'As far as I can see they were near Plymouth for a few years. They came to Cornwall when they built their house here a few months ago.'

'Did they convict anyone? For the death of the wife. Victoria.'

'No.' Jayden shifts on his feet, his energy palpable. 'There was a gang operating in Surrey at the time, varying degrees of aggravated burglary. Two weeks later they were caught breaking into a mansion half a mile away, firearms possession, assault, the lot – but they denied having anything to do with the Hunters. And definitely denied killing anyone. There wasn't enough evidence to link them in the end. But they went down for a load of other stuff.'

'How did you find all this out? On the internet?'

'Plus a late-night chat with my mate Fatima,' says Jayden. 'We trained together, and she ended up joining Surrey Police.'

Ally takes a sip of coffee and looks to the water. 'I don't think that can be something you'd ever get over – a death like that. In your own home. Knowing, probably, that if you'd been there, as you should have been, then it might not have happened at all.'

'It's guilt on top of guilt,' says Jayden. 'And . . . shame. Big-time. No wonder they moved away.'

'The trauma of it,' says Ally.

Jayden paces the boards in his skinny jeans and big white train-ers, hands gesturing. 'Exactly. His first wife was murdered, now his second wife is missing . . . he must be thinking *I can't go through this again*. Wouldn't that have come across when he turned up here? If he was getting emotional, you know?'

'We hardly talked. Perhaps I didn't give him a lot of room. I didn't like the way he came barging in. Maybe, unfairly, I . . .'

'Helena's been gone for nearly twenty-four hours now.'

There's a couple of surfers out on the water and Ally watches them bobbing, lifting and dropping with each passing wave, wait-ing for their moment. All patience and purpose.

'And the police still have nothing to go on?' she says.

Jayden shrugs. 'Don't know. The watch you found though, that can't look good.'

'I know it doesn't. But Jayden, I don't think Lewis would have hurt anyone. And I don't think he jumped off that cliff. I know I have nothing to base that on except . . .'

'Your instincts.'

And the way he says it, it's like he trusts her.

She presses her hands to her eyes. 'Hold on. Would Roland Hunter have known what Lewis was in prison for?'

Jayden stops; rocks back on his heels.

'Yeah, maybe. If Maggie Pascoe told him he was in prison, I'm sure she'd have said what for. You don't just leave that hanging, because people's imaginations are going to go to the worst places, aren't they?'

'Then perhaps he's prejudiced against anyone who's been convicted for burglary.'

'Keep talking.'

'Well, when Lewis turned up out of the blue, late at night, it could have provoked an extreme reaction. It could have felt like an intrusion all over again. It wouldn't have mattered that Lewis was upset, confused – Roland could have felt threatened simply by his presence. Don't you think?'

She hears herself: the words sound nothing like hers. But Jayden doesn't seem to notice.

'I definitely think it could have felt complex,' he says.

'Or perhaps very simple. Here was someone walking free, when his first wife was dead at the hands of burglars. He might have seen red. Mightn't he? God, listen to me, what a stretch . . .'

She sits back; she's said more than enough. And who is she to speculate?

'It's not a stretch, Al,' says Jayden. 'I reckon it could be motive.'

20

Gus stares at the blank page. This morning the words won't come. It's as if the real-life drama unfolding around him is revealing his own attempt at crime to be feebly fabricated; distasteful, even. That sort of reasoning is enough for his head, which always seems to welcome a bit of self-sabotage. He claps his laptop shut.

What now though?

He wanders across to the window and looks over to Sea Dream. The woman at the window, Helena, is missing. And unless anything has changed, she's been missing for twenty-four hours. He's learnt from his writing research it's a significant marker in a missing persons case: twenty-four hours, and then seventy-two. You don't want to get to seventy-two. Or is that more for children? An adult can just walk on out of their own life, can't they, if they so wish it? In an odd way, that's what it feels like he's done sometimes.

But the police are taking it seriously. He's been trying to stay off the news since moving down here, but he caught the report last night. An appeal for information.

Does Gus have any information? Should he tell them what he knows? Is it, in fact, anything worth knowing?

And how exactly do you know that this nakedness was a regular occurrence, Mr Munro?

Then a thought crosses his mind: what if Helena was communicating with someone, and her twilight striptease had an intended audience? He stops himself. He's trying to make a story out of it. Maybe Helena Hunter is just uninhibited. Perhaps when she stood upstairs, behind all that plate glass, staring out at the sea, it wasn't about anything except feeling good in her own skin, in her own home: she can't have known anyone else could see her. Or perhaps she didn't care.

Gus knows one thing for sure: Roland must be going out of his mind.

Gus has never been an interfering person, but it's a question of doing what's right. The neighbourly thing would be to go over, to check in and ask if there's anything he can do. It's strange not to, isn't it? Suspicious, even, to stay hidden in his house, just metres away?

The complicating aspect is whether Roland has any idea that his wife has been standing naked at the window – at least three times that Gus can count. And if Roland doesn't, is that something a man ought to know? Perhaps, in this situation, it is. Because what if someone saw her, and that same someone has now hurt her, and Gus knows this tiny scrap of information and does nothing with it on account of his own embarrassment? He wouldn't be able to forgive himself.

Gus rubs his face with both hands. He thought Cornwall would be simple. It doesn't feel terribly simple anymore.

As he steps outside, Gus turns his face to the morning sun. It's mild for early spring, with a lively breeze. Decent-looking waves are rolling into the bay. He's immediately nostalgic for all the days when he wasn't carrying this particular burden; yesterday, the day before, all the ones before that. Did he even appreciate it? I mean, really appreciate it? Just him and his book and his sore little heart.

116

Then he gives himself the thinking equivalent of a short, sharp slap. Helena Hunter is missing, and Lewis Pascoe is lying in Intensive Care. Gus's moral dilemmas really are small fry. He'll talk to Roland Hunter, neighbour to neighbour, man to man, and simply offer him any help he can. He knows he's up and about, because he saw him put the bin out earlier.

Gus cuts across the dunes and is at Sea Dream in just a few seconds. Compared to the towering glass and brickwork, his own place feels like a toy house. The front door is a barricade of dark polished wood. Gus presses a buzzer, and immediately a voice crackles in reply.

'Yes?'

'Oh, good morning. It's . . . it's your neighbour. From across the way. I hope it's not too early, only I wanted—'

The door flings open just as Gus is still tilted uncertainly towards the intercom. He straightens up, immediately awkward.

Roland looks as if he hasn't slept. There are dark scoops beneath his eyes and his thick hair is dishevelled. His neck is a vivid red. Perhaps it's too early for a Saturday morning. Has he got him out of bed?

'Do you know something?' Roland barks.

Gus stammers. He never stammers. 'K-know something? About what?'

'About what? About *what*? You're not serious.'

Start again, Gus.

'I just wanted to see if you, well, see how things are. If there's anything I can—'

Roland is scrutinising him; his eyes are tiny and probing.

'You do, don't you?' he cuts in. 'You know something.'

'No, not at all, I was concerned and just wanted to offer . . .' Gus rubs his hand on his jawline; hears the stubble crackle.

'Shifty,' said Roland. 'You look *shifty*.' He draws out the word, his lip curling.

Gus knows then that it was a bad idea to have come. Very bad.

'Tell me what you know. Because you saw something, didn't you? Spit it out, or I'm calling the police.'

'I don't know anything,' says Gus. 'Only that . . . well, you never know who's out on the beach at night, do you? Or in these dunes, I mean. Anybody could be—'

'What an insightful observation, Mr Book Writer.'

'What I mean is, if someone was watching . . .'

'Watching?' Roland comes closer, and a puff of sour whisky-breath hits Gus. He tries to subtly step back, but there's something about Roland's gaze that makes it suddenly very difficult to move. 'Watching Helena, you mean? Why would someone be watching Helena?'

Gus shakes his head. Speaks quickly. 'Sometimes she stood at her window not wearing very much.'

'What?' The colour drains from Roland's face, leaving it as white as seafoam. Then red, rushing back in. Fast. 'What? Say that again.'

Gus really doesn't want to say it again.

'Your wife. Standing at the window. She didn't have much on.'

Roland just stares at him. His face is on fire now. Gus swallows.

'I think she probably did it a few times. And she was mostly naked. I mean, when I saw her, when I happened to . . . catch a glimpse. In passing. Altogether naked, actually. Which of course is her prerogative. I mean, it's her house. Her windows. But, you know, given what's happened, you never know who might be watching, that's what I mean. Who might be going past? It feels so quiet, out here, you think it's just you and the sea, but . . . I just thought you should know, in case it had anything to do with anything . . . In case someone saw, the wrong person, and . . .' He hesitates. Loses his way.

The silence from Roland is deafening.

When the punch comes, it's out of nowhere. A quick, sharp jab – and it catches Gus full in the face.

He takes two steps back, sways. His hands, belatedly, go to protect himself, and they come away bloody.

'You come here, telling me something like that?' shouts Hunter.

Gus's mouth tastes full of metal. He can already feel his lip swelling. He's pretty sure that if he tries to speak, it'll come out wrong again – worse than before, even. Meanwhile, Hunter's fist is still clenched. A ring glints on his littlest finger; so that's the added sting that Gus can feel at the corner of his mouth.

'And what else do you know? Hmm? Apart from what my wife looks like naked?'

Gus goes to touch his face again; winces. He doesn't know anything. Nothing about anything. But these words bounce around inside his head like balls in a busted pinball machine.

'Hmm? Mr Book Writer? *Fifty Shades of Grey*, is it?'

Gus was never playground bait as a child, and once upon a time he held his own on the rugby pitch too. But as Roland looms over him he can feel his insides twist and he realises that he's frightened. He can't remember the last time he was frightened. Sad: well, a little. Uncertain: probably. Anxious: sometimes. But actually scared?

'I'm calling the police,' says Roland.

And it's the last thing Gus expects him to say. Immediately fear is replaced with relief. And then, a wave of uncertainty. What if Gus's words come out wrong then too?

21

PC Tim Mullins lifts Snuffy from the hutch and cradles him in his arms. He can feel the rabbit's heartbeat right beneath his palm, and sometimes it makes him feel strange, too aware of his own power. It's a bit like standing on a train platform when one of the non-stopping services goes by, and you feel your insides rattle and know all it would take is one step, just one step. Mullins doesn't have suicidal thoughts, nor is he a fluffy-animal killer, but the line between life and death feels a little bit thin sometimes.

Just look at someone like Pascoe. Or Helena Hunter? Things round here are getting heavy.

He adjusts his grip and strokes Snuffy's long ears. He is in fact Snuffy V, the fifth in a line of rabbits called Snuffy at 7 Ocean Drive. If anyone asks, Mullins pretends it's one of his mum's things, another of her little obsessions like collecting anything to do with William and Harry and 'those two lovely girls'. Mullins's whole life has been spent in the shadow of William and Harry, the big brothers he never had – and never wanted. Too many of their types descend on these parts in the summer, and everyone knows the price of that; the fact he's still living with his mum, for one.

But his living arrangements do have their upsides. The full English he's just tucked into, for instance. Lashings of HP sauce. Toast on tap. And no one makes tea like Ma Mullins: strong enough that the spoon stands up in it, and just the right amount of sugar.

He can't touch the stuff down the station because it doesn't come close. And he's never been much of a coffee fan – though Saffron Weeks doesn't need to know that.

Hippy-Dippy. He can still remember the biro daisy chains around her tanned ankles in Year 10. How once he came home, shut himself in his room, and drew the same up and down his arm, then spat and rubbed each petal off one by one. *She loves me, she loves me not.* Always bloody not. And you'd think if he was the one drawing the petals, he could load the dice.

He lowers Snuffy back into the hutch, and the rabbit does a half-arsed hop, noses around in some lettuce leaves. Mullins watches him wistfully. It's alright for some. He needs to get to work, but he doesn't really want to.

In cop movies there's always a buzz about the station when something big is going down. People stride about with crackling energy and theories fizz like cola bubbles. Down their place, it just means Mullins's every minute is being watched. Like now, he should probably be at his desk already, not-drinking their crappy tea and flicking through hour after hour of CCTV or something. Suddenly no one wants the banter anymore; and there's no cream horns from the bakery, and they always have afternoon horns from the bakery. All because that lot from Newquay are on their way: the major incident team.

The truth is, Mullins likes the small stuff. Parking violations. Speeding – oh, he loves speeders, parking up in a lay-by and getting his big measuring gun out. Moving on the rough sleepers: he doesn't love it, but he'll do it, no sweat. He knows where he is there; the uniform counts for something. Something like this, though, what good's the uniform? It just puts you on the receiving end of pressure. Maybe that's why detectives wear plain clothes.

Take Roland Hunter. He has no respect, that's for sure. He's already hauling Mullins over the coals, just because he can. Even

Roland's snooty brother, Nathan, agreed: Roland had been out of line before.

Mullins straightens up, and brushes white rabbit hair from the front of his shirt.

He's got no one good to learn from, that's how it feels to Mullins if he really thinks about it – which most of the time he manages not to. Sergeant Bill Bright would have been a good teacher, by all accounts. And he went into this wanting to learn; he actually did. For the first time in his life, it felt to Mullins like he'd stuck his head above the parapet and thought, *I'm going to have a proper crack at this*, knowing full well that trying probably meant failing. But he hasn't failed, has he? Somehow, he made it through training. And now here he is. It's official. He's declared to faithfully discharge the duties of the Office of Constable. He's a servant of the Crown. And that's a line that makes him feel like he's in *Game of Thrones* or that video game Teg's into, *Call of Duty*, not plodding the same streets he grew up on, closing his ears to the shouts of *Oi, Muzzer!*

He swore to *well and truly serve the Queen*, which is more than William and Harry have ever had to do, isn't it? They're too busy going to rugby matches and having kids and whatnot – though of course his mum likes to remind him of their gleaming military careers, and even has a picture of William in camo, pretending to give orders to a squad out in the desert. Photoshop probably. Mullins sniffs, his nose twitching like Snuffy's. Anyway.

He sees the flicker of a net curtain and knows it's his mum watching.

Always watching. She can't have been watching when his dad left all those years ago though, can she? Because she didn't have the foggiest clue where he was going then. Mullins found the note on the mantelpiece before school; he thought it was an early birthday card because there wasn't a name on the envelope, and well, wasn't he going to be eleven in two days' time?

What a happy birthday that was. Not.

Some people just disappear and that's how life is. Hippy-Dippy didn't even know who her dad was, though it never seemed to bother her; not that they ever talked about that kind of stuff. You can't make people stay, not if they don't want to – and Mullins had felt like telling Roland Hunter that yesterday. But there was something about the man that made him feel like he wouldn't want to hear it. Especially after what happened to his last wife; they know all about that down the station. Hunter would have to be pretty unlucky for history to repeat itself though. And not much about Hunter – these days anyway – seems unlucky.

Rumour is the chopper will be out later. Coastguard too.

His mum raps on the window and Mullins knows it's time to go. As he walks back up the path to the house, he tries to put a kick in his step and stick his chest out. He wants to feel like he's in the movies – and he's the one who's going to crack this case wide open.

Then he realises he forgot to change Snuffy's water, and doubles back to the hutch. When it comes to the bunny, he never neglects his duties.

22

Saffron has made it to Truro. She cycled to the train station first thing, then stood with her bike in the rattling carriage. Once there, she cycled a confused loop before she finally found the hospital. It isn't like the clock is ticking, but she doesn't like the thought of too many people turning up at Hang Ten and seeing the 'Closed' sign on the door, especially on a Saturday morning. Actually, it says 'Gone Surfin'!' – a silly touch for the tourists but often enough true. She keeps her board out back for just those moments. And she'd like to be surfing right now, perfect peelers out there today, but instead she's standing outside the hulking hospital, holding a bunch of flowers that she's already thinking twice about. They're daffodils from the lane; nicer than anything the BP garage had to offer, with their spray-painted chrysanthemums and aggressive-looking roses, but are flowers even allowed in the ICU?

Is *she* allowed in the ICU?

She looks up at the building again; takes a breath. Why do hospitals always have to look so much like *hospitals*? Saffron and hospitals are not a good mix. For the lucky, they're a place of healing, where life gets better, not worse. Well, not *that* lucky, maybe, because you're still there in the first place, right? But, relatively speaking. Only it didn't work out like that for her mum, did it? Sometimes Saffron feels older than twenty-three. Way older.

She's here for Lewis, but really she's here for Maggie Pascoe. Maggie, who hardly had anyone. And Lewis, who now has even less than that.

You have to look after each other, she thinks, when you're in a similar kind of boat. Hell, you have to look after each other anyway.

Saffron dips her head and strides in; acts like she's on her board, paddling with intent.

~

Five minutes later, and she's back outside, gulping in the fresh air. Mission totally non-accomplished. She looks down at the flowers in her hand and wonders what to do with them. She decides to leave them by the revolving doors, just in case they're what a passing stranger needs.

Family only.

Of course. How could she have forgotten?

She should have tried to blag it. He *has* no family. It didn't help that she'd said that.

'He's wanted by the police,' the girl on the desk said, in a half-whisper.

'He's not wanted by the police,' Saffron shot back. 'The police know exactly where he is. And they're trying to find out who did this to him.'

But even as she said it, she knew it wasn't really true.

'Helena's still missing,' the girl said, holding up her phone to show the news section of Cornwall Live.

For a minute Saffron wondered if the girl knew Helena Hunter, but then realised she was doing what people always do when a certain sort of person goes missing: that overfamiliar, first-name thing.

As she'd picked the flowers in the lane this morning, Saffron had looked over her shoulder. She'd felt a prickle of unease, to be on her own, on a lonely road. A missing person was like sea mist: it changed everything. Ordinary places suddenly felt eerie. Even people you thought you knew looked different. Even if you made your brain rattle off all the ordinary explanations – even then.

But what it went to show was something that Saffron 100 per cent knew – in her heart, anyway: that Lewis didn't have anything to do with Helena's disappearance. Because otherwise, why would she be feeling creeped out when the chief suspect was as good as under lock and key, hooked up to machines in a room that only someone in a uniform was allowed into? Which was good and bad.

Good for Lewis. Well, not exactly *good* for Lewis. Not good at all.

And bad, because it meant that whatever had happened to Helena was down to someone else. Someone who was still out there. Didn't it?

Saffron's thinking on this again as she's jumping on her bike and wheeling out across the car park. Her head's busy with the image of a woman jogging alone along a beach – jogging, or running away? – and the soundtrack she's hearing isn't her favourite sea song but the wheeze of the machine that Lewis might be hooked up to; the one she couldn't see, but doesn't have to imagine, because her mum had the same and Saffron feels like she'll remember that sound forever.

Wheeze – press.

Wheeze – press.

The next thing she knows, hard asphalt is coming at her. Somehow, she lands like a cat, in full crouch mode, but her bike clatters on to its side. Front wheel still turning; Spokey Dokeys clack-clacking. She gets to her feet and brushes her hands against her jeans. It's all over as soon as it started. A lifetime of getting smashed in the sea has quickened her reactions.

But then a man's bending down beside her. He puts his hands on her shoulders and peers into her face.

'Are you alright? I didn't see you. You came out of nowhere. But you're okay?'

'I'm fine,' she says. 'Honestly. No worries. I'm fine.'

He's being kind enough, but she still pulls back from him. 'I'm great,' she says with more force. 'No harm done.'

'Your hands are bleeding.'

She looks down and sees a peppering of grit in her palms.

'It's nothing.' She plasters on a grin. 'And I'm already late for work. I've gotta jet.'

Turning to pick up her bike, she winces as she takes hold of the handlebars.

'You've had a shock,' he says, his voice all concern. 'It'd be dangerous to get back on that now. Let me drive you where you need to go. Least I can do.'

Saffron hesitates as she takes in his encouraging smile. She blinks, then, as stars suddenly fizz at the edge of her vision. Maybe it is shock. Or is she just totally suggestible? She was fine a few seconds ago, until this good Samaritan – though, to be fair, if he was really good then he'd have avoided hitting her in the first place – hypnotised her with his over-the-top concern. She can feel her throat start to burn and she thinks, *Oh man, am I going to cry now too?*

'Come on, get in,' he says, and he's picking up her bike in one hand and taking her lightly by the elbow with the other. It feels like he's crowding her space but, well, maybe she does look a bit wobbly.

His car is like a spaceship, one of the bright white new Range Rovers, and okay, maybe it would be nice to sink into those leather seats, to skip the cycle ride, the train, the ride again.

'But I'm all the way down in Porthpella,' she says. 'It's like thirty minutes away.'

'Are you now?' he says. 'I'm headed in that exact direction. In fact . . .' He narrows his eyes. 'You're familiar.' His hand taps his head. 'The pink streaks. I've seen them. I've seen *you*.'

'I run a beach café,' says Saffron. 'Hang Ten?'

And he's starting to look familiar too, now he's mentioned it. Maybe he's been to the café.

'What's your name?' he says.

'Saffron.'

He claps the boot shut and throws open the door for her. 'Need a hand getting in, Saffron?'

She catches his aftershave, something spiced and expensive-smelling. She wrinkles her nose. Says, 'No thanks.' He takes off the baseball cap he's wearing and shakes out a thick thatch of brown-grey hair.

It's only when she's in, when the door's slammed, when he's behind the wheel and they're swinging through the car park barriers, that she realises exactly who he is.

And it's too late to do anything about it.

23

'Ally Bright again, eh? This is becoming a little habit.'

DS Skinner's voice booms into the phone, and she doesn't particularly appreciate the edge it has to it.

Ally looks over to the picture of Bill set in its frame on the mantelpiece. In the photo, he's standing at the barbecue in a striped apron, a straw hat on his head. He's holding a beer in one hand and tongs in the other. It wasn't a special occasion, just a happy sunny evening when they lit the coals and draped the length of a bass over the grill, and sat out in the garden at the edge of the sea feeling like the richest people on earth.

She wonders what Bill would have made of DS Skinner.

'I've got something I think might be relevant,' she says.

She tells Skinner about the article Jayden found, and their thoughts on the burglary connection. She glances at Jayden, who's sitting across the table from her, another cup of coffee in his hands. His face is all encouragement. Though he deliberately asked that she didn't mention his name to Skinner.

'Hang on, you're saying you think Lewis was involved in what happened back in Surrey?'

'No, no, not at all.'

'Well, that's a relief, because I was going to have to tell you you're joining two dots and making five, my dear.' He gives a thick laugh, and Ally can see how easily he would have belittled Jayden before too. 'It's like I said before, Mr Hunter's under a lot of stress. Not only the Pascoe kid throwing himself off the cliffs just after he's been ranting and raving round at his house, but his wife's missing. None of it's good. And until Pascoe comes round, *if* he comes round, we've got nothing to go on.'

'You can't only be looking at Lewis,' says Ally. 'There must be other avenues?'

'You sure Bill's not there?' He laughs again. 'No. Bill was a beat bobby, you wouldn't catch him asking questions like that. You wouldn't have him doubting the *brass*. Mrs Bright, everything points to Lewis Pascoe. In fact, you helped us yourself there, so I hear – very much so, in fact, thanks to you and your beachcombing. I can't tell you anything more than that. In fact, you're getting far too much out of me here already,' he says. 'Plus, I've got a cup of tea going cold at this end. If you hear a helicopter out today, throw us a wave. We've got the Major Crimes lot down from Newquay, including the DCI himself, and let's just say they're making their presence felt. You keep your eyes peeled for Helena, that's what you can do. The general public are more trouble than they're worth with most missing persons – more spots than a Dalmatian, and we have to follow up every single one. So, here's a tip: think before you call us, alright?'

Before she can answer, he's rung off. Ally imagines him in his office, kicking back in his chair, feet up on his desk. One of those people who talk more than they listen. And the way he weighted the word *DCI*, with a combination of respect and disdain. Bill always said he had no interest in rising up the ranks, that he did the job where he felt he could make the most difference – and for him that was being in the community. This community.

If he were here now, he'd be going door to door. He wouldn't rest.

'I heard most of that,' says Jayden. 'He gave you more time than he gave me. Just.'

She takes a moment before she replies, trying to get her thoughts in order.

'Did you hear the part where he said I'd helped them? I don't understand that at all. What have I done, Jayden? I haven't done anything.'

'You did find the watch. It could be about that. He mentioned beachcombing, didn't he?'

'The watch?'

'What if it had Lewis's prints on it?'

Ally shakes her head. 'He didn't say that.'

'Well, he couldn't. He's not going to reveal details to a member of the public. Ally. . .' And she hears the caution in his voice. 'I know you feel responsible for Lewis, like you could have stopped it or something, but . . . if his prints *are* on the watch – and I know that's a big if – that would directly connect him to Helena. If he was troubled, out of his mind, he could have done something stupid. Couldn't he? Then panicked. Stepped off that cliff thinking it was a way out. Again, only guesswork. It could be a whole other story. And whatever happened, Lewis isn't going anywhere right now. He's as safe as anyone can be in the ICU. It's Helena who needs to be found.'

Jayden's on his feet now. Pacing. He goes on.

'And if they're sending out a chopper, that's a big deal. They'll have looked at phone records, they'll have looked at bank activity. Weighed up the push-and-pull factors; the things people might be running away from or towards. If it was a simple case of her walking out on Hunter, then she'd have prepared for that in advance. Maybe she had a blow to the head, became confused, or lost her way? That's possible. But she'd have popped up on CCTV . . .'

'Not all the way out here she wouldn't.'

'Or she'd have been spotted by now. A member of the public would have seen her. So, all that's plausibly left is . . . something happening to her. Isn't it?'

Ally watches the way he turns his hand as he sets out different scenarios. A clear thinker, a straight talker. Bill would have liked Jayden. Even if what he's saying is difficult for her to hear.

'You're sure you don't want a job down here? They could use you, I'd say.'

'The quiet life, that's me now. Glamping overlord.'

'You loved it though, didn't you? The police work?'

Jayden looks faintly startled. 'Loved it? Well, yeah . . . I guess I did. Kind of. For a bit. But I wasn't cut out for it in the end. Not with everything. Once you start feeling that . . .' He shakes his head. 'You've got to leave it to someone else.'

'Like PC Mullins and DS Skinner for instance,' says Ally, with a half-smile, trying to lighten the tone. Because she knows Jayden isn't telling her the full story, and she wants him to know that that's okay; she'll never press to hear it.

'You got it.'

Ally goes to the window. She picks up a perfectly formed Venus shell, caramel-smooth, and holds it in her hand.

'I live quietly here,' she says. 'At the edge of things. But I don't feel at the edge of this. I feel right in the middle of it.'

She turns. Jayden's crouched down, fondling Fox's ears.

'And I remember seeing Sea Dream when it was just built. It was almost like it appeared overnight. It didn't, of course, I just hadn't been paying that much attention. I wondered what had happened to Maggie Pascoe, but I had other things on my mind. I was very . . . inward. I think I've always been rather like that. It didn't seem to matter when Bill was here, because he'd get involved for both of us. For more than both of us.'

'And it was around the time your husband died, that Maggie left?'

'A few months after. I'm not a prejudiced person, Jayden, I've only met Roland Hunter once, but to me . . . he's a bully. All I know for sure is that when Lewis turned up at his door, Roland managed to make him feel worse, not better. Not one shred of sympathy – that was clear enough from the way he then talked to me.'

'Yeah, I agree. But remember the burglary connection. A convicted burglar turns up late at night, and, sure, I can see Roland losing it, because of what happened before. In fact, I can kind of understand that a bit, from his perspective. It's the sort of thing that might make you lose it.'

'Enough to push Lewis off the cliff? I don't think the police are looking at what might have happened to Lewis at all. They're only focused on Helena.'

'Which is right. It's a question of time, of urgency.'

'And I hope to God they find her. But what if they're not looking in all of the right places?'

'If they're getting a chopper out, they're looking everywhere.'

Ally runs her fingers over the ridges of the Venus. Such secrets the shells held; you found the empty houses, and you could only guess at what went on inside them.

'Oscar Wilde said that "to lose one parent may be regarded as a misfortune; to lose both looks like carelessness".'

'Lit quotes. Okay, now you sound like my mum and dad. But what's it got to do—'

'Could that be applied to wives, I wonder?'

Jayden gives a low whistle. 'That's cold, Ally Bright.' Then, 'You think Hunter has something to do with his own wife's disappearance?'

'What I think,' says Ally, 'is that there could be more to this. Couldn't there? Lewis is going to come around – I hope he's going to come around – and he's going to face a barrage of questions. And I'm not sure that he's terribly well-equipped to answer them. Especially after what Stewart said, about him being easily led. And he's especially vulnerable right now. If Helena could be found before then, wouldn't that save a lot of pain?'

'Well, yeah,' says Jayden, 'of course it would. She needs to be found.'

'So perhaps we could look in the places that the police aren't.'

'To be fair, I don't think we're getting that accurate an idea of what the police are or aren't investigating. They're not going to tell us, are they? But . . . okay.' He rubs his hands together. 'Let me think.'

'There's a holidaymaker,' says Ally, 'staying in the house nearest to Sea Dream. I met him on the beach yesterday. We could speak to him.'

'The police will have spoken to him already, Ally.'

'But people remember things after the fact. Don't they? Or things that don't seem unusual end up taking on a new light. Bill always said that.'

Jayden looks at his watch. 'Look, Cat told me to go surfing this morning, even though she knew I'd lost her board. *Me Time*, she called it. But I don't think I can stretch out this non-surf too much longer. Why don't you go and talk to the holidaymaker? Report back?'

Ally hesitates. It was ridiculous of her to think that they're in this together. He has a life of his own to live, he doesn't need to be picking over the tangled threads of other people's.

'Of course, of course. You must go. I've kept you far too long already.'

'Then how about a post-lunch coffee in Hang Ten? I can get down there, once I've cracked on with the farm jobs on my list for today.'

'Your wife won't mind?'

Jayden rubs the back of his head again. 'She worries I don't have any friends here, I think. Not friends of my own, anyway. She'll be pleased. So long as . . .' He seems to stop himself. 'So long as I don't go losing any more surfboards.'

But Ally can feel herself smiling. *Friends of my own.* 'It's a plan,' she says.

24

Roland didn't intend to pick up the girl – Saffron – but suddenly he'd wanted to. Because isn't it just the sort of thing that a respectable citizen should do in the circumstances? And he'd already seen enough for the Truro trip to have been worth it. The receptionist confirmed that the only visitors to Lewis Pascoe's bed had been the police. Then the sheer luck of it: just as he was coming out of the men's room, that pink-haired girl standing there with her flowers, asking after the little jailbird.

Talk about exquisite timing.

Roland becomes aware that he's gripping the steering wheel too hard – his knuckles are bright white – so he consciously lightens up. Rolls his shoulders. Then he looks sideways at her.

Her tan seems to have paled since she got in the car, and she's rapidly tapping a message into her phone, her mouth in a tight line. She looks up and catches his eye – and her own are as startled as a child's.

Ah, he thinks. *She's figured it out.*

There are some people who thrive on the crises of others, and there are others who act like those crises are contagious. *Look at her now*, he thinks – her hand pushed to her mouth as if the air in the car is polluted. It isn't a power he wants but he feels the effect of it anyway. He puts his foot down, feels the surge of the engine.

'You've seen me on the news, then, have you?'

'I don't watch the news,' she says. 'It's depressing.'

'The jungle drums then.'

'What?'

'The Porthpella bloody grapevine. My wife is missing. And I'm going a little bit crazy, if I'm honest. Which no one around here really seems to grasp.' He shoots another look at her. 'I'll do anything to find her,' he says. 'I'll stop at nothing, as the saying goes.'

'The police. . .' begins Saffron, as if the word itself is reassurance. As if it's some kind of cavalry, blue lights flashing in the rear-view mirror.

'I need you to tell me how you know Lewis Pascoe.'

Roland hears a quick little intake of breath – and that's when he knows he's on to something. He makes a quick decision.

There's a lay-by up ahead, with a sorry-looking food van that's always closed. He pulls off the road, a move that requires an exaggerated twist of the wheel, which he knows will make this look like something it's not, but what choice does he have? In the back, the girl's bike shifts and bumps as he slams to a halt. He twists in his seat and gives her his full attention.

Roland notes the glinting line of her star-shaped earrings. The tiny plaits threaded through her loose hair; the bright pink streaks. Her mouth is gaping, like she's a fish on land. That's when he realises, it's not the drama she's frightened of – it's him. And, again, he feels that quickening of power in his gut.

'It's okay,' he says, 'you don't need to look so worried, but you do need to start talking to me about Lewis Pascoe.'

And despite him using his soft voice, he sees her shrink back. It's as if his words are knives and he's pointing them right at her.

'I don't know Lewis Pascoe,' she says, defiance in her voice. 'But I knew his nan a little bit. And I liked her. And if she's not here to look out for him, then I will. That's it.'

Roland grits his teeth. 'Just you and Ally Bright, huh?'

'People care about each other around here,' she says.

'Oh, they do, do they? There didn't seem to be a whole lot of caring going on when Maggie Pascoe was selling up to me.'

Saffron hesitates, and he sees he's hit a nerve. 'Maybe she wanted to keep it quiet. Selling to a . . .'

'A what? An incomer? You people haven't changed. I came here twenty years ago – stag party; about the only thing that's keeping Newquay afloat if you ask me – and it was just the same then. You've always hated us, but you'll always need us.'

'I wasn't going to say that,' says Saffron. She stops. Frowns. Tugs at her tacky little seashell necklace. 'Twenty years ago?'

'Anniversary of my introduction to this charming county.'

'Can we drive on now?' says Saffron. 'Or I'll take my bike and go.'

'Funnily enough, we even wound up in Porthpella.' He rolls his eyes at the memory. But life was simpler back then – before Victoria, before Helena. Even Nathan seemed like slightly less of an asshole in those days. Speaking of which, there's been something off with his brother; Roland just doesn't buy the whole supportive thing. If he's come down here to view houses, why the hell isn't he going on about square footage and knockout vistas and infinity pools? That's the Nathan he knows: rub-your-face-in-it. This Nathan feels idle; purposeless. Roland realises the girl is asking him a question, and her insistence makes his irritation flare.

'Say what?'

'I said, why were you in Porthpella back then?'

He starts the engine back up again. Eyes her sideways.

'My wife's missing,' he says. 'You'll have to excuse me if I'm not in the mood for reminiscing about holidays gone by.'

And he swings back out into the traffic.

25

Gus stands looking at his suitcase. He's gone as far as to take it out from the wardrobe and set it on the bed, but he hasn't put anything in it yet.

He doesn't really want to go, but how can he stay now?

He can still hear the thrum of the helicopter tracking back and forth. There are dogs out there too; rangy German shepherds followed by serious-looking officers. Amid all this activity someone called DCI Robinson talked to him too.

It was soon obvious that Robinson and Hunter knew one another, not just from the case, but because of some charity golf thing a while ago. Which is surely why the DCI turned a blind eye to Gus's fat lip; emotions running high, boys will be boys – all that. Which was probably a factor in why he had decided not to press charges. The inspector seemed disappointed in the account of Helena that Gus gave him, as if he'd thought there might be more to it. Gus at least got his words out properly this time – thanks, probably, to the fact that he'd written it all down this time, to fix it in his head. He could see why people cracked under pressure, how someone might come to believe they were, in fact, in the wrong; their own reasoning trampled by someone else's far heavier boots.

The police must have done their checks on him too – and found not so much as a speeding ticket in all of his sixty-six years. A hopelessly law-abiding retired teacher, and geography wasn't even one of the subjects that occasionally raised eyebrows, like literature or drama; romance was suspicious in an unconventional-looking man of a certain age.

Not that Gus is unconventional-looking, with his head as smooth as polished stone and a rotation of knitted jumpers. There's nothing much to get hold of there. And if the police cared to plunder the pages of his novel-in-progress, they'd see nothing to get anyone excited.

Which obviously isn't great, in a novel.

Gus stares down into his empty case. There's still three weeks left on his rental, and he's come to be happy here. Okay, *happy* is perhaps too strong a word but there's been definite spells of contentment. But nobody likes to be branded a peeping Tom. And nobody likes to be punched to the ground by their nearest neighbour. These aren't ideal conditions for the inspiration – creative or otherwise – that Gus hoped to find at the beach.

Let alone the fact that a young lad tried to kill himself and a woman is missing.

He's just pulling the first of his shirts off the rack when there's a knock at his door.

Oh no, is his first thought, *what now?* He's been rattled. And he hates being rattled. He's never been one to thrive on confrontation. Mona, on the other hand, she lived for it; he can just picture her, hackles rising, eyes flashing, provoked by the slightest thing. And his mate Clive: when he was younger, he always liked a *rumble*, as he called it; didn't even need a reason why. Gus has never understood it, personally.

He heads downstairs with heavy steps. And when he pulls open the door he's standing as far back as it's possible to be.

But it's the woman from the beach.

Even then, he still thinks, *What have I done?* And braces himself for a reprimand.

'Oh, hello there,' she says. 'We meet again.'

The way she puts it, it's as if this knock at the door is quite by chance. An accidental – and perhaps even quite pleasant – crossing of paths. He sees her notice his lip, but then she glances quickly away again, as if embarrassed to be caught looking too hard.

He relaxes an iota.

'Good morning,' he says. He realises he doesn't have much more than that, but she looks kind, this woman, and he can feel himself being pulled towards her in the way that flowers turn their faces to the sun. 'How can I help?'

'It's a slightly strange request,' she says, and is it his imagination or do her eyes dart right, to Sea Dream? 'I couldn't come inside, could I?'

He steps aside, gesturing with his arm, and it's overblown, this welcome, but he's chock-full of relief at this point.

'I should introduce myself. I don't think I did at the beach. I'm Ally. Ally Bright.'

Her eyes are pale green and her hair is grey-blond, cut short, falling just below her ears. A soothing wash of colours, like the ocean first thing in the morning.

'Gus Munro.' He holds out his hand and he's sure it's formal and odd of him – maybe he's still feeling tarnished, Roland's accusation of *shiftyness* – but she shakes it warmly enough.

'Can I offer you tea?' he says. 'Or coffee?'

She gives a brief shake of her head. 'Thank you, I'm fine.'

'A seat?'

She takes the wicker sofa, while he perches on a dining chair. He sees her note the nautical paraphernalia in the room; her eyes linger on the huge and highly polished conch shell on the bookcase.

'I'd like to say I found it, but it's part of the fixtures and fittings.'

'You'd be hard pushed to find a conch on these shores. But plenty of smaller treasures.'

'I did the message-in-a-bottle thing as a boy,' he says, not knowing why he's telling her this. 'I can't remember what I wrote but I'm pretty sure I'd cringe to read it now.'

Of course he can remember: it was a love letter to a girl he met on holiday but couldn't quite find the words for. So far, so Gus.

'I suppose back then we weren't thinking so much of rubbish in the ocean. It seemed innocent enough,' he says.

He's aware that she's listening, but her thoughts seem elsewhere.

'Sorry, Ally, I'm prattling. I don't get too many visitors.'

'And I don't pay too many visits, so we're a fine pair. I'm not sure where to begin, so I'm going to just launch in. Like I said, it's slightly strange. Can it be in confidence?'

'Of course.'

'It's not normally like this around here, this sort of activity on the beach. And I'm not normally . . .' She hesitates, as if uncertain how to finish the sentence. 'But I'm looking for some answers that the police perhaps aren't . . . well, I don't think they're asking the same questions.'

Here it comes, he thinks. *She's heard somehow.*

'How well do you know your neighbours at Sea Dream. The Hunters?'

'Hardly at all,' he says. 'I just came here to write. I wasn't looking for company or anything like that.'

'But I wonder if perhaps you've seen them come and go. Maybe even formed an impression of them. I sound like I'm clutching at straws . . . I mean, I am, I know I am, but . . . I want to try and understand what kind of a relationship they had.'

He lets out a gust of laughter; he can't help himself. 'How can anyone ever know that? The inside of a marriage is a mysterious place. The last of earth's secrets, surely.'

Ally blinks. Smiles. 'Well, yes. I told you . . . straws.'

'I'm not the person to ask. I'm sorry.'

'No, okay.' She folds her hands in her lap. 'But do they have many people coming and going? Friends and things?'

'Well . . .' Gus thinks on it. He's admiring her persistence – rather likes it, in fact. 'Now you mention it, no. Not generally. Though there's a car there at the moment I don't recognise. A Lexus. I suppose I imagine that people who choose to live out here want the isolation, don't they? I know that's my excuse.'

'What about Helena? Do you ever see her with friends?'

Gus hesitates. Is this a stealth approach to the peeping Tom accusation? He shifts in his seat.

'I know this is all very strange,' Ally says, 'but I thought I had to at least ask. I'm sorry if it feels intrusive.'

And suddenly he wants to tell her about Helena at the window. To just have it out there – and, importantly, understood. So, he does. The nakedness. The punch. The police.

When Ally reacts without theatrics, he's pathetically grateful. Or maybe he just spent too long living with Mona: his expectations for reasonable responses are set outstandingly low.

'I did wonder,' she says, gesturing to his lip. 'Are you alright?'

He blusters a grin. 'Oh yes. Apart from appalled by how easily I went down.'

'I'm sorry. From what I've seen of Roland Hunter I think he's rather a volatile man.'

'I'd spoken to him before, when I first got here, and I just didn't pick up on it. But I did know he wasn't someone I particularly wanted to be pals with.'

Gus tells her about the offer of whisky. How Roland called him one of these 'arty-farty types', and although the way he'd said it was far from a compliment Gus had rather enjoyed the moniker, having never been thought of in that way before. Arty-farty Gus Munro.

'Oh,' he says, his memory suddenly jogged, 'there was someone I saw.'

Several weeks ago, and just down from the house, there was an artist, painting outdoors with an easel on the beach. She was wearing a puffy black jacket and a hat, because it'd been colder then. And he saw Helena bring her cups of tea and stand there talking, with her back to the house. He can remember thinking he'd have liked to wander down and join them, but it was not long after he'd arrived and he was still drawn up in his own shell.

'She was there for three days, maybe. Perhaps more.'

'When was this?'

Gus counts back. 'Early February, maybe. They looked friendly, the two of them. Like they had a connection. They talked while she painted.'

He can see Ally thinking; her brow is crinkled, her head tilted. He feels boyishly pleased to have given her something.

'It's not at all unusual to see artists on the beach,' she says. 'It's a popular view, with the island, the lighthouse, the curve of the bay. Sometimes in the summer there are nearly as many easels set up in the dunes as windbreaks on the beach. She was painting by Sea Dream, you said?'

'Just down there,' says Gus, gesturing to the window. 'And you're right, it's the perfect view.'

Ally's lost in thought. 'I had a rotten cold at the start of February, and it made me miss a couple of walks. I just took Fox down to the shore and back.'

'She was quite distinctive, the woman,' says Gus. 'She wore one of those hats I think of as Australian. A little bit Crocodile Dundee somehow. And she had long red hair.'

'Oh!' says Ally. 'Hold on. I think I know just who you mean.'

She rummages in her bag for her phone. A moment later she's holding it up, and a picture of a flame-haired woman in a chequered shirt and wide-brimmed hat fills the screen.

'Yes! That's her. I mean, I'm not sure I ever saw her face, but that's the hat. And that's her hair. I'm sure it is. How did you . . .'

'Fiona Penrose,' she says. 'An artist over in St Ives. And a very successful one too. Her paintings go for thousands.'

'So, mystery solved,' says Gus. 'That was impressive.'

'Fiona Penrose,' says Ally again, as if turning the name over in her mind.

'You don't think she's got anything to do with . . . anything?'

'If she was at all friendly with Helena Hunter then she could be useful to talk to.'

Ally stands up. Gus finds himself standing up too. For a moment they face each other, and he has a ridiculous desire to say, *Shall we go to St Ives?*

But, of course, he doesn't.

26

Jayden crests the hill, and as the view opens up in front of him, he winds the windows all the way down. The sea glitters, and the horizon – darker blue sky above, brighter and lighter below – is so straight it looks computer-generated. Moments like this, he gets why they're here. Being surrounded by the great wide open draws you out, not in. In the weeks and months that followed Kieran's death he paced the Leeds flat like a cage-bound tiger, anger and sorrow turned in on himself. There were days when he didn't think his head would ever be straight again. Cat took control in eventually getting them to leave, and he let her; it felt good, loosening his grip. After all, she had double votes by then: two people to his one.

'Not just for a holiday?' his mate Ty said when he told him.

'Not just for a holiday.'

'But not forever, right?'

He clapped his mate on the shoulder. 'Come visit. Learn to surf. Eat a pasty.'

His phone rings, breaking the reverie, and he expects to see Cat's name. He's been gone longer than he planned, but there was something so nice about Ally's place: The Shell House. Most of the time he can't imagine what their baby will be like as an actual outside-the-womb human being. He can't picture being one of those dads with a sling, walking about with a swagger of pride, or one day even having actual conversations with this person he helped make. Sometimes Jayden wonders if this inability of his to imagine is because it's not going to happen for them after all, and he has to press this thought all the way down, because it's the last thing he'd ever voice to the shining, swelling Cat. That's what he does: he pushes it down, like he's pushed other things down too. And then he screws the lid on tight. But this morning at Ally's place – a place where he weirdly felt more at home than at the farm – he imagined crouching with a tiny girl beside him, pointing out all the shells; shells he might even know the names of by then; shells that would be part of her beach-babe birthright.

And he liked it. It felt peaceful.

Instead of Cat, the screen says Fatima. And he can't help but smile, thinking of the night they went dancing, years back, when they were all training. That one kiss. Life before Cat feels like another country, one he has no desire to visit again – but every so often you could look at the holiday pics, right?

'Fatima, hey. Hang on, I'm pulling over.'

From here the road dips down, roller-coaster style, and phone reception will soon be lost. He tucks into the gateway, and on the other side a handful of sheep scatter in wild alarm, then carry on their grazing just a few feet further on. They must have decent reset buttons, sheep – or else just tiny minds. He clicks off the engine.

'Are you out on the tractor?'

'You think I'm allowed near the tractor?'

Fatima laughs, and he realises he's missed this in particular: the easy chat with workmates. She messaged him after what happened to Kieran, just like a lot of people messaged him, trying to find words when there were none; he can't remember if he even replied. It felt good yesterday, connecting with her on something else entirely; something that's only about the here and now. The here and now, and five years ago.

'So, look,' she says, 'I did some more digging.'

147

'Fatima, yes! And what did you find?'

'Something interesting. John Hunter was never under suspicion for his wife's murder because he had a clear alibi.'

'Yeah, his now-wife, Helena. Classy guy.'

'Very classy. But at the time, his brother-in-law, Sebastian Lyle, pointed the finger pretty heavily in Hunter's direction. Gave a statement, which was pretty far-out to be honest, not the most coherent thing you'll ever read, but very clear on one point – he'd never trusted Roland.'

Jayden shifts in his seat. He watches as the grey hulk of a tanker edges into view on the horizon. Weird to think there would be people aboard it, going about their business, just as he's here on land, going about his. So many ways to live a life. Is this his now? Sleuthing by sheep fields?

'Anything to base that on?' he asks.

'Not really. Nothing concrete. But Lyle thought it was a marriage of convenience. Convenient because Victoria was loaded, and John Hunter wasn't.'

'A bit thin,' says Jayden. 'That it?'

'That's pretty much it. You feel sorry for Sebastian though, reading it. He doesn't sound like he's got anything left except for a whole lot of anger. But I thought you'd want to know the full picture.'

'What are you saying, that you think there's more to it?'

'I listened to the tape of Roland Hunter's interview. The guy sounds pretty devastated. I don't think you can fake that emotion.'

'You listened to the tape?' he says with a smile.

'The streets were quiet first thing this morning, Jay – crime was lying low. I listened with my coffee. Beats yet another podcast.'

'So, the brother was basically tilting at windmills.'

'Windmills? That a countryside thing? This how you talk now?'

'Don Quixote, baby. Curse of parents who make you read the classics.' A thought crosses Jayden's mind. 'You know what though, it'd make this Sebastian Lyle an enemy of Roland Hunter, right? And definitely an enemy of Roland Hunter's new wife. She was sleeping with his sister's husband.'

'There is that. It's been five years though, Jay, and no contact – or none that we've heard about anyway, and Hunter doesn't seem the type to keep quiet. If he or Helena were getting hassle from Lyle, if it ever came close to escalating, we'd know about it, I'm sure.'

Jayden's mind ticks over. 'Okay, thanks, Fatima. I appreciate it.'

'Happy to help.'

He hears the smile in her voice. 'What?' he says. 'What is it?'

'Welcome back, Jay,' she says. 'That's all. Welcome back.'

27

'This is what we know about Helena Hunter,' says DCI Robinson.

PC Mullins rocks back in his chair and chews the end of his pen. DCI Robinson is part of the Major Crimes Unit that's been shipped in from Newquay, bringing a whole lot of noise along with them. But Robinson himself is a softly spoken man, who looks like he might be somebody's dad: a fixer of broken things; maybe a kicker of footballs when the sun is out.

Yo, weird thought, Mullins – he's just a bloke.

He straightens himself in his chair. Finds a listening face. The room is stuffed full of people, and he doesn't want to be the weak link. DCI Robinson stands in front of the smeary whiteboard, passing a marker pen from hand to hand, eyes watching them all.

'She moved down here with Roland Hunter six months ago. Before that they lived in Torbay and Bournemouth. She was having an affair with Hunter when his wife was killed in a burglary gone wrong in Godalming in 2018. They married in 2019, in Swindon.'

'That's a lot of moving around,' says Mullins, then afterwards regrets it. Just because he's hardly crossed the Tamar.

'You're right, Tim, it is. As far as we can see she didn't make friends in these places either. She worked as Hunter's PA, so had no work colleagues. He's a freelance management consultant, which is basically a licence to do whatever you want. The two of them coming down here was about a forever home, according to Hunter. It's in the name, Sea

Dream: this was their dream and they wanted to set down roots. That said, Helena didn't make a lot of effort to get to know anyone in the community. Was a bit of a stay-at-home, by all accounts . . .'

'Sir,' says Mullins. 'Um . . . why are you saying *was* – shouldn't it be *is*?'

DCI Robinson blinks. 'Quite right. *Is* a bit of a stay-at-home . . .'

'Do you think we're too late?'

Silly, really, that it's the first time he's felt it. It was the description of Helena, the story of her life, cooked down to a few lines. He feels a little chilly suddenly and tugs at his shirtsleeves. She can't actually be *dead*, can she? He glances around at the other faces, to see if anyone else is feeling it too.

DCI Robinson pushes back his shoulders as he eyes the meeting room. 'It's been more than twenty-four hours since Helena was last seen. What we know is that, according to her husband, she left her home in the dunes for a run, sometime between 7.30 and 7.45 yesterday morning – and that's something she does most days. And, like most days, she left all of her personal possessions at home – including, this time, her phone. Presumably she simply forgot it. The unusual thing about this occasion is that Lewis Pascoe had been to the house – upset, angry, making tangible threats – not once but twice. Both the night before and that very morning. The last words he apparently said to Roland Hunter, corroborated by Nathan Hunter, were: *How would you feel if you lost the only person you loved?*

Robinson holds up his hands, as if to say, *Go figure!*

'Pascoe would still have been in the area that morning as Helena went for her run – that's more or less guaranteed. He had no transport of his own, and we've found evidence of a rough sleeper in the dunes – fingerprints on a can of Foster's, and they're Pascoe's. Just like the fingerprints on Helena Hunter's watch, which was discovered further along the shore, not far from the cliff he eventually fell from. From there we don't know. A motorist has come forward saying they saw someone jogging further along the beach road sometime after 8 a.m. but can't confirm if it was a male or female; nor can they confirm their clothing. Lewis Pascoe was wearing a grey hoodie and tracksuit bottoms: to all intents and purposes similar sportswear to Helena Hunter's attire of Lycra bottoms and a hooded top. It could have been either one of them, I suppose, or someone else entirely. We also have a more accurate sighting at 7.45 a.m. – a full description that matches Helena Hunter, running on the coast path near the cliff car park. Plus the added detail from the witness that the jogger appeared to be running away from something rather than just running. Potentially a smart observation, given the circumstances.'

'Which direction was she running in?' asks one of the other officers who's been drafted in from Newquay; a string-thin man, sitting with one leg hooked over the other. 'And what made them so sure she was running away, if she was in sportswear? She could have just been a decent athlete.'

'Something about the action. He noticed it, the witness, before he knew anything untoward had happened, but then he put it out of mind. The potential significance occurred to him afterwards. And it was eastward. Away from the spot where Pascoe was found.'

The Newquay bloke writes in his notebook, and Mullins wonders if he should be writing something down too.

'Anyway,' Robinson goes on, 'Pascoe was found by surfers just after 8 a.m., having fallen from the cliff. It's unclear how long he'd been there, but paramedics at the scene, assessing the blood loss, estimate no more than ten or fifteen minutes. Which means we're looking at a maximum thirty-minute window in which Pascoe and Helena could have crossed paths.'

Mullins chews at his thumbnail. He can't see how it adds up. There are better heads than his in the room, he can admit that, but not people who know the area like him. And there isn't anywhere round there that Helena could be. Anyone can see that, can't they?

'It's already been established that Pascoe was on foot,' Robinson continues, 'so his means were limited. If he attacked Helena, or was holding her somewhere, then we're talking about a small area. We've gone door to door. We've gained access to the shut-up holiday homes. We've even had sniffer dogs going around the fixed caravans down the other end. Nothing. The Coastguard know what they're looking for – they're out on the water.'

'Why would he hold her somewhere and then try to kill himself?' pipes up Skinner, and it's only then that Mullins realises how quiet his boss has been until that point. 'What would be the use in that? And all within half an hour? I don't buy it.'

'Pascoe wasn't of sound mind,' says Robinson. 'I think we can say that with some confidence. If he'd taken things too far, started to regret it, he might have panicked. Then gone for what he thought was the easy way out.'

'Do you mean he was pissed off and upset,' says Mullins, 'or, like, mentally whatnot. Unwell like that, I mean. Depressed and that.'

Mullins feels uncomfortable even saying it, though it's supposed to be okay to talk about that kind of thing these days. Depression. But how can you tell if someone is just a bit down because life isn't all that A1, or if it's something more?

'According to prison officials at Dartmoor he wasn't clinically depressed,' says Robinson, 'but he was said to be emotionally immature, which could affect how he handles difficult situations.'

'The system failed him,' says DS Chang, another of the Newquay lot, a serious and impressive-looking woman with a shiny bob. 'The shock of his grandmother's house not being where he left it, abruptly learning of her death from a third party who, let's face it, probably wouldn't have delivered the news in a sympathetic manner, combined with the heightened feelings of being newly released and the sometimes difficult adjustments . . . it's a perfect storm of emotion. In my opinion, Lewis Pascoe was failed.'

The detective's words land with Mullins, in a way that he's not used to. *Lewis Pascoe was failed.* Suddenly, what's happening here feels bigger than any of them. He's never been involved in anything like it, and he almost feels nostalgic for the speeders, for the drunk and disorderly: you know where you are with them.

'All efforts were made to contact Lewis after Maggie Pascoe died,' says Skinner, his chest pushed all the way out, like a beer barrel. 'The Guv up at Dartmoor. Us here. If the kid gets out and doesn't answer his phone that's on him, not anyone else. That's not the system.'

'It's still the system,' says DS Chang.

'It was a perfect storm of emotion, you're right,' says Robinson, cutting in. 'And in the middle of all of that you had the Hunters. The very people Pascoe probably sees as being responsible for the whole mess – or at least emblematic of it.'

'*Emblematic*,' huffs Skinner.

'What about the old mine shafts?' says Mullins suddenly, the words *Lewis Pascoe was failed* still ringing in his ears.

'Initial searches have turned up diddly. We'll go deeper, and further, today. No stone left unturned but . . . it's unlikely. The fact is,' says Robinson, 'Lewis Pascoe went off the exact same cliff where his dad committed suicide twenty years ago. That doesn't feel like a coincidence to me. But what was the nature of the inter-action between Pascoe and Helena before that moment? That's the million-dollar question. If we can answer it, there's a good chance we'll find Helena.'

'What, so Hunter's putting up a reward?' Mullins blinks.

He hears a snort of laughter from one of the Newquay lot.

Mullins flushes. Recovers. 'Yeah, okay, okay. I know we're not a fan of them. But isn't it a bit odd that he hasn't even suggested offering one? If he's as rich as all that?'

28

Ally stands outside Hang Ten, taking it in as if for the first time. It's a purple and yellow beach hut with a wooden balustrade, planters full of French lavender and rosemary. There's a bench fashioned from a sun-bleached old bellyboard, and the curtains at the window have a palm-leaf print. It's a place made with love; Ally can see that now.

She presses her nose to the glass to look inside. There are no lights on, and the chairs are stacked on the few tables.

'Oh,' says Jayden, appearing behind her on the boardwalk. He nods to the sign on the door, 'Gone Surfin'!'. 'Occupational hazard round here, I guess. Shall we wait? Or we could head to yours? The Shell House sounds like it was designed to be an HQ.'

'An HQ?'

'For the Shell House Detectives, of course.'

Ally laughs and shakes her head. 'You're in good spirits.'

'I've got something interesting to share with you. Something *very* interesting. Plus, Cat's got some old schoolfriends round. They're eating cake and drinking something that's supposed to be non-alcoholic but they're flying high, if you ask me. There's a lot of shrieking. I got out of there while I could.' He grins. 'It's nice to see her so happy. This is what she wanted – reconnecting, all that. It's good. And . . . yeah. Like I said, I might have something. I spoke to Fatima again. My Surrey friend?'

'Doing some reconnecting yourself?' She sees his face, adds, 'I mean with the police.'

'What? Oh, yeah. Not really, but . . . she called me.'

She sees Jayden look sideways as two dog-walkers pass, their anoraks rustling in the stiff breeze. Another man hovers nearby, fiddling with his phone. Ally does a double take. He's wearing chinos and a polo shirt and has a tangible air of self-satisfaction.

'Actually, shall we wait until we get to The Shell House?' he says. 'It might be better. More private.'

'What's that? Oh, yes. Of course.'

'Ally, you alright?'

Her brow furrows. 'I'm seeing things. I just thought that was Roland standing over there. It's not. Come on, let's go.'

Jayden points out his car, parked up just behind the café. They're making their way to it when Ally stops and looks back at Hang Ten again. The man's moved out of view.

'Still thinking about Roland?' he says.

'No, no. Just . . . the girl who runs it, Saffron. Is it like her, to open and close when she likes? I wouldn't have thought she'd want to miss Saturday trade.'

'Don't know, I've only been in a few times. What are you thinking?'

'Overthinking, probably,' says Ally.

Jayden nods, and she can tell he's caught her drift.

'She lives in a house-share in the village,' he says. 'I don't know any more than that though.' She watches him scan the beach, checking out the scattering of surfers on the water. 'Hang on, she keeps her board behind the café. One sec.'

He nips round the back while Ally bends down to stroke Fox. She doesn't want to think this way, but when one woman was missing, perhaps you couldn't help it.

156

'The board's not there,' he says. 'She's probably doing exactly what the sign says.'

'Let's walk along the beach. If you're okay with that?'

'Sure.' He nods to the water. 'And I'll bet she's one of that crew. We'll take a look. Come on, little mate.'

Fox trots beside Jayden like he's an old friend. Ally follows, her hands pushed deep into her pockets. Should she be ambling along, when all the time the clock is ticking for Helena? She called the police earlier, after talking to Gus, because she felt she had to, and told them about the artist working outside of Sea Dream a few weeks ago. PC Mullins – not Skinner this time, to her relief – noted it down with what seemed to her like excessive courtesy; as if obviously humouring her. Or maybe she's just oversensitive now. And perhaps it's a long shot, but Fiona was seen speaking with Helena, the two of them seemed friendly, and weren't all possible connections worth exploring?

As they take the sandy path down the cliff side, she tells Jayden about the artist. They pause to let a young family pass in the other direction, and Ally sees the way that Jayden glances at the baby riding high up in a carrier. She notices how the two of them trade smiles; the baby showing a gummy grin, his podgy hands waving, Jayden waving back.

'So, it was worth speaking to this Gus guy then?' he says, turning to her. 'That's good info. Hey, what? Why are you smiling?'

'You and that baby.'

'That's my people.'

And she thinks what a lovely dad he'll make. Bill did so much for them, but he left all of the tending to Ally; it was women's work, back then. Not that her daughter's husband has the same excuse. But there's something about Jayden that makes her think he'll be in it all the way up to his eyeballs, and willingly too.

157

'You know, I'm wondering if we should just go there,' she says. 'To St Ives. To speak to Fiona Penrose.'

'Ally, yes,' says Jayden. 'I like this kind of talk.'

'I did pass the information on to the police, but they didn't seem terribly interested. And perhaps that's fair. Even as I was telling them about Fiona, I felt myself losing faith in it meaning anything. But still.'

'Who was it, Skinner again?'

'I got through to the young chap. PC Mullins.'

'Okay, cool, so you've done the good citizen bit,' says Jayden. 'Now we follow it up, see if there's anything in it. Shell House Detectives vibes, Al.'

'Will you stop saying that?' And while her laugh feels out of place, given everything, it's a relief, too.

As they reach the beach, she thinks how nice it is to be walking beside someone here. How different it feels.

'So, what did you have to tell me?' she asks.

Jayden stops and shields his eyes with his hand. 'Hang on, out there, that's Saffron, isn't it?'

They watch as a svelte surfer dances across a wave then steps off into the shallows. Her hair is slick against her head, darkened by sea water – but, surely, pink?

'Saffron!' yells Jayden, making Ally jump beside him.

The woman turns. Waves. Then runs back into the sea, her board under her arm.

'It's her,' says Ally. And she can feel something relax in her chest.

Jayden nods. 'It's her.' Then, 'St Ives, huh? Well, let's do it. What if we talk on the road instead of at your house?'

'Are you sure you won't be missed, Jayden? When I said *we*, I was really just . . .'

He checks his watch. 'Cat and the girls were just getting going when I left. It's all good.'

Ally throws a stick for Fox. In truth, she's already thought how they might go about it. They'll first head for the gallery that represents Fiona Penrose – Salt Air Gallery, she double-checked online – and ask for her there. She's pretty sure Fiona lives out towards the moors, but better to go to the gallery and do it properly. It won't be that different to turning up at Gus's door this morning, and that went well; he didn't call her a busybody or any such thing. She even accepted a cup of tea before she left, and one of those Tunnock's teacakes she hasn't had since Evie was a girl.

Although, it is a Saturday afternoon. Bill would have said she was barking mad going into St Ives on a Saturday afternoon.

Meanwhile, Jayden has walked on ahead. He turns, calls back, 'Ally, yes? We're on?'

She hesitates; nods. She gives Saffron a quick glance again, far out on the water, then – satisfied – she catches up to him. Fox is there already, as if they're a trio. An unlikely trio: that surely must be what Jayden's young wife thinks.

'And this thing I've got to tell you,' he says. 'It's kind of big. But I'll wait till we get to the car now. Spoiler alert though: it's about someone who has a reason to hate the Hunters.'

29

Saffron duck-dives under the waves then comes up the other side. Hauls air into her lungs. Beneath her, her board is reassuringly solid. When she makes it out beyond the breakers, she floats, looking back at the far-off shore. She can see the undulating dunes, and specks of people moving. Everything feels so far away from here.

She recognised the pair from yesterday – Ally and Jayden and that cute little dog – but she didn't want to stop and talk, even with them. She needed to be in the water.

She feels safe out here, as if she's above and beyond everything. She didn't feel safe in the car. But she stood her ground, didn't let herself be intimidated, and in the end, it was Roland Hunter who shut down the subject of Lewis. She saw the anger in his eyes though; the pulsing at his jawline, as if something in his head was going to burst wide open. Then he took hold of the steering wheel like he wanted to rip it from the dashboard, kicked the accelerator, and they drove back to Porthpella in silence.

'I'm so sorry that your wife is missing,' she said as she got out, 'but you can't blame Lewis for it. No one knows what happened. His nan said to me that he might be in prison, but he wouldn't hurt a fly.'

'Fortunately, the police don't share your view,' he said. Then, 'He must have friends around here, other little ASBOs he kicked around with before he was banged up?'

She didn't even bother replying to that.

As Roland drove off, sand flying from beneath the wheels, Saffron realised her fingers were trembling; she leant her bike against the wall and pushed her hands together to make them stop. She'd got him to drop her at the village rather than outside Hang Ten – a crucial bit of distance. Saffron knew, then, that she didn't want to open up the coffee shop today. She didn't want to be available to anyone who walked in the door, a smile at the ready, welcoming all-comers.

Most of the time she travels through the world like it's a good place to be, like most people can be trusted. But what if she's too busy hanging out on the sunny side of the street? Catching waves and frothing milk and making chit-chat with anyone who wants it. What if she needs to get real?

Walking home from late-night beach parties, of course she's aware of the shadows. She's always held her body strong, ready for fight or flight. It's never mattered how well she knows the paths, or how most of the time all she's startled by is the sudden dart of a rabbit or the shriek of a gull; she's still primed for it – all women are, aren't they? This threat that they all feel; this injustice that's so engrained it's almost normal.

Did Maggie Pascoe ever feel scared, in all those years living out here on her own? Does Ally Bright now?

Saffron closes her eyes, lets the sea's song wrap around her. Beneath her wetsuit her heart bangs like a drum. She turns over in her mind the other thing that Roland Hunter said: that he'd been right here in Porthpella twenty years ago.

Didn't Ally Bright say that Lewis's dad killed himself twenty years ago?

She wonders if that's the kind of thing the police would be interested in. Not that she's trying to stir anything up. Or get involved. Hell, no. She does not want to get involved.

Seeing Roland Hunter up close brought it home to Saffron more than anything that Mullins had said, more than hearing the whirr of helicopter blades and seeing the police dogs sniffing over the dunes: Helena is missing. A woman went out running and, more than twenty-four hours later, she still hasn't come back.

She'll open up the café tomorrow, but not today.

Saffron glances over her shoulder and sees a new set rolling in. She drops to her front and starts paddling.

Twenty minutes later, Saffron calls it a day. She's heading back up the beach, board under her arm, when someone calls out to her.

'Hey, you, pink-haired girl!'

A middle-aged man in a salmon-coloured polo shirt and cream chinos stands with his arms folded across his chest. Everything about him screams out-of-towner. When she makes eye contact, his smile shows all of his teeth, and maybe it's just because it's today, but she feels a ripple of unease. The fact that he bears an uncanny resemblance to Roland Hunter doesn't help either. Nor does the use of *pink-haired girl*.

She quickly scans left and right. There's a young family tucked behind a striped windbreak twenty yards away; a boy running with his dog through the shallows; a scattering of surfers further out. No one's paying any attention to this man.

'What is it?' she says.

She thinks of adding *grey-haired man* but doesn't want it to seem like banter. She's so over banter.

'I tried to get a beer at the café, but it's all shut up. An urchin on a skateboard told me it's your place. Even pointed you out. Nice surfing.'

'Yeah, sorry,' says Saffron – politely enough, but without much apology – 'we're closed for the day. And we're not licensed anyway. If you head into Porthpella, you can get a pint at The Wreckers.'

'Oh, it's not the alcohol I'm after; my brother's got a truckload of that back at his. More the *ambiance*.' He says it with an exaggerated French accent, his lips twisting in a way that she's pretty sure he thinks is attractive but is mainly gross. 'A bit of local colour, that's what I want.' His eyes blatantly go to her hair. 'I'm down for a long weekend, but things are a little miserable Chez Bro-ski. My sister-in-law appears to have done a runner.'

Saffron plants her board in the sand. Only just rid of one Hunter, and here's another.

'You don't mean Helena Hunter?'

'You two are friends?'

Saffron shakes her head. 'No, but . . .'

'No, I wouldn't have thought so. She's a bit of a princess, is Helena. And you, you're a . . . well, you're a too-cool-for-school surf chick, aren't you?' He laughs, eyes flashing. 'I'm not sure the two mix.'

'Aren't you worried about her?' And it's a pretty spiky voice for Saffron. But if this guy notices, he doesn't show it.

'What harm could she have come to round here? Except for getting shat on by a gull. Or pulled out by the tide. Or there's the cliffs, I s'pose.' He grins. 'But, perils aside, I'm finding the locals to be thoroughly charming. How much for surf lessons?'

'There's a surf school opening here next year. For now, you'll have to head round the bay. . .'

She makes to walk on, and he holds up his hand. His heavy-looking watch glints in the sun.

'A one-on-one lesson, I mean. I'm one of your favourite Londoners: the kind that's quite happy being ripped off. Name your price.' He laughs, then says, 'Oh, don't look so serious. I'm just amusing myself. I told you, it's a washout of a weekend. I'll be back at the office on Monday and . . .' He hesitates, runs his fingers through his thinning hair. And the look that passes across his face takes Saffron by surprise: half-angered, half-pained. Then he seems to physically shake himself. 'Anyway, I'm not a novice. I've been surfing in Newquay. Years ago, but it's like falling off a bike – isn't that what they say?'

Was the reference deliberate? But then a thought occurs to Saffron: was it the same trip that Roland mentioned in the car? Because here's a chance to get a bit more info, before she goes to Mullins and is told, *Yeah, thanks Saff, but, er, newsflash, people like to come on holiday to Cornwall.*

'How long ago are we talking?'

'Let's see.' He counts off on his fingers. 'Nineteen. No, twenty. Twenty years. That's nothing, is it? A decent vintage.'

'What was it, a stag party?'

'How did you guess?' He grins. 'Bloody good one too.' He gives a blurt of laughter. 'Cheese!'

'Say what?'

'We were all dressed as cheese. Martin, the groom-to-be – divorced now, obviously – came as a stinking great wedge of Stilton. Genius.'

Saffron forces a smile, although behind it her teeth are gritted.

'And me and Jonno were the Laughing Cow. Naturally it was my brother as the rear end. Sorry, *Roland*, that's how you all know him. Gallivanting around in a cow suit in the heat of the summer, things got a little foisty, I can tell you. You couldn't argue with the commitment though. We stayed in that suit all damn weekend. Even when we came down here to some piddly little beer festival.'

Piddly little beer festival. If anyone would remember that happening, it would be Wenna at the shop.

'You and your brother were dressed as the Laughing Cow, right here in Porthpella?' she says.

'One of the boys had pulled a girl from here. Can't remember her name. I hope to God it wasn't your mother.' He holds up his hand again and rolls his eyes. 'Sorry, locker-room humour. Apparently that's illegal now. Can't say a bloody thing.'

'And you were in your outfits all weekend long?' It sounds too probing, so she adds, 'Even when you were surfing?'

'You don't think we actually went in the water?' He laughs. And it's an exaggerated boom of a sound, the opposite of infectious. 'The intention was there, but the action never quite materialised. Hey, time to make up for it now, what do you say? Show me some moves, Mermaid Girl?'

And he's reaching for his wallet.

'Sorry,' says Saffron, tucking her board under her arm and carrying on up the beach. 'Like I said, we're closed.'

'What did I say?' he calls out after her, a rougher edge to his voice now.

She catches the words *knickers* and *twist*. But she doesn't look back. Suddenly she's got a different kind of wave to catch.

30

Ally and Jayden are in a queue of vehicles sitting bumper to bumper. The car park is jam-packed and it's the third one they've tried. So far, so St Ives. *If you're going to go, you've got to go early*, was what Bill always said. *Afternoon's a mug's game.*

'What now?' says Jayden.

'Nothing for it but to wait.'

They're high up above the town, in a slanting car park behind the Tate gallery. Until they can get a space, St Ives itself is like a secret garden they can't find a way into. The sea lies beyond, a tantalising haze. The rooftops of the town, slate grey and set at every angle, beckon like a Ben Nicholson painting.

'What if I wait here,' he says, 'and you go on to the gallery? I'll come meet you when I get a spot.' He holds up his phone. 'Stay in radio contact.'

Ally climbs out, Fox jumping down with her. Then the dog promptly hops back in and curls himself up in the seat beside Jayden.

'Looks like someone wants to be my wingman,' he says, stroking his ears. 'I'm happy if you are.'

Ally hesitates. She's never left Fox with anyone before, but the dog looks so contented.

'I'm very happy,' says Ally.

She cuts across the car park and takes the steep alleyway down towards Porthmeor Beach. To her left is the cemetery, a place where art lovers hunt out the grave of Alfred Wallis. When Evie was small, they used to come to this graveyard; there was always a quiet bench for them among the tilted stones, and the ocean view was serenity itself – a place of respite, in a town where tourists clogged the narrow streets and in summer the beach was an intricate jigsaw of towels and windbreaks.

Now Ally walks on, the impressive geometry of the Tate rising to her right, and suddenly she rounds the corner and there's the full view of Porthmeor, golden sand stretching all the way to The Island peninsula. It's a blustery afternoon but blowing offshore, and the water's busy with surfers. Day trippers amble along the seafront, and a crocodile of international students is lined up by the gallery steps. Ally hurries along the narrow pavement, then swings around the corner and into the back roads leading to Salt Air Gallery. As she weaves between people, she feels her pulse quickening; she's never felt comfortable in crowds.

She knows St Ives well, although these days sporadic trips are enough, and every time she hits the coast road, leaving the glitter of the town behind her, she always finds herself drawing breath. She wouldn't go near the place in the height of the summer season. But now, on a sunny March afternoon, here she is, part of it.

And this isn't exactly an ordinary trip.

As she walks, her mind is full of Jayden's information. The name Sebastian Lyle, Hunter's former brother-in-law, repeats in her mind like a tattoo. Was there anything behind Lyle's accusation other than sorrow? Is it possible that his animosity could have flared again now, with Lyle seeking revenge for something that happened five years ago? It seems unlikely – but, Ally is realising, a lot of things are unlikely until they happen.

Salt Air Gallery is just off Island Square. In a town full of galleries, it's one of the newer ones, and its elegant signage and measured window display suggest fine art rather than seaside-souvenir paintings. It's the kind of place Ally has always been far too intimidated to approach with her own work, though the thought has crossed her mind a few times over the years. One of Fiona Penrose's paintings is front and centre in the window. Ally recognises her style right away: a bold and splashy seascape in the kind of vivid colours you want to drink, not just look at. Confidence and vitality leap from the canvas.

When Evie was younger, Ally thought that her true passion might have been for art. They spent many happy times walking the halls of the Tate together, or sitting among the tropical plants and immaculate sculptures in the Hepworth Garden, the pair of them with their sketchbooks balanced on their knees. For a while, the romantic in Ally – the mollusc in her, admittedly – imagined her daughter staying down here forever, maybe working from a beach-front studio, Ally dropping by for tea among the easels. Cornwall was a fine place to be an artist, so why not? And Evie had the personality to throw herself into the cut and thrust of it, whereas that was never Ally's style. But at some point, Evie dropped talk of art college and switched to marketing instead; an about-turn that she never looked back from, and that took her, eventually, to the other side of the world.

And now the pressure is on for Ally to follow her there too. As much as the question of Sydney is currently being crowded out by other things – Lewis, Helena, Fiona, Sebastian – it's still there, running beneath it all. Like a patch of uncertain weather out on the horizon that can't be ignored. There will be quiet spots in Sydney where she can take her grandsons to go sketching, won't there? If they're interested, that is. They could have so many nice days. But it isn't just about that, is it?

Ally steps inside the gallery, feeling trepidatious suddenly. An old-fashioned shop bell jangles incongruously, announcing her arrival.

'Hello,' says the young man behind the counter.

He wears horn-rimmed glasses and a raucous flowered shirt; his smile's courteous enough, but he gives her a quick look up and down as she returns his greeting and it's clear that he doesn't consider her a serious proposition. Not a buyer. He goes back to what he's doing, behind his sleek white computer.

Ally makes a show of looking at the work on the walls. Actually, it's not that much of a show, as there's something about the white walls and the riot of colour that centres her – she can't tear her eyes away from the work. The floor is polished stone and there's a cathedral hush to the place. Why doesn't she spend more time in galleries these days?

'Can I help, or are you happy looking?'

He says it on autopilot, already anticipating the answer. She feels a ripple of pleasure at being able to surprise him.

'I'm actually interested in one of your artists, Fiona Penrose.'

'Oh, really?'

He takes his glasses off, wipes them, returns them to his nose. Now, it's as if he sees her differently.

'Fi? Yes, she's really something else. This is all brand-new work, hung just last week.'

He comes and stands beside Ally, points out the painting directly in front of them. 'That's Zennor. Has it ever looked more delectable?'

'Doesn't she live out that way?'

And she's surprised at the way it trips off her tongue.

'She does. Perfect spot, between the moors and the sea.'

'I wanted to speak to her,' says Ally. 'Is that where I'll find her now, do you think?'

'At home, you mean?' He checks his watch. 'She'll likely be in her studio. But it's not open to the public. All enquiries go through us here.'

'I'd wanted to look her up as a surprise.' Ally smiles. 'I'm an old friend, you see.'

She hasn't dressed for this – that's what she thinks as she says it. She's wearing her old wax jacket with the ripped pockets, and hiking boots that are clogged with sand. But she does have on her sea glass necklace, which Bill used to say brought out the green of her eyes, and perhaps it's an age thing – an air of trustworthiness – or perhaps she looks the part as one of Fiona Penrose's slightly dishevelled artistic friends, because now the man's nodding, and for a second Ally thinks he's going to go along with it.

'How do you know each other?' he says, his head tipped, something catlike in his expression.

'I'm an artist too.'

It's a simpler statement than she thought. And certainly no lie. Is it her imagination, or does his nose wrinkle just perceptibly though?

'I'm sorry,' he says. 'I can't give out any personal details. Fiona's a very private person. As I'm sure you know.'

His phone rings then, and he makes an 'excuse me' face, and Ally knows that's the end of the conversation. 'Marcus, hello,' he gushes. And he's off, walking through to the back room, talking fast, one hand pressing the phone to his ear, the other swiping the air as if conducting an invisible orchestra.

Ally sighs. She's just about to leave when she catches sight of a Rolodex on the man's desk. Clearly, what with the shop bell too, he has a taste for the analogue. She feels a quick spark of possibility. She glances over to the back room, which presumably leads to another, because the man is now out of sight. His voice is still just audible, muffled laughter reaching her ears, and she looks back at the desk.

No, it's too risky.

She hurries to the door, and the bell clangs again as she opens it.

Then she closes it again – and stands in the silence of the gallery. If he's kept one ear on her, he'll think that she's left.

Ally tiptoes back to the desk. She notes the card that the Rolodex is open on – *Harrington Frames* – and then flicks through, hunting for P, her fingers fumbling with a mix of nerves and excitement. She sees Parkinson, Patel, Penrose. *Penrose!* And then the address: *Sealark House, Zennor.* Her eyes are darting around for a piece of scrap paper and a pen when she remembers her phone; she slips it from her pocket and quickly photographs the card. The sound of the camera snapping seems to echo throughout the gallery. Ally freezes, breath held. But there's no movement from the back room. She hurriedly turns the Rolodex back to the original card and makes for the door. This time the clang of the bell is like a victory cry as her feet hit the street, and she keeps on moving. Her heart is racing like she's just stolen something – which she supposes is exactly what she's done.

But Helena. She's trying to find Helena. Doesn't the end justify the means?

Ally checks her phone and there's a single message from Jayden: Still no spaces!

She taps a message back: No need to park anymore, we're bound for Zennor!

Ally doesn't even notice the shoals of tourists this time; she hurries back through the town, head high, the name Sealark burning a hole in her pocket.

31

Jayden settles into the drive, the moorland roads opening up before him, the sea beaming to his right. The landscape changes so quickly around here. Cat's family's farm is all softness, with rolling fields and cotton-wool sheep and geese traipsing about like they're out of a Disney film. It's beautiful out here on the moors, for sure, but there's also a harsh edge to it: maybe he's too much of a city boy, but the vast emptiness unsettles him.

He quite liked the noise of St Ives: the lines of traffic and crowds of pleasure seekers felt friendly. Everyone just wanted to have a nice time, so why not bundle in and have it on top of each other? Maybe he and Cat can take the baby there, sit in one of those over-stuffed cafés and eat a cake that'll probably be less good than his mother-in-law's. That could be fun? Or is that strictly for tourists? He still can't figure out where he sits.

In Cornwall, you're an incomer, her dad said last week, completely straight-faced, *but give it twenty years and we'll review your file.*

'Here,' says Ally, 'can you stop a second? Those trees. I recognise them from a painting in the gallery.'

Jayden draws up beside a clutch of windblown trees, their trunks slanted. They mark the entrance to a narrow track.

'Want to try it?' he says.

But the track runs out after twenty metres or so, the way ahead swallowed up by angry-looking brambles and giant ferns; the stone carcass of a ruined barn just visible ahead.

'Red herring,' says Ally. 'Sorry. We're close though. Try the next turning.'

'Y'know,' says Jayden, 'it's not exactly protocol, just turning up like this.'

'Whose protocol?'

'I mean, we're not police. I know I was all for it back on the beach but . . . just saying. We need to make sure we get our story straight. If we ever find the place.'

He clicks into reverse, foliage swishing the sides of the car as they bump backwards down the track. Presumably Mullins would have passed the name Fiona Penrose on to Skinner, but who knows how long it'd take for them to follow it up, given everything else. It *is* a longshot – he can see that. But here they are. And the fact that the guy in the gallery was happy to pass on Fiona's address, well, that was on him, right?

'It is an intrusion,' says Ally, 'I do know that, but . . .'

'I think we just need to watch how we handle it, you know?' he says, as they rejoin the road. 'Okay, where to now? Carry on towards Zennor?'

'So, you do want to keep going?'

'Sure. Of course. We just have to tread carefully.'

'Okay,' says Ally, her voice doubtful now, 'but perhaps if we can't find it, we take that as a sign that . . .' She throws out her arm suddenly. 'Look!'

A boulder with *Sealark House* engraved on it marks the start of an overgrown lane.

'Well, you wanted a sign, Al. Good enough?'

They take the turning, the car bumping along a lane that's so narrow tufts of grass sprout in the middle. There's no house in sight – just a band of sea up ahead. Then, suddenly, the track dips. Jayden spots a grey roof, a chimney pot.

Beside him, Ally fidgets in her seat. 'I'm a little nervous now.'

'It's all good.'

'And, you're right, we shouldn't be here. I expect it's very different in a uniform?'

A beat. 'Yeah, maybe. Though it can close as many doors as it opens, you know?' Then, 'Your husband ever feel like that?'

'I think sometimes. But he worked hard to get to know everyone. To build bridges. But, of course, that didn't always work.'

And Jayden reckons she must be thinking of the Pascoe family.

He eases the car through a narrow gateway, gravel crunching beneath the tyres. The house looms large, grey stone and as tall as a church. Potted palms explode out of terracotta, and what looks like a mill wheel is propped against the wall, half swallowed by some kind of prehistoric-vibe creeper. An unseen dog starts barking loudly, and Fox squirms in Ally's arms in response.

'There goes our stealth arrival,' he says.

'And that must be Fiona,' says Ally, as a woman rounds the corner of the house.

She wears a loose shirt and a pair of gardening gloves, battered rubber shoes on her feet. Her red hair is tied back in a headscarf.

'You should do the talking, Al.'

'Really?'

'I'll back you up.'

Ally nods. They share a quick conspiratorial glance that out of nowhere makes him think of Kieran. He unballs his fist; Ally probably isn't into knuckle bumps.

'Hello there,' he hears her saying cheerfully as she climbs out of the car. 'So sorry to come by unannounced.'

She told him she was shy, but he's immediately struck by Ally's ease. Maybe it's easier when you're playing a role; well, that he understands.

As Jayden gets out of the car too, he turns his attention to Fiona; she's guarded, that much is clear, but wouldn't anyone be, if strangers pulled up at their hideaway? Living all the way out here, she can't have too many people randomly dropping by.

Fiona takes off her gloves, wipes a streak of soil from her cheek. 'Are you lost?' she says.

And it almost sounds like more of an accusation than a question.

'In a manner of speaking. My name's Ally, Ally Bright. And this is Jayden. I'm not sure where to start but . . . it's about Helena Hunter.'

He looks for a reaction in Fiona's face, but he doesn't see one. Her eyes are as still as a pond.

'Helena Hunter?' Fiona pushes a strand of hair out of her face. 'I was commissioned by her just a few weeks ago. It was a lot of fun.'

'But you've heard the news?'

'News?' Fiona shakes her head. 'What news? I live more or less off-grid here. It's how I like it. I . . .' Her eyes narrow as she looks at Ally, then to Jayden. 'Is everything alright?'

'She's missing,' says Ally.

'Missing?'

'Since yesterday,' adds Jayden. 'She was last seen running in the dunes out by Porthpella, early Friday morning.'

'I don't follow the news,' says Fiona, passing her gloves from hand to hand. 'I don't like the intrusion into my space.'

Jayden feels Ally shift beside him, taking – and feeling – the hint.

175

'What are you telling me?' says Fiona. 'Are the police looking for her? Are you with them?'

'Yes, the police are looking for her,' says Jayden. 'And . . . no, we're not with them.'

'But we are trying to find her,' says Ally. 'And we thought perhaps you might be able to help. As you know her.'

'I hardly know her very well. She's a client.'

'Fiona, even the smallest piece of information might end up proving useful. Even if it feels insignificant,' Jayden says.

Fiona stares at him, as if he's said something really stupid – and she looks like she couldn't care less about being useful.

'I know we've no business turning up out of the blue like this,' says Ally, carefully. 'And I'm sorry for the shock. Really, I am.'

Generous of Ally, or a tactic? *Shock* isn't an adjective Jayden would have used to describe Fiona's reaction.

'But no stone unturned,' she goes on, 'and . . . I heard that the two of you were quite friendly. You'd have spent a bit of time around the Hunters' house, while you were working on their commission? So, I thought you might have been able to give an insight into what her day-to-day life was like. I know, it's not exactly much to go on, but . . . it might be something. And I always think of artists as being particularly observant.'

And Jayden thinks how good she is at this. Gentle but firm. But Fiona's eyes narrow.

'Heard we were friendly? And who said that? The husband?'

'Not at all. Another neighbour.'

'So you're not teamed up with him for this?'

'No, no,' says Ally. And she leaves it there.

Ally's vagueness is necessary – they can't give too much away – but it doesn't go over well with Fiona.

'I don't understand why you two are looking for her. Hmm?' Then, without waiting for an answer, she says, 'I'm sorry, but I really can't assist you. Like I said, I hardly know Helena. She struck me as a nice woman who likes her art. That's about the size of it.'

'What about Roland though?' says Jayden. 'Did you meet him?'

'Only briefly. Now, if you don't mind . . . I'd like to go back to my gardening.'

'One moment,' says Ally, and she digs in her bag, pulls out a receipt. A pen. She quickly scribbles, then hands the receipt to Fiona. 'My number,' she says. 'Please, feel no pressure, but just in case anything else comes to you.'

Fiona looks at her studiedly, but Ally looks straight back with nothing but openness and encouragement in her face.

'How did you get my address?'

'It's a small world down here,' says Ally.

And there's something about the way Ally hesitates that makes Jayden wonder how she got the address after all.

Fiona grunts. Then she turns on her heel and disappears.

He looks to Ally, eyebrows raised. 'That's our cue, I guess,' he says.

From inside the car Fox barks, as if in agreement, or in warning, as just then a humungous hound gallops around the corner of the house. Tongue swinging, jaws open, it heads right for them. Jayden jumps in front of Ally, his arms thrown up instinctively.

The dog skids to a stop three feet away and lets loose a volley of barks.

'That's definitely our cue,' says Ally. And very slowly, steadily, without taking their eyes from the dog, they climb back inside the car.

32

'So, that didn't quite go as I imagined,' says Ally.

Jayden slows to carefully pass a rider on a piebald horse, and the coconut scent of gorse wafts in through the open windows. Ally loves the emptiness of the moors, but today she's looking at them differently. She's looking at it all differently. The rider lifts her crop in acknowledgement as they pass.

'How did you imagine it going?' he says.

'We were intruding on her,' says Ally, glancing back at the horse and rider in her mirror. 'And I suppose there's a chance the chap from the gallery phoned her.'

'Fiona would have mentioned that though, right?' Jayden glances sideways at her. 'What are you thinking?'

'Something just seemed off about it,' says Ally. 'If she had no idea that Helena was missing, I'd have thought she would have been more shocked by the news, wouldn't you? That's all. It felt like she was more bothered by the fact that we'd turned up asking questions than something potentially having happened to Helena. Don't you think?'

'It's hard to say,' says Jayden. 'Yeah, okay, she seemed a bit . . . mechanical. But maybe that's how she is, you know? If she's living off-grid, the way she likes it, then I guess unexpected visitors are never going to get a big welcome.'

And he's right, of course he is. But she can't quite let go of it.

'But . . . where was her passion? Her paintings are so vibrant, Jayden, all that colour and energy. Don't you think it's strange that a person who expresses themselves like that on canvas can give so little reaction in real life?'

But as the words are out of her mouth she thinks of her own pictures. Would someone connect them with her own outward personality? Perhaps not.

'Maybe she just processes things differently, Al. We can't judge her on that.'

Ally's quiet for a beat. The moorland is falling away behind them, and the first rooftops of St Ives are coming into view.

'Well, what do you think we should do now?' she asks.

'I guess . . . help join the search in Porthpella? And keep hoping Lewis wakes up.'

'And everything that happened with Roland's first wife?'

Jayden shrugs. 'I've been thinking about that. The police have all that info, right. The statements, case report, the lot. Maybe we could try talking to them again, draw attention to Sebastian Lyle . . . but more than that? I honestly don't think—'

Ally's phone rings, cutting him off. She hesitates, not recognising the number, then answers.

'Where are you now?' a voice demands. It's taut; loaded.

'Who is this?' says Ally.

'Fiona.'

It takes Ally a second to compute. She shifts in her seat to face Jayden, who – as if a mind reader – immediately finds a spot to pull over.

'We're just coming up on St Ives.'

'Could you stop and turn around?' says Fiona.

Ally holds the phone slightly from her ear, and Jayden nods. He's getting it all.

'Ally Bright, you said your name was,' says Fiona. 'You were married to the sergeant, weren't you?'

'I was.'

'He was kind to me once. Years ago, now. My car was broken into, and my bag was stolen. It had my sketchbook in it, and I was devastated. Well, you can imagine. Your husband hunted for it, searched every inch of the vicinity, because he said the thief would probably dispose of it when they'd taken anything of obvious value. And sure enough, he found it in a back alley. I don't think many people would have done that.'

It isn't even a story Bill bothered to tell her, because there were so many things like that: going above and beyond, because he cared. It can't be why Fiona has called though – to reminisce about a not-so-petty theft?

'So, you're looking for Helena?' Fiona surges on. 'Why? Concerned members of the public are ten a penny, but this is a higher form of devotion. Why drive all the way out to find me? Isn't that a terrific long shot?'

Jayden's talk of processing time has hit the mark; Fiona has evidently been thinking.

'Yes,' says Ally, 'it probably is. But we've got to do something. I live out in the dunes. This feels like my doorstep. The thought of a woman not being safe—'

Fiona cuts in. And her voice is a notch warmer this time. 'You've had a piece hanging in the Bluebird for the last year or two, haven't you? A seascape made of plastics? I thought there was something in it actually. Totally wrong place to show it, mind. Sunita's a darling, but people go to her for the cosy stuff, not statements. You should think about somewhere more cutting-edge if you're serious. And who's the sidekick? The young chap?'

'Jayden's a friend of mine,' says Ally, trying to keep up with the way Fiona flits from subject to subject.

There's a pause on the other end of the line. Fiona says something, but Ally doesn't catch it.

'What was that?' she says.

'I said turn around and come back again. We'll talk this time. You caught me unawares before. And I think I was probably rather rude.'

'Only if she calls the dog off,' says Jayden beside her, and Ally can't tell if he's joking or not.

Fiona clearly hears, as she says, 'Vinny's all mouth and no trousers. Like most menfolk, I find. Though your young friend excepted, I'm sure. Wait, does anyone know you're here?'

'I called in at the gallery,' says Ally, thinking she's not going to mention Gus. After all, she didn't say she'd be making the trip herself.

'It wasn't Petr that told you where to find me?'

'Not at all.'

'Anybody else?'

'Nobody else knows we're here,' says Ally, and she looks across to Jayden as she says it. An uneasy feeling is building in her chest; it's non-specific, more of a circumstantial reaction. She wraps her arm tighter around Fox and breathes in his reassuring scent. 'Why?'

But she says it to an empty phone; Fiona has already clicked off the line.

Fifteen minutes later they're back at Sealark, and they're being shown into a vast space. The roof above them is domed, almost like in an orangery, and there are giant polished flagstones beneath their feet. The room is full of the sea, with Fiona's paintings sitting at regular intervals on the lime-washed walls, as ordered as a gallery. The effect is beautiful – but a little intimidating.

'Please sit,' Fiona says, gesturing to a chestnut leather sofa. 'I'll make coffee.'

The dog, Vinny, lies in the middle of the floor, resplendent on an intricately woven rug. His head is on his paws, watching them, and Ally's glad she left Fox in the car. Jayden lowers himself down beside her. His phone buzzes in his jeans pocket as he does, and Ally sees the way Fiona's eyes dart to it instantly.

'Look, this might not be my best idea,' says Fiona, 'having you both here. But frankly I'm rather out of them. So . . .'

'So why are we here?' says Jayden.

'Because of me,' says a voice.

The dog gives a low whine.

And Helena Hunter walks into the room.

33

Helena is used to turning heads, but the way that the man and woman on the sofa look at her it's as if she's the final flourish of a magic trick. She hovers in the doorway, unsure what to do next. Fiona beckons her in, and she's trying for one of her encouraging smiles.

'Helena, you're safe.'

It's the grey-haired woman who says it; she must be Ally Bright. And the young guy beside her must be Jayden. Fiona fully briefed Helena, before Helena decided that they should make the call. She looks at the two of them now, still wondering if this is a good idea. They just seem like ordinary people. How can they be of any help to her? And more to the point, why would they want to be?

Helena chews her lip. 'You're definitely not with the police?'

'We're not,' says Ally.

Helena sits down, drawing her legs up beneath her. She feels like a self-conscious schoolgirl, not knowing where to put herself. It's unreal, seeing the expressions of these people she doesn't know, looking so relieved to see her. Relieved, and probably a little confused.

'I know there's a lot of fuss,' says Helena, fiddling with the hem of her shirt; Fiona's shirt, more accurately. 'I didn't expect it. It just got bigger and bigger. Until it was too late.'

She glances over at Fiona, who says, 'I'll make coffee. Helena, you . . . say what you want to say. It's all going to be okay, darling.'

And Helena feels a surge of gratitude for this woman who took her in without question – she'd never met kindness like that before. She brought trouble to Fiona's door when it was the last thing she was looking for. Fiona lived out here so calmly, so independently – and Helena was a bundle of chaos in comparison.

And, of course, someone as good as Fiona would never have done what she did in the first place.

'I really didn't plan any of it,' Helena says to Ally and Jayden. 'I want you to know that.'

Ally gives a small, close-lipped smile that Helena might have found reassuring were it not for the nerves, the way they twang inside her like an instrument gone haywire.

'We haven't been properly introduced,' she replies, with a soft smile. 'I'm Ally, and this is Jayden. I live out in the dunes, a mile or so west from you. Jayden's a little inland, on his wife's family's farm.'

Ally talks calmly and steadily, and Helena feels like she could listen to her forever. Only, sweat pricks at her palms, and there's a pounding in her chest; it will be her turn to speak soon. It has to be. She listens, her breath held.

'Lewis Pascoe came to my house the night before he went off the cliff. He was asking for help, and . . . I didn't feel in a position to give it. I've regretted it ever since. Jayden was there when they found him the next morning. We've both felt involved, in one way or another, from that moment.'

At the mention of Lewis Pascoe, Helena's hand goes to her mouth.

'He hasn't died, has he?' she says. 'I heard on the radio that he was in Intensive Care . . .'

'He's holding on.'

Helena closes her eyes. She wants everything to just go away. But it can't. It won't. It never could.

'That's why we're here,' says Ally. 'Because we started asking questions that the police weren't. Or didn't seem to be.'

'There's a lot of people who are worried about you, Helena,' says Jayden. 'They're afraid you might have come to harm.'

He says it kindly enough, but Helena shrinks back, the blame pushing at her, even if it's coming up from her own insides, even if it's all of her own making – and isn't that just how it should be? Because she is to blame.

'But can't you see that harm has come to her?' says Fiona, coming back in with a tray of rattling cups and a cafetière that's dribbling coffee grounds. 'Of course it has, or she wouldn't be here at all.' She stands back, her hands planted on her hips, her face puckered with concern.

Helena doesn't know where she'd be without Fiona. Or perhaps she does. And the thought of it makes her throat burn, her stomach churn. Is this alternative better? Fiona has convinced her that it is, but she doesn't know, not really; her mind has never felt much like her own. But in the last day, being here at Sealark, she's felt a little more in control of it.

It was Fiona's idea to ask Jayden and Ally for help, but it was Helena who had the final say. And she said yes. Given everything, it didn't really feel like a choice at all.

'I don't know where to start,' she says, her voice a croak.

'Helena,' says Ally, 'we're very grateful that you're talking to us at all. That you trust us means such a lot.'

'Yeah,' says Jayden softly. 'Thank you.'

Helena slowly exhales. The currents in the room have softened. She looks to one of Fiona's pictures – it's an ocean of calm. So many layers of blue. Blues that she's seen in Fiona's studio; that she, Helena, swirled a brush through just this morning, though she'd

185

never painted before in her life. *Because there's nothing more calming*, Fiona said, so she sat mixing blues she didn't even know the name of, the colours darkening, brightening, transforming, and all the time she felt her heart slow, her breathing grow steady. But she can't hide away doing that forever, can she?

'I need to know,' she says, 'that whatever I tell you doesn't go anywhere. You need to promise me that.'

'No police,' says Fiona. 'That's what you said, wasn't it, Helena?'

Helena nods. 'No police.'

'Not yet anyway,' says Fiona. 'Not until we have everything clear. Not until Helena wants.'

Fiona sits down beside her and Helena tries to draw strength from this woman's presence. But was that even possible? In a lasting way? Or were you just who you were and that was it, washed about on tides you had no control over? She wraps her hands around the coffee cup that Jayden passes across to her. She has no idea where to start.

'Why don't you tell them how you first met Roland,' says Fiona. 'Because that's what this is all about.'

34

The atmosphere in the room feels delicate. Helena sits on the sofa, looking as if she might wisp away if anyone makes too quick a movement.

No police.

Ally can understand why some people feel they haven't been well served, but she wouldn't have expected to hear those words from someone like Helena, who looks to be the picture of privilege.

She glances at Jayden. She didn't mention his police background to these women, and now she's glad of that. She wonders how he feels, sitting here. Bill didn't have very long to enjoy his retirement, but even then *enjoy* wasn't quite the word. He never really took off the uniform; not inside. Is it the same for Jayden, for all that he says?

She feels a rush of emotion. They've actually found Helena Hunter. Perhaps it was pure luck, but they've done the thing the police couldn't: they've found her. The questions she wants to ask Helena are lining up in her mind, one by one, but she knows they have to be patient. *What were you running from, when Jayden saw you from the car park? What happened to Lewis Pascoe? And why no police?*

No police. Just Ally and Jayden. Okay, then.

'I met Roland in a bar back in Guildford,' Helena says. 'I was working. He was on his own and we just got chatting. I thought he was charming. Not like a lot of the customers I had to put up with. He asked me to dinner the next night, and I said yes.'

Ally notes the white press of her fingers against the mug she's holding; how the coffee tilts inside.

'He wasn't wearing a wedding ring,' she says, 'but later, in daylight, I saw the paler strip on his finger. I ignored it. I told myself he was newly divorced. Because the thing is, I liked him. I liked his attention. He made me feel special. But when I think back over everything, that was the moment when I could have walked away. When I should have walked away.'

Ally sees Fiona's hand squeeze Helena's knee and the two of them swapping a meaningful look.

'But I didn't. I started seeing him. And it was like out of a movie. Flowers all the time. Presents just because. Amazing hotels. And I wanted all of it. There was this one day when he was wearing his ring again, and it wasn't even that much of a surprise to me. I don't know if he'd forgotten to take it off, or if it was kind of a test, to see if I'd say anything. And I didn't. Because I knew that he knew that I knew, and . . . at that point I didn't even care. I didn't want any of it to stop. And I didn't want to ruin it with a hard conversation.' She rubs her nose. 'I've never been any good at hard conversations. Just like my mum. She always let my dad dominate. I remember as a little girl, watching him going for her, and his tongue was always worse than his fists.'

She stares at an indefinable point on the floor. She appears, to Ally, utterly desolate.

'Helena and I have talked a lot,' says Fiona. 'She didn't have the easiest start in life. And Roland Hunter preyed on all of her weaknesses. Men like that, they make me sick.'

'In the beginning though,' says Helena, 'he treated me like a princess.'

Ally watches her carefully as she talks on. Helena is very pale; she sits stiffly, with her hands placed on her knees. Her hair hides half her face. It's glossy, well-cared-for hair; not the kind to be blown about by the elements down on the dunes. She has no idea where this conversation is going to go, but Ally knows one thing: Helena is safe – Lewis didn't hurt her. But did she hurt Lewis? Does she know who did? She noticed the shock in Helena's eyes as she said his name, her urgent enquiry after him, and she knows Jayden saw it too.

Ally glances at him now and Jayden raises his eyebrows. She shakes her head, just perceptibly. She knows he's itching to ask Helena all the same questions that she is, but just as the sea reveals its secrets in its own time, Ally has a feeling that this woman will too.

'When the man came to the house, it was . . .' Helena brings her hands together, knots her fingers. 'It brought a lot of things together in my head. It was a shock, you know? We were just finishing up dinner, and there was this hammering at the door.'

Helena tells them how Roland went to answer, and how she shrank back. But she listened; she heard everything.

'He was in panic mode, this Lewis Pascoe. Roland hates panic. He just doesn't get it. I don't think he's ever panicked about anything. Anger, oh yes. But not panic. But I understood it with Lewis. I could hear what he was saying, and I was thinking, *Yeah, that's bad. That's really bad.* He had no idea his nan had moved house, let alone died. I mean, how would any of us feel? Roland mentioned to me a couple of weeks ago that she'd died, the lady we bought the land from, but . . .' She shakes her head. 'I guess I didn't think about it that much. But you could tell this Lewis knew nothing about it. And the way Roland told him, there on the doorstep, was . . .'

'Cruel,' says Fiona. 'That was the word you used.'

189

'It was cruel,' says Helena. 'It was. He just wanted to get rid of him. But why not give him a kick when he was down? That's what it was like. To Roland he was this . . . inconvenience . . . and so he wanted to get rid of him as quickly as possible. He just shut it all down. Sent him away. Yes, it was cruel. And, of course, he wouldn't miss a chance to show off in front of Nathan.'

'Nathan?' asks Jayden. 'Who's Nathan?'

'Roland's brother. He's staying for the weekend, down from London. Nathan said he wanted to buy a house in Cornwall, which obviously irritated Roland because it's like he's trying to get in on his patch. He came down for some viewings.' She gives a small shudder. 'I've never liked him. One of those men who . . . just makes you feel uncomfortable. He can't just look at me normally; it's like he's thinking something every time he does, you know?'

Ally remembers the man she saw outside Hang Ten. The man who, at first glance, she thought was Roland. She swaps a look with Jayden.

'Do they get on, Roland and his brother?' asks Jayden.

'Not really. But I'm an only child. Maybe I don't understand how it's possible to love someone but . . . also not like them very much at the same time.' She looks down at her hands. 'Or maybe I do know something about that. Though I'm not sure it was ever real love.'

'Helena, did Lewis tell Roland that he'd just been released from prison?' asks Jayden.

She gives a sad little laugh. 'It was one of the first things he said. He didn't know that Roland knew already – Maggie had told him, you see. Though maybe Lewis didn't know what kind of response he was going to get. Anyway, the way Roland was with Lewis, I saw this other side to him. I mean, I always knew it was there. I did. I'd seen it before, in flare-ups over little things. Like once a waiter spilt some wine on him when he was pouring. And another time the Range Rover got scratched by someone's car door and . . . well, there were enough times with me, when I was being stupid about something or other, of course I saw it then. But I know that's not what we're talking about.'

'Helena,' says Fiona. 'You were never being stupid. And it is what we're talking about – it's all relevant.'

She squeezes Helena's arm as she says it, and Ally figures that they've talked about this; that, probably, Fiona knows all there is to know about what's gone on behind Roland and Helena's closed doors.

'Was he violent towards you?' asks Jayden.

And Ally realises she's holding her breath, waiting for Helena to answer.

'What I'm saying,' says Helena carefully, looking down, 'is that it never took much to set him off.' She pauses. 'But this time it was different, because . . . I saw it differently, I suppose. I finally saw it for what it was. His . . . temper. And how, afterwards, he just didn't care.'

'What did he do, Helena?' says Ally.

'Roland just got rid of Lewis, sent him packing, and then he came back to the table, sat down like it was all nothing. Like Lewis had been some bloke from Amazon dropping off a parcel and that was that. But I could see this . . . this *rage* just beneath the surface. His neck was red. It does that. And Nathan sat there smirking. Said something like, "Nobody messes with my little brother, do they?" but kind of all sarcastic. I said to him, to Roland, "Is it because he was a burglar?"'

'Because of what happened to his first wife,' says Fiona, quietly. 'Do you know about that?'

Ally nods. 'We do.'

Helena's lips are trembling. 'I thought it might have pushed his buttons, you know? This convicted burglar turns up out of

191

nowhere.' She sucks in her breath. 'And Roland just said, "Eh?" That was it. *Eh?* It was like he didn't even know what I was talking about. Like that meant nothing either.'

She looks at Ally, and she looks at Jayden, and then she looks at some indeterminate point between the two of them.

'He didn't even know what I was talking about.' She gives a laugh that's completely empty of humour. 'And I knew then, I just knew. I'd been thinking it. I had. I'd been thinking it for weeks, months; God, maybe even years. Pushing it all the way down inside. I thought it'd be different moving down here, but it . . . came with me. Got even bigger, until it was pretty much all I could think of. I thought it was going to be our happy place, Sea Dream, but it became the opposite. But that night was the moment when I actually knew for sure. Because of Lewis.'

'Knew what for sure?' says Ally gently.

But Helena is lost in her own story. 'After I mentioned him being a burglar, Nathan just tipped his head back and had a good laugh. Said something about Roland having a very short memory when it suited him. Like it was all a joke to him too. I just felt . . . I went completely cold. Because I *knew*. I didn't sleep at all that night. Not one wink. Then Lewis came back the next morning, didn't he? Probably wanting to have more of a say. I was getting up for my run anyway, but when Roland went to answer the door, spitting blood, I just . . . hid. I hid in the bathroom. I couldn't listen, couldn't watch.'

'What were you afraid of, Helena?' says Jayden.

'I was afraid he was going to really hurt Lewis this time. So I hid in the bathroom. And then I thought, *My God, this is what you always do. You bury your head in the sand.* And I felt so ashamed of myself. So, I eventually went down. But by then Lewis had gone, and Roland was in the kitchen. I could hear him banging about. And I just felt this surge of . . . hatred. I just wanted to run. To shake it all off. But as soon as I was out of the house, as soon as I was moving and I felt the air all around me, saw all that sea, I just wanted to keep on running. I'd held it together the night before, but being out, being away from the house, from Roland, I just broke. I was crying, crying like I couldn't stop. And that was when Fiona saw me.'

'It was a perfect morning, and I'd taken my camera to the point,' says Fiona. 'I was driving back when I saw Helena. I recognised her straight away and stopped to say good morning. And she was distraught. I just said to get in – and she did.'

'I did,' says Helena.

'So,' says Jayden, 'you didn't see Lewis again after you left the house?'

'No. I didn't see him at all.'

'But you're certain he left? There's no way he could still have been there? Like Roland had invited him in, and you'd missed it?'

'Roland was on his own. And there's no way he'd have let him come in.'

'What time was it when you left, Helena? Can you remember?' says Ally.

'Maybe half past seven? A bit later? I can't remember exactly. I left in a rush, I didn't have my phone with me. I almost went back to get it but then I just thought, *I don't care.*'

'What about your watch?' says Jayden.

'I never wear my watch to run.'

'It was found down on the sand. The face was cracked.'

'My watch was? But that doesn't make sense.' Helena shrugs, as if a lost Rolex is the least of it.

Ally knows they have to tread carefully; that they're near the edge of something, and too quick a movement could send it crashing. And Jayden knows it too, because his voice, when it comes, is gentle – but sturdy.

'Helena, just before, you said that you knew something. You knew something for sure. What was it?'

Helena puts her hand to her mouth. Her perfectly painted nails are shocking pink against her pale face.

'I know that he killed her,' she says. 'My husband killed his first wife.'

Ally flinches. Jayden, calm beside her, quietly asks, 'How do you know that, Helena?'

Helena looks to Fiona. Fiona's mouth is a straight line; she nods. 'If you want them to help . . . you need to tell them.'

Helena bows her head. 'Because I lied to protect him,' she says.

35

The bell clangs as Saffron pushes open the door of White Wave Stores.

'Sweetheart!' trills Wenna. 'Run out of milk for your cappuccinos?'

Saffron grins, relaxing instantly. She's been coming here her whole life, and it's stayed reassuringly the same. Even the glass jars of sweets behind the counter, with the sugar-dusted toffees and the foam shrimps that her mum used to buy her a little paper bag of on the way home from school on a Friday. Wenna has stayed the same too, with her peroxide-grey hair and runaway tongue; plus, she's quietly rad, taking her wooden bellyboard out even in the dead of winter.

'No, I'm all good. How's it going here?'

'Oh, wonderful, wonderful, you know me. Though of course we're worried sick about that poor woman from the big house. The glass monstrosity, Gerren calls it, though you can't hold that against her. Heard anything, have you? Down there at the beach?'

Saffron shakes her head.

'Nobody ever knows,' says Wenna, 'what's going on in a marriage. That much I will say. Or inside a family, for that matter. I hear there's a brother staying down there too. Been making a nuisance of himself up at the vineyard, Gerren said. Drank half a bottle's worth in the name of "tasting" and then got in his car after. But then, if you will offer tasting to anyone who walks through the door, you make your bed, don't you? I've always said that.'

Saffron leans on the counter and cups her chin in her hand. Wenna will talk and talk; you just have to let her.

'Not that I'm saying that poor man's had anything to do with it. Either one of them. More than likely that little lad who went off the cliff, Lewis, is tied up in it somehow. Not that he's talking yet, so I hear. Terrible thing. He must be going spare though, the husband. But you can't help wondering, can you? Human nature, that is, Saffron. Love thy neighbour and all that, but sometimes it's suspect thy neighbour too, isn't it? I don't know the Hunters from Adam. If they came in here from time to time, I might have more of an opinion, but—'

Saffron has always imagined Wenna's mind as being like a giant spider's web, all these interlacing threads of thought, one spun after another. It's easy to get tangled up in it if you don't watch it.

'Hey, Wenna,' she cuts in, 'do you remember there being a beer festival at The Wreckers, one summer? Way back. Like, twenty years ago.'

'Well, that would have before Ben and Lou took it on. And before Paddy had it. You're talking Janner and Maddy. It was Janner and Maddy who did the festival. Not quite the success they'd hoped, as I remember. Decided it wasn't worth the effort, not after they looked at the takings, so it was a one-off. Don't blame them. You have to think about the takings. Your mum would have been there I expect. Joining in with the shanties.'

'Which means I probably would have been too.' Saffron smiles. 'But I'd have been three years old, Wenna, my memory doesn't stretch that far back.'

The woman gives a snickering laugh.

'Ah she did love a giggle and a drink, your mum. God rest her. Why are you asking after all that anyway, Saffron? Are you thinking of putting something on at the beach?'

'I'm just curious. I heard there was a stag party down from London. They were staying in Newquay but they came across to Porthpella for the beer festival. A bunch of idiots – well, I'm pretty sure they were idiots – dressed as . . . wait for it . . . cheese. Does that ring a bell?'

'Men dressed as cheese?' Wenna throws back her head to laugh. 'I've never heard the like. Though things did get a little bit rowdy. There were a lot of blokes there, like there always is. You know what they're like, Saffron, when they egg each other on.'

'There was a cow with this stag group. A red cow. You know, like one of those pantomime ones you get, where someone's the front and someone's the back. It would have stood out, I reckon.'

'A red cow?' Wenna suddenly claps her hands together. 'Well, that I do remember. Absolute fools, they were, inside of that thing. Charging about knocking over people's pints and whatnot. Obnoxious, that's the word I'd use. And I don't use it lightly. I like a laugh as much as anyone, but this was different. Oh, course I remember that damn cow. They got short shrift from Janner, I can tell you. But then one of his own staff – not a regular, but one of the lads he'd hired as extra help – got in a bit of a rumble with one of their mates.'

'The red cow's mates?'

'I suppose he might have been a piece of cheese, now I think about it. Though I couldn't tell you what type.' Her face changes. 'Oh, you know who it was, don't you? The staff? It was Paul Pascoe. And how sad that his own son's gone and tried to kill himself now too. I can't get over that. It was Ally Bright who told me, and I thought it must have hit her hard – though why it would, I don't know, because when was the last time she came looking for a chat? A very long time, I can tell you.'

Saffron tries to keep her face still, but it's proving difficult. 'So, hang on,' she says, 'Paul Pascoe was working at the beer festival and got into a fight with a friend of . . . the red cow's?'

'Oh, not a proper fight. Nothing much to see. Fisticuffs, you'd call it. Course, anyone round here was used to seeing Paul get in fights – but this time? I'd have said Janner should have thanked him, those drunken emmets making trouble, but he got the sack for it, did Paul. There and then. I remember that. Course, Janner had no choice. Not really, you can't have staff going around throwing punches, can you?'

Wenna takes off her glasses. Cleans them with the hem of her cardigan.

'Do you know what, you're taking me right back, Saffron, my love. I saw Janner, oh must have been a week after the festival, just outside here in the square, and he looked like he'd seen a ghost, poor bloke. He said he didn't like thinking he had a hand in making anyone's life feel like it wasn't worth living.' Wenna blinks. 'I didn't know what he was talking about, but it was Paul, of course. They'd just found him down at the beach. We all knew Paul was in and out of trouble, anyone round here could have told you that, but I suppose what none of us stopped to think about was the fact that he was troubled in himself. Do you see what I mean?'

36

'Okay,' says Jayden. 'So now I get why she said no police.'

They're in the car, parked two minutes up the road from Fiona's house, in a moorland lay-by. Jayden chews at his thumbnail. His mind spins.

Helena has been found. And now she's accused Roland of murder.

This has been some afternoon.

He looks steadily at Ally. It's not like he knows that much about her life before, but surely this is a long way out of her wheelhouse? Yet the deeper it all goes, the more firmly she seems anchored. He's not sure the same can be said for him.

'Giving a false alibi is serious stuff,' he says. 'Helena signed that statement. That's jail time.'

'It didn't sound like an outright lie. She said she was knocked out on sleeping pills. In theory, Roland could very well have been beside her in bed all night long, couldn't he?'

'Then she should have said that.'

'But she said she didn't want to admit to Hunter that she was taking them. And more to the point, if she told the police about the pills, then they'd know she couldn't swear to him being there. And she knew that if she couldn't swear to it, there'd be repercussions from her husband. Who we know she was afraid of.'

'How bad do you think that got?' says Jayden.

'Well, she didn't answer when you asked if Roland was violent towards her, and I think that's telling in itself, isn't it?'

'I think you're right. So, if Helena hadn't given Roland an alibi, maybe she thought he would have held that against her, whether he was involved or not.'

'And I believe her, Jayden,' says Ally.

He draws a deep breath. 'Okay . . . let's think. So, Helena's agreed to phone the police, right, and tell them that she's okay. Apologise big-time for the misunderstanding. That'll probably be straightforward. Though when she says she had no idea anyone was out looking for her it might not fly.'

'If pushed, Helena is going to admit that she'd been having doubts about her relationship. That she needed some space, so she went to Fiona. Fiona's a solitary artist; she's practically living off-grid. Easy to forget the real world, in a place like that.'

'It's still lying to the police though.'

'Not in comparison to the false alibi.'

'Okay, sure. Hierarchy of lies, it's lower.'

Jayden shakes his head; this is all pretty crazy. And they, of all people, have found Helena.

'And I guess she doesn't know anything about what actually happened to Lewis,' he goes on, 'so they won't have further questions for her there. And they've no reason to suspect Roland of anything either right now.'

'It's not a crime to walk out on your husband. Or ask for privacy.'

'I still don't like it,' says Jayden. 'I mean, I get it, I feel sorry for Helena, but I think she should be coming clean now. On everything.'

'All she wants to know,' says Ally, 'is that Roland can be incriminated.'

'Yeah, I get that. She doesn't want to admit the false alibi and then have the case reopened, only to see it fall apart.'

'Because that would leave her in an incredibly vulnerable place with him.'

Jayden rubs his face with his hands. 'So, what, we're supposed to prove that Roland's a murderer? You and me?'

Fox turns in Ally's lap and Jayden sees her rest her hand on the dog's back. What she doesn't say back, is *I know, how crazy is that?* In fact, Ally seems to be taking it all in her stride.

'Here's the thing,' he goes on. 'There's no evidence against Roland. I talked to Fatima about this, before I even knew it was going to be so . . . relevant.'

'Helena said he inherited a large amount of his money after Victoria died. Money that he promptly used to set up home with her – his lover.'

'Okay, so call that a potential motive. For sure. But there's still no evidence, is there?'

'Talk me through it,' she says, 'just like you used to with your partner in Leeds, Jayden. How it might have happened.'

'I was just a beat cop, Al. I'm as out of my depth as you are.'

'I don't agree. Tell me.'

'Okay. But . . . this is hypothetical, right?' He drums his fingers on the steering wheel as he puts it together; one way it could fit, anyway. 'Roland Hunter stages a burglary. Luckily for him – or maybe he went and did his homework – there were a spate of similar crimes in the area. No one killed, but violent break-ins, which is enough for it to look like it might be part of the pattern. Hunter leaves no prints. At least, not in any suspicious places, because it's his house, and his prints are everywhere anyway. And then he does a really good impression of being the distraught husband. But the only one who doesn't buy it is the brother-in-law, Sebastian Lyle. Helena provides the alibi – and it's watertight. So then Roland does a good impression of being ashamed of that too: caught with his pants down while his wife's being murdered is probably the worst kind of look, right? But he takes it, because he knows that what he's actually done is a whole lot worse . . . That's how it *could* have happened. Or could not have happened. Because without any evidence, it's just a story, you know? All we've got is Helena's word for it, and we already know she's lied.'

'But we understand why she did. In her situation.'

'Yeah, okay. But it's still just supposition – that he actually murdered his first wife. If there's something more going on here with Helena and Roland, if he's been violent towards her, and that's the issue, that's what we should be focusing on getting her to report. Right?'

'I agree. But for her, the Victoria accusation seems to be looming largest.' Ally shakes her head. 'What I don't understand, is how Lewis fits into this.'

'That's the thing,' says Jayden. 'I don't think Lewis does. Her watch seems to link them, but only if his prints were on it, right? Which we don't know for sure, but it's definitely a possibility because of what Skinner said to you. But Helena said she wasn't wearing that watch yesterday morning. She's got no reason to lie about that.' He turns to face her straight-on. 'Ally, I know you're still looking out for Lewis, but I don't think this is about him anymore. Or, even if it is, it's become something else completely. It's become about a crime that happened five years ago, and a woman accusing her husband of murder. And Helena thinks we're the ones to fix it, just because we tracked her to Fiona's? I don't think so. We're in way over our heads here.'

But even as he's saying it, he can feel something inside him. A flicker that's almost unrecognisable: it's challenge – and the desire to rise and meet it.

But that's not the Jayden that came to Cornwall.

'What if Roland Hunter really did kill Victoria?' says Ally, a tremor in her voice.

And it's like the reality of it all is sinking in. The newspaper coverage wrapped it up, distanced it, just like it always does. Five years ago, a woman was murdered in her own home, and now Ally's feeling it.

'I know,' says Jayden. 'But it's still a what-if.'

'I love my corner of the world. It's a privilege, to live in a place like this. I know a lot of people feel the same. They want to look after it, appreciate it. Roland Hunter doesn't deserve to be here; I knew that much already. He doesn't deserve to wake up every morning to that view.'

And it's the only thing Ally's said that's got under his skin.

'Oh, come on, since when did "deserving" something ever come into it? You think the good things in life only belong to the good people? Nothing's fair. Haven't you noticed that yet?'

She looks at him, faintly startled.

'You're right,' she says, holding his stare. 'I'm sorry. I don't really think that way.' Then, 'Helena's afraid that if she tells the police nothing then will happen, isn't she? And I've a horrible feeling she might be right. Roland will get off scot-free.'

'She's also afraid of getting into trouble with the police – remember that.'

'But isn't she already in trouble? The poor woman's scared. What if we just . . . spent some time looking into this. In a quiet way, a small way. So Helena has something more to take to the police when the time is right. That's all it'd be.'

But it isn't all it'd be, is it? It'd be so much more than that. Jayden's thoughts churn.

'I don't think I can keep doing this,' he says. 'Cat doesn't love it, the idea of me getting involved. She thinks I left it all behind when we left Leeds.'

'But what do *you* want to do, Jayden?'

And it's a question that's about as simple, and as complicated, as any he's ever been asked. His hands grip the wheel, but he doesn't start the engine. Out of nowhere he suddenly feels like crying. And he knows if he catches Ally's eye, it'll tip him over the edge.

'You said before,' says Ally softly, 'that the police wasn't the same for you after your friend died.'

He blinks. 'Yeah. No, it wasn't. But you don't want to hear all that.'

'If you want to tell me, I do.'

And he could leave it there, because Ally isn't the poking or prodding kind.

'Well, okay,' he says. He shifts in his seat, turning towards her. 'It was a Saturday night. We responded to a call. A fight had broken out between two men outside a pub in the city centre.'

His voice is low, and doesn't sound much like his own.

'We were just a couple of streets away, but when we got there it was already escalating. We had to move through a crowd to get to them. One complied with our instructions. He was already badly hurt, and I went to help him. The other was yelling and waving this broken bottle, so Kieran drew his taser. It's enough, a lot of the time, just seeing it drawn, right? The verbal warning, that red dot, any of that can be enough to stop it. But not this time. So, Kieran fired. The suspect went down. But then Kieran was on the ground too. He'd been stabbed. Stabbed in the neck by someone else. Someone from the crowd, that we didn't even see. I tried to stop the bleeding. I tried. But there was just too much, you know? The ambulance was there fast, but he died on the way to hospital.'

He glances away, at the expanse of moorland that surrounds them; somewhere beyond, the blue. He doesn't look at her as he says, 'Sorry. That was a lot of detail.'

Then he feels her hand on his, a feather-light touch. When he meets her eye, the kindness in her face makes his throat ache.

'It was eight months ago,' he says. 'Eight months ago – and, some days, I'm right back there, in the middle of it, you know? And maybe that's right. I shouldn't push it to the past.'

'You know it doesn't help anyone,' says Ally quietly, 'thinking like that.'

'Yeah. I know it doesn't. Anyway, I couldn't stay on after. I mean, I had all the support, the counselling, I had all that. My bosses were cool. But . . . I couldn't shake the fact that I was alive, and Kieran wasn't.'

He leans his head back against the seat. Closes his eyes for a second.

'The report concluded that in that situation we did everything right. We were focused on the immediate conflict, the two men. We couldn't have seen the other one, the perpetrator, or known he had a weapon. He was chased and arrested by a patrol team. I testified in court. He went away for life – murder of a police officer. But . . . after, I just couldn't put the uniform on anymore.'

He hears Ally take a breath, as if she's trying to contain her own emotion. 'I can understand that,' she says.

He glances across at her. 'I was kind of a mess for a bit. I really put Cat through it. She's been amazing, but . . . Kieran had two little daughters, a wife.'

He can feel his words running out, so he stops talking. Turns the key in the ignition.

'Anyway,' he says, over the soft purr of the engine, 'that's why I left, Ally. So please don't say anything. You don't need to. I just wanted to tell you. So that you know. We should get going, hey?'

'Alright, I won't say anything. Except, thank you for telling me. And I'm just so sorry.'

He nods. Quietly thanks her.

'Wait . . . Jayden, doing all this, with me, the investigation . . . I didn't make you, did I?'

'I wanted to,' says Jayden. 'I don't know what that means, but I really wanted to.' He puts the car in gear and pulls out on to the road. 'And I still want to. It's just . . .'

'It's okay. You're right, perhaps we should . . .'

'I think we could give it a day,' he says, before she can finish. He puts his foot down, feels the surge of the engine; the window's wound all the way down and the moorland air blows in. 'You and me.'

'A day,' says Ally. And he can hear the smile in her voice. 'Are you sure?'

'I'm sure.'

'Tomorrow, do you mean?' she says. 'We're not counting today?'

'Tomorrow is our day.'

'Then I think we need to go and speak to the brother. Don't you? Victoria's brother. You said he lives in Somerset, didn't you?'

He looks sideways at her. 'Ally . . . you really just left your husband to it, back in the day? You didn't try and get yourself involved in investigations?'

She gives a small smile. 'Of course I didn't get involved. And he was a beat cop too, remember?'

'What, never?'

'Well, we talked. Kitchen-table stuff. Bits and pieces. But Bill was always very discreet.' She shakes her head. 'I liked it though, when he did want to chat something over. I really liked it.'

'And now it's one of the things you miss.'

'I didn't even realise it was,' she says. They sit in silence for a moment, just the sound of the road, the air gusting in. 'Well, that and his fish stew. It had the best part of a bottle of wine in it. It was glorious.'

She laughs, and the sound of it lightens everything. Jayden smiles back at her, feeling like he's known her a lot longer than a couple of days.

'Jayden, Lewis asked me for help,' she says, 'and look how that turned out. And now Helena's asking us for help. I think it's that simple. I don't think I've ever been called on to help before. Not as far as other people are concerned. Bill was like an octopus, you see – he always had a spare pair of hands, did everything for everyone. He was never off duty. Whereas me, I don't think I've ever been *on* duty. Not outside the home, anyway.'

She's looking straight ahead, and her voice has dropped.

'And what happens,' she says, 'is that you slip into a life that's so quiet, that if you left it, there'd be almost no one who'd notice. My daughter said there was nothing here for me anymore and I thought how sad that was, but also, perhaps, how true. And then came Lewis. And now Helena. And because of them, I came to you.'

The landscape opens up ahead of them. Jayden can see the distant stem of the lighthouse, and the slim band of yellow sand that's Porthpella. This otherworldly place that, a lot of the time, he can't help feeling he's randomly washed up in.

'Actually,' he says, 'I think we came to each other, Al.'

37

Fiona's bathroom is just as beautiful and calm as the rest of her house. The tub is sunk into the corner and is surrounded by fat buttermilk-coloured candles and glossy-leaved plants, and there's a wide window that looks out over the garden and down to the sea. Its elegant simplicity makes Sea Dream look garish, with all its shimmering marble and double sinks and mirrored walls – things that she once thought were part of her happiness. Helena shivers. Steam billows in the air and she sinks lower in the water, letting it swirl around her. If she could disappear, she would.

Actually disappear.

Anyone who thinks she disappeared in coming to Fiona's is mistaken; she's never felt more face-to-face with herself.

Fiona is, she's realised, one of life's confronters; not in an aggressive way, just in a look-a-problem-in-the-eye kind of way. They're opposites, like that. And maybe that was the attraction she felt, as soon as Fiona arrived with her easel and paints – that here was a woman she could learn from. Fiona looked so free, standing there in her wide-brimmed hat and skinny jeans and workman's boots. Her hair bright red against the blue of the sea and the yellow of the sand.

Helena was shy taking that cup of tea down to her the first time, wanted to tiptoe away, but Fiona set down her brushes and seemed happy to talk. She said she always liked to get to know the people who commissioned her, and that she didn't always uncon-ditionally agree to a request. *You got lucky though*, she said, *I was just thinking the other day how I hadn't painted Porthpella in ages. The stars aligned. So, Helena, tell me, what brought you to Cornwall?*

And in that moment, with the water sparkling and paint on the canvas and Fiona's wide-open smile, Helena wanted to actually tell her. *Really* tell her. But, of course, she didn't. Not then.

Roland had indulged her with the commission, like he always did with the things that he didn't think mattered. It was as if he'd said, *Have anything you want, except for that one thing: truth.* And that suited her for a long time. For five years that suited her; she had to admit that. But she had been so many different versions of Helena in those five years, and maybe the one thing those different Helenas had in common was that they didn't ask the questions they were too afraid to know the answers to.

Get whoever you want to do it. More artists than you can shake a stick at round here. But for God's sake, don't pick one of those up-their-own-arse abstract ones.

How ironic that the innocent commissioning of painting would prove the catalyst for everything.

Helena stretches and turns the hot tap on with her toe. She keeps her foot as close to the burning jet as she can bear. She wants the pain. Pain is controllable; the self-inflicted kind, anyway. What isn't controllable is people. Ally and Jayden. *But what if they can actually help?* she said to Fiona after they'd left – and after old Vinny, the dog that was more horse than hound, had calmed down. *And they found me here, didn't they? They did find me.*

Helena reluctantly made her call to the police, just as Ally and Jayden had told her to. She'd been worried it'd ignite too many ques-tions about the past, but she played her role well, the emotional wife needing a friend's shoulder to cry on – she'd just happened to choose a friend who lives off-grid. And how sorry she was for all the fuss.

209

It didn't surprise her, she said, that Roland had been too proud to admit to the police that their relationship was in trouble. And yes, she could see now how it looked, leaving her phone behind. But it was spontaneous, she just hadn't thought it through, and she was scatty like that. She was very sorry. And could she make a donation to a police charity, to apologise for wasted resources? That last bit had been Fiona's idea. The only slip Helena made was in mentioning Ally's name as the person who told her about the police search. But it seemed to be okay, because Ally was an artist, just like Fiona was an artist, and the two of them knew each other – she'd just happened to stop by the house. That was what she said.

It still shook her though, the phone call.

She'd known she couldn't lie low indefinitely. Although in moments like this – lost in steam, the heavy wooden door closed to the world – wasn't it possible? It almost feels possible. But as Fiona said, *It's not sustainable. Not with all the clamour. You've got to look the tiger in the eye at some point, sweetheart.*

She's grateful to Fiona. Beyond grateful. But she can't help feeling a little envious of her too. How did you get to be that independent? That free? Fiona hasn't traded stories of her own relationships; Helena's account of her marriage has gone unreciprocated. And there are no photos of significant others on the walls. Perhaps there has only ever been Vinny the dog – although Helena finds that hard to imagine of someone who has as much to give as Fiona.

There's a tap at the door.

'I come bearing tea.'

'Oh, thank you!' Helena sits upright quickly, water sloshing over the sides of the bath.

The door pushes open and Fiona steps into the steam. She draws up a little table and sets down the tray. There's an ornate teapot, and a plate with Florentine biscuits.

Helena has her arms crossed over her chest, and she knows it makes her look like a prude. Back at the beach, during one of their chats as Fiona was working on the painting, Fiona had told her she often swam at the naturist beaches down the coast, and that's when she, Helena, started stripping at her window. She'd stand naked, looking out to the water, imagining slipping into it as if the ocean were one great bath. Every time, she felt a ripple of pleasure and power. But this is different.

'I think it was brave, what you did today,' says Fiona. 'Impetuous, but brave.'

Helena can feel her cheeks burning up. *Brave.* Has anyone ever called her that?

'But you know, if Ally and Jayden can't find anything, you'll still have to decide what to do next.'

'I know.'

She slips back under the water. Fiona means tell the police the truth. With no guarantee that it will be worth it. And this is when Helena knows she can't claim any bravery. Not at all. Because she's certain that confessing her false alibi, without there being any evidence against Roland, will only bring trouble.

And who will protect her then?

38

Mullins is trawling through CCTV footage when the call comes in. Helena Hunter is the needle in several hundred hours of haystacks, and the footage from the holiday park, which connects to the road heading out of Porthpella, is making his eyes cross. But a member of the public has just reported seeing a woman in sportswear running along this road yesterday morning, and maybe the CCTV caught her. They're following up every single one of these so-called leads – and it's a long, long list. It'll be some time before they get to that distinctly cold lead that Ally Bright phoned in earlier: so, a few weeks ago, Helena was seen talking to an artist woman? Mullins didn't even bother telling Skinner about that one. He just logged it, along with all the others, and then got on with the grunt work. If the choppers and the sniffer dogs felt a little bit Hollywood, then everything else was anything but.

Then in comes DCI Robinson. Arms going like a windmill.

'Everybody stop!'

Mullins sits up and listens, and his teeth bite straight through the end of the biro he's chewing when he hears the words *she's found*. He puts his hand to his lip, and it comes away blue. He wipes it on his trousers. None of it makes much sense to him. Helena Hunter has been found. She's safe. But is she being brought in for questioning? No. He rubs hard at his lips with the heel of his hand.

'Waste of bloody time,' he hears one of the Newquay lot say, pushing back his chair. 'Waste of bloody time, resources and money.'

'At least she's safe,' says Mullins. And he almost has to check behind him to see if someone else said it. But no, it was him.

The other officer gives him a look he can't make head nor tail of, and then starts throwing things into his rucksack. A Mars bar. Headphones. A stapler – one that Mullins is pretty sure belongs to their station.

'She only became aware of the scale of the operation when a neighbour dropped by the house of the friend she was staying with,' says Robinson. 'She's asked that we respect her privacy and don't reveal her whereabouts to her husband. This will be problematic for Roland Hunter, who filed the missing persons report, but, of course, it is not in fact a criminal offence.'

'What about Lewis Pascoe?'

And it's the woman who spoke up for him before, DS Chang. With the glossy black hair and the knack of saying things that no one else round here does.

She goes on. 'Lewis was prime suspect for Helena's disappearance. What about the fingerprints on her watch? Shouldn't this switch our focus? Lewis as potential victim, not perpetrator? I've consistently said that the assumption that he attempted to take his own life is exactly that, an assumption, and we all know what they say about that.'

Mullins doesn't know what they say about that, but he decides now probably isn't the time to ask.

'So, what, Helena Hunter is now wanted in connection with the incident involving Lewis Pascoe?' pipes up Skinner, a bemused smile on his lips – and in no way reaching his eyes.

'Pascoe's fingerprints are on the watch,' says DS Chang. 'That unequivocally connects them.'

213

The officer from Newquay pauses in the packing of his bag. He takes out the Mars and rips off the wrapper; bites its head off.

'Helena wasn't wearing the watch when she left the house that morning,' says Robinson. 'She says she has no idea how Pascoe came to have it. My best guess is that he stole it from the house somehow.'

'Ally Bright's fingerprints were also on the watch, remember,' says Skinner.

'She's the one who found it on the beach,' says Mullins. 'She turned it in.'

'Did she though?' says Skinner. 'Maybe that's just what she's saying.'

'It was someone called Ally who told Helena that people were out looking for her,' says Robinson. 'Another artist mate of this woman Fiona, she said.'

'And it was Ally Bright phoning me with theories about Lewis Pascoe,' says Skinner. 'That's a whole lot of Bright, if you ask me.'

Mullins's eyes widen. What, so Ally Bright could be mixed up in all this too? That seems like a stretch. He knows she lives way out in the dunes, a mile or so on from the Hunters' place. Everyone knows she keeps herself to herself. Surely she'd be the last person around here to get mixed up in anything?

'I think it's worth a conversation with her,' says DS Chang. 'And I think it's worth following up that Helena Hunter phone call with an actual statement. In person. With a few more questions about Lewis Pascoe.'

'Agreed. First thing tomorrow morning, you go and see Ally Bright, Skinner,' says Robinson. 'Take Mullins with you.'

'Just don't let Roland Hunter see us,' says Mullins. 'Or his brother.'

'What's that?' says the DCI.

214

'Roland Hunter,' says Mullins. He coughs awkwardly. 'Just thinking. He won't be best pleased, will he, if Mrs Bright knows where his wife is, and he doesn't.'

Just then he feels his phone vibrating in his pocket. He slides it out. It's Hippy-Dippy, and an instant grin lights up his face.

Then the thought: *But why would she be calling me?*

39

Jayden has been trying to work out what to say, ever since he dropped Ally off at The Shell House. He's chewed over his lines like an amateur actor, and he thinks he's got it straight in his head. More or less.

As he pulls in, daylight's just fading. There's only the old green Land Rover parked there, so he figures Cat's friends have left. As he steps into the farmhouse it's quiet inside, and he's struck by the smell of the place, in that way you notice in other people's houses but never your own. Here it's woodsmoke, and usually the English comfort food that's Sue's speciality, lingering in the air: her batch-cooked casseroles and shortcrust tarts. She's a great cook, his mum-in-law, but she's asked if Jayden can show her some new moves. Cliff will probably be the sticking point there. Jayden suggested they make a paella the other day and Cliff held up a hand to stop him and said, *Now pie sounds just the ticket – none of that ella stuff.* Cat collapsed in peals of laughter that Jayden felt obliged to join in with; though he threw in an eye roll for Sue's benefit. Upper Hendra is a house of predictable rhythms, and at this hour, coming up on 7 p.m., Cat's mum and dad are usually sitting down to dinner; but then he remembers that they're at a neighbour's this evening. No food wafts.

Talking of predictable rhythms, he's about to rock everything. 'Babe?' he calls out. 'Cat?'

'Through here.'

The muffled voice comes from the room that the family call the 'snug'. It's a small space, with a sagging sofa and a half-empty bookcase – personally, Jayden has never understood half-empty bookcases – and a window looking out over the back fields. If you're in the snug, it is generally understood that you want to be left alone. Cat used it a lot as a teenager, apparently. When she wasn't up at the bench, or down on the beach.

'Oh, hey,' he says.

'Hey, Jay.'

Her eyes have a drowsy quality, and her hair is tousled. She's curled up on the sofa, a magazine on the floor beside her.

'You've been napping.'

'People are exhausting. Even the good ones.'

He drops down beside her. Greets the bump like he always does.

'How were the girls?'

'Full of the joys of spring. Especially after the news of Helena Hunter. Did you hear?'

Jay rubs the back of his head. 'I did. Yeah.'

'They didn't say much, only that she's been found safe and well. What is it? Your face.'

'What face?'

'That face.' Cat shifts, one arm wrapped around her bump. She fixes him with her eyes. 'I know you've been following it. I know you and that woman Ally have been . . . actually, I don't know what you've been doing. But if she thinks you're some kind of freelance policeman or something . . .'

'It's not like that,' he says.

And he tells her what it is like. He says it just as he planned to – more or less. But his wife's gaze is more interrogative than the

217

view through the windscreen was in his practice runs. He's not sure he's explained it as well as he wanted to.

'So, what we've said,' says Jayden, 'is that we'll just use tomorrow, use tomorrow to . . . see what we can do.'

Cat is completely silent. His hand reaches out for her bump and she grabs hold of his fingers; pushes him away.

'Jay, don't. This is crazy. Can you actually hear yourself?'

'It escalated quickly,' he says, trying for a grin.

'I *knew* you wanted to get involved in it all. I knew it.'

'I was involved. I found the body.'

'You didn't find him. Someone else called you over. And "body" – he's not dead, is he? You're being dramatic.'

Is he? But it is dramatic, isn't it? The whole thing. If it didn't start out that way, it is now, that's for sure.

'And it's dangerous! So you're saying that Helena Hunter actually thinks that her husband has murdered someone and she's asking you to find out if that's true? I mean, come on. How is that a good idea?'

Jayden says quietly, 'And I'm such a bad choice, am I?'

Cat's face instantly softens. 'You know I don't mean it like that.'

And he knows she didn't too, but even so, it's pulled at the thread that's always waiting to be unravelled.

'Jay, you *know* I don't mean it like that,' she says again. 'But the only people that should be going anywhere near this are the police. And . . . I just don't think it's good for you. Getting your head caught up in this stuff again. I mean, it's literally the reason we came here, to get you away from all that.'

Jayden sits up. 'That's the reason we came?'

Cat stares back at him. Two spots of colour have appeared in her cheeks.

'So, not because you want to be near your parents when the baby comes? Or because you want to raise her by the sea, to have all the things that you had? Or because you want to open up a fricking campsite? Not those reasons?'

'I was happy in Leeds,' she says. 'I would have carried on being happy in Leeds.'

'*Seriously?* You want to do this?'

'You were broken, Jay. Understandably, but you were. Something had to change. And you weren't the one who was going to do it. I had to do it for us.'

'I left the force because I wanted to,' he says. 'That was a choice I made when I was clear-sighted. I sat down and thought it through. We talked about it. It wasn't just about Kieran dying.'

'I know.'

And he sees how her eyes are swimming, how she hates this as much as he does. He feels his own eyes fill in response.

'You like talking about fate,' he says. 'Signs, right? I didn't go looking for any of this with Lewis Pascoe or Helena Hunter, Cat. It found me. And you know what, it actually feels good. I feel good.'

'That's because you've had three months of playing on the beach, Jay.'

'No, it's because I'm *doing* something. I spoke to Fatima earlier.'

'Fatima Reddy?'

'It felt like old times. I felt connected.'

'Connected to Fatima Reddy?'

'Yeah. And with Ally, today, it was like we were partners . . .'

'Oh God, Jay.' Cat rubs her face with her hands. 'She's not your partner. She's . . . lonely. She's a lonely woman who lost her husband and now she's trying to do what he used to do, probably to make herself feel connected to him or something. And you're trying to do what you used to do – but not even that, because it's not like you were a detective, is it? It's not like you had murder cases on your desk.'

'We found Helena. We managed what the police couldn't.' Then, 'I was thinking of going for detective. I never told you that.'

'What? When?'

'It doesn't matter.'

She pushes her hair from her eyes, gives him a look of incredulity. 'You think it doesn't matter? How can you say that?'

He shrugs, and he knows he's going back in on himself. Shoulders rounded.

She makes a click of exasperation. 'And now there's the two of you running around together, being . . . commissioned . . . by a woman who's clearly pretty desperate and possibly unhinged. It's all such a bad idea, and the fact that you can't even see that says everything. I mean, doesn't it?' She gives a squeak of what sounds like laughter – but he knows is far from it.

'I know Ally's not my partner,' he says. 'Kieran was my partner.'

'Yes, he was,' she says. 'And you were brilliant together.'

The tears are streaming down Cat's cheeks now, and they're streaming down his too. He leans into her, presses his forehead to hers, and their arms wrap around each other.

'I'm sorry,' she says. 'I'm really, really sorry.'

'Today, I felt almost like myself again, Cat. You don't know what it's like – you're always the same, nothing gets to you. But me? I lost myself for a while back there.'

'I know you did.'

'And some days, even in your miraculous Cornwall, with all the things that we have to be happy about, I've been worried I'm still not back to myself yet. Like . . . sea air only goes so far, you know?'

'I know. I'm not that stupid. It takes time. It was a horrendous, tragic thing. And I hate that it happened. Not just to Kieran but to you too.'

'When Ally asked me to help, I just thought . . . *yes*. I didn't even have to think about it. I wanted to. And wanting to, felt . . . like such a relief.'

They sit with that for a moment. Cat presses her fingers to her eyes.

'You were really thinking of CID?' she says.

'Yeah. I was. But that's over now.'

'For what it's worth, I think you'd have been brilliant. Just like you were a brilliant PC.' She bites her lip. 'Do you hate it here, Jay?'

'Hate it here?' He catches one of her tears with the edge of his thumb. Gives a low laugh. 'I don't hate it here, babe. It doesn't feel much like my home yet but . . . you do. And that's all I need. All I'll ever need.'

'Because if you hate it here, we can go. I mean that. We can get our old flat back.'

'I don't want our old flat back,' he says. 'It was damp and smelt of takeaway. And I don't want to go anywhere. But I do want just one more day. Just one more day with Ally and this case. Just to see . . . if I'm right.'

'What do you mean?' she says.

'If I'm right about this being something that makes me happy,' he says.

'Chasing a murderer across the dunes?'

'I think the plan is to drive to Somerset actually.'

'Jay, seriously?'

'Just one day.' He holds up his finger. 'Pinky promise?'

'Okay. Pinky promise,' she says. And they're hooking fingers, and she's cracking up laughing at how grave their tones are, and he knows, then, that they're going to be okay.

40

Saffron is making dinner for her housemates. Here on Sun Street it's Thai green curry night – with butter-soft monkfish and fat prawns – and she focuses on it; loses herself in the comforting rhythms of cooking. She'd love to do more than cakes at Hang Ten. She can imagine cook-outs down on the sand, the summer air crackling with the scents of ginger and lemongrass and the catch of the day. She and the girls are all going to go to Thailand together one day. And Sri Lanka – that's definitely on the list too. And wouldn't she love to bring those flavours home with her. Spice things up a bit down at the beach.

Whenever Saffron talks of travels, she always means the winter months. She couldn't leave Hang Ten in the summer. In fact, it's hard to think of leaving it anytime – someone else flipping the sign, firing up the coffee machine, cutting the carrot cake. Today is the first day she hasn't opened since, well, since she first opened. Her phone has been pinging with messages as a result, from Hey, where's my coffee? through to Saff, you okay? She doesn't want to get anyone worrying. After all, she's doing enough of that herself.

She felt uneasy about Roland Hunter as soon as she realised who he was back at the hospital. And his brother, Nathan, sent out all of the wrong vibes too. Now Wenna has confirmed – without even knowing the significance of it – that their group had a run-in with Paul Pascoe the very same week he killed himself. Well, what was that about?

Maybe Saffron should have thought more on what it might have been about before she phoned Mullins, because while he listened, and said he was making a mental note, he didn't exactly sound excited to have the information.

But hey, that was Mullins. Maybe he didn't like that it was her detective work that'd figured it out.

Figured what out though?

'That Helena Hunter woman,' says Jodie, walking into the kitchen and opening the fridge. She takes out two beers and passes one to Saffron. 'Guess what? She's found. It's all good.'

Saffron has to strain to hear over the music, fast-paced electro that's doing just what she needs it to do: filling all available space. She drops the knife. Spins round. Turns the music all the way down.

'What, really? They've found her?'

'She just wanted to do her own thing, I reckon,' says Jodie. 'Hey, want help there?'

'But where was she?'

'They didn't say. It was all really vague in the piece. Like, one paragraph.'

Jodie goes to the window and starts ravaging their coriander plant. She tosses a handful in Saffron's direction. But Saffron is wiping her hands on her leggings, looking around for her phone. Scrolling.

'You're right. Super vague. But this: *the investigation into Lewis Pascoe's accident continues.* Damn right it should continue.'

She reaches for her beer. Takes a long drink. Turns the music back up. A female vocal kicks in over the beat.

'I went to try and see him this morning. Lewis Pascoe.'

Her friend leans close; wrinkles her nose. 'Er, why?'

223

'Because who else would?'

'Oh babe, you and the waifs and strays.'

'I knew his nan a little bit. And I remember her telling me his mum died of cancer, so, you know . . .'

Jodie nods. She gives a little smile of understanding.

'Where is he even? Truro?'

Saffron nods. 'Then this guy knocked me off my bike in the car park.'

'Whaaat?'

'I'm all good, I'm fine.' She holds up her hand. 'Just a tiny scratch. But anyway, he was acting like he felt all bad, and offered me a lift back to Porthpella, so I was like . . . yeah, okay.'

'Dumb.'

'Dumb? Why, dumb?'

'Stranger danger, Saff. What are you, like, eight? Did he offer to show you some puppies?'

'Okay, whatever. It all happened quickly.'

'Do we need to talk? Because I thought you were pretty clued up. And then you tell me that?'

'Anyway, turns out it was Roland Hunter. Helena Hunter's husband.'

Jodie drops her face into her hands. 'None of this is good. What was he doing there?'

'Tell me about it. I got a really bad vibe off him. Honestly, I was holding my phone in my hand all the way back here, my finger like right over that emergency button. But he was just . . . angry. Scared, I guess. Blaming it all on Lewis Pascoe. I just stayed really quiet, and after a while, so did he.'

'You should have phoned me.'

'Why? There was nothing to say.'

Kelly walks in then. Wrapped in a towel, her hair done up in a turban. 'Nothing to say about what?'

'Saffron hanging out with the missing woman's husband. Who, by the way, has now been found.'

'What?' Kelly drops into a chair. 'I don't have a beer. I need a beer for this.' She promptly gets back up again. 'She's been found? What's Saffron got to do with it?'

'So, anyway,' says Saffron, 'that's why I didn't open up today. I felt horrible. Like, it was all just too much reality. So, I went for a surf, and then I came home and just . . . I don't know what I did. Cleaning. Therapeutic cleaning. Oh, and baking. I did a load of baking.'

'For the café or for us?'

'Both.' She nods to the stack of tins. 'Dig in.'

Kelly takes the lid off the top one. 'The toffee nut cookies?'

'The toffee nut cookies.'

'Just what this beer needs.'

Saffron feels her friends on either side of her. Jodie's hand on her shoulder.

'You should tell us, okay?' says Jodie.

'Tell you what?'

'Tell us if you're thinking of doing something like going off to Truro, to go see a suspect in a missing persons case, and then accepting a lift home from a man who's directly involved in that case – who may or may not be another suspect, depending on who you talk to. And then being so freaked out that you shut up shop and spend the day baking sweet treats on your own back here. Though that last part *is* kind of your usual vibe, but . . . without the undertone. Next time you do that kind of thing, you need to tell us. *Before*.'

Saffron laughs – but there's a tear somewhere in there too. After her mum died – her lovely mum, who'd brought her up all on her own and who'd been the best friend she'd ever had – these girls saved her; they filled this suddenly empty house with music and laughter and love. She became a landlady almost overnight, and it was their rent that helped her make a go of Hang Ten. She's grateful to them for pretty much everything.

'Okay,' she says, a creak in her voice. 'Deal.'

'And just so you know, we'll say don't do it,' says Kelly, chomping the cookie as Saffron picks up her knife and starts chopping again. 'We'll say no way.'

'I saw his brother too,' says Saffron, casually. 'Seeing as we're on the subject.'

'Whose brother?'

'Roland Hunter's brother. And guess what, charm runs in the family. Not. He was gross. And he wanted to pay me for surf lessons.'

'How much?' says Kelly.

'Tell me you didn't say yes,' says Jodie.

'Of course I didn't say yes. Anyway . . . there's a weird coincidence. About those brothers and Porthpella. And Lewis's dad, Paul Pascoe. I got chatting to Wenna about it. Or, well, you know Wenna, she got chatting to me – and then some. Anyway, I phoned and told Mullins, in case it connected to anything.'

But Kelly's got a text on her phone, and Jodie's squealing at it, and Saffron supposes that it doesn't sound all that interesting, not now the big drama is over: Helena Hunter has been found. But she can't help thinking about Lewis Pascoe lying there in that hospital. And whether this is all just a case of history repeating. Or something worse, even, than that.

41

Gus loads another cracker with a hunk of Cornish Yarg and a good spoonful of onion chutney. A decent enough dinner. He really needs to get back in the kitchen – he can't help feeling it's lame of him not to enjoy cooking for one – but until he's seized with inspiration, the cheese counter at White Wave Stores will do him fine. Maybe it isn't the most balanced diet in the world but the Yarg is wrapped in nettles; at least he's getting his greens.

He brushes the crumbs from his shirt and goes back to staring at the blank page. Not writing is rather like feeling your lids growing heavy in an avalanche and thinking maybe *I'll just sink into it; that way lies peace* – accept the all-white oblivion of the unwritten. Not that he'd actually know; he's never been in snow past his ankles, and he's certainly never skied – or done anything particularly daring, come to think of it. Maybe that's why this crime novel is proving itself so hard to write. He has no experience of extremity.

Even his reaction at the end of his marriage was muted: he retreated, rather than battled. Perhaps battling was what was needed all along.

He finds himself wondering how Ally Bright reacted to her husband's death. It's a whole different thing, of course, and it's insensitive to even compare the two. But even in their short meeting earlier she just seemed so calm, so level, as if she let life swirl around her, her own anchor set good and fast. Ever since she stopped by, he's been wondering if she went to St Ives to find the artist lady in the wide-brimmed hat, or if she simply told the police this detail instead. He looked Fiona Penrose up himself, All Swell's slow-churning Wi-Fi revealing her paintings strip by strip; all that colour, splashed on the canvas with what seemed like extraordinary freedom and, probably, deceptive ease.

Maybe painting would be a simpler thing for him to tackle than novel-writing? But it does offer less of a place in which to lose yourself. Here he is, writing a whole other world.

Or not writing, as it happens.

How can he make up crime, as if it's some kind of fun diversion, when the real thing is happening right under his nose in Porthpella? Gus's literary efforts have never felt so insubstantial – or misplaced.

But he's unpacked his suitcase. He isn't leaving yet after all.

Funny that, Gus, how you changed your mind after a visit from Ally Bright?

He tells his interior monologue to pipe down; but not without a smile.

His thoughts are interrupted by a loud knock at his door, and his first thought is *Ally!* But as he sets down his cracker and pushes back his chair, the knock comes again – insistent, impatient – and he knows that probably isn't her style.

He glances at the clock. It's after eight o'clock: only just within the bounds of reason for unsolicited visiting hours – by his not-very-bohemian estimation, anyway.

'I know you're in there!'

Gus stiffens. It's Roland Hunter.

What should he do? Open up – or lie low, hoping he'll just go away? Unconsciously his hand goes to his mouth where his lip still hasn't recovered from their last encounter.

I know you're in there. Not the most enticing entreaty. Not by a long chalk.

'Everything alright?' Gus says, through the door, regretting it the moment the words are out of his mouth. Of course everything isn't alright.

He pulls the door open, simultaneously gathering himself up to his full height of five foot nine and a half inches.

Roland has his arms folded across his chest. He wears a rugby shirt, a red that seems too bright. His eyes fix on Gus and he looks him up and down.

'You haven't heard?'

Gus gives a brief shake of his head.

'She's been found.'

'Helena?'

Roland sucks in air, as if to cool whatever rage is burning inside.

'My wife. Yes.'

'Oh,' says Gus, the sarcasm in Hunter's tone obvious. 'Oh, thank goodness for that.'

'Thank goodness? *Thank goodness?* I'm a long way from thanking anyone.'

A horrific image suddenly descends. Found alive, surely? Not dead? Because you wouldn't say it like that otherwise, would you? You wouldn't say *she's been found*?

'Found,' says Roland. 'But not returned.'

Gus gives a brief shake of his head. It's as if he's been thrust into a conversation that's in a language he can't understand.

'Not exactly what you'd call law enforcement, is it?' says Hunter.

Gus shrugs. Then quickly tries to turn it into something else: an adjustment of his entire body, because any suggestion of indifference, or incomprehension, might go over very badly in this moment.

'What can I do?' he says.

By which he really means: *What do you want from me? What have I got to do with any of this? I'd really prefer it if you left me alone.*

'All your curtain-twitching. Ever see a man with her?'

At last, a question he can answer. 'No. No.' He's so relieved he says it twice. 'And you have to know, that was never how it was. I only told you what I'd seen because—'

Roland holds up a hand, as if stopping traffic.

'Never? Never a man sniffing around? Not once? And don't mention my brother, because he's here this weekend, being no use whatsoever.'

Gus has indeed seen a man he presumed to be Roland's brother, striding about on his mobile phone outside the house, elbow cocked high.

'No. But I was hardly watching, I—'

'Not interested.'

Roland slams the conversation shut like a door. Just like Gus wishes he could do himself right now. To his relief, Roland turns, and starts to walk down the path. Then he swings round, and Gus sees how he sways, wonders if he's drunk.

'What about your own wife, Book Writer? Where's she?' He says it suddenly, as if the thought has only just occurred to him. 'Or don't you have one?'

'In Oxford.'

'With someone else?'

'Yes.'

'You alright with that, are you?'

So many answers to that question, but none he'll be giving Roland. 'It's like that sometimes,' he simply says.

'Oh, is it? Is it like that sometimes?' The sarcasm is back – in spades. 'Because I didn't know that. I didn't know that it was like that sometimes.'

Then Roland kicks out, a scuff of sand, the hard clunk of shoe against the cast-iron anchor – which doesn't budge an inch. He stumbles, giving a yelp of pain. Followed by a volley of curses. Roland rights himself, turns on this new opponent. Gus watches as he grapples with the anchor in a furious embrace. With all his strength, and a whole lot more cussing, Roland pulls it away from the wall and tips it over. He jumps clear as it lands with a thunk, sand puffing up in a cloud around it. Then he wipes his hands on his chinos and turns to Gus with a look of victory. A lock of hair hangs in his face, and he appears, thinks Gus, demented. Sweaty. Maybe even laughable – but he doesn't think that now, only later maybe, with the door safely locked. And not really laughable at all; not if you're Helena.

'Waste of space,' spits Roland. Then he turns and limps down the path.

Gus breathes out. He gives silent thanks for the human ability to withhold information.

Not a man, but a woman. He'd answered Roland's question honestly.

Then he thinks of Ally again, on her own further along the dunes. Roland's rampaging won't take him in her direction, will it? Does Roland have any idea that she's been asking questions? Gus realises he has no way of getting in touch with her. The only thing to do is knock on her door himself, and he can't do that at this time of the evening. He's no Roland.

He looks again at the fallen anchor; the mess of footprints in the sand around it. Safety has to override propriety, doesn't it? Because he has a horrible feeling that Roland isn't done yet.

42

Mullins looks across at his mum. She's sitting on the opposite sofa, and although it's only early evening she's ready for bed, in her raggedy pink dressing gown and fluffy slippers. There's a cup of tea balanced in her lap, and an open packet of custard creams beside her on the cushion. The television prattles on, some drama with a bunch of posh actors putting on accents and pretending their lives are going up in smoke.

His mum's hooked.

It occurs to Mullins that she's paying this fiction way more attention than the reality unfolding right under her nose, here in Porthpella. Part of him wonders if she's just blocked it out: maybe someone walking out of their life without a backwards glance – just like his dad did – isn't a story she wants to tune into.

Mullins feels his insides knot at the thought, and he glances at her again. All the things he can't say. He takes a slurp of beer, and instead offers, 'Maggie Pascoe moved away without anyone round here knowing about it.'

'Course she did,' says his mum. 'Last thing she would have done was tell anyone.'

Since Helena has turned up alive and well, Mullins is thinking more and more about Lewis. The theory they were all so quick to believe – that Lewis hurt her, then tried to kill himself – doesn't work anymore.

What if they've got other things about Lewis wrong too?

And what about the thing that Saffron told him, that the Hunter brothers crossed paths with Paul Pascoe the same week Paul went and killed himself? Mullins told Skinner and Skinner told Robinson and then Skinner reminded Mullins – in a way that really got up Mullins's nose – that in an average year something like five million people came on holiday to Cornwall, so it wasn't so very strange that the Hunters were among them, was it?

Nevertheless, Robinson suggested that they go and talk to Roland and Nathan about it tomorrow. Then Skinner said that Mullins could do it himself. *Just a friendly chat, like.* Not that he expects either of the brothers to be particularly friendly or willing to chat. And he, Mullins, turning up at their door . . . well, it isn't exactly sending in the big guns, is it? Even he can see that this is his boss's not-so-subtle way of showing just how significant a lead they think it is.

Lead. Is it even still a case? They needed DS Chang to remind them about Lewis's fingerprints on Helena's watch: that they couldn't presume it was attempted suicide.

And now, what if Lewis goes and dies without any of them ever knowing the truth about what happened on that clifftop? He came to Porthpella thinking his life was about to start over – but it was the opposite.

'Didn't you feel sorry for her, Mum?'

'Sorry for her?' His mum sniffed. 'Who, Maggie Pascoe? We've all got our problems. She wasn't special.'

'But her son killed himself.' He wants to say something else – *Doesn't it matter, when your own son is so unhappy that he does a thing like that? And you couldn't even see it?* – but he doesn't want to go there. 'If you were her, and Roland Hunter made you that offer, where would you have gone with all that money?'

'Spain.'

She seems to say it without thinking, as if it's the question she's been waiting to be asked forever. He has a sudden image of his mum in a flamenco skirt, twirling round and round. All that life not lived. It's a far cry from Ocean Drive and the rabbits.

'You could go on holiday there,' says Mullins. 'Couldn't you?'

'What's the point in that?'

And he's not sure how to answer that. 'Sunshine?' he offers.

'I need more than sunshine,' she says. 'Shh, Tim. I'm missing this.'

'Paradiso Heights,' he says, 'that's where Maggie Pascoe went. Outside St Austell. It's like a residential home, but you live in your own flat.'

'Tim, shh now.'

He looked it up, trawled through images online, and it seemed like whoever had come up with the name had a sense of humour. It was a blockish building surrounded by a strip of lawn that was about as interesting as a school field. He phoned them and had it confirmed. Maggie Pascoe had been a resident. And then, just a couple of weeks ago, she'd suffered a fatal stroke.

'We couldn't get hold of her next of kin,' the girl on the phone said. 'We tried everything. The police got in touch with the prison he'd just been released from too. But I think they said his number wasn't working, and he hadn't seen his probation officer yet. Does Ally Bright work with you? She asked the same questions.'

Ally Bright again.

'Maggie can still be properly laid to rest,' the girl said. 'She's still at the funeral home. It's such a good thing her grandson can be there. I mean, not a good thing, but . . . you know what I mean. The right thing.'

The line went quiet, and for a moment Mullins thought the girl had rung off. But then she spoke again.

'And now he's in hospital? In a coma? Did he really try to . . .'

'Yeah,' said Mullins. 'It's actually kind of a sad story. His dad killed himself in that same place, like, twenty years ago. I think his dad probably had some head stuff going on, but no one was helping. Round here they just thought he was bad news.'

There was something quite nice about talking on the phone to someone who didn't know him. His voice sounded softer than he'd thought it could: not much like PC Mullins.

'Maggie's grandson is called Lewis, isn't he?'

'Yeah, he is.'

'Look, don't think I'm a snooper, but . . . hang on, I've forgotten your name.'

And she didn't sound like she was talking to a PC either.

'It's Tim. PC Tim. I mean PC Mullins.'

'Okay, Tim PC Tim PC Mullins. I'm Naomi.'

And she was sort of laughing at him – but he sort of didn't mind it.

'Her flat here's still got all her things in it. We figured that her grandson would eventually come and get them. But I went in, just to clear out the fridge, make sure nothing was rotting. And I saw this amazing photograph. It just stopped me in my tracks. And now . . . after what you said . . . well, I think Lewis might want it. Shall I nip back and get it? We hold all the keys. I can send it, and maybe you could get it to him?'

'Er, he's kind of in a coma. Can't he just have it when he goes to the flat?'

'But what if he doesn't wake up, Tim?'

Then, duh, he won't see the photo anyway, Mullins thought.

'What I mean,' she said, 'is that I think it might help him, when he's lying there in hospital. All on his own. You'll see what I mean when you see the photo. It might even help him pull through – feel the good vibes.'

Of the many things Lewis Pascoe might have wanted, Mullins couldn't imagine an old photo would be high up on his list. But she sounded like she wanted to help, the girl, even if she was a bit weird. Like, Hippy-Dippy-style weird. So, Mullins gave her his address. Afterwards he wondered if he should have given the address of the station, but it was too late. Ocean Drive it was.

'Oh, wow, Porthpella,' she said. 'I used to go there as a kid.'

'I reckon it hasn't changed.'

'Reassuring,' she said, with a laugh. 'Everything else does.'

There wasn't much more he could say after that, so he just thanked her, and she thanked him, then they both hung up. Afterwards there was a spring in his step like he'd done something useful.

Now he takes another slug of beer and glances at his mum. She couldn't care less about Maggie. Nor Lewis. But here she is now, her eyes filling up with tears at some made-up drama on the screen.

Why does he still look to her for his cues? He doesn't have to. The fact is, this case is something different – and maybe it's making him see a little bit differently too.

Mullins gets up to fetch another beer. Just one more though; tomorrow he's going to talk to the Hunter brothers, and he'll be doing it for Lewis, and for Lewis's dad. He'll be needing a clear head for that, won't he?

43

Ally sits with an evening glass of wine, staring at the jet of flames in the wood burner. It's not a cold night, but she wanted the comfort of it, and a fire has always felt like company. Fox lies in his basket, sound asleep, breathing rhythmically. Beyond comes the faint push-and-pull of the sea.

She's thinking on death. How can she not, after what Jayden told her? The scene he described plays out in her mind, but also his own quiet telling of it. His bravery and emotion. The fact that he told her means more than she can say.

Ever since she met Jayden at the foot of the cliffs, he's surprised her. People round here, they don't seek out her company, or confide in her. It hadn't even occurred to her to want that, she's been pulled up in her own shell for so long. Far before Bill died, her ways were set. But then Lewis fell – and there was Jayden.

And now they've gone and found Helena.

The extraordinary events of the day are still settling within her. Her reaction – the determination to stay with this – is still settling within her.

From the picture on the shelf, Bill is looking at her with his steady grin, and she can't for the life of her guess what he'd be thinking right now.

'What would you have done?' she asks.

She has a distinct feeling that he would have disapproved of her and Jayden playing detective, as Skinner – and probably anyone else around here – put it. The words *no police* would have set his alarms going: his blues and twos. *That's just when we're needed most, Al, when people say a thing like that.*

The thing about Bill was that he was compassionate: nothing was ever too much trouble for him. In darker moments she's thought that this is why his heart gave out – that he simply did too much caring for one lifetime; there wasn't enough to go around. She's pretty sure that if he'd sat across from Helena Hunter and seen her fragility, he would have wanted to help her. And if helping her meant doing things differently, well, maybe he would have done that too. Only the truth is, he wouldn't have been there in the first place, would he? Helena would have been frightened by the uniform, just as Maggie Pascoe had resented it too.

Ally was trusted precisely because she *wasn't* Bill. And this is an extraordinary thought.

Roland Hunter as a murderer, though? And up to her and Jayden to prove it?

She takes a sip of wine and shifts in her seat. She's just starting to relax when the knock comes. It's soft, respectful, so as she gets up and goes to the door, she's not unsettled. She half wonders if it's Jayden, changing his mind about tomorrow; doing it on her own would be very different and she's not sure she can. But when she opens up, she sees Gus.

'Sorry,' he says, 'I didn't want to disturb.'

And she realises she's smiling. Gus sees the smile and returns it with one of his own.

'Oh, Gus, I meant to contact you,' she says, 'but I realised I didn't have your number.'

'You wanted to contact me?'

She starts to say 'Fiona Pen—' but Gus puts his finger to his lips.

He glances over his shoulder at the dark dunes, the navy sky above. Says in a low voice, 'I'm probably being . . . overcautious. But could I step inside for just a minute?'

As Ally closes the door behind him, he makes all kinds of apologies for the intrusion, for the time of the evening, for the spontaneous nature of his visit. To hear him, it's a wonder he's come at all. His discomfort makes her feel, bizarrely, more at ease; for once, she gets to be the cool one.

'But if you didn't have my number how else could you get in touch?' she says. And she sees his shoulders relax.

She thinks of offering him a glass of wine, but he said he was only stepping in for a minute and she doesn't want to make him feel obliged. She's still thinking this conundrum over as Gus rubs at his stubble and speaks.

'My neighbour paid me a rather agitated visit a short while ago.'

'Roland Hunter?'

'He said that Helena's been found, but – reading between the lines – she's not coming home.'

Ally nods. 'I heard that too.' She almost adds something like *it's a relief* – that would be the expected response here, surely? – but it feels inappropriate, given what she knows. And Gus deserves honesty.

'He's not taking it well,' he says. 'Not at all well. My anchor bore the brunt of it.'

Ally throws him a confused look and he gives a low laugh.

'The maritime design feature by my front stoop,' he says. 'It's taken rather a battering. As I watched Roland going at it, I couldn't help feeling he'd rather it was me.'

Ally feels a shiver run through her. With the image of Roland Hunter attacking a piece of cast iron, she says, 'Do you want a drink? It sounds like you might need one.'

'Do you know,' says Gus, 'that would be . . . just right.'

Fifteen minutes later and Ally has heard what happened, blow by blow. Gus sits in the armchair by the fire – she doesn't want to call it Bill's chair, but it was, it still is – and every so often he reaches down to stroke the sleeping Fox's ears.

'You did well not to mention Fiona to Roland,' she says.

'Well, he did only ask me if I'd seen her with a man.' Gus shrugs. 'Did you make it to St Ives to find Fiona?'

Ally takes another sip of wine. She finds her glass is almost empty and sees that his is too. 'Do you want . . . another?'

He rubs the bridge of his nose. 'I don't want to outstay my welcome. I really only meant to drop by and warn you that Roland's in a bad place, so if there was a knock at the door, then . . .'

'It was good of you to,' she says, standing up, 'very good of you. But I'm used to it, being on my own out here. Really I am.'

'But these last few days, it's not normally like this round here, is it?'

'Well, no,' she says. 'That's true.'

'And Roland Hunter, you don't know him very well. He's new-ish, as a neighbour?'

'I'm getting to know him better,' she says carefully, 'what with one thing and another.'

And as Ally's walking through to the kitchen, to take the bottle from the fridge, she's wondering how much to say – or whether to say anything at all. She knows she'd like to, but that isn't the point, is it?

'He's got his brother staying,' says Gus. 'Though I haven't seen much of him.'

Helena mentioned Nathan staying for the weekend, and it was pretty clear what she thought of him too. Could he be involved somehow? He does keep popping up.

'I've heard he wants to buy somewhere round here,' she says. 'Did Roland mention that to you? Or anything else about his brother?'

'It wasn't really a chatty sort of chat, Ally.' Then, 'I don't mind admitting I'm intimidated by him. Roland, I mean.'

'Roland's not suspicious of you, is he? On account of what you said about . . . seeing Helena.'

She notes Gus's hesitation. Helena clearly believes that her husband has the capacity for violence, and here's Gus, already with a fat lip. Is he here to warn her, or because he prefers not to be so close to Hunter himself this evening? But then she bats the thought away. Anyway, if he wanted to, he could leave Porthpella. It's the holidaymaker's privilege, to go back to their real lives, wherever they may be.

It strikes her, then, how little she knows about Gus Munro, yet here he is in her sitting room, here she is filling up his glass, and then her own, as if it's the most natural thing in the world.

'Helena is Roland's second wife,' she says, in a rush. 'They were having an affair. They were together one night, at Helena's, when Roland's house was broken into. His wife – his first wife, Victoria – was home by herself and she was killed by the intruders.'

Gus near enough spits out his wine.

'He told you all this?'

'Jayden came across some newspaper articles. It's all online.'

'No wonder Roland's . . .'

He appears to lose his thread.

'What?'

'I don't know. I don't actually know what word to use.'

'And you, a writer,' says Ally.

'I never said I was a good one.' He looks towards the fire. Takes another sip of wine. 'That's a very sad story.'

'It is,' says Ally.

'But the way you told it, you didn't . . . you didn't sound all that sympathetic. Towards Roland, I mean.' His brow's furrowed. 'Is that because you judge the affair, you think somehow the consequences . . .'

'Not at all,' says Ally.

'My wife had one,' says Gus. 'Had a couple, actually, as it turns out, but we went our separate ways as a result of the last. I knew for a while. She wasn't exactly subtle, not in the end. But I thought it might just go away. It didn't. But she did.'

'I'm sorry.'

'Oh no,' says Gus. 'It was the right thing. How it turned out, I mean. In the end.' He takes another sip of wine; resettles in his seat. 'Did Roland's first wife have any idea about it?'

The same question Ally asked of Helena.

'Not according to Helena.'

'Sorry. I'm just . . . the choices people make. Plodding on, versus . . . not. I think about it a lot. Far too much, probably. The ink's still fairly wet on the divorce papers, you see.'

Ally looks up at him sharply.

'What if Victoria knew?' she says, and she realises she's said it out loud.

'Ah, you see, I used to think ignorance was bliss,' he says. 'Well, perhaps not bliss as such. I wouldn't go that far. But ignorance as preferable? Anyway, the jury's still out on that one for me.'

'But when you know something, you have a choice,' says Ally. 'Don't you? You have some sort of power.'

'I didn't, as it happens,' says Gus, lost in himself. 'Or it didn't feel like I did, anyway, but . . . no, that's not quite true; I did make decisions. I mean, I'm here, aren't I? I did come here. To Cornwall. And the book . . .' He trails off. 'Ally? Are you alright?'

And just like that, she knows what she'll be talking to Sebastian Lyle about tomorrow: whether there was any proof – anywhere at all – that Victoria knew about her husband's affair. Because if she had plans to divorce Roland, then that could be seen as motive, couldn't it? If Sebastian was right about Roland and his gold-digging intentions, he wouldn't have wanted to lose a penny.

44

First thing on Sunday morning, Mullins stands looking up at Ally Bright's house. Skinner is inside the car still, finishing up a call, and so Mullins has a minute to take it in. It's pale blue weatherboard, with a wide veranda and hundreds of seashells set into the low stone wall. The name *The Shell House* is painted on a piece of driftwood, by someone who, it looks like, really knew what they were doing. A path winds up to the house, and there are seashells decorating its edges too. It looks too pretty a place for a burly local sergeant; Bill Bright was a good copper – that's the word on the street, he was one of the best – and Mullins can't imagine him here, somehow. Or maybe he can. Because it's nice. And what's wrong with nice?

He squats to look closer at a glinting top shell – his grandad was into his shore life, good old Grandad Jack – and as he touches its pearly outer layer, it comes away in his hand. He glances furtively left and right and drops it from his fingers. Then nudges it with the toe of his boot. There are loads of bloody shells, what does it even matter?

'Well, don't hang about, lad, knock on the door.'

Skinner slams the car door shut behind him, and Mullins thinks that if Ally isn't already aware of their arrival, she will be now.

He walks up the path, and as he climbs the creaking wooden steps a funny thought comes to him: he wishes he wasn't here on business.

Mullins is never a welcome sight on anyone's doorstep – even if someone has called him. After all, something has to be going wrong for the boys in blue to show up. What he'd really like is to be visiting this house just because: maybe for a weekend barbecue or an afternoon cuppa. It's one of the friendliest-looking places he's seen, which is a weirdo thing to say, a Hippy-Dippy thing to say – again! – and immediately he thinks not of Saffron for once, but the girl on the phone, with her talk of old photos and good vibes. It was different for girls, he thinks. Girls could say what they wanted. For a bloke, one bum note and they threw the whole piano at you.

'Stop dithering, lad, what are you waiting for – an invitation in a little white envelope?'

He can hear the heavy tread of Skinner's boots behind him, so he hustles on up to the door, puffing his chest out; hammers at the pane.

No response.

He knocks again, even louder this time.

Still no answer. Mullins turns and surveys the dunes. The low-tide beach looks smooth as a pack of butter before you stick the knife in. Beyond the bay, the bright white island lighthouse watches over things. And it's all totally deserted.

'Admiring the views?' says Skinner.

'She might be out with her dog.'

That's where she was two days ago, when Lewis was found at the foot of the cliffs. She probably walks the dog at the same time every morning.

Skinner grunts and takes out his phone. He dials and waits. 'No answer.' He dials again, and this time leaves a voice message.

He sounds sugary and fake and Mullins knows Ally Bright's not going to fall for that.

'Tell you what, Mullins, let's station you here. Take a pew on the veranda. Build yourself a sandcastle. And when Mrs Bright gets back, tell her we need to talk to her. If she holds out on you, bring her in for questioning. You think you can handle a sweet old lady?'

'She's not actually that old,' says Mullins. But, really, he's thinking, *What if she doesn't want to come in for questioning?* But he doesn't voice it. To be honest, it all feels very unlikely to Mullins. But here's what could have happened: Helena goes for a run, Lewis sees her, they argue, he goes off the cliff, she's frightened and does a runner – which is why she's lying to the police about it. And, what, she dumps the watch, because maybe it's the part of her that he grabbed on to? And what did Ally Bright have to do with any of it?

But okay, sure. He'll wait.

'Hang on, there's no car here,' he says suddenly.

'Ace detective, you are,' says Skinner. 'Trying to impress Robinson, are you?'

'What if she's gone out for the day? That's what I mean.'

'Then you'll get yourself a nice little suntan, won't you?'

Mullins blinks up at the sky, which is basically mackerel.

'And when you're done here, you can have a chat with Roland Hunter and his brother about holidays in Cornwall in years gone by. They might even get their photo albums out for you.'

'DCI Robinson thought you might want to be involved in that after all, sir.'

'Oh, he did, did he? Well, after a little chit-chat with Helena Hunter, DCI Robinson is on his way back to the Major Crimes Unit, so he doesn't need to worry about us down here anymore.'

As Skinner drives away, Mullins settles himself on the wooden bench on the veranda. It feels a bit like trespassing, even in the uniform. He keeps an eye on the 180 degrees in front of him, because as soon as he spots Ally Bright's grey head and that little red dog he'll get to his feet and stand to a kind of attention. But then he's distracted by a row of mobile-type things, strings of driftwood and seashells, and the way they turn slowly in the breeze keeps drawing him in; he feels like a baby in a crib. There's a cushion on the bench and he leans back against it. He looks past the mobiles to the white horses – that's what Grandad Jack always called waves like that – running into the bay.

He feels a strange sensation – or more accurately, a realisation – coming over him.

Skinner has no urgency for this case anymore. Not really. He's going through the motions. Is it because he's so certain Lewis jumped? Or is it that Helena's life has been deemed more valuable than Lewis's? With her big house and bossy husband and squeaky-clean record.

Sitting here on The Shell House veranda, this thought suddenly strikes Mullins as all kinds of unfair. But instead of slumping even more with this depressing realisation, he sits bolt upright; sharpens himself right up. Because he's still on the case, isn't he?

He just wishes someone else was too.

45

'Is this it, do you reckon?'

Jayden peers through the windscreen at the grey stone cottage. It sits in a puddle of shade, rangy trees clustered on both sides, hillsides rising steeply behind. A scraggy wisteria half chokes the dilapidated porch, and there's a piece of hardboard in place of a windowpane.

Ally nods, pointing to a piece of partially obscured slate. The name *Sunnybank* is etched on it, and a crack runs right through the middle.

It reminds Jayden of the kind of house in old-fashioned kids' storybooks, where you'd come home to find a bunch of bears in your bed, or a wolf dressed as your gran, and all the time Jayden would be thinking, *Well of course they're all crackers, look at them, living out there in the middle of nowhere*: what did anyone expect?

It was fun, meeting Ally in the lane this morning. Stopping to get breakfast pasties – *Is that a thing? Breakfast pasties?* To which she replied, *It is now* – and then the drive inland, counting the moors: Bodmin, Dartmoor, Exmoor.

It had been easy enough to find Sebastian Lyle's number. Ally made the call from the car, and she flipped it to speaker so Jayden could hear the faint slur to his words – in the middle of the morning. Lyle was cautious at first – then, at the mention of Roland Hunter's name, animated.

Somehow that voice doesn't fit with the cottage in front of them now. It was a grandstanding voice, comedically posh, and Jayden pictured a huge old manor house, or a smart townhouse, not this tumbledown spot, with an ancient Polo parked askew, its dashboard littered with screwed-up receipts.

The door opens and Sebastian Lyle appears. He throws up an arm and waves as if they're long-lost friends. He's wearing cords and a knitted jumper that's full of holes. His feathery blond hair is caught by a lick of breeze.

'Greetings,' Sebastian says heartily, 'come in, come in,' and it strikes Jayden that he's way too cheerful for the occasion. Fox seems to agree because he lets out a small growl. Up close, though, there's something insubstantial about the man, and as Jayden shakes Sebastian's proffered hand his fingers almost slip from his grasp.

Sebastian pushes the cottage door wide open and a mushroomy scent escapes: damp, probably, mixed with an unidentifiable sourness. Jayden glances back at Ally, who appears admirably unfazed. He ducks his head to avoid the low beam and follows Roland Hunter's former brother-in-law inside.

'I've never trusted that man. Not from the very first day he turned up in my sister's life.'

Jayden and Ally are sitting side by side on a low sofa that creaks every time they move a muscle. The room around them is striped with shadow and sunlight, and Jayden can feel himself squinting. It's a small space, crowded with heavy old furniture. An enormous television is on low in the background, the racing commentator's weirdly lyrical tones providing the soundtrack to their conversation. *And it's Muddy Waters, Muddy Waters in the lead, with Back Track coming up on the near side.* Jayden attempts to tune it out – and tune in to Sebastian. The man showed so little surprise at their intended visit that they had to remind him that they weren't the police.

Of course you're not, Sebastian said, *because the police are bloody useless.*

Nor did he seem to care who they were – there were none of the questions that Fiona had rightfully asked. All that seemed to matter, all that Sebastian fixed on, was that here was an opportunity to talk about Roland Hunter. Now he sprawls in an armchair, one leg draped over the other, a drink in his hand.

Jayden's eye is drawn by a mousetrap in the corner, just behind Sebastian's chair; it's upturned, as if there was a struggle, and a pair of tiny legs and a stiff tail are sticking up in the air. It makes him feel nauseous. *Mate, you've caught one*, he thinks of saying, because what kind of person doesn't clear their traps?

'Absolute gold-digger, anyone could see that,' Sebastian says with gusto. 'Anyone except for Victoria, of course. He was after our family's money from the off.'

'Did Victoria know about the affair?' asks Ally.

Straight in – nice one, Al. She obviously hasn't noticed the mouse.

'What you have to understand about my sister,' says Sebastian, 'is that she wanted so badly to believe that Roland loved her. It blinded her. Don't ask me why – some defect arising from our childhood probably. What's that line of Larkin's about your parents fudging you up? Anyway, Victoria was very much fudged up. Oh, she pretended to be all together, ever so' – he waves his glass, puts on a high-pitched voice – '*I'm in control here, Sebby*, and she liked to think she was, she absolutely did, but anyone could see that she and Hunter were a fundamental mismatch.'

Jayden glances at Ally, sees her open her mouth to say something, but Sebastian's jumping to his feet. His sudden movements make Fox shrink back and Jayden feels the press of the dog against his legs. Sebastian grabs a photo frame. 'I mean, look at her.' He pushes it closer to Jayden. 'You look. Tell me what you see.'

There's a shaft of sunlight coming directly from the opposite window, and it's showing just how thick the air is with dust; Jayden fights the urge to clap his hand to his mouth. He leans closer to look, his lips pressed tight together.

In the picture, Victoria is standing beside a horse. She's wearing an old-fashioned-looking flowered dress and isn't quite smiling.

'And here's another,' he says, 'when we were teens. Look, will you? That's me on the left of course.'

It's Sebastian and Victoria in a garden, side by side on a bench, a grand old house in the background. Her arms are folded across her chest and she's glaring into the camera as if she doesn't want this picture taken at all. The breeze is throwing her curly hair up at a bizarre angle. Sebastian's laughing about something, and there's a cigarette dangling from his long fingers.

'Met Hunter, have you?' he says, pointedly.

'Not properly,' says Jayden.

Sebastian turns to Ally. 'You've got to admit he's a good-looking man. Or has a certain . . . charisma. My sister though?' He spins back to Jayden, shaking his head. 'It can't be said. The same, simply, cannot be said.'

Jayden looks again to Ally. Her eyes are narrowed, and he's willing to bet she's fighting the same urge to say something that he is.

'She was never one of the radiant girls, Victoria. She wasn't even one of the passable girls, if we're honest. None of my friends would've touched her with a bargepole, I can tell you. Oh, I know what you're thinking, just nasty brother talk, nursery stuff, but the fact of the matter is, it's relevant here. Ho yes. My sister was not attractive. That's a fact. Nor, I'm afraid to say, was she charming, or especially pleasant-natured at all. Very little sunshine in Victoria

Lyle. So why on earth did she catch a man like Roland Hunter's eye? Hmm? Perhaps it was something to do with our fantastically wealthy parents departing this earth, and my dowdy sister suddenly looking a lot more attractive to an unscrupulous stranger. What do you think, detectives? Could it by chance be that?'

Jayden wants to speak up, to cut this man short. But maybe there's a point to it; maybe it's relevant. He swaps another look with Ally, and it's clear she's no Lyle fan either.

'It's so bloody obvious,' Sebastian goes on, 'but no one else could ever see it. He was always after her money. *Our* money. And he got it too. All of it – near as damn it. And you tell me there's nothing suspicious about her death? That it was the work of a random break-in? He'd simply had enough of her, hadn't he? I said all of this at the time. Shouted it from the rooftops. But no one listened. No one.'

'We saw your statement to the police,' says Jayden, 'where you express your concerns over Hunter.' His voice is gruff, and he consciously resets himself. Sebastian can help them; they need to keep him on side. 'It was a week after her death. Why the delay?'

'I had to pick myself up off the floor,' says Sebastian. 'I was heartbroken. She was my sister, the only family I had. But as I started to get myself together, got myself thinking straight, the more it became clear as day to me. And I've never got over the fact that no one else could see it. No one! But you' – he points at them both, his finger waggling – 'you two can see it. Can't you? Are you reopening the case? Tell me you're reopening the case. Five years, it's been. Five unbearable years.'

Ally speaks softly, and instead of setting him straight, reminding him – again – that they aren't the police, she says, 'Did Victoria have any idea of Roland's affair with Helena Hunter?'

'And now she goes missing!' Sebastian rolls on. 'This new one. This other woman. And no one thinks that's suspicious either! Do we really believe that she's been found safe? I'm not so sure. Not so sure at all. He's up to no good again, if you want my opinion. Sitting there in his palace in Cornwall, surrounded by his ill-gotten gains. Porthpella, is it? Huh.'

Ally tries to get him back on track. 'Sebastian? It could be important. Whether Victoria knew.'

He sags back in the armchair, tired after his tirade. Jayden glances at the trap again: the mouse, of course, hasn't moved.

'Don't know.'

'Victoria didn't talk about her relationship with you, ever?'

'We weren't close like that.'

Sebastian dips his head in obvious regret. For the first time, Jayden feels a pang of proper sympathy for him; grief and anger is a mix that does strange things to people.

'Victoria always thought she knew best. Stubborn as an ox. Wouldn't listen to anyone, except for him. She was a docile lamb in his presence. My sister, officers, was a whole farmyard of different animals.'

He's rambling now, moving from one point to another without connection.

'We're not officers, Sebastian,' Jayden says.

'Of course you're bloody not.'

Jayden glances to Ally. She looks as gutted as he feels.

'What about friends?' she says. 'Did Victoria have many friends?'

'Always a loner. Nothing like me.'

'Well,' says Ally, and it's a wrap-up kind of voice, 'I don't think we should keep you much longer. Jayden, is there anything else you wanted to ask Sebastian?'

'What about Roland's brother, Nathan?' asks Jayden, with a sudden thought. 'Did you know him?'

'We didn't go in for family gatherings. No Christmas lunches with the Hunters and the Lyles gathered round, pulling crackers and carving ham and dousing puds with brandy. No, none of that.'

Jayden nods. *Let's get out of here.*

'Thank you for seeing us,' says Ally, 'we won't keep you any longer—'

'Hunter got everything. Or near as damn it. Which was what he was always after from the off. Anyone sane could see that. Meeting that tart Helena just hurried it all along, didn't it? He had to do something. How could he exit the marriage but walk away with every last penny? Well, he found a way, didn't he?'

Sebastian blinks; wipes his eyes with the back of his hand.

'And now he's at it again,' he says. 'What does he stand to gain this time?'

46

Roland sits on the edge of the white-stone bath, inspecting his toe. After last night's run-in with the anchor, he wonders if it might in fact be broken; every time he tries to wriggle it, he yelps like a baby. It's insult to injury. And all the time that puny tourist was looking on. Roland feels a rush of fury – not just at his neighbour, who saw his wife in the nude and has a face that just asks to be punched – but at the whole damn world.

The police: they're on the list; useless, pathetic, waste of time.

Pascoe: senior and junior. The old crone because she was too proud or useless to get word to her jailbird grandson that she'd moved and was on her last legs. And the no-hoper who turned up at his door and started this whole thing off.

But most of all Helena. Don't even get him started on Helena. *You can run but you can't hide.* That's what he's thinking when he hears Nathan's footsteps in the corridor. And guess what? He's mad at his brother too.

'Nathan,' he calls out. 'Get in here.'

Nathan pokes his head around the door. 'We're a little old for bathtime together,' he says with a half-grin. 'I was thinking we should get some lunch. Anywhere decent for a Sunday roast round here?'

They rowed last night, when Roland limped back in from his neighbour's place. Mostly because Nathan had his 'I told you so' face on and, with everything else, Roland couldn't handle it. Helena had left him. *Well, of course that's the obvious explanation. That's why I was never worried*, Nathan said. *I had to let you get there on your own.* As if he were somehow in control of the whole thing. As if a PC Plod turning up on Roland's doorstep was Roland getting anywhere. Well, he's had about enough of Nathan now. And this pretence of a stay.

'Why did you even come here?' he says, trying to draw himself up to his full height, while avoiding putting weight on his toe. 'Because it sure as hell wasn't to view houses.'

Nathan lets out his bellow of a laugh. 'What are you talking about? Course it was.' He holds up his phone. 'Do you want to talk to Monty at Savills and check up on me?'

'You fixed your brake light because you had to. But other than that, you've hardly left the house since you got here.'

'Moral support. That phrase mean anything to you? No, thought not. Where were you when Clarissa left? Or Wendy?'

Roland narrows his eyes. He's deflecting: a classic Nathan move. 'Were you in on it?' he says. Because, frankly, he wouldn't put it past him.

'In on what?'

'Helena. Her little getaway plans. Did you help her?'

Nathan laughs again. 'Oh, brother, you really are losing it now.'

'Or did you needle her, push her over the edge to make her do it?'

'Total utter paranoia. Let me get you the number of a shrink . . .'

Roland takes a step forward and winces as his toe skims the ground. In response, Nathan squares his shoulders – and his eyes dare him. Roland has a sudden vision of the two of them rolling around together like lion cubs as kids, only the claws were out – and Nathan always ended up on top. Suddenly Roland doesn't care; the toe hurts to hell and back anyway, and so does his heart – what's more pain on top of that? He just wants to have at Nathan. And maybe it's the look on Roland's face – the pure, bristling intent – but his brother lifts his hands up in surrender.

'Helena never told me a damn thing, okay?' he says. 'She wouldn't have. She's never liked me. Honestly? You're better off without her. They're nothing but trouble, women.'

'Says the man who can't keep one.'

'And why would I want to? There's always more.' Nathan claps his hand on Roland's shoulder. 'Why don't we go out tonight, you and me, see what passes for totty around here?'

Roland presses a hand against the wall. He feels old, suddenly. Old and hurt and tired.

'Aren't you leaving? It's Monday tomorrow.'

'I'm a free agent. I told you, it's a long weekend.'

'Why did you come, Nathan?' he says levelly.

And maybe, just maybe, his brother will cut the crap for once.

'Because I wanted to get out of London.'

'You love London.'

'Yeah, well, London doesn't love me. Not my corner of it, anyway.' His hand passes across his mouth. 'HR have got their knickers in a twist. Some junior's trying to stir things up.' He flashes a grin but it's failing. 'I'm on a break.'

'Sacked?'

'As soon as anyone cries sexual harassment it's game over, mate. That's where we're at. It's ludicrous. Rigged.'

Roland feels a pulsing at his forehead. 'And did you?'

'Did I what?'

'Harass sexually?'

'Talk to me again about how you got together with your wife – sorry, ex-wife-to-be. Pulled her in a bar, wedding ring on your finger. What was that?'

'A good old-fashioned chat-up. And don't you call her my ex . . .'

'It's all six of one and half a dozen of the other, bro. Just depends on who's counting the eggs. And, right now, the people who appear to be counting the eggs are—'

The knock comes then. And Roland swears, of course he does, because he's caught off balance, and as his damn toe touches down pain jets up his leg and all the way to his balls. He cries out; bites his fist.

'Want me to get that?' says Nathan.

'I'll answer my own damn doorbell.'

As Roland hobbles from the bathroom, the knock comes again.

'Coming! For pity's sake, just wait,' he hurls back.

He takes the stairs gingerly. The bare heel of his injured foot smacking down despite himself, each impact sending reverberations through his body. That anchor was a health hazard and he'll report that too; serves whoever owns that little holiday hovel right.

He throws open the door, his face burnt red with effort.

'PC Mullins,' he practically growls. He exerted himself for this loser? 'What is it? Unless you've got her with you, I don't want what you're selling.'

Mullins gives a brief shake of his head. 'I wanted a chat, if that's alright with you.'

'A *chat*?'

'Sergeant Skinner plans to join us,' says Mullins, glancing down at his watch.

His cheeks flush red as he speaks, and he looks like an over-grown schoolboy, stuffed in just another uniform.

'Like I said,' Mullins goes on, taking off his hat and rubbing the back of his neck. 'Just a quick chat. Can I come in?'

Roland's about to say that there's nothing wrong with the door-step, but then he glances down towards All Swell and decides he doesn't need the audience. He abruptly turns around and Mullins follows him in, his cheap shoes clomping on the tiles.

'What happened to your foot?' asks Mullins.

'Tripped,' says Roland. 'Now, what did you want to *chat* about, Officer?'

Mullins scratches his head again. Roland watches as his eyes comb the room, taking in the sleek furniture, the chandelier, the light pouring in through the vast glass windows illuminating every inch of the square footage.

Well, let him look.

'I thought you were new to Porthpella when you had this place built,' says Mullins.

'I was. We were.'

'But you'd been here before, on holiday?'

'To Porthpella? No. More of a Maldives man. A Marbella man, at a push.'

'I don't mean recently. Like, twenty years ago. On a stag weekend, wasn't it?'

'Who have you been talking to?'

'Your brother mentioned it.'

'I mentioned what?' says Nathan, sauntering into the room.

He stands by the fireplace, posturing as if he's lord of the manor. But he came here on a lie. Lost his job. And, what, now he's been pointlessly stirring things up with the police?

'Your stag weekend to Porthpella, sir,' says Mullins.

'Oh, that. Yeah, it was a good laugh.'

Roland stares hard at Nathan. He wants him gone. 'It was a lifetime ago. And it was Newquay. Why are you—'

'There was a beer festival, and your group came to Porthpella,' says Mullins.

'Did we? I honestly can't remember,' says Roland. 'Believe it or not, Officer, Porthpella's not the centre of anyone's universe. Though I appreciate that's an unpopular opinion in this neck of the woods.'

'But you'd remember if you'd been before, wouldn't you? If you then went and had a house built here?'

Roland's head is starting to ache: a dull thud, in comparison to the piercing sensation in his toe. He can feel the fight ebbing out of him. He wants to sit down, but if he sits down then Mullins will take it as an invitation to do the same, and he's damned if he's going to let him and his substantial rear end get comfortable.

'We did come, as it happens,' says Nathan. 'Like you said though, it was twenty years ago. And it was a stag. Therefore, as is tradition, we were drunk for most of it.'

'There was a beer festival at The Wreckers Arms,' says Mullins, 'and one of your group got into a fight with a member of staff.'

'A fight? I can't remember that, can you, Roly? But then I refer you to my previous point. It was a stag. There were drinks.'

'It was Paul Pascoe. The member of staff. And he lost his job over it.'

Roland leans back against the counter. Glares at Mullins.

'Paul Pascoe was Lewis's dad,' says Mullins.

'What, the kid who tried to kill himself?' says Nathan.

'Yeah, yeah, whatever point you're trying to make, Officer,' says Roland, 'stop this pussyfooting around and get on with it. It's embarrassing. Not to mention time-wasting.'

Mullins purses his lips. Roland sees a flash of uncertainty – and seizes on it.

'Or is that the point? That there is no point?' He grins, and he feels his dry lips crack. 'Neither of us remembers the incident in question, Officer Mullins, because quite honestly it was inconsequential. Men go out. Men drink. Men fight. If one of those men happened to be Peter Pascoe . . .'

'Paul – and he wasn't drinking. He was working. He was doing his job. And your group were rowdy, causing trouble. He tried to put a stop to it, and—'

'And was then sacked for his trouble?' says Roland. 'Sounds like he was a valued member of staff. A regular employee of the month.'

Nathan gives a snort of laughter.

'A week later he killed himself,' says PC Mullins. 'He jumped from the same cliff where we found Lewis.'

Roland shakes his head. 'And what does any of this have to do with me? With us? You think I'm going to remember some casual worker in a pub? Sorry, but that's just not going to happen. What about you, Nathan? Any of this ring any bells?'

'Absolute bell-free zone,' says Nathan.

'There you go, Officer. Paul Pascoe means nothing to us. *Less* than nothing.'

'Less than nothing?' repeats Mullins.

'The name, I mean,' says Roland.

'He means the name,' chimes in Nathan.

And Nathan's looking like he's enjoying this just a little bit too much. Because it's all a game to him; a diversion from his own substantial troubles.

'Look,' says Roland. 'Helena said she'd always dreamt of living by the sea. And so I made that happen. Picking this place was like sticking a pin in a map. Who cares? The sea is the sea is the sea. Did I remember I'd been here before? No. Do I now? Yeah. Okay. Just. Do I remember the fight you're talking about? No. I was drunk. My brother here was drunk. All of our friends were drunk. Do I feel guilty that, a week later, someone who worked in a bar that we happened to go into, decided to step off the edge of a cliff? No. Not a bit. Do I feel responsible for the actions of my friends, in case one of them somehow may or may not have contributed in some miniscule and unprovable way to the man in question's eventual – and might I say self-inflicted – demise? No again.'

Mullins blinks.

'I think we're done here, don't you?' says Roland, pleased with himself for the first time in days. 'Unless you have something useful to tell me about my wife?'

Anger surges again as he says it. Do they know where Helena is? Well, he'll be damned if he's going to beg. He looks at Mullins's wide ears and thinks how he'd like to grab him by them and pull – hard as you like.

'Thought not. So, thank you for your visit, Officer Mullins. We're done.'

As he closes the door on him, Roland hears a slow hand clap.

'Well played at the end there, brother. Nicely done.'

'Pack your bags. I want you gone too.'

'What?'

'You heard.'

Maybe some people in Roland's situation would want the company, someone to get drunk with and put their busted world to rights. Not him though.

'But . . .' Nathan hesitates, his face serious suddenly. 'You might need me.'

And that gives Roland his first proper laugh in a good few days. Need Nathan? As if.

47

'Victoria's brother really had nothing to give us, did he?' says Jayden.

'No,' says Ally. 'I don't think he did. He just wanted to be heard.'

They're driving fast over the moors with the windows down. It felt so good to step outside of Sebastian's cottage, back into the sunlight and the lane and the greenness of the trees. The visit to Sebastian has left Ally feeling slightly outside of herself, in a way she can't quite describe.

'Imagine if he knew that that alibi of Helena's was false,' says Jayden.

'Don't,' says Ally. 'I've been thinking the same thing.'

Sebastian Lyle seemed to be a man who was burnt out. But as they left, Ally saw the embers glowing in him – and she realised then that they wouldn't take much to catch light. Holding the knowledge of Helena and her alibi inside her had felt like a physical weight to Ally. What a relief it was to climb inside the car and slam the door and be away.

'He made me uncomfortable,' she admits. 'Or rather, the situation did. I suppose it's something you have to get used to in the police? Entering people's lives, and then exiting them again. Seeing them at their lowest and then just . . . leaving them to it. Did you ever struggle with that part of it?'

'Sometimes,' says Jayden. 'But you just had to do the best you could do, you know? No one signs up for the easy life. What about Bill? How did he manage it, all those years? The balance, I mean.'

'Well, Bill was pragmatic,' she says. 'Not one of life's worriers. When Evie used to get in a tizz about something, he'd just say very calmly that there was no use worrying about it – and he was right. I think that was how he approached all things, including his job.'

Except for the Pascoe family. He'd worried about them.

'I wanted to feel sorry for Sebastian,' says Jayden, 'and I kind of did. But the way he talked about his sister . . . man, that was cold.'

'I think his anger at Roland is so huge that it's twisted everything. Don't you? And he has such a bee in his bonnet about the money side of things.'

'A bee in his bonnet? A swarm, more like. Okay, so Helena and Victoria are two different-looking people. But it's a mean observation to make. And no kind of evidence.'

'I agree,' says Ally.

'The way he lives, it doesn't look like there's a lot of cash about. That's going to play into it too, right? The bitterness? There's Roland, muscling in on the family fortune. If there ever actually was one. I'm not sure I believe a thing he said, Al.'

'It can't just be sour grapes, can it?'

'I don't know,' says Jayden. 'People are weird about money, right?'

As Ally drives, she feels the pull of the sea, drawing her onwards. She misses it; even when she's away for just one day, she misses it. But going home to Porthpella feels like the end of the road with this case. Almost. And she can't bear the thought of that. What are they supposed to do after? Wait and hope with Lewis? While all the time Roland lives happily in the dunes. She turns something over in her mind.

'Jayden, I might have something.'

'Go on.'

'What if we make some phone calls? Contact all the solicitors we can find within a certain range of Godalming, and ask if a Victoria Hunter ever made any enquiries about divorce? If there is evidence that Victoria did know about the affair, and had been looking to end the marriage, that would be something to take to the police, wouldn't it? Put together with Helena's false alibi.'

'Maybe it would,' says Jayden, 'but it's not going to fly, Al.'

'What, you don't think it'd be enough to reopen the case?'

'There's no way solicitors would give up that kind of confidential information. Even the police would need a warrant.'

'Even if we asked them nicely?' says Ally.

'No way. To be honest, I couldn't believe the guy in the gallery gave you Fiona's details just like that. That's a breach of confidentiality, right there.'

Ally grips the wheel a little tighter. 'Ah,' she says. 'He didn't exactly—'

Jayden swivels in his seat. 'Do I want to know this?'

'Probably not. I just thought, well, it's plausible that I might have known where Fiona lived. I mean, it is a small world down here, in a lot of ways.'

'Yeah, okay,' says Jayden, in a voice that says he doesn't want to hear any more. She glances sideways at him, sees him rub his face with his hands. 'I think maybe this thing has run its course, Al. I think maybe we should get back to our day jobs. Or whatever.'

But she doesn't want to give up on this line of thought. She doesn't want to give up at all.

'Would it have been done at the time of the investigation, do you think? Contacting the solicitors, I mean?'

'I don't know. But if it was, it didn't turn up anything significant, or I reckon Fatima would have said. It would've been in the file.'

'Because Roland had an alibi. So the divorce factor wasn't relevant.'

'Exactly. The alibi.'

Ally sighs heavily. 'I think we both know that, objectively speaking, there's nothing to say Roland wasn't beside Helena in bed all night. Not if she was knocked out by pills. Is there?'

'Nope.'

'But I believed her, Jayden. Didn't you? I believed that she's afraid of her husband. And that she thinks him capable of murder.'

'People can escalate things. Especially if they're anxious. Small, everyday things can take on a completely different shape.'

'You think she's got it all wrong?'

'Yeah, I'm not saying that, but it's a possibility. It's *all* just possibility at this point. But . . . let's say that Helena had a gut feeling. And then you come along, and you're clear-sighted, and you have a gut feeling too . . . so you trust her, and what she's saying. That's okay, that can be enough to justify a line of enquiry. But then you've got to find the evidence. And make sure it's admissible when you do. So, stuff like breaches of confidentiality . . .'

'You're right. I'm sorry, I really didn't . . .'

And she doesn't know what else to say. Maybe it is the end of the road.

They drive on, and the silence feels flat, defeated. Eventually the sea appears on the horizon, and they move towards it.

48

Saffron is sitting on the terrace, her feet resting on the wooden balustrade, the sun on her face. It's been a quiet day so far. And a day where she's been, she has to admit, a little on edge. Every time the café door has opened, she's expected to see Roland Hunter or his wannabe-surfer brother. She's worrying about nothing probably, but they just seem like the kind of men to follow up on a thing; whatever that thing is.

Enough people do stupid stuff when they're drunk, she can't exactly hold that stag weekend against them, but Wenna's story has lodged in her head and she can't shake it out. Even after a night at home with the girls, with the Thai curry, the beers, the mucking about on their garden skate ramp, it's still there. The fact is, Paul Pascoe's last week on earth included the Hunter brothers. And what if losing his job was the final straw? Maybe it isn't that simple, but Wenna reckoned the landlord of the Wreckers at the time had definitely felt the weight of guilt.

Now that Helena has been found, it's this thought that nags at Saffron. It was too sad, that you couldn't all look out for each other, especially in a little place like this.

She had her usual early surf crowd this morning, and most didn't notice she was anything other than the usual chirrupy Saffron. But when she passed Broady his coconut flat white, he said, *Hey, you okay, babe?* She turned on a grin, said, *I'm always okay.*

Afterwards she regretted it. She didn't want to just kick about in the shallows, not with Broady.

She spots a figure down on the sand and realises it's Mullins – trudging, head down.

'Mullins!' she calls out, and waves.

Okay, so now she's willingly drawing Mullins into Hang Ten. She must be desperate.

'Patrolling the rock pools?' she says, as he comes up to the deck.

He really needs to sort his walk out, she thinks; there's no energy or authority in it. Or maybe he just doesn't spend that much time down on the beach. She can't quite imagine him in board shorts, the sun on his back. Or, more accurately, she doesn't want to. It's an uncharitable thought, and she knows this. Why is her sympathy boundless for some, and barely existent for others? Because it's about power. The powerful can look after themselves. And as much as she suspects Mullins is full of bluster – maybe he's nothing but a lost little boy under all that show – he's still one of the powerful.

But she doesn't know what's going on in his head either. She has to remember that.

'Haha, yeah, yeah, Saff. Sting operation on a bunch of jellyfish. You seen Ally Bright today?'

Saffron shakes her head, thinking, *That was quite good for Mullins.*

'Why are you looking for Ally? Is she okay?'

'I reckon so.'

'What about the thing with the Hunters?' says Saffron. 'Have you looked into it?'

'Ah, yeah.' He rubs the back of his neck. 'Nothing to report there, Saff. Just a coincidence. We spoke to both the brothers and they were here, sure enough. They could remember one of their mates rubbing a bloke up the wrong way, and that would have been Paul Pascoe alright. But that's it. They had no clue who he even was.'

'So, there's no connection?'

Saffron realises she's disappointed, and by the look of him, so is Mullins. But isn't it better this way, that Roland Hunter had no idea who Lewis's dad was when Lewis came calling at Sea Dream? That when he bought Maggie's house, he was just another out-of-towner snagging a piece of beachfront real estate? Less sinister, for sure.

Mullins sniffs the air like a dog. 'Is that a fresh batch?'

'Maybe.' She rolls her eyes. But there is something quite nice about predictability – especially when other things are unpredictable. But then she pushes back her shoulders. 'Brownies for public servants are at the discretion of the management.'

Mullins looks confused.

'That's me, by the way,' says Saffron, folding her arms, a grin at her lips. 'The management. You're the servant. So, what, there's nothing else to be done about Lewis?'

'Not until he wakes up,' he says, '*if* he wakes up. I called the hospital for an update earlier – there isn't one.' He stuffs his hands in his pockets, rocks on his heels. Then says in a voice that's so quiet you'd almost miss it, 'I'm starting to feel a little bit sorry for Lewis Pascoe.'

'Jeez, Tim. Better late than never.'

'It was talking to Roland Hunter,' he says, louder now. 'Seeing how he doesn't care at all. And I reckon a lot of the reason he doesn't care is because of who Lewis is. And who his dad was.' He shoots a careful look at her, then kicks out at the sand. 'Like their lives are worth less than his, you know?'

'Yeah, I do know,' she says. 'In fact, I think you've got it in one. Question is, what are we going to do about it?'

49

It's early evening by the time they're back in Porthpella. The beach is filled with a golden, almost neon, glow: a sharp contrast to the dark clouds looming on the horizon. Fox leaps from the car and darts across the garden; lifts his leg by the palm. As they walk up to the house Ally notices a line of seagulls on the roof: a sign of a storm coming.

She turns her phone in her hand. 'Three missed calls. I really should return them. Or they'll be sending the helicopters out for me too.'

'What will you say though?' says Jayden. He lopes up the steps and un-fixes a note from the door. Passes it to her. 'Looks like they've been here too.'

Mrs Bright, please contact us as soon as possible. It's important. PC Mullins.

'Well, I can't lie,' says Ally. 'Not if they ask me directly.'

'No.'

'So . . . I think it's better to say nothing. Under the circumstances. And then tomorrow, go and see Helena again. Me, I mean. I know not you.'

Jayden looks down. 'It's just because of Cat. I promised her I'd only do one day.'

And in that look, Ally sees the conflict in Jayden. He's trying to do the right thing. But the right thing by who? She suddenly wonders if she's keeping him.

'Did you want to get going now?' she says.

'Hey, it's not midnight yet, Al. I'm still pre-pumpkin.'

She smiles. 'Okay, well, what I'm thinking is that we need to find a way to persuade Helena to come forward regardless.'

'But there's nothing else to try. If Victoria Hunter was sounding out divorce lawyers, then yeah, that's relevant. But there's no way you and I can find that out. Hey, is there coffee going? Can I get the kettle on?'

'There's always coffee going,' she says. 'Or there's some wine open?'

'Tempting,' says Jayden, 'but coffee's good.'

She thinks of telling Jayden about her impromptu visitor yesterday evening, but what is there to say, really? Although it was Gus who gave her the idea of following up the divorce line. The idea that felt at the time like a lead – but now doesn't.

God, listen to you, Ally. You're not Bill.

Jayden sinks down in a chair. 'Ally . . . maybe this is where we both have to call it a day.'

Ally's spooning coffee grounds and her hand shakes, spilling them on the counter. She doesn't want to stop – that's the trouble. But she says, 'I've a horrible feeling you're right.' Then, 'Was it even real, what we were doing?'

'Damn right it was. The look on Helena's face as she told us what she thought about Roland was real,' he says. 'And knowing Lewis is still in Intensive Care. That's real.'

'Yes. And then today, seeing those photographs of Victoria, witnessing how troubled her brother is by her death still . . .'

'Very real.'

'But the fact that we're looking into it,' says Ally, 'that's what I mean. And the fact that we haven't got anywhere.'

271

'Apart from finding Helena, you mean?'

Ally offers the biscuit tin and Jayden stares into it.

'You're right. I don't know if I've earned a ginger nut,' he says.

'Take two.'

'Ally, a week ago, if someone told you that this is what you'd be doing, what would you have said?'

She thinks. It feels like the answer she gives will matter. When she and Bill used to chat about his work, she knew there was a lot that he didn't say too – and she never pushed it. When Evie was at home that was probably the right thing to do and after she left, it was as if the rhythms were set. *When the uniform's off*, Bill used to say, *I like to switch off too*. But she knew that wasn't really true, because he was always ready to serve his community. He left enough dinners halfway through, or rolled out of bed in the dark enough times, for Ally to know he was never truly off duty.

What is she doing here, exactly? Trying to take up his mantle? Fulfilling a promise that he'd made? Or, maybe, exercising a muscle that she didn't even know she had.

'Well, Jayden,' she says. 'The truth is, it doesn't feel half as strange as it probably should.'

'Yeah, I'll second that,' he says.

She takes a sip of coffee. Already, it feels like so much has changed.

Last night, as Gus left The Shell House, there was the suggestion that they might do it again some time. She can't remember who it first came from, or quite how long it hung in the air for, or whether, in fact, it was even spoken out loud at all – all she knows is that the thought of it is rather nice. But, of course, Gus will be gone soon. What did he say, three weeks left on the lease? The beach will fill with holidaymakers, and he'll go back to his ordinary life. And she'll be left with hers. Whatever that looks like.

Evie and her entreaties. Those words that ring on in her head: *There's nothing there for you anymore, Mum.* She told Jayden about Australia in the car and he looked disappointed – said, *But you're my only mate here!* But then went on to talk with such animation about year-round sunshine that it sounded like he was almost trying to sell it to her.

'What I do know,' she says, 'is that I want very much to see it through. It feels simple to me, in a way. A wrong, or several wrongs, need to be righted. So, why not us, if we're the ones being trusted with it?'

Jayden sits forward in his chair. His face looks grave.

'But this isn't about what's happening on our doorstep anymore, Al. It's about Surrey. And Somerset. And it feels too big.'

'It's about Lewis not having anyone. And Helena being too frightened to do the right thing. And they're on our doorstep.'

Jayden puffs out his cheeks. And she knows he feels, at least in part, the same.

'I think you would have made a really good detective, you know,' he says. 'Once we'd schooled you on the rules and regs, anyway. Better than a bunch of the people I worked with back in Leeds, that's for sure.'

She doesn't feel much like laughing, but she does laugh at that. 'I very much doubt it. And I did note your use of the past tense, by the way.' Then, 'It's not too late for you, though. You could do anything you wanted.'

Jayden shakes his head. 'Today's a one-off. Just . . . I wish we'd done more with it. Going all that way to see Sebastian, and for what?'

'We had to try.'

'But if there'd been any proper evidence, he wouldn't exactly have been sitting on it, would he?'

'It's like you said to Fiona, sometimes people don't realise the significance of things,' she says. 'It was worth trying. And the day's not over yet, is it? There must be something else we can do. Something else that we can take to Helena to convince her to come forward to the police.'

But as she picks up and puts down her reading glasses, she can't think of a single thing. Outside, rain pitter-patters against the darkening window. As dusk rolls in early, the sea sounds closer.

'Okay, here's an idea,' says Jayden. 'And it's back on your divorce line. Cold-calling solicitors is out, but what about we check in with Sebastian and see what firm their family used? We don't want to get him riled up again, but maybe he could sound them out for us – that might get around the confidentiality issue . . .' He loses steam. 'Though if Victoria was a separate client, then it's still going to be a problem.'

'I think it's worth a try,' says Ally.

Sebastian seemed so scattered that he might not have thought to ask the most basic questions. She picks up her phone, scrolls through the numbers.

It's answered on the second ring. But for two, three beats, no one speaks. Then at last Sebastian says, 'Yes, hello?'

It's a snappish voice, fraught with impatience.

She's momentarily thrown off course, but then quickly rights herself. 'Sebastian. It's Ally Bright. From this morning. I just wanted to—'

'Can't talk now.'

And the phone cuts off.

Jayden's watching, his eyebrows raised. 'Short and sweet, Al.'

She turns the phone in her hand.

'What is it? What's wrong?' says Jayden.

'Seagulls,' says Ally. 'There were seagulls in the background.'

50

Roland lies on the red leather sofa, his leg hoisted up on a cushion. He's wallowing but who cares? There's no one here to see. He takes another slug of whisky. Swills it round his mouth before swallowing.

The room's over-lit, because he doesn't know the configuration of spotlights they usually have in the evening. That's a Helena thing. He closes his eyes against the glare.

The idiotic Mullins took him right back with his questions, dredging up blurred memories of that stag. He can't remember where they stayed, or where they partied, but he can feel the clammy confines of that red cow suit like it was yesterday, his head uncomfortably close to his brother's rear end. Well, they were young and stupid. Plus, he and his brother got on slightly better in those days. Roland was poorer and Nathan was richer – and obviously that was the way Nathan liked it.

He takes another hefty slug of whisky. What is his life now, if this thing with Helena is actually permanent? He hates his head for throwing up that stupid question, because the truth is, he loves her. Sure, his temper gets the better of him sometimes, but she's maddening. They all are, aren't they? Women. And it's the way he's built. His old dad was the same. It's never taken much to press a Hunter man's buttons. It isn't like he really means it, is it?

Thoughts of the stag rear up in his drunken memory again. That was all well before Victoria. She turned out to be his pot of gold at the end of the rainbow – eventually. Life moves in mysterious ways. Sometimes it does feel like the universe has a plan for him. The way it ended with Victoria – the way it ended *for* Victoria – was a terrible thing. But if you look on the bright side – and you have to, don't you? – it saved a lot of mess and pain on the Helena front. Not that he'd admit that to anyone; he isn't that callous. Or that stupid. But Nathan saw it. He ribbed him over it, at the time: *Made things very easy for the pair of you, didn't it? And, of course, all that money . . .*

Whatever other thoughts are rattling about in his head, Roland's pretty sure that Helena will come snivelling back. In no time at all, probably, because what is she without him? Nothing. Again, he hears Nathan piping up: *Actually, she's fifty per cent of your assets, mate.* To which Roland had smirked his response: *Two words, big brother: pre-nup.*

Every penny that Roland gained from his marriage to Victoria he earned fair and square, to his mind. And Helena won't be getting her manicured little hands on any of it.

His phone pings with a message and he makes a grab for it. His hand slips – whisky fingers – and the phone clatters to the floor. He retrieves it, cussing.

When he sees Nathan's name flashing up instead of Helena's, he snarls. He opens the message, bitterness stinging the insides of his mouth.

Little brother. Helena will see sense. And if she doesn't, you'll still come out on top. You always do.

Is that a jibe?

You're right about that, taps out Roland in reply. Hunters are winners.

His finger hovers for a moment, then he hits Send. There's nothing more to say. Nathan can go home to his own mess and leave Roland to sort out his. It was the right thing to do, telling him to go. He laughs humourlessly, thinking of Nathan's suggestion that he might need him around. That guy as a shoulder to cry on? Not likely.

Roland picks up his glass but it's empty. He grabs the bottle from beside the sofa and is sloshing the glass full to the brim again when the doorbell rings. The sound of it cutting through the silence of the room makes his heart jump.

Is it?

It has to be.

He takes another quick drink, then gets to his feet. The room spins, and when his toe touches the ground his vision fizzes. But he makes his way over to the door as quickly as he can, wincing with every step. He's still not sure how he'll react when he's face-to-face with Helena. Frankly, it could go either way. But then it always could, couldn't it? He throws the door wide.

And his mouth drops open. Standing there on his doorstep is the last person he ever expected.

51

'But Sebastian would have had to leave right after we did,' says Jayden.

'What if he did?'

Outside, the rain has started coming down harder. It sounds like handfuls of shale thrown against the pane.

Jayden just can't see it. 'But why? Why now?'

'Because we shook him up,' says Ally, on her feet. She moves to the window and stands silhouetted, looking out at the rapidly blackening sky. 'We brought it all back to the present. What if we got this wrong? Rushing in with our questions. As we left, he just had this look in his eye . . . did you notice it? I didn't like it, I felt . . . like we'd started something up again for him.'

'What, and you think he's come down to confront Roland?'

'We never said we were from Porthpella,' says Ally, her hand going to her head. 'We never mentioned Sea Dream. Did we?'

'No,' says Jayden. 'Definitely not. But . . . he'd seen Helena on the news. He knew the Hunters lived in Porthpella.' He sees the look on her face, and quickly adjusts. 'But look, he could have just driven out to the coast. Any coast. Somerset has coast, right? Hell, it could even have been the TV on in the background. Okay, okay, maybe not the TV. But there's nothing to say he's come to see Roland Hunter. There's nothing to say that Lyle's in Cornwall.'

'No, you're right.'

But still. Jayden thinks of Sebastian as they left, and the look in his eye that Ally described. Had they re-awoken something? Were they a match-strike?

Once, in the early days of the job, he'd been called to an estate where a group of kids had set fire to a car. It was blazing when he turned up, flames as tall as a house, and the kids scattered. But they didn't get far, and Jayden remembers their scared white faces. They said they hadn't thought it'd go up like that, not in a million years. It isn't a particularly helpful memory. But he does remember how cool and calm Kieran was; and how kind he was to the older boy, the one with the burns all the way up his arm. And, for once, the thought of Kieran is centring.

Jayden gets up, joins her at the window. He can feel Fox twining round his legs. Outside, the palm in Ally's garden is swaying, its fronds outlined eerily. He squeezes her shoulder.

'Let's think, Al. Let's see it from Sebastian's perspective. For years he's thought that the man who killed his sister got away with it. And all that time no one else believed him. And then we turn up out of the blue. And we listen to him, you know? It doesn't even matter to him who we are – do you remember, how confused he was? He talks anyway. He's seen the news about Helena and thinks it's happening all over again: Hunter getting away with it. He said he didn't believe she'd really been found safe, didn't he? Maybe . . .'

'Maybe what Jayden?'

Ally's turned to face him. She's lifted Fox up into her arms and suddenly she looks older, smaller.

'Maybe he wants to do something about it. I don't know what, but . . . maybe Helena's disappearance triggered memories of Victoria.'

'I didn't anticipate this,' says Ally, 'not for one second. If I'd thought . . .'

'But that's all just guesswork from me, Al. One possible reaction, out of, like, hundreds. Look, why don't we phone the guy at the house by Sea Dream. Gus. He's been helpful, right? Get him to keep an eye out. Neighbourhood-watch vibes.'

'And look for what? He'll think we're mad.'

'A tall blond stranger from Somerset on the approach.' Jayden gives a low laugh. 'Al, seriously. Maybe we are mad. There are about a thousand seagulls on the British coastline. No, a million. There's no way you can tell that was a Porthpella gull.' He stops, waits for her smile. But it doesn't come. He adds, 'Or we could always go down there ourselves?'

'I don't want to be seen by Roland Hunter. Not right now.'

And he thinks how flustered she looks; how un-Ally-like.

'Okay, so let's phone your buddy Gus.'

'Jayden, I can't help feeling that any meeting between Roland and Sebastian is going to end badly. Gus said Roland's blood's up, he's spoiling for a fight. Sebastian will have no idea what he's walking into . . .'

'The brother's there too, remember. He'll calm it down, if anything kicks off.'

But Jayden reckons he's probably being optimistic here. After all, he knows nothing about Nathan Hunter.

52

Gus attempts to roll up the starfish-patterned blind – like everything else in All Swell it has an oceanic twist – but the cord is caught, and it won't budge. He still closes the blinds every day at dusk, a force of habit from when Helena stood at her window, and now he's ruing it. He tugs with both hands and it releases at last. Picking up his phone, he cranes forward, breath misting the window.

'I can't see anything,' he says. 'The lights are on but . . . wait, there is another car. I don't think it's Roland's.'

'What kind of car?' says Ally, and there's a sense of importance in her voice that he rises to.

'A small car. Hold on, let me get my binoculars.'

'Or you could pop out and look?'

'Oh yes. Yes, I could.'

Idiot that I am.

He hears someone say something in the background to Ally, and then she's asking, 'Is it an old VW Polo? A black one?'

'It could be. It's definitely dark. I'm going out to look.'

Gus hurries down the stairs. He doesn't have a single clue what all this is about, but the sense of urgency is palpable. Later he'll admit that he was disappointed when he realised Ally was only phoning him for surveillance duties, but beggars can't be choosers and really, it's nice to have the interruption, isn't it? He left The

Shell House yesterday evening feeling like the visit was one of his best decisions in years. He didn't often applaud his own efforts, but the quiet sense of pleasure he experienced afterwards was something to be noted.

'Be careful, Gus,' Ally says now.

Such a simple thing to say, throwaway really. And yet.

He pauses in the porch to pull on his shoes and grab his anorak. The rain on the flat roof sounds thunderous, and he pulls up his hood. It takes a minute for his eyes to adjust to the gloom outside. Evening has rolled in early, on the coat-tails of a drenching sea mist, and the tide's up too, bringing with it a sharp wind. Altogether it's an assault, especially after the cosy interior of the house, but tonight he welcomes it. He ducks his head as he moves towards the lights of Sea Dream.

'Are you still there?' he whispers into the phone.

'We're here,' says Ally.

'I'm close,' says Gus. 'Hang on. Yep.' He holds his phone up to the badge on the car, and it lights up the VW.

'Affirmative,' he says, 'VW Polo. A knackered one, by the looks of it. Hang on.'

He looks at the number plate, his hood flapping. Cold water trickles down his ear as he holds the light of the phone close to the car again.

'Timpson's of Somerset. There's an old garage sticker I can just make out.'

'Jayden, it's him,' says Ally.

'Him who?' says Gus. And as he's straightening up, he hears a shout. He catches it over the swell of the sea, over whatever Ally's saying in the background to Jayden, over the rush of wind through the tall grass. *A shout.*

'Did you hear that?' he says. 'That shout? There was a shout.'

'What, from the house?'

'From the house. I'm certain of it. Or thereabouts. I . . .'

'Okay,' says Ally, 'Gus, go back indoors. Can you call the police?'

Another shout rings out, and Gus backs away, his feet sinking in the wet grass. 'The police. Right. Okay. What am I saying to them? That there's a disturbance?'

He suddenly wonders if he should be volunteering to knock – if that was what Ally really wants of him – but he's now had a total of two doorstep encounters with Roland Hunter and neither went well. He's really not keen for a third.

'Or I could always knock . . .' he begins.

'No,' says Ally, 'no, don't do that. Yes, report a disturbance. And . . .' She breaks off, and he hears a muffled conversation in the background. Hears, 'No, Jayden. No, you mustn't.'

'Ally?' says Gus.

'Jayden's coming,' she says. 'We both are. And Gus, hurry up and make that call.'

53

Something clicks in Jayden as the car bumps down the track: muscle memory. Front-line response was what he did. Ally's driving as fast as conditions allow. The windscreen wipers squeak, the rain lashes down. A seabird swoops low, illuminated by their headlights, and they miss it by a fraction.

'What do we do when we get there?' she says.

He looks across at her: his partner, gripping the wheel in full concentration.

'Assess the situation,' says Jayden, his voice calm. 'We'll be there before the police.'

'Which means?'

'Knock on the door. Defuse it. Distract. I don't think Roland knows who I am.'

'But Sebastian does.'

'All we can do is make something up on the spot. Then, when the police come . . . they can handle whatever there is to handle.'

'Whatever Sebastian's here for, he's walking into the lion's den. I'm afraid for him, Jayden.'

'Yeah,' says Jayden. 'I'm with you on that.'

And he feels the surge as she puts her foot down.

In the distance, Sea Dream burns with light; an alien spacecraft landed in the dunes. As they get closer, the huge plate-glass windows reveal the interior like it's a stage set.

'Okay, Al, you stay in the car,' says Jayden. 'Or head to Gus's place.'

'No,' says Ally. 'I'm with you.'

Jayden cranes to see. From here, the inside of the house looks deserted, but the men could be deeper inside. He jumps from the car and hears the click of Ally's door.

'Ally, seriously. I've got this. You stay well back.'

The outside lights of the house flick on automatically as Jayden draws closer. The rain comes down like needles and he puts his hand up to shield his eyes, squints through it.

The front door is wide open. Never a good sign.

A shout comes then – a friendly one, but nevertheless it's shot through with alarm. 'They went that way!'

A man he presumes is Gus is making his way towards them. His arms are thrown wide and his coat flaps like a sail in the wind.

'They went over the dunes! A minute ago, less!'

He catches Jayden's arm, speaks breathlessly. 'The police are coming. But . . . he had a knife.'

'Oh God,' says Ally, her hand to her mouth.

'Okay,' says Jayden, and he gestures for Gus's torch. 'Give me that. And stay with Ally. Gus, how many people? Was the brother there too?'

'The brother? No, just Roland. Roland and this other man . . . the one with the knife. And Roland was all over the place. Drunk, I think. He couldn't walk properly.'

'Wait, what? So, it's not Roland with the knife?'

'No! No, Roland's the one being chased. I should have stepped in, I should have . . . But he's a madman, this other one, he's . . .'

Jayden thinks of the Sebastian they saw at his house; he was prickly, bitter and erratic. Erratic could be scary. Erratic with a knife is a whole different level of scary.

He can feel Ally looking at him meaningfully – and he knows what she's thinking. Hell, it's what he's thinking. But he meant it when he said *I've got this*. And he means it still.

'Which way did they go, Gus?'

Gus points off into the blackness.

'Jayden, wait for the police,' says Ally, 'please, you must—'

'I've got to go, Al,' he says.

'Then I'm coming with you.'

'You're not.'

Ally opens her mouth to protest, but then nods. He can see the tears in her eyes. Jayden squeezes her arm; mouths, *It's okay*.

Then he's away and moving, the puny beam of the torch bouncing over the dunes. He scrambles up and over, his feet slipping in the sand. At the top of a dune he stands, turns, listens; tries to get the wind out of his ears. It's raucous up here: the tide is high, throwing itself at the beach, a rush and fizz of water. He can feel the strength of it, the black body of water beyond. The Porthpella he knows is gone, and in its place is a wild and wicked place; one made of pure elements. He turns, trying to orientate himself and shake the glaring, corrupting lights of Sea Dream from his vision. He looks into the darkness, finding his focus. They could be anywhere, the two men, but losing them is not an option. It's clarifying, this thought, and the thunder of his heart in his chest just makes him all the more certain.

And he's recalibrating his perceptions: Roland as prey, not hunter. It's Sebastian with the knife.

As Jayden listens hard through the roar of wind and water, he hears a faint shout. He can't tell the exact direction, but he strikes off, trusting his gut. He pauses, listens again. Catches the sound of another cry – no more than a wisp, but he follows it. And he's moving on instinct now – that's what this is – the body taking over, the mind following close. He slithers and skids, up and down, up and down, tall grass sweeping his thighs, his feet catching in holes and sudden drops. As he crests another dune, he hears a sharper cry, and his adrenalin surges. He's close.

With the slam of the sea and the tilt of the ground, it's like he's on the edge of the earth – the rim of the planet – as it spins through space. But he holds on. Looks hard.

Then he sees them, the outlines of two men.

'Hey!' he shouts, moving towards them. 'Hey, stop!'

He immediately recognises the skinny frame of Sebastian, his shock of blond hair bright in the torchlight. Hunter opposite him. They're circling each other, an ill-matched pair. Hunter's limping, already carrying an injury, though whether it's from Sebastian, Jayden can't tell.

'Stop!' Jayden yells again, with more authority this time. His voice cuts through the sound of the sea, the whistling in the grass, the roar of the wind. 'Put the knife down!'

'Help!' Hunter squeals. 'Help me!'

Gus said Roland was drunk, and it's there in the high shriek of his voice, his stumbling movements. Drunk and terrified. Perhaps, on any other day, Roland might easily have seen off a man like Sebastian: slammed the door in his face, or punched him to the ground or, if it had still got this far, sprinted ahead of him to safety. But not today. Not tonight. It's as if Sebastian has him on a string and he's toying with him: yanking him back and forward, enjoying his fear.

And when Jayden's torch passes over the pair of them, he sees the glint of metal in Sebastian's hand.

Ally was right: their visit wound Sebastian up, reignited the old pain. It's on them. Which means it's on them to fix it.

Jayden quickly calculates; he knows his play. He sprints forward, launching himself from the dune. But as he lands, the sand disappears – and he feels his ankle give way beneath him. It twists sharply, pain slicing through him. He stumbles on to his knees, plants his palms on the ground as his ankle burns white-hot.

This is not the play.

Jayden looks up, teeth gritted. 'Drop the knife,' he shouts. 'Drop it now.'

Sebastian spins round, eyes tracking over him. He half smiles. 'I know you. You came to see me. You and your lady friend.' Then, in a voice that's pure steel, 'This is what happens, you see. This is what we do when we're pushed.'

'Sebastian, it doesn't have to be,' says Jayden. He winds his hand round tall grasses and hauls himself back up to his feet, feeling a swell of nausea at the effort. He takes a limping step forward. 'Sebastian, just give me the knife. It's okay. It's over. Give it to me.'

'Look at that despicable man over there,' says Sebastian, jabbing the air with his blade. 'Just look at him. And he still thinks he's getting away with it.'

'Getting away with it?' hurls Roland, his hands thrown up. Even in the dim light Jayden can see the fear splashed across Roland's face, the slur of his words. 'Look at you now! You're not—'

But Sebastian has returned his attention to Jayden, stabbing at the air, moving closer towards him. Jayden braces himself, watches the knife's darting movement.

'Where's your lady friend? She understood me. She understood all of it.'

'We both do, Sebastian. We know how much it hurts.'

But Sebastian only laughs at that, a sickening sound, as the knife darts closer. Jayden tracks it all the time, waiting for his moment. If *erratic* seemed like the right word for the man they met in Somerset, this version of Sebastian is something else: he's out of control. Jayden watches as Sebastian spins on his heel, dancing on his tiptoes back to Roland, easy on his feet. Jayden inwardly curses his ankle; he's pretty sure it's broken. But there's no way that's going to stop him.

'You want to know what this is called, Hunter?' screams Sebastian. 'This is called comeuppance. And my money's not going to save you now.'

What happens next is so fast that time twists, distorts – and falls into slow motion.

Sebastian darts forward, hoisting his arm so the knife is aimed like a spear at Roland. Jayden launches himself into a dive, grabbing Sebastian's jumper and taking him down, in the same moment that Roland yells out, sways, jumps back, then disappears completely.

There's a beat of absolute quiet from the three men; nothing but the landscape upping its tempo: rain, wind, tide.

But then the present slams back in.

The move should have been easily executed, but the pain in Jayden's ankle makes his vision slip-slide, stars dancing at the corners of his eyes. Sebastian is snake-like and surprisingly strong, his long body flinging back and forward like a sidewinder as they grapple. Then Sebastian strikes, kicking out at Jayden's foot; whether it's a wild flounder or a calculated aim he doesn't know, but the pain makes Jayden cry out. He falls forward, face in the sand. But, somehow, he keeps his grip on Sebastian, the thinnest handful of his knitted jumper. With sand in his mouth, sand in his eyes, it's in this moment that Jayden realises Sebastian could actually get away from him – or turn on him with the knife.

His mind goes where it needs to go.

Jayden thinks of Kieran, who was always in it with all his heart. He can hear him say, *Let's do this*. It was what Kieran said whenever they responded to a call. He'd turn to Jayden, and no matter what it was – loitering teenagers, a stolen car, a fight outside a city centre pub on a Saturday night in July – he'd nod and say those words.

Jayden thinks of Cat, at home at the farm, knowing nothing of where he is or what he's doing. And he thinks of their baby, who doesn't even know yet how much they love her but will soon, very soon; the second she's out and with them, she'll know. And it's this last, this thought of new life, that makes Jayden gather his strength.

Let's do this.

With a roar he launches himself at Sebastian again, and this time the man folds beneath him. Jayden pins him and – using only the force he needs – pulls Sebastian's arms behind his back. He gets a hold of the knife and takes it from his hand, as Sebastian's whole body shakes with angry sobs. After all this fight, this last move is nothing. Nothing and everything.

The pain in Jayden's ankle makes his head spin, but he holds tight on to the knife, and holds tight on to Sebastian. Whatever happens, he's letting neither one go.

He refocuses; shouts, 'Roland!'

No answer.

Shouts again: 'Are you okay? Roland?'

The dunes are like rollers, and the man's probably hiding in a dip. If mobility's not on his side, then it's the smart move. And maybe Roland doesn't trust him enough to shout back. But honestly? Jayden could use a bit of assistance right now.

Then comes a sound that's like the sweetest music: sirens. Over the noise of the sea, he wills them on and on. Beside him, Sebastian tries to shift, but Jayden has him held.

Soon, criss-crossing torch beams move towards them.

'We're here,' Jayden shouts out. But his voice cracks at the end; he's got nothing left.

As officers click handcuffs on Sebastian and pull him to his feet, Jayden rolls on to his hands and knees. His chest heaves. He tries to get up and can't do it. Mullins, the officer from the beach two days ago – was it really only two days ago? – claps his hand to Jayden's and gently pulls him up.

'Good job, man,' he says. 'You okay? What've you done to your leg?'

'Hunter's still out here. He went off the back of the dunes. I think he's hiding.'

He watches as Mullins strides off, the beam of his torch bouncing over the ground. Meanwhile Sebastian is led away in the opposite direction, supported between two officers; a picture of defeat.

Jayden tries to see where Mullins has gone. He follows the light then sees it stop, less than twenty yards away. The beam hovers over one spot.

'What is it?' Jayden shouts.

Mullins calls back something that he can't quite catch. The torch beam continues to hover.

Jayden's gut twists as a bad feeling comes over him. With wincing effort, half hopping, half dragging his foot, he makes his way over to the spotlight of Mullins's torch. He can feel the blood roaring in his ears and, somehow, he knows just what he'll see. Even though he doesn't understand it. This isn't a cliff edge; the dunes are like a soft-play zone. Though he knows it himself – you can still land hard.

Jayden looks down, and there's Mullins, just three feet below on the beach. And his torch is trained on Roland Hunter.

Mullins looks up at Jayden. Says, 'Er, yeah, he didn't get very far.'

He passes the beam over Roland's body, pausing at his head – and the sizeable rock he must have struck when he fell; a one-in-a-million chance, surely.

'Have you checked his pulse?'

'Dead,' says Mullins.

'Are you sure?'

'He's bloody dead.'

Jayden sinks down on to the sand. He focuses on the searing pain in his ankle, the rain landing on his cheeks, the thrash of the tide. He tries to think of these basic, uncomplicated things, and not the fact that he didn't manage to stop anything at all. That it was all pointless. Then an even worse thought: *Did we do this?*

54

Ally sits on a hard plastic chair in the waiting room. She's been here before. A little over a year ago she sat, perhaps even in this exact chair, and waited, just like you were supposed to, because what else was there to do?

She thought she'd left this room behind: the sharp, detergent smell of it; the raw strip lighting; the dread coiled in every corner. But now she knows that it was just waiting for her, all this time, and as soon as she stepped inside it, she was hauled back here: to the place where Bill's life ended and her own fell apart.

Jayden is having X-rays on a suspected broken ankle. He didn't want to go in the ambulance, but after he fainted Mullins called it and suddenly there it was, blue lights turning. Ally followed behind all the way to the hospital, her heart in her mouth. She'd offered to call Cat, but Jayden had wanted to do it himself. The knife-wielding brother, Jayden's intervention, Roland's sudden, awful death . . . these wouldn't be easy things to explain to a woman who hadn't wanted him anywhere near anything like this again.

'You do know he's more or less fine, don't you?' Gus said to Ally in the car, his voice all kindness.

'Try telling that to his wife,' she replied.

Ally didn't tell Gus about what happened to Jayden in Leeds – it's not her story to tell. And she didn't tell Gus about her trepidation in walking through these hospital doors again either. She kept this last pushed down inside her, hoping it might be okay, but as soon as their headlights picked out the sign for Accident and Emergency, as soon as they swept into a parking bay, climbed out and saw the brick building lit up like a cruise ship, she knew it wasn't. Currents of unease pushed and pulled inside of her; it's a wonder she made it inside at all.

Now, Ally presses her fingers to her forehead. She's glad of the coffee Gus brought her – even though it's one of the worst she's ever tasted – because it's something to hold; something to do. In fact, she's glad of Gus, full stop. Now he's gone in search of a vending machine, *some chocolate to take the edge off*, he said, and she's anxious for his return. For someone who seems easily flustered by small things, Gus's presence beside her is surprisingly reassuring.

When Ally told Gus that they knew where Helena was, he reacted with barely a flicker.

It makes sense to me, he said, *that she'd want to tell you of all people*.

Ally's eyes roam the other people in the waiting room: the child curled in a chair playing a game on his phone, his head resting against the shoulder of a woman whose eyes are red from crying; the thin man holding his arm as though it's something he carried in, not connected to his body at all. The room vibrates with pain and boredom. Stress hangs in the air like an actual cloud.

Had people looked at her that day with Bill, and thought, *Oh dear, that poor woman*?

She wishes Fox was with her now, just as she wished it then. Distressing thoughts push in, one after another.

Roland is dead. And while it was an accident, Sebastian's intent had been murderous: Jayden was in no doubt about that. And here's another certainty: if they hadn't gone to talk to Sebastian in Somerset, Roland would still be alive. So, doesn't that make it their fault?

Ally looks again at her phone. She tried calling Fiona, left her a voicemail, asking that Helena ring her back as soon as possible. That was well over an hour ago. She phoned again after that, and in another message she gave the barest details of what had happened to Roland. Helena would be notified by the police, if they have a contact number for her at Fiona's. But Ally can't count on that.

And there's still no response.

Ally senses Cat before she sees her, as if Cat's energy is flashing ahead of her, crackling the air. She looks up as the automatic doors make their shushing sound and she sees Jayden's wife stride in, one arm wrapped around her pregnant belly. Her hair is pulled up in a messy ponytail and she wears a long cardigan and tracksuit bottoms. She looks like a young girl, wrenched from the comfort of home.

'You're Ally,' she says, as Ally stands to greet her. Her voice is frayed. 'Where is he?'

'Getting X-rays,' says Ally. 'But he's fine. I mean, he's not fine, his ankle's taken quite a knock, but considering—'

Cat holds up a hand. Her cheeks burn red. 'Don't. Just don't. He should never have been near any of this.'

Cat's not just worried; she's furious. Ally feels herself recoil as guilt rushes in like the tide.

'He's a bit of a hero, your man,' says Gus, appearing then with a handful of chocolate bars. He holds them out to Cat and Ally as if fanning a deck of cards; no idea what he's walking into. 'Things could have been a lot worse. Take your pick.'

Cat blinks. 'Worse than a knife-wielding psycho and one man dead? Yeah, you're right, I suppose it could have been worse than that.'

'Have a sit down,' says Ally, trying for a calm she doesn't feel. 'I know it's upsetting, the shock of it, but really, he's alright, he—'

Cat pushes her fringe out of her eyes. 'You have no idea how vulnerable Jay is. He was a mess before we moved down here. But it was working – being here, taking it easy, away from everything that reminded him of what he used to do. And then he gets mixed up in this. With you.' She points her finger, and Ally feels it as sharply as if it were jabbed into her chest.

'I'm so sorry,' she begins to say, 'I did know, but he—'

'Jay told you? About Kieran? Then that makes what you've done even worse. What are you playing at? You've got no authority, no reason, to be running around after murderers. But, oh yeah, it's not actually you doing the running is it? You've got Jay for that. But what—' She stops, winces. Puts a hand to her stomach.

'Cat?' says Ally gently.

Cat's mouth twists. 'It's . . . ahh.'

'Here, sit down,' says Ally, a hand to her shoulder, carefully guiding her into a chair. 'Okay?'

'Braxton . . .' says Cat. 'Just Braxton Hicks.'

'Who's Braxton Hicks?' says Gus.

'Take a breath,' says Ally. 'That's it.'

'Ahh . . . okay. Okay. That's more intense than Braxton's.'

'How far along are you, Cat?'

'Thirty-six weeks,' she says. 'Due date's not until . . . Ow. Oh, ow. Okay.' She puffs out. 'This isn't happening. Not now. It can't be.' She grabs Ally's arm. 'Where's Jay? I need Jay.'

Ally takes her hand. Holds it tight. 'It's all okay,' she says. 'We're here. Gus, can you fetch a nurse?'

Gus's eyes are as wide as saucers. He nods. Surges towards reception.

'Oh God,' says Cat, her hand squeezing Ally's so hard she almost cries out with her. 'I think my waters just broke.'

55

Mullins is writing his report when the message comes in, hunched over the keyboard tapping it out word by halting word. He hates report-writing, it feels like schoolwork – always someone picking holes in it – but tonight, it feels different. More like one of the Boys' Own adventure stories his grandad used to read to him: the storm, the chase, the knife, the man smashed against a rock.

He can't quite square the fact that Roland Hunter is dead. Men like Roland Hunter don't just trip and die.

But it was a decent whack of granite. And on those dunes, the sand could disappear from beneath your feet, so you'd tumble into space. Nothing to stop you. Except for that rock. You couldn't argue with it, could you?

Bloody dead.

Roland was unlucky, sure, but maybe it was a life of luck coming undone at last. After all, Roland hadn't been in the house five years ago when the murderous burglars came in, had he? Instead, he'd been wrapped around Helena. That was kind of lucky – though also not; definitely not, if you were Victoria Hunter. Or her brother – the skinny bloke with the knife. The same bloke who right now is in a cell, having *no commented* his way through an interview with DS Skinner.

It was Ally Bright who filled them in – telling them that Sebastian Lyle thought Roland Hunter had murdered Victoria. It was all there, in the reports from way back, but nothing had come of it at the time. Ally Bright and Jayden Weston are the only ones who seem to think it's relevant now. Sure, Hunter came into a lot of money when his wife died, but that was his anyway, wasn't it? Share and share alike? And right now, Lyle isn't saying anything at all. Maybe he's in shock at what unfolded at the beach. Maybe he never meant for Hunter to die, just wanted to scare him by waving the knife about. The fact is, though, Lyle is looking at an attempted murder charge.

Mullins stops. Rubs his chin.

It's a right mess. Lewis in the ICU. Helena missing then found – but was she really telling the truth when she said she had no idea anyone was looking for her? Sebastian Lyle and his vendetta. Roland Hunter dead. His brother, Nathan, is on his way from London to identify him, and he sounded proper distraught on the phone; like a totally different man to the one Mullins met at Sea Dream.

And then there's Ally Bright and Jayden Weston: slap bang in the middle of it all.

Talking of Jayden, that guy did a decent job in the dunes – even if he did wind up clobbering himself. The talk at the station is that he used to be a big city cop, and that he's seen a thing or two – like being right there when his partner was killed in the line of duty. Mullins's imagination runs out at this point; he literally cannot think how that would feel. Would Jayden want to join up with them after all this, because once a copper always a copper? Maybe it wouldn't be so bad if he did. Though does he have the banter? Banter should be on the essential skills list. If it was, Skinner would never have made it past interview.

Mullins pulls himself back to the report – and the case. He has no idea what any of it means, in truth. And he's pretty sure Skinner doesn't either. With a bit of luck Robinson will make it down here again; bring some common sense. Skinner's face was a picture when Ally said she'd talk to him later, that right now she had to follow Jayden to the hospital. But Skinner's hands were full of Lyle at the time, so he couldn't really argue. Or maybe it was just that you couldn't really argue with her full stop. For a small, quietly spoken woman, she's weirdly commanding.

Mullins's phone beeps. It's Skinner.

Lewis Pascoe has woken up. Get down there in case he does a runner.

He jumps up, leaving his chair spinning behind him.

56

This isn't how Jayden thought it'd happen. But really, all the times he imagined Cat going into labour he just couldn't picture it, so perhaps this is every bit as plausible as anything else. Leaning on crutches, a freshly cast plaster around his ankle, dosed up on painkillers. Painkillers that Cat could really do with but is so far refusing, as she paces and bellows in the small, dark room.

But it's too soon. That was his first thought when Ally appeared in the corridor. Followed by a rush of something that felt like excitement and fear mixed together. He hugged Ally – and she hugged him back; good and hard, too. Then they pushed him in a wheelchair to the labour ward. Surreal scenes, as if he were the one it was all happening to.

'Ah, here's Dad at last,' the midwife said as he poked his head around the door.

And something went off inside of him then – a firework at that word, *Dad.* Then panic: 'Is she born?'

'We're just getting started,' the midwife said with a laugh. 'Settle in.'

He crutched his way to Cat's side and kissed her hair.

'It's happening, Jay,' she said. 'It's happening, so, you'd better forget everything else and do this with me.'

Everything else? What else was there? Nothing. Nothing but this room, this woman, this child – who, incredibly, was getting ready to make her way out.

Their daughter.

Now Cat leans up against the wall, palms flat, feet apart. She's breathing in heavy whooshes. She's finding her rhythm – and she's magnificent. When she turns to look at Jayden her face is creased with pain, and he knows she's somewhere else in these moments – somewhere he can't reach her, no matter how hard he tries. And he definitely tries. Then the contractions pass, and she's left panting, clutching his hand. Her forehead wet with sweat.

If I could do this instead of you, he thinks, *I would. I'd do it in a heartbeat.*

But he also knows that this moment is hers. That she is deep in this ocean, and all he can be is her anchor; she leans into him and he wraps his arms around her.

'Does it hurt?' she says. 'Your ankle.'

'It's nothing,' he says. Then, trying for a grin, 'I'll be back on a surfboard in no time.'

'I can't think about what could have happened on the beach, Jay,' she says. 'I can't . . .' She stops, lets out a low animal moan.

His eyes fill. He's not thinking about it either, because it's a complicated truth. Guilt over Roland's death sits heavy in his gut. Maybe Sebastian was a firework, ready to go off at any moment, but no matter; however inadvertently, their trip to him lit his fuse.

And here's another complicated truth. As Jayden chased through the dark of the dunes, hell-bent on one thing – stopping trouble – he didn't feel afraid. He felt alive in a way he hadn't in a long time. And, in a weird way, so did Kieran.

He rubs her back in slow circles; focuses on the here, the now. The immaculate intensity of this moment.

'Our baby's coming, Cat,' he says, 'our baby's coming to meet us.'

57

'What do you want to do?' says Gus, stifling a yawn.

They're in a different corridor. On different chairs. Different cups of equally grim coffee in their hands. Gus offers Ally a finger of KitKat and she takes it.

'I'd really like to leave this hospital,' she says. 'But . . . I don't think I can. Not until I know that everything's okay.'

She tells him then, about Bill. She finds herself, surprisingly, giving him the long version. The version she hasn't really ever told anyone, not even Evie; especially not Evie, because no matter how old your children were, you still sought to protect them. She tells him about the perfect crescent moon over the hospital car park, and the look on the doctor's face as he came down the corridor towards her. How she was still holding Bill's coat in her hands, and when she pressed it to her face the collar smelt of his aftershave, and she realised, then, that that was all she had of him. Of course, it wasn't, really – but in that moment, it felt like it. And as she walked back out into that car park, the moon still slicing the sky above, she thought about how she had to tell Evie, all the way in Australia, that her dear dad was dead, and how was she supposed to find the words for that?

'I'd like for something good to happen here,' she says, 'Cat and Jayden's baby.'

'So, we'll stay,' says Gus. 'I thought we could take a bit of a walk? The rain's stopped out there.'

'Gus, I can't stop thinking about what could have happened to Jayden out on those dunes. How I'd never have forgiven myself.'

'Jayden wanted to go. You tried to stop him.'

'And I can't stop thinking about whether Roland Hunter's death is . . . blood on my hands.'

She drops her face into her palms.

'Let's walk, Ally,' he says, gently.

It's getting on for midnight and all the stars are out. The rain clouds have been blown away and the air is so fresh you could drink it. Ally tries to breathe deeply, but it's not easy.

'You don't really feel responsible for what happened to Roland, do you?' says Gus.

'He'd still be alive if we hadn't gone to see Sebastian,' she says.

'You don't know that. Just seeing Roland in the news again, with Helena missing, might well have been enough for it to have brought everything back for Sebastian. He could have made up his mind to go to Porthpella the minute he saw that headline.'

'But he also knew that she'd been found. That was all over the news too.'

'It still would have been emotional for Sebastian, I'd say. Like history repeating itself, only his poor sister wasn't as lucky as Helena. That's how he might have seen it.'

Ally thinks on this. And whether it's true or not, she's grateful to Gus for saying it.

'Helena was so sure it was Roland who killed Victoria,' says Ally.

'This frees her, doesn't it?' says Gus.

'I don't know if it's that simple.'

How would Helena feel? Bereaved, or liberated? Ally doesn't know her well enough to guess.

'No one will ever know the truth of it,' says Gus, 'not now. She can believe what she needs to believe.'

Ally feels a shiver come over her and wraps her coat around herself. 'I keep thinking about Victoria too,' she says. 'And how much I wanted to find some kind of evidence that she was divorcing Roland.'

'Because it would have given him motive?'

'Because . . . it would have given her control.' Ally stops. 'I know that's a strange thing to say, given what happened, but . . . she was being taken for a fool. And her own brother had written her off. He thought she was nothing without her money. I like to think that Victoria might have had the prospect of a different life, even if she was denied it in the end.'

'Perhaps she was, Ally. Perhaps she was only looking forward.'

And maybe it's the night, the stars, maybe it's the swirling mix of life and death, but Ally has a sudden impulse to touch him; to place her hands on Gus's shoulders and hold on tight.

But then she's distracted by the sight of someone hovering at the hospital doors. A wisp of cigarette smoke.

'Isn't that PC Mullins?' she says. 'What's he doing here?'

58

There's a digital alarm clock in the room Helena sleeps in, and the time seems to mock her. She's pretty sure she's seen every hour of the night. Now 4 a.m. glints at her. It's normally when she pulls herself from bed, wraps herself in the dressing gown Fiona has lent her and pads downstairs. Makes herself a cup of tea and sits waiting for light to flow into the sky, waiting for the dog to wake, waiting for anything to take her out of herself and her thoughts.

Normally.

She's only been here two nights, but already her movements feel established. Her life has shrunk to these four walls, and if she had her way, she'd keep it like that forever. Except without the sleeplessness. But maybe that's the price you pay, thinks Helena; maybe that's just checks and balances.

She goes to the window and pushes it open. It's basically the middle of the night still. But the air smells of the sea in a softer way than out in the dunes and there's greenery too; the sweet scent of clematis and jasmine. Helena inhales it all.

Roland is dead.

Dead.

The police called the house. Then she listened to Ally's message too. Helena tried to picture it: Victoria's brother, Roland running, the chance slip and fall. The hard, hard rock.

Was it fate? Roland's punishment?

And if it was, what does that mean for her? She who lied, and hid from the consequences?

Part of her wants to let go: to take what's coming to her, for her own score to be settled by forces beyond her control. As she looks up at the night sky, pricked with so many stars, she can almost imagine slipping out of her skin and melting into it all.

Is that what Lewis Pascoe felt?

But another part of her wants to hold on to the life she has – or the life she could have; these last two days with Fiona have taught her that. She thinks of the extraordinary peace she felt as she moved blue paint across the canvas. Was that hiding – or living in a moment she didn't feel she deserved? Can she find a way to deserve it?

'Roland is dead,' she says out loud, hardly believing it to be true.

It's up to you now, Helena, Fiona said earlier. *It's up to you what happens next.*

And the thought of that is terrifying. But not *worse*, surely? Surely not worse.

59

The buzz of a phone wakes Gus. For a moment he's bewildered, no clue where he is, certain only of the crick in his neck and a sharp need to pee. He blinks, blinding sunshine filling his eyes, but, as he adjusts, he realises it's only the delicate light of morning, and the sun is, if anything, a tentative one. He rolls his shoulders, stretches. Turns his head to see Ally.

'Sorry, did it wake you?' she says, holding up the phone.

He smiles a slow smile. 'No. Not at all.'

They spent the night in the car. That's a first for Gus. But, really, it's all a first, isn't it?

Last night, PC Mullins telling them that Lewis had woken up was the boost that Ally needed. *If they let me*, she said, *I want to see him.*

'Is it news?' Gus asks now.

'She's here, safe,' says Ally, her whole face glowing. 'A little girl. Oh look!'

Gus looks down at the picture of a tiny wrinkled creature, wrapped in a blanket and wearing a knitted hat.

'Look at her,' he says.

And he can only just get the words out.

He'd have liked a child, but it was never to be. Whenever he let himself think it, down the years, he reckoned he might have made a nice dad. Maybe not the joker in the pack, or the cool one at the gates, but other things: patient, trustworthy, kind. And he's pretty sure he could have pulled off being an even better grandad – though of course the one has to follow the other. If Gus thinks he's missed out on anything, it's the experience of loving another human being unconditionally, knowing you'd lay down your life for them without the slightest hesitation. How must that feel? Maybe some have it with their spouses, but it was never quite like that for him and Mona, even in what might have been considered their glory days; she always felt like her own person – never his heart, walking round outside his body.

'Does it take you back?' he asks, gathering himself. 'Back to your grandchildren being born?'

Ally nods. 'That's certainly one of the things that would be nice,' she says. 'Being an active part of their lives. About Sydney, I mean.'

Last night in the car they talked and talked. When Ally told him about the pressure from Evie to move, he felt rebellion rise up in him: *Don't go!* Ridiculous, really. Why should it matter to him, Gus, if she stayed or went? As Ally drifted off in the seat beside him, he examined his reaction: was it that the existence of her family made the lack of his own more obvious? That he was unmoored, whereas she had a port to call her own? Or something else altogether?

He winds down the window and birdsong fills the car; not the screaming of gulls but the chirruping of garden birds. He can't stop a smile.

'Did you want to see if we can pay a visit to the maternity ward?'

'Cat was so upset,' says Ally. 'I don't think I'd be welcome. Plus, it's too soon anyway, they'll want their privacy.' She shakes her head. 'There's nothing more on Lewis yet either.'

'I imagine the police will speak to him first, won't they? If he's coherent.'

He sees Ally exhale.

'I want to tell him I'm sorry. For not listening to him better when he came to me.'

'You've got nothing to be sorry for, Ally.'

'No word from Helena either. She must have got my message. I don't know whether to ring again, or . . .'

'You can't do any more,' says Gus. 'You've already done far more than most.'

'But what about everything Helena told us?'

'That's for her, not you. She'll work it out.'

Ally heaves a sigh. 'So, it's time to . . . walk away?' she says.

'Perhaps.'

Just not all the way to Australia.

Beside him, Ally lifts and drops her shoulders. She gestures through the windscreen. 'This is the first time I've not woken up beside the sea in . . . I don't know how long.'

Gus looks past the cars, the thicket of trees, the sky beyond. Not an inspiring view, not by any stretch, but it's already dear to him.

He looks sideways at her, says, 'Shall we go in search of coffee?'

'I need to get back for Fox,' she says. 'He'll be wondering where on earth I am.'

Her phone buzzes again then. Insistently this time – a phone call, not a message. She answers, just as Gus looks at the time on the dash: 7.05 a.m.

'But why?' he hears her say, then, 'I don't understand.'

A minute later she hangs up. Confusion is etched on her face.

'Sebastian's still in custody,' she says, 'and apparently he wants to speak to me.'

60

Jayden is in a room with two sleeping people, and they're the most beautiful humans he's ever seen. He sits in a chair beside Cat's bed, their tiny daughter curled on his chest. She wears just a nappy and a knitted hat. *Skin to skin*, the midwife called it. Jayden sits barechested, another heartbeat pushed against his own.

Meanwhile, Cat sleeps, the night's labour having drained her but also somehow filled her up. Is such a thing possible? To be completely spent, but totally radiant? She couldn't have been braver. It seems to him like there's nowhere to hide in childbirth; you have no choice but to confront it, to become one with it – and then, somehow, through some miracle of humanity and strength, one becomes two. To think that his mum did this. His sister too. And his eyes fill up just thinking of them. He takes his sleeping wife's hand and holds it.

'Thank you,' he whispers again.

They're a trio now, a little three-person family, and Jayden has never felt surer of his job in life: to protect and serve these precious people.

The broken ankle situation isn't ideal but he's already pretty tasty on the crutches and at least it's better than breaking an arm; at least he's able to hold his daughter. At least he can do nappies.

Jasmine makes a snuffling noise, and he watches her tiny features crease then settle. He doesn't think he'll ever get tired of looking at her face. Or those tiny seashell ears. Or her hands: those tiny fingers, those nails! He's not sure he'll ever be able to have a regular conversation again.

Did you see the game last night?

No, but look at her foot! Have you ever seen a foot like it?

A sense of peace flows through Jayden and he lets himself stay within it. It feels like stepping into sunlight or slipping into a pool of still water. A tear rolls down his cheek, but he's never been happier.

What he'd give to be able to text Kieran now. *Meet Jazz!* That's who she's become already. *Jazzy.*

He knows that the thought of Kieran in the dunes helped power him on to stop Sebastian. *Let's do this.* It's a new thing for him – to use his memory of his friend as a force for good. The tears run freely now, but he's not bothered about wiping them away. They're mostly happy ones. And they're all love.

Cat's parents are on their way in, and he spoke to them both by phone just after the birth. Cat's dad sounded different; a lot less certain than usual. Jayden was just about to ring off when Cliff said, 'Hold on there.' Jayden heard a pause, a cough, then, 'Whatever went on in the dunes last night, they're saying you saved a life.'

'But he died,' Jayden said. 'I didn't stop anything.'

'Not true, son. You stopped that bloke with the knife from making a mistake he'd regret for the rest of his life. You stopped him from being a killer.'

Jayden drew in a breath. He hadn't thought of it that way.

'I'm proud of you, Jayden,' Cliff went on, 'and I always have been. Sue says I don't show it enough but I'm saying it now. That little girl of yours is lucky to have you. And so is that little girl of mine.'

Now Jayden looks at his phone to see if his own parents have messaged again. His softly spoken mum sang out her delight earlier,

311

and his dad said they'd be filling the car with petrol for the drive to Cornwall just as soon as they got the nod. The thought of them meeting their granddaughter makes him grin from ear to ear.

Instead there's a text from Ally. The sweetest message of congratulations. He immediately taps one back.

So far she's the world's most peaceful baby. She's going to stay that way, right? Then he adds, **Any news on anything else?**

He puts the phone down. What news does he expect to hear exactly?

His phone buzzes almost straight away.

Lewis is awake. And Sebastian wants to talk to me. I can't imagine why.

Jayden's eyes widen. Lewis! And why does Sebastian want to talk to Ally?

The moment in the dunes crashes back in. He closes his eyes. Despite everything, it doesn't take much to send him back there, and adrenalin jags through him. Sebastian with the knife held high. His bitter words to Roland. Roland's yelped response.

Any sense of triumph or relief that Jayden felt at taking the knife from Sebastian disappeared as soon as Mullins found Roland's body. It felt like the opposite of saving a life, in that moment. But Cliff was right. There was no showmanship in Sebastian: he was pure intent. Perhaps Jayden did save Sebastian from becoming a murderer.

He sits with the thought.

Placing one hand on his daughter's tiny back, he feels her stir. He glances at the sleeping Cat, wanting to give her more rest. He starts to sing the softest song, his lips brushing Jazzy's warm head.

'Hush little baby, don't you cry . . .'

But how does it go after that? Weird lyrics, that's for sure, like so many of those old songs. *Papa's gonna buy you a . . . diamond ring?*

Is that it? Seems like a strange promise to make a baby – talk about making them money-obsessed from the get-go. That said, right now, Jayden's pretty sure – no, scratch that, absolutely certain – he'd do anything for this child in his arms, so if it takes a diamond ring, then hey.

He gives up on the lullaby and drops to humming instead. Closes his eyes.

My money's not going to save you now. Sebastian's last words to Roland come sliding back into his consciousness; now there's a money-obsessed man. Sebastian was so sure that Roland had been nothing but a gold-digger when he married Victoria. It was a strange phrase to use though: *My money*, not *my sister's money*. Why would he say that? Jayden closes his eyes, tries to see the nuance. They say hindsight's twenty-twenty, don't they?

But there's something nagging at him. It bothered him in Somerset – Sebastian's casual disdain for his sister, his cruel assessment of her looks. There was real bitterness there. So, maybe there wasn't a lot of love lost between the Lyle siblings. But what if part of Sebastian's sorrow, part of his anger – maybe a pretty big part – is for the family money? The fact that his sister's share of the inheritance went to Roland. Sebastian's falling-down cottage in Somerset is a world away from the silly luxury of Sea Dream. *My money.* And if it was the money that Sebastian was upset at losing, then what actually changed with Victoria dying? The way Sebastian might see it, wouldn't her marriage have signalled the loss of the Lyle family money?

Jayden stops humming. He can see Sebastian's face, and the glint of the knife in his hand. Sebastian definitely meant business. So, wasn't it weird then, that in the dunes he never once said Victoria's name? If this was about revenge, and Sebastian finally giving Roland the comeuppance he thought he deserved, wouldn't he have wanted to hear Roland confess to Victoria's murder before he stuck the knife in? Wasn't Sebastian killing Roland in her name? That conversation could have happened at Sea Dream before he and Ally got there, but . . . what if it didn't?

Jayden's amazed that the crash of these thoughts isn't waking up his tiny daughter. But she's sleeping peacefully, with those pouting lips and so-perfect lashes, even though beneath her, around her, he's practically sparking.

What if Sebastian didn't need to force a confession from Roland, because he knew Roland hadn't been the one to murder her?

Helena could have got it all wrong. Marrying someone for their money is a long way from killing them for it.

Jayden glances at the sleeping Cat, then – in a careful move, trying not to shift Jazzy one millimetre – he reaches for his phone. Hits the Call button.

'Ally?' he says, his voice low. 'Have you got two minutes? There's something I want to run by you.'

61

The key is just where Ally said it would be, beneath the scallop shell in the earthenware pot by the door. Before Saffron lets herself in, she stands on the veranda and slowly turns; she thought the view from Hang Ten was good.

What's special about Ally's place, The Shell House, is that it's the last in the dunes before they run on down to the nature reserve. Out that way, you can't see another building – unless you count the lighthouse. Her garden has somehow survived the batter of onshore winds and is stuffed with plants. There's a fat-bottomed palm, plump as a pineapple, sitting by the gate. A magnolia tree, in crazy-beautiful bloom, each petal like a luscious pink wedge of soap; and hanging from the branches are slow-turning mobiles made of intricate slithers of driftwood and seashells. Lobster pots have been used as planters, succulents bursting out of them, and there are shells everywhere, set into the stonework by the pathway, along the hem of the house itself.

'Oh man,' murmurs Saffron, 'I could be happy out here.'

It's not that she doesn't love living with the girls. And it's not like she wants to spend her whole life in Porthpella – after all, there's a world out there, and it seems a shame not to see it. But she was born in a place of incredible gifts, and it will always have a hold over her. It will always be her compass point.

As she sticks the key in the lock, excited barking erupts from inside.

'Hey Fox,' she says, wanting to warn him she isn't Ally. 'Hey Foxy, it's Saffron. Remember me, from the café?'

As the little red dog skitters to a stop and looks at her quizzically, she produces a dog biscuit from her pocket.

She squats down, tickles his ears. 'Oh wow, you're cute. Ally asked me to come take you for a walk. She's gotten held up. But she'll be home soon, okay?'

As Saffron straightens up, she looks around.

It's calm: that's the first thing she thinks. It's peaceful. And it's also the beach brought inside. White-painted wooden floorboards. Wicker furniture. Sky-blue walls and vivid paintings. A table that looks like it's made from a hunk of found wood, its surface smooth as toffee. A jug – the blue and white Cornishware her mum always liked too – sits in the middle, full of spring flowers: white-petal daffodils, a fat red tulip, grape hyacinths.

It's a table you want to sit down at. Spread out your things and roll up your sleeves. A place for hatching plans or dreaming dreams. Or, if you were Ally and Jayden, doing whatever sleuths do. There's a notebook open and she goes to it; runs her fingers over the thick creamy paper. There's a list of phone numbers written in blue fountain pen. A note:

What if Victoria wanted a divorce? Would that be enough for Roland to kill her?

Saffron catches her breath. She's heard all about the scenes in the dunes last night. It's pretty crazy. And maybe the craziest part of all is that Ally and Jayden were right in the middle of it.

Or maybe not. The moment the two of them walked into Hang Ten for the first time together, she thought, *Okay, they fit.*

She just hadn't known they were going to turn out to be detectives.

Her eyes are drawn, then, to a flash of colour on the back wall, and as she rounds the corner, she sees a huge picture. It's Porthpella Beach, with the island lighthouse and the peninsula. In the foreground the dunes are bursting with sea pinks; the sea and the sky are almost one. She moves closer, and it's only when she's right up to it that she sees it's all made of plastics. She sees a Smarties cap and a Lego piece, ribbons of carrier bags, drinking straws, bottle tops; unidentifiable wave-battered bits and bobs.

'I love it,' she murmurs.

If only Hang Ten were bigger, she could have a bunch of pictures like this hanging on the walls. Or even just one would look amazing. She thinks again of her dreams of extending: the feast nights and cook-outs; tea lights and wildflowers and the running tide. And Broady's surf school, set to open next year if the money works out. How cool would a picture like this look in there? With a bunch of litter-pickers by the door, for people to use on their way out. When she sees Ally again, she'll ask her who the artist is.

Saffron hears a sharp little bark and sees Fox standing by the door, tail wagging.

'Mate!' she cries. 'I'm right here.'

As she's moving to the door, she hovers by the fireplace. There's a scattering of seashells on the mantelpiece – periwinkles, and perfect little helter-skelter tower shells – and quartz-streaked pebbles as smooth and round as hens' eggs. A postcard of Sydney Opera House, with a child's crayon drawing on the back. There's a photo too: and she can't stop looking at it. It's Ally and Bill on their wedding day, she guesses, though there's no puffs of meringue or stiff suits. Ally has seed-pale blond hair that tickles her shoulders, and is wearing a simple turquoise dress. She's holding a bunch of sunflowers and her smile is just as bright. Bill is in a pink shirt and a quiff, leaning into her and laughing: the happiest man in the world.

They both look so young.

Bill Bright wasn't very old when he died. She remembers hearing about it; he'd only just retired from the beat. He should have had ten, twenty more years, easy.

But there's no *should* about it, is there? Just look at her mum. Her amazing mum.

And Paul Pascoe.

Wenna's account of Paul's suicide has stayed with Saffron: the fact that everyone around here knew he was always in and out of trouble, but no one stopped to think that he was troubled himself. She thinks of her crew of girlfriends, how they're always there for each other, how they split their hearts right open like pomegranates and share the jewels – the good, the bad and the ugly. Life is more open these days, isn't it? Conversations more honest. But maybe not for everyone.

Bill Bright had got a kickboxing club going in Porthpella a few years ago, and it was never just about the kickboxing, anyone could see that. It got the kind of boys going to it who might have drifted off and done something destructive instead. She thinks of Broady, with his beanies and grin, his coconut flat whites and poppy-red surfboard – his little brother was one of those boys. She wouldn't mind a reason to take her conversations with Broady a little deeper than *How's the surf?* or *Brownie with that?* Maybe they could put something on for the community on the surf side. Time in the water has always beaten her blues. With Hang Ten hot chocolate and a beach fire after?

Saffron closes the door on The Shell House, Fox by her side. It's definitely something to think about. And now that Lewis Pascoe has woken up, everything seems a little bit more hopeful, doesn't it?

62

It's the third time that Ally's seen Sebastian Lyle, and on each occasion he's looked different. In his Somerset cottage he appeared eccentric, walking wounded. In the dunes last night, as he was led to the patrol car, he looked like a man split wide open by his grief, reeling from his desperate act. And this morning, through the window of the interview room, he looks . . . unreadable.

Is there a fourth version – the one that Jayden suggested just now on the phone? A brother so resentful of his sister and her share of the family money going into her marriage with Roland that he killed her?

Ally was outside the police station when she took Jayden's call. Part of her reason for agreeing to speak to Sebastian – a big part, if she's honest with herself – was to try to find out whether it was their visit that made him come to Porthpella. For all Gus's reassurance, it felt important to know. But Jayden's phone call has changed everything.

'Al,' he said, 'what if Sebastian presumed there was a prenup? So if Victoria died, the money wouldn't go to Roland, but to Sebastian, as the last member of the family. So, he killed her, making it look like a burglary.'

'You mean everything he told us about Roland getting all her money was a lie?'

'No. I think that was him speaking the truth. I don't think it went his way. Maybe there was no pre-nup after all. And that's why he's hated Roland all these years. And publicly blamed him for her death.'

There was a beat of quiet.

'Al, you still there?'

'I'm still here. And I'm just wondering why on earth Sebastian would demand to speak to me, if he's got something to hide.'

'He's looking at attempted murder. Maybe he thinks you'll support him and help prove Roland's guilt.'

'But Roland's dead.'

Jayden paused, then said, 'And . . . maybe he thinks it'll help him, lessen his sentence or something, to have you in his corner.'

'Why? That makes no sense.'

'Because of your connection to the police.'

Because of Bill. She felt a flare of anger in her chest at the thought of it. 'You think that's it? He wants to use me?'

'Sebastian's a wildcard, Al. I couldn't call it. But I think he's manipulative. He'll want you in there for a reason.'

How Ally wishes that Jayden were here with her now; his presence galvanises her in every way.

She steps back from the door, turns to DS Skinner.

'Any advice, Sergeant?'

Skinner shrugs, his voice gruff. 'Oh, now you're looking for advice? This wasn't my idea, to get you in here, Mrs Bright. But if I hear another *no comment* from him, I'll go spare. And Robinson, who's sitting on his laurels in Newquay again, seems to think it couldn't hurt. When you're finished with Lyle, I want to talk to you as well.'

Ally feels like a schoolgirl, dressed down by the headmaster.

'I hear Lewis Pascoe is awake,' she says. 'Isn't that good news?'

'Yes. The prodigal son is awake. And as soon as we're done here, I'm going over there. Don't get any ideas about gatecrashing that party too, okay?'

'I'm just grateful Lewis will have the chance to be heard.'

'It's a shame the same can't be said for Roland Hunter. Now go on. We don't want to keep his lordship waiting.'

'You're not coming in too?'

'I'm indulging him. He wants just you, and he'll get just you – for no more than three minutes. Okay?'

Ally steels herself. Bill walked these halls like it was a second home, but even knowing that, she can't take comfort in it. She places a hand on her chest and her breathing is quick, shallow. She couldn't feel further from Porthpella. She thinks of Fox. He'll be skittering about the house wondering what on earth's happened. Thank goodness for Gus's idea about Saffron.

'Jayden called me just before I came here,' she says, carefully. 'He's been thinking about Roland and Sebastian in the dunes. What Sebastian said to him. And what he didn't say too.'

She fills him in on Jayden's theory, watching for a change in Skinner's expression, that clicking on of a light. But he only makes a small noise of frustration and shakes his head.

'But don't you think it's worth considering?' she says.

'The Victoria Hunter case is closed. Has been for years.'

'Sebastian always claimed publicly that Roland did it. The only evidence to link Victoria's death to that spate of burglaries was circumstantial. But what if Sebastian—'

'Enough, Mrs Bright. I've had it up to here with this amateur hour. And that Jayden boy should know better. Give Lyle his three minutes, then we're done.'

Ally holds her tongue, but her mind whirrs. *He doesn't think I'd dare ask Sebastian the question*, she thinks. *Or any questions, in fact.* It could be useful, being underestimated.

'One thing: does Sebastian know that Roland is dead?'

Skinner nods. 'Oh, he knows.'

She goes in, and the door clicks shut behind her.

'I owe you a thank you,' says Sebastian.

As a greeting, it sets Ally on edge. She takes the seat opposite him. She has her hands in her lap, then folds them in front of her on the table. Her fingers go to her wedding ring and she turns it. For at least the tenth time since she walked through the door of the station, she wishes Jayden were here too.

'That's why I wanted to see you,' he goes on. 'To express my gratitude. I was hiding. I'd absented myself from the world. But you sought me out, Ally Bright. My battery was flat, I'd done my raging, and no one had listened, but then you came along and gave me just the jump-start I needed.'

His mouth twitches with a smile, and Ally's heart drops.

'All we wanted to know was why you suspected Roland. That was all.'

'But don't you see? To even be asked that question was . . . a beautiful thing. I was wasting away in that cottage. Forgotten. Overlooked. And there you were . . . listening. The wife of a police officer, too. He was quite the man of the people, wasn't he, Bill Bright?' Sebastian's voice is syrupy, bordering on sarcasm. 'I read his obituary after you left. Rather beloved in this little backwater, it seems. I don't mind having the wife of a man like that in my corner. Oh no, not at all.'

Ally shifts in her seat, fighting every temptation to get up and leave. Jayden was right about Sebastian's motivation to talk to her. Was he right about the rest too?

'You must miss him such a lot, Ally Bright,' he says, his head cocked, watching her.

Show him you get where he's coming from, Jayden said on the phone. Then, *You can do this, Al. I know you can.* But Jayden can't have anticipated she'd be on her own in a room with Sebastian – or that his words would feel so goading. Bill was too precious to be talked about by just anyone.

She moves her hands beneath the table and squeezes them into fists. She makes a quiet resolution: if this man really killed his sister, then she's going to make him admit it.

'Sebastian, I can't imagine how it must have felt to lose Victoria so brutally. And then to be left with so much anger and injustice. Believing what you believed must have been very difficult to live with.'

'I knew you'd understand,' he says.

'But there's something that's been bothering me,' she says. 'I didn't like the way you talked about your sister, Sebastian. There was no respect there.'

'Respect? She's dead, Ally Bright. Uselessly dead.'

'Uselessly dead?'

'Pointlessly dead.'

'Not pointless if you're Roland Hunter – not according to you, anyway. There was very much a point. Her money.'

'Ah yes.' He steeples his hands. 'Yes, indeed. He got everything.'

'But wasn't it family money?' says Ally. 'Didn't you have some share in it?'

'Oh, you would have thought so, wouldn't you? Thank you for asking that question.' He shakes his head. 'You have an uncanny ability to ask just the right questions. I suppose that's on account of your husband. Was he the world's only upstanding policeman? I rather think he must have been. Now *he* would have put Roland behind bars long ago, wouldn't he?'

He smiles at her again, and there's something wolfish in it. She can't bear the way he keeps aligning himself with her, with Bill. But if Jayden's right, it might just play to their advantage.

'The family money,' she says, nudging him back on track. 'You were telling me about it . . .'

'Our parents died when we were scarcely out of our teens,' says Sebastian. 'My father first, in a hunting accident, then my mother after a short, cruel illness. Mummy made certain provisions. And, ridiculously, it was Victoria who was given the purse strings. And by God she held them tightly.' Sebastian gives a tight little laugh. 'I wasn't a terribly responsible person back then. And Mummy either had remarkable foresight or was rather of the belief that a leopard couldn't change his spots. Victoria always made sure she gave me my pocket money: no more, no less, Ally Bright; no more, no less. And Roland Hunter enjoyed the rest.'

'So, when Victoria died, you expected to inherit your fair share?'

'Bingo.'

Ally slowly turns her wedding ring. She goes back over what Jayden said on the phone. It was like wandering the shoreline then suddenly seeing something in a tangle of seaweed. You didn't know what it was, but you knew it was worth investigating. So, you went straight to it. Peered close.

'What happened in the days following Victoria's death, Sebastian?'

'Sorrow, Ally, that's what happened. Sorrow and fury.'

'What about the reading of the will?'

'Ah. Ah yes. The reading of the will. For a terribly officious sort of person, she hadn't got her house in order before her death.'

'I expect that's because she wasn't planning on dying.'

'She hadn't updated that will since after she married. The stupid . . .' He puts a hand to his mouth; wipes his lips. 'Couldn't she see Roland was cheating on her?'

'So, Roland inherited the lion's share, despite his infidelity?'

'King of the jungle,' says Sebastian. 'Top of the tree. Not anymore though, eh? So I'm told. Not anymore. Poetic justice, I call that. I knew his days were numbered the minute I saw the news that he'd lost his wife in Porthpella. Basking in all that luxury by the seaside, pretending to be aggrieved she'd gone "missing". Oh, I knew there'd be a reckoning, one way or another.'

At your hands? Ally thinks of what Gus said, about when Sebastian decided to go after Roland – how perhaps it was before she and Jayden even turned up in Somerset. As much as she wants to press this, as much as she wants the absolution, she can't lose focus. This is about Victoria.

'And it was after the reading of the will that you made your statement about Roland being responsible for her death?' she says.

'I believe I called it cold-blooded murder at the time. *Responsible* sounds like a traffic accident. Or a faulty rung on a ladder.'

'A week after she died.'

Sebastian looks down at his hands. Pulls at a fingernail.

'Sorrow and fury,' he says, tearing off a slither of nail. 'It's rather paralysing.' Ally watches him place it on the table, a pale crescent, then set to work on another.

'And the reading of the will,' she says, pulling her eyes back to his face. 'It must have been a shock for you. I mean, even with the tightly held purse strings, you must have thought you'd finally be getting your hands on what was rightfully yours.'

'Exactly. My fair share. All I ever wanted. Not much to ask, is it?'

Ally gives a brief shake of her head in agreement. She glances at the tape recorder: Skinner set it turning before she came in. Perhaps he didn't think their conversation would be so inconsequential after all. She draws in breath through her nose, her lips tightly shut.

'Not at all,' she says then, with effort. 'Why did your family think you were irresponsible? You seem very responsible to me.'

'Thank you for saying that. My father was a great sportsman, and so was I. But my interest was in strategies and outcomes, rather than getting sweaty, if you know what I mean.'

'A betting man?'

'Exactly that. And none of them respected it. Victoria acted as if I was shooting heroin or smoking a crack pipe. I'm a perfectly respectable country gent who likes a flutter. There's a great tradition in this country, you know.'

Ally thinks of the TV playing horse racing in the middle of the day. The disrepair of the house. His obsession with money.

'That must have hurt,' she says.

'My sister was stupid enough to marry an obscenely obvious gold-digger and yet I was the one who couldn't be trusted with cash.'

'Did you ever try to talk to her?'

'Oh, she was a brick wall.'

'What, she couldn't see your point?'

'Impenetrable.'

'But you tried to convince her?'

'Oh yes.'

He's sweating at his temples, as if reliving the force of will it took to present his side of the story to his sister. Ally glances again at the tape recorder. It's Jayden's words that shape what she does next: *Sometimes they just want the credit, Al. They want people to know how clever they are.*

'And meanwhile Roland still escapes justice,' says Ally. 'Sebastian, you must feel as if nobody ever listens to you. As if what you think doesn't matter.'

'Oh, but they do listen.'

'Do they? It seems to me like the only reason you want me here now is because I'm listening. But I don't matter, Sebastian. I'm not anybody important.'

'You're Mrs Bill Bright. Round here that counts for something, so I'm told. *Survived by his wife Ally and daughter Evie*, it said in the obituary. And now *his wife Ally* is here with me.'

She ignores him. 'But the really important people – people like your parents, your sister, the police – they don't listen to you. That must be hard to cope with. To feel so invisible.'

'Hah!' He gives a shrill laugh. 'Invisible? Oh, you don't know the half of it.'

'So, tell me.'

'I leave no trace, Ally. A regular will-o'-the-wisp. Why are you looking at me like that? I'm cleverer than everybody thinks. What you have before you is a very dark horse indeed.'

Ally forces a low laugh; it's the last thing she feels like doing – but she does it.

'Don't laugh,' he says. 'Never laugh. You don't believe me?'

Ally makes herself hold a smile. She shakes her head, her neck stiffening with the effort. 'I'm sorry, Sebastian. I see before me someone who has been dealt a series of blows by life and who, finally, tried to take matters into their own hands' – she hesitates – 'and last night was denied even that.'

Sebastian stares her down.

'People write me off,' he says. 'They've always written me off.'

'Perhaps because you don't give them a reason to think otherwise.'

'Ah, that's where I'm clever.'

'Okay,' says Ally, glancing down.

'Oh, you don't believe me?'

'I believe that that's what you'd like to think. But thinking and doing—'

'I am!' Sebastian slams his hand down on the table. 'Oh, I am. I am, alright.'

Ally looks at her watch: it's time for the boldest move of all. 'I have to go now. I'm sorry.'

She stands up. Thinks *if it's going to happen, it'll be now.*

'People write me off,' he says again. 'They don't know what I'm capable of.'

And the look in his eyes chills her. It's in that moment – exactly that moment – that she knows Jayden is right. It was Sebastian who killed his sister.

'And isn't that dispiriting?' says Ally, meaningfully. 'Don't you want them all to know? To see what you're really made of? I would, I think. I'd want people to know.'

She makes for the door, and, behind her, she hears him muttering to himself. She carries on, slowly, one foot in front of another. Feeling adrenalin like never before. In her head she counts: *Five, four, three . . .*

'It was perfectly planned,' he hisses. '*Perfectly.*'

She stops. Now what? Keep moving towards the door, maintaining this show, or turn – and risk him dropping the thought altogether? She glances to the camera. She's never been one for an audience, but she hopes to God that Skinner is watching – and that, any second, he'll come bursting in. She follows her instincts and turns to face him.

'You mean with Victoria?' she says very gently.

Sebastian stares back at her silently.

I've blown it, she thinks.

'Planned to the letter,' he says, at last. 'I did my research. Quite the scholar. It takes real intelligence to execute something like that.'

Ally watches as a strange sort of excitement moves across his face. He very carefully pats down his hair.

'What, you don't think I could? Everyone always overlooks me, Ally Bright.'

'You were with Victoria the night she died?'

'I covered my tracks. Perfectly. Immaculately. Indisputably . . .'

'Were you trying to make her understand why you needed more money?' And then she sets the trap: she pretends to underestimate him, just as he hates. 'The police said she died from a blow to the head. That can happen so easily. One little push, one trip. I mean, look at Roland. Accidents happen.'

Sebastian looks up at her. His eyes are bloodshot – and sparking with fire. And no matter how much it scares her, Ally knows it's coming. He won't be able to help himself.

'There was nothing accidental about it,' he says. 'I killed her. I planned it, and then I killed her. I killed my sister.'

For a moment the room spins. Ally puts her hand to the wall. She stares at Sebastian, and he stares right back at her; his look is so triumphant he's practically glowing.

'But, Sebastian,' she says – quietly, but no less forcefully – 'you didn't check the will. In all of the planning you speak of, you didn't check that her death would, in fact, lead to you inheriting. You only presumed it. It was all for nothing.'

A shadow moves across his face.

'I planned it. It worked. It did.'

The door opens then and it's Skinner. Although his entrance seems perfectly on cue, the quick look he shoots Ally is one of pure astonishment.

He rearranges his features as he faces Sebastian. 'Sebastian Lyle, I'm arresting you for the murder of Victoria Hunter.'

Sebastian folds his arms across his chest. His cheeks bloom red. Perversely, he's back to looking victorious.

'You do not have to say anything, but anything you do say will be taken down in evidence . . .'

Ally turns away, and she can feel her legs shaking as she makes for the door. She doesn't want to be in a room with Sebastian for a single second longer.

'Can I go now?' she says quietly to Skinner.

He nods. 'You can go, Ally.'

She's just walking down the corridor – slowly, all the adrenalin drained from her body – when she hears her name called out. She turns wearily, tears threatening.

'PC Mullins is talking to Pascoe this morning,' says Skinner. 'I'm tied up here now, but if you want to be there, and I've a feeling you do, then I've got no complaints.' He looks at her sideways. 'Seems like you have a way of getting to the truth.'

'Not me,' she says. Then, pointedly, 'It's all Jayden. You might want to think about that.'

63

Helena sits with her legs folded beneath her, beside the mermaid statue in Fiona's garden. She looks up at the smooth curved stone, the flick of her fish tail, the way her arms are thrown wide. She looks so wild and free.

Helena holds Fiona's phone in her hand. Her finger hovers over the Call button. She bites her lip so hard she's tasting metal. Then she hits it. She's on the verge of hanging up when Ally answers.

'Hello,' says Helena. 'I'm so sorry it took me so long to call back.'

'I understand,' says Ally, and her tone is so kind that Helena's eyes fill. But there's something else in Ally's voice: she sounds different; fainter.

'Were you there?' she says. 'Were you there when they found Roland?'

'I was nearby,' says Ally. 'He—'

Helena cuts in. 'I've been thinking it over. I'm saying it quickly, now, because if I don't I might . . . I just need to get on and say it. And stick to it. Even though he's dead, I should talk to the police. I want to talk to the police. I want to tell them that I lied to them five years ago.'

'Helena —'

'I should never have done it,' she says. 'And I know I can't undo it. But I can admit it. I think that would be the right thing to do. Sleeping pills or no sleeping pills; I lied. I said Roland was definitely with me.'

'Helena—'

'I'll take whatever punishment comes my way, Ally.'

'Roland didn't kill Victoria.'

Helena stops. Shakes her head. 'I know you might not have been able to prove it, and I know I was asking too much of you and Jayden when I—'

'Sebastian Lyle confessed to the murder, Helena. Literally moments ago. He killed his sister.'

'Sebastian?' breathes Helena. 'Victoria's brother? But . . .' Her hand goes to her mouth. 'And you're sure he's telling the truth?'

'He's telling the truth,' says Ally. 'He killed her for her money. Their family money. But it all went to Roland anyway.'

Helena begins to cry. Not slow tears, but great shuddering sobs that crash through her, wave after wave. It's a storm of feeling, and she doesn't know what it means, only that it's too much. They subside and, remarkably, Ally is still there.

'It's okay,' says Ally gently. 'You're going to be okay.'

'But it doesn't change anything for me,' says Helena in a whisper. 'I still thought him capable of murder. I truly did. I can't . . . grieve him. I hated him, by the end. I hated who I was when I was with him. What he did to me. Oh God, Victoria. Poor, poor Victoria.'

After a little while, Ally says, 'I have some good news about Lewis. He's woken up.'

And Helena feels a swoop of relief. Ally tells her that she doesn't need to rush into anything. To take her time to process what has happened. 'But Helena,' she says, 'you can go home now. You can go back to Sea Dream.'

And Helena doesn't know what to say to that.

She ends the call with Ally, and then she stays where she is, hardly able to move. She hugs her knees, rocks gently back and forth.

Roland is dead. Victoria was killed by her own brother.

She doesn't know how long she's been there like that when Fiona finds her. She sits down beside Helena, wraps an arm around her shoulders and draws her close.

'You know you can stay here as long as you need to,' says Fiona. 'As long as you want to.'

And she knows she needs to tell Fiona everything that Ally said, and she knows she still needs to decide about the police, but for now Helena just leans into this other woman and closes her eyes and feels her warmth. And the warmth of those words: *As long as you want to.*

64

Mullins does a showy full stop at the end of his sentence and claps his notebook shut.

'That about clears it up, Lewis,' he says. 'The watch is straight up theft, and that was an idiot move right out of jail, but whether Helena Hunter presses charges is up to her. The way she's lying low, I reckon not.'

Lewis gives the briefest nod in response.

For a man who's been sleeping for the last however many hours, Mullins thinks Lewis looks completely knackered. All he can reckon is it's a good job it's taken Lewis this long to come around, because he'd have had much more taxing questions to answer otherwise: while he's been out cold, a missing person has been found, and a murder from five years ago has been solved.

Not that they can take much credit in either department.

He looks at Lewis's arm and leg in plaster, his bandaged head, and winces. Although, it's kind of a miracle that the guy is still in the land of the living at all – Mullins is pretty sure if he were to topple over that cliff he wouldn't bounce. Then he thinks of Lewis's dad, and that this is actually all pretty rubbish for Lewis Pascoe, whichever way you cut it.

Mullins has decided not to tell Lewis what he knows about Paul losing his job at The Wreckers, or the run-in with the idiot stag group from London. He's talked to Wenna at the shop about it, and it seems like losing jobs was what Paul did: the event didn't have any special significance except for it was the last time it happened. *He can't have been well*, said Wenna, *but I'm not sure anyone noticed.* Mullins rubs the side of his head. There are a lot of different feelings going on in there right now.

'I'm sorry again about your nan, Lewis,' he says. 'And I'm sorry you didn't get to speak to her before she died.'

Lewis has explained what happened. As he was leaving Dartmoor, he was given a hook-up, the promise of some work, and he wanted to come good, to get it all in place, so he could return to Porthpella with good news for his nan; show her that he'd changed, just like she wanted him to. But it didn't quite work out like that. Instead it was two weeks crashing on the floor of a dingy flat in Swindon, realising the work these guys had for him was definitely the kind to land him back in jail. *I told them I wasn't interested*, he said. *I told them I wanted to stay out of trouble.* Somehow he lost his phone in the middle of it all too. So Lewis had got on the train to Cornwall two weeks after he should have, with no idea of what lay in wait for him here. And somewhere his phone – in a back alley or a railway siding or a random pub's lost property box – was stuffed full of messages, from the prison, the police, the retirement home. Perhaps even his nan herself, before she died; maybe welcoming Lewis out into the blue sky – and telling him how she'd sold up, and how it was for the best.

They could only guess at that part of it.

Mullins told Lewis that he found out where Maggie had moved to, and that they seemed like a nice bunch up there. He has nothing much to base that on, apart from the voice of that girl Naomi. You couldn't argue with her enthusiasm about the photo, even if it was totally random of her and, in fact, a kind of low-grade breaking-and-entering. Though he hasn't mentioned the photo part to Lewis, in case it still comes to nothing.

Mullins also explained that Maggie Pascoe's body was being kept safe at the funeral home, and that Lewis could say a proper goodbye when he was back on his feet. Lewis looked like he might cry at that, and Mullins shuffled in his seat, not sure what to do with himself.

'And that bloke who bought her house,' says Lewis now, his lips barely moving, 'the one who told me to get lost. Roland Hunter. He's really dead?'

'Gravely so,' says Mullins, and suppresses a titter. Saffron would like that one. Or would she? Hard to tell. 'Look, I'm going to let you get some rest here, okay?'

Lewis is already closing his eyes.

Mullins closes the door as quietly as he can and stands for a second in the dimly lit corridor outside. He feels a bit weird, kind of like he's stepped outside of himself and isn't sure how to get back in. Who's going to look after Lewis once he's been discharged? If anything like that ever happened to Mullins, his mum would be there like a shot; sure, he moans about her, but he can count on her for that kind of thing. But Lewis doesn't have anybody. No one at all. And the whole time that Lewis was talking to Mullins about what had gone on that morning in the dunes, the big elephant in the room was what was going to happen to Lewis now. A massive great pink elephant, that right now feels like it might be looming over Mullins, flicking its trunk and lifting its tail. But it isn't that he cares. Is it?

65

When Lewis opens his eyes again, there's a woman sitting beside his bed. She looks a bit familiar. Short grey-blond hair. Cat-like green eyes. A smile that makes you want to dig deep and find one of your own. She's wearing one of those tunics the old fisher blokes wear, but it suits her.

'It's good to see you, Lewis,' she says.

He remembers then.

'You're here,' he says. 'Bill Bright's wife.'

'I'm very glad you're going to be okay,' she says.

Lewis tries hard not to cry, but then what's the point? He feels a trickle run down his cheek. A salty taste on his lips. She just smiles kindly, which makes it worse: now it's like Niagara Falls.

Since the policeman had left (he was alright, was Mullins), Lewis has been slowly putting all the pieces together in his banged-up mind.

If he really stops and thinks about it – and what else is there to do right now? – it doesn't surprise him that Nan would have wanted to leave Porthpella. She stuck it out all those years because she was tough as boots, and stubborn with it. But the truth is she had nothing but bad memories of the place. She didn't even like the sea. Always took seagulls personally. Maybe Lewis would have felt that way too, if he'd had a son who killed himself on the beach, but even so. Maybe it made a kind of sense that when she got the right offer for the house, she finally let go of whatever she was holding on to.

And it isn't just that, is it? Lewis let her down too. He knows that. He felt it every single day of his sentence, a sharp pain like a just-made blister. He understands why Nan told him that she didn't want to hear a single peep from him until he was out and ready to behave properly. Not to expect any phone calls or visits or anything like that. No matter how much it hurt, he's never held that decision against her. She'd had more than enough pain, had Nan. She'd have been saving telling him that she'd moved away from Porthpella until he was free and out, he knows that, just like he'd been saving telling her that he was free and out until he got that job lined up. Peas in a pod, that way.

Well, some job that turned out to be. But he was proud of himself for turning it down – though the time it took to figure that out had cost him: two stupid weeks when he could have been down here with her. She was all he had left. It was Nan who'd taken him in, straight after his mum died. She didn't have to do that, but she did it anyway. And then he messed it all up by getting involved with those blokes from Plymouth. And the stupid thing was, he'd seen how things could have been alright in Porthpella. The window of his bedroom had opened right up on to the sea, so you could lie in bed at night and see it, all silver and black and glowing under a big fat moon, the sound of it sending you off to sleep as easy as a little kid. He'd loved staying with her back in the old days, even if it was strange that they were just down the beach from where his dad – his dad who he'd never met, or not that he could remember, anyway – had killed himself. But it was probably even stranger that he looked at that cliff like it meant something; better than a churchyard or whatever, he knew where to go to find his dad.

He must have been saying all this out loud, or some of it anyway, because Bill Bright's wife is nodding, her head tipped to one side. But at least Niagara's stopped.

'I went there again in the morning. To Nan's house. Or where it should have been.'

'The new-build?' says Ally.

'Yeah. I argued with him again. Roland. He's really dead, yeah?'

She nods.

'He was storming, raging, not even looking at me, and I saw that posh watch just glittering on the shelf in the entrance. Just chucked there, like it was nothing. So, when he wasn't looking, I took it. Just put it straight in my pocket. I didn't want to hurt anyone, did I? But as soon as I was out of there I just thought, *Lewis, what are you even doing? You just got out.* So, I threw it about as far away as I could. I know it was stupid. But I figured someone would find it. They'd get it back.'

'Then you went to the cliff?' says Ally.

'I just wanted to speak to Dad. Because here's the thing, yeah – I never knew him, but I also sort of did. Because I had my version of him, didn't I? And the version I had of him was useful. Probably more useful than the real one would have been, though that's a bad thing to say, isn't it? But I could tell him my problems and he wouldn't chat back, you know? Just listened. Wouldn't try to fix it, or reckon he knew best. I know all that sounds stupid.'

'I don't think it sounds stupid at all.'

'And even though that cliff is supposed to be the place I hate most, I sort of like it, because it's his. It's one place where I know he went. And I know that doesn't make sense. Not at all. But when I stood there, what I said was, *I'm not going to give up, Dad. No offence, Dad, but you gave up. I'm not going to do that.*'

And Bill Bright's wife is listening to him as though he's saying something important, so he keeps on going. Even though his head's aching now. Even though his mouth is dry. And his eyes are getting wet again.

'I was nearer the edge than I thought, and it was windy – that's what I always noticed over at Nan's, how windy it was, and there was this sudden smack of it, like a proper gust, and suddenly I was caught out. I lost my footing, didn't I? That was all it was. A nothing kind of trip, but I was going over and I couldn't stop.'

It didn't take much, because for all Lewis's talk of not giving up, his head had been hammering all of that morning: from the cans the night before, from the lousy night's sleep in the dunes, but mostly from the anger and grief that was ripping through his body as he looked at that house built on top of where Nan's should be, and that man telling him she was dead like she was nothing. Like she didn't even matter. How could she be dead? You could have knocked him down with a feather right then – let alone a gust of wind on a clifftop.

'And the next thing I knew, I was here. And it was, like, two days later. That's what they said.'

He hauls in a breath. It's not that he wants to be dead. But it's not like being alive is all that great either.

'I guess I just wouldn't take the hint, right? That I shouldn't have come back to Porthpella? Nan, Nan's house, the cliff. Quite a few signs, really.'

'Lewis, I'm sorry that Bill wasn't here when you came looking for him.'

'That copper who was just here, Mullins, he said he died. I think you told me that when I came, but I didn't really listen.'

'He did. A little over a year ago.' She looks kindly at him. 'I miss him a lot.'

'He was nice to me.' He rubs his eyes. 'I'm sorry he died. I didn't say that before. It was Sergeant Bright that found Dad, did you know that? That's what he told me, after he arrested me for that dumb break-in. He said he wished he could have helped my dad. Look, I know Nan hated the police, but I didn't feel like that. And I knew that when Bill said he wished he could have made a difference to Dad, he meant it.'

'He never said anything he didn't mean.'

'Yeah, and you don't either.'

He sees her shift; her mouth starts to open.

'That Mullins, he said you were the one sticking up for me, all the time I've been in here. So, you're just like him, like Bill – you want to help people too. And you know what, I think that's the best thing someone can do, isn't it? Want to help?'

Lewis feels very tired suddenly and sinks back into the pillow.

'So, thanks,' he mumbles. 'That's all.'

'You know, Lewis,' she says, 'you said you thought there were all these signs that you shouldn't come back here. But think of it this way. Roland Hunter just stumbled in the dunes – and he died. You went off the side of that cliff, fell all that way, and yet you survived. You've been given another chance.'

His eyes snap open. 'You think someone was looking out for me?'

And it's a good thought, that maybe his dad somehow had a hand in it. Held him, as he fell.

He feels Ally's hand cover his own, and he closes his eyes again then; breathes low and slow. For the first time in ages, he's not thinking about all the people who aren't here anymore. He's just in the moment with someone who is.

66

DS Skinner would probably have kept him at it, but DCI Robinson is back in town and said that Mullins should go home and catch up on some sleep. So here he is, trudging up his path, dog-tired, still thinking about Lewis lying there on his own – when he stops. There's a girl standing on his doorstep.

She has curly brown hair and a bright blue hat on her head – a beret? Is that the word? – and when she turns around, she smiles at him. It's not the kind of smile he's used to seeing.

'Are you Tim? Hey Tim, you've got snail mail.'

'Snail mail?'

'Naomi,' she says, holding out her hand.

And when was the last time he shook hands with a girl? Woman. Ever?

'We talked on the phone. About Maggie Pascoe? I work at Paradiso Heights.'

'Oh!'

'I had the day off, and I couldn't resist. Porthpella!' She throws open her arms. 'I used to love this place back in the day.'

And unlikely as it is, it's as if, in that moment, it's the Mullins' front garden that holds all the charm. With its crazy paving and arrangement of gnomes in various leisurely poses, and him, PC Mullins, in the same uniform he wore to go puffing over the dunes last night.

'I thought I'd hand-deliver the photo I was talking about, and then . . . go see the sights.' She wrinkles her nose; grins. 'I'm gabbling. I do that. It's cool. I know that about myself.'

Mullins glances at his watch. It's Monday morning, so his mum's out doing the shop. She's regular as clockwork and won't be back for forty minutes. There's no one else around. No one to be seeing this. So he can be whoever he wants to be. He can be whoever this Naomi seems to think he is. Which is definitely not Tim Mullins. Tullins. Tuzzer. Muzzer.

'It's nice of you to bring it,' he says.

She beams. 'Felt like the least I could do. It's such a sad story. If I can give a bit of good energy, then that's all cool.'

Mullins starts. She doesn't know Lewis is awake! He tells her, and before he can budge out of the way she's planted a hug on him. So quick you could have missed it. But he didn't – he caught it good. He can feel his face go crimson.

'Sorry.' She grins. 'But wow. Awake.'

'What's the photo of anyway?' says Mullins, recovering, focusing on the brown envelope she's holding. 'The one you thought Lewis would like? Or is it, like, private?'

'I don't think it's private,' she says, drawing it out of the envelope. 'I mean, I think it's okay for us to see it. Because I rescued it, and you're an officer of the law.'

She twinkles at him, then reads from the back. '*To Mam. Whatever else I've stuffed up with Jenny, whatever else I've got wrong, I have the most beautiful son. He's called Lewis and he's pure love.*'

Naomi's eyes are glistening as she passes over the photo. Mullins takes hold of it carefully. And he immediately sees why she wanted Lewis to have this picture with him as he lay there in his coma. Why she came all the way here to bring it safely.

It shows a dad cradling a tiny baby. You can barely see the baby – he's bundled in a blanket like a sausage in a roll – but oh boy, the way that the man's looking at him. *Pure love.*

So, this was Paul Pascoe and his baby son.

He coughs. Croaks. If he, Mullins, had one picture, just one picture of him and his dad like this, he feels like everything might have been different for him. Or, maybe not. Because here's Paul Pascoe, looking like he was feeling all there was to feel, and by the end of the year he'd taken himself off that cliff, thinking he had nothing to live for.

'Life's cruel,' says Mullins, before he can think to stop himself.

'Uh-huh. But beautiful too, don't you think?' says Naomi.

And she sounds like Hippy-Dippy. But maybe all the best people do.

'I'll make sure he gets it,' he says. 'I was at the hospital earlier. I'll go again.' Mullins rubs his nose. 'Lewis doesn't have anyone. When they want the bed back, there's nowhere he can go.'

'Maggie's flat's still empty, you know. She'd paid up for another six months.'

'What – Lewis could move in? Isn't it sort of an old people's home?'

'Retirement complex, actually. Anyway, so what? I reckon we could do with a bit of fresh energy about the place. He can get his jigsaw groove on.' She waves her hand. 'It's an idea, anyway. And I reckon I can persuade management as they're still feeling guilty about Lewis never getting word about Maggie.' She smiles at him, and it's total sunshine. 'So, hey, what are you doing now, Tim PC Tim PC Mullins?'

Mullins thinks, *Crashing out. Getting out of these stinking clothes. Bumbling around the house until Mum gets back and the telly goes on.*

'I've just come off a night shift,' he says, his hand rubbing the back of his head. 'So, I need to freshen up. But after that, I was maybe going to head down to the beach. Get a coffee. My friend Saffron runs this café that does killer brownies.'

Killer brownies? Who even is he now?

'That sounds like a sight I need to see. The café bit, I mean,' she laughs. 'Not you freshening up.'

'I owe you,' he says with a grin, 'for bringing this picture all the way here. So, my treat, yeah?'

He cringes. It sounds like something his mum would say, scrabbling around in her purse with one of her pals.

'I'd love that. I'll wait out here, soak up the sun.'

'There's a rabbit round the back.'

Mullins, seriously? Is she five years old? He should just give up. Stick to not catching criminals instead. Parking tickets. You couldn't go wrong with a parking ticket. Actually, you could, but . . .

'Oh my God, I love rabbits. Is it yours?'

He stands blinking on the path – holding the photo that he feels like he's still got a good cry in his system about – thinking, *This is a day not like any other.*

'Yeah,' he says, his cheeks pink and happy. 'It's mine.'

67

When Ally lets herself into The Shell House, Fox thunders to meet her. She kneels down and buries her face in his fur; says sorry for leaving him so long.

'You can't want another walk,' she says, 'or do you? Do you?'

On the table there's a note from Saffron.

All good! If you ever want to put him up for adoption I'm first in line!

Then Ally sees a box, and when she lifts the lid there's a pile of delicious-looking homemade cookies, glinting with toffee and nuts. She realises how hungry she is; it's past lunchtime and she hasn't even had breakfast.

'Let me just make a coffee,' she says, 'and we'll head out to the beach.'

There's comfort in the familiar ritual of unscrewing the pot, scooping the grounds, setting it on the stove. She's home at last. A wave of fatigue washes over her, but Fox is turning circles by the door and the sky is wide-open blue, and she knows that what will restore her more than caffeine is what's outside: the blast of salted air, the lick of the sea at her feet.

She pours her coffee into a mug, picks a cookie, and together they step out.

It's a walk she's done every day, often twice, for nearly forty years. But still, she never crests the dunes without her heart catching, without the sight of the bay unfurling before her making her pause to take it all in. There's a spry breeze, and only the most delicate wisps of cloud in the sky, like sheep's wool caught on a fence. As she moves down on to the beach her feet sink into the sand. After the hospital waiting rooms, after the police station – my God, the police station – after the dimly lit ward of the ICU, to be here feels like a gift.

Fox skitters towards her, dragging an absurdly large piece of driftwood, looking for congratulation. She admires his find, tells him he's a very clever boy, then she takes a sip of coffee and a bite of cookie. As she nears the water, she slowly finds her way back to herself. Basks in all that reflected light.

The last three days – has it really been only three days? – have been filled with so many people. So many people, and the mess and wonder of their lives. And their deaths too. Alone is what Ally's always loved, even with Bill; the stillness of her own world. Right now, this state of solitude feels like a homecoming in itself. But she can't help feeling a little altered. Like something is missing.

I'd like to try cooking you something one day soon, Gus said as she dropped him in Porthpella before going on to the police station. And Ally wasn't sure if the *try* part was the cooking itself or the cooking for *her*, and so she hesitated – not from lack of enthusiasm, just turning over the words he'd used. Then he looked bashful, said, *I don't think this should go unmarked, that's all. I think you deserve to raise a glass to this.*

He said he'd drop by to set a date.

She wonders if Cat and Jayden and baby Jasmine will be home soon too. The exact day she brought Evie home from the hospital is blurred in her memory – that tiny Falmouth flat, the ache in her body and her ratcheting anxiety – but she remembers bringing her here to Porthpella. Oh yes. Walking into The Shell House for the first time, sunlight pouring through the wide windows, the sea singing in every room. She held her daughter tightly and said, *I think we'll be okay here.* And Bill's face, sheer hope, as he wrapped his arms around his family.

She wonders if Jayden knows yet what a magic place Porthpella really is.

She hadn't wanted to bother him, and she was still nervous of getting it wrong with Cat, but she was so excited to tell him about what had happened with Sebastian Lyle. That Jayden's hunch after talking to Cliff had been right: *Ally, what if I didn't save Sebastian from anything? What if he was the killer all along?* The smart thinking was all his: realising the importance of the money issue, and how Victoria herself had seemed to be a long way from Sebastian's thoughts in the dunes. Maybe one day she'd be comfortable rerunning the interview with Sebastian in her mind, reliving the moment where he admitted to the murder, but not yet; maybe not ever. It had been a strange sort of feeling: sadness as much as triumph; and an overriding disbelief that it'd come from her questioning.

As Jayden answered his phone, she heard the high-pitched squalling of his daughter in the background. He moved somewhere quiet. Then, at the news, he let out a low whistle.

'Ally Bright, you just cracked a cold case.'

'You mean we did,' she said. 'Without your theory on Sebastian, we'd be nowhere.'

'Yeah okay, I'll take that. *We.*'

And he sounded different – so bright, so happy.

Now Ally presses her fingers to her eyes. It's time for some quiet. She goes to turn her phone off, thinking how strange it is, this feeling of connection. Before Lewis came to her door, her days were as empty as the beach at dawn.

But now, what if Jayden calls again?

Or Gus?

Or Helena?

Or Lewis?

Even Evie, breaking her schedule? Alright, that's unlikely, but even so. And they do have things to talk about, her and Evie. There are plans to make. The last few days have made Ally's mind up about Australia once and for all.

68

Jayden leans his crutch against the car and lifts his daughter from her seat; it's been no time at all, but he's glad to have her back in his arms. It's weird with the two of them up front and Jazzy all on her own in the back. *Maybe we should have another?* he said earlier, then at Cat's look, he hurriedly added: *Not now, or not anytime soon. Not for, like, years. Or never. Never's good.* She's still so tiny and she curls into his shoulder like a hedgehog. Three days old and the girl is a gift.

He passes her reluctantly to Cat, hating that he can't walk and hold her at the same time. But it's a small price to pay, considering. He keeps reminding himself of that.

Cat pushes her sunglasses on top of her head. Squints up at The Shell House.

'I'm not sure Ally's going to want to see me after what I said.'

'Babe, it was the heat of the moment,' says Jayden. 'And Ally's not exactly the type to hold a grudge. She's cool.'

He thinks of how they met last Friday morning, Lewis lying at the foot of the cliff looking like he was dead and gone. Ally's face. Her little red dog. He was drawn to her then, he knows that now; inexplicably, he wanted to stay in her orbit. Maybe that was how it worked: certain people came into your life at just the right moment – only you didn't know it was the right moment, not at the time. That only came later.

He pushes open the gate with his crutch, and Cat and Jasmine go through first.

Ally appears at the door. She smiles, waves, but there's a hesitancy to her as well. He saw it in her messages, when he suggested coming. I'd love to meet your baby, but don't you have lots of other people you want to see? It was like she didn't believe she mattered enough to him. Well, screw that. They've known each other less than a week but so what? If he thinks about the people who've made a difference to him, she's right up there. And he's pretty sure he's made a difference to her too.

He crutches up to her at high speed, canes tapping on the veranda, and pulls her into a one-armed hug.

'Meet little Miss Jasmine Weston,' he says. Then, turning to his wife and daughter, 'Jasmine Weston, this is Ally Bright.'

'Oh, my goodness,' says Ally, stepping forward. She reaches out and holds Jazzy's tiny hand. 'Oh, look.'

'Ally,' says Cat. 'Thank you. Thank you for helping me at the hospital. I don't think I got to say that, in the middle of it all.'

'You were wonderful,' says Ally.

'I was pretty rude too, before it all kicked off. I'm so sorry for that.'

Cat looks kind of appalled, and that's not a look she wears often. Ally lays a hand on her arm.

'You were absolutely right,' she says. 'Everything you said was true.'

Cat and Jayden exchange a look.

'Yeah, about that,' says Jayden. 'I know the way it's all turned out is . . . a win. Well, kind of. That's how DCI Robinson described it in his email. Did you get one too?'

Ally nods.

It was an official note of thanks from Devon and Cornwall Police that made Jayden feel oddly proud. Was it a win though?

351

Not so much for Roland Hunter, who was a long way from one of the good guys, but even so. Victoria before him, not appreciated by anyone at all, by the sounds of it. Helena, attaching herself to the wrong person and being unable to unstick until she literally thought her husband had killed his first wife. And Lewis, losing the only family he had, and the only home too.

Jayden frowns. 'In a solving-it sense it's a win,' he says. 'In a life sense, it's all pretty rubbish.'

'I don't know about that,' says Ally. 'Sebastian will be brought to justice. Helena's free, and I've a feeling the choices she's going to make will be very different from now on. And Lewis – Lewis can get on with the business of living. He's been given a second chance.'

See, this is why he likes being around Ally Bright.

'We saw Saffron on the way over here,' says Cat. 'She's going to visit Lewis later.' She turns to Jayden. 'And didn't she say she was hatching some plan?'

'She said she always needs another pair of hands for the summer season. And that if he's up to it by then, and if he wants to stick around in Porthpella, then the job's his.' Jayden laughs. 'I was kind of eyeing that myself. Damn.'

'No you weren't,' says Cat.

'No. Exactly. Yeah, so, what I was saying, Al, is that these last few days I've been thinking. I've really enjoyed working on this case with you.' He rubs the back of his head. 'That's kind of an understatement, to be honest. And . . . anyway, it's settled things for me. About what I want to do next. See, I've got this idea.'

'Alongside the campsite, obviously,' says Cat.

'Oh yeah, obviously. The campsite is . . . king.'

Jazzy makes a sound that can't be a giggle, it's way too soon, but it breaks him off and he has to give her a kiss right there and then. How is he supposed to get anything done in a day when his daughter is this cute? When she has his heart so entirely?

Jayden throws out an arm. 'I mean, we're the Shell House Detectives, right?'

It's then that he notices the travel guide to Sydney on the table. Ally's passport beside it. Dismay hits him with a thud.

'You're going?' he says.

'Evie's been asking me for a long time,' says Ally.

He didn't exactly know what he was imagining, but in the middle of the night, as he took his turn with Jazzy, he was googling detective agencies. In the last few days he and Ally had solved a missing persons case and a murder from five years ago. Maybe it was a lucky break. Maybe most of the time it'd just be stolen surfboards and camper van break-ins, but hey, it was still a puzzle. And it was about working with a partner. As dawn flowed into the sky and Jazzy nestled in his arms, he pictured him and Ally on the veranda of The Shell House – notebooks, phones, ginger-nut biscuits. And the best thing was, when he talked about it with Cat over breakfast, she loved it. Well, maybe not *loved* it. But she definitely quite liked it. She said that all she'd ever been worried about was him not being okay, and she could see how okay he was right now. Even with the busted ankle. And the no sleep. *You've got your mojo back*, she said, *and I don't know if that's our daughter or Ally Bright or the pair of them together. But I know that I'm very glad.*

But now Ally is leaving.

'Hey, isn't that Gus?' he says suddenly, spotting a figure down on the beach, the sun glinting off his head. Isn't Gus another reason for Ally to stay? Jayden's heard the way she talks about him, and it isn't without a little something extra. He's started to get his Cupid vibe on. 'Who's that he's with?'

There's a dark-haired woman strolling beside him. As they draw level, Jayden sees Gus glance up towards The Shell House then turn back to his companion. They walk on by.

'That's his wife,' says Ally.

'I thought they were divorced.'

'They are. Apparently, it didn't work out with her new partner.'

As she says it, she's impossible to read.

'And you're moving to Australia,' he says. 'Damn.'

69

Saffron wipes down the table in a swift figure-of-eight. Twenty minutes until she closes up and she can hit the surf. It's not perfect out there but she's never needed it to be. It's about being in the blue. The dunking. The drift. The occasional moments of out-of-body elation.

Today is a good day.

She went to see Lewis this morning and, with him out of Intensive Care, they let her in this time. She brought him more flowers, and a bag of brownies – a fresh batch, as they've been flying out the door lately. Mullins and the girl in the blue beret had nailed two each the other day, then Mullins had gone and bought all that were left. He'd even asked Saffron to put them in a white box and tie a ribbon on it.

There'd been an awkward moment at the till, Mullins taking out his wallet, glancing back at the girl, but then leaning in to Saffron and saying, 'So what shall we call it? Just the ones in the box, yeah?'

'I call it ten brownies. The four you two just had, plus the six in the box.'

'Come on, Saff, just because I'm not in uniform today. Give me a break, eh?'

'Pay up,' she said with a sweet smile. 'And if you're not careful I'll start counting backwards too. See what your lady friend thinks of that.'

Mullins had reluctantly handed over his money, then after a quick glance at the tip jar, pocketed the 20p change.

Some people never changed. But maybe that wasn't quite true. Because when she visited Lewis Pascoe, and they talked about Maggie, Lewis showed her the photo. He said that Mullins had brought it in for him – and on his day off too.

'Nan'd had this all that time and never given it to me,' he said. 'I don't know if she'd forgotten, or just thought I wouldn't want it. Or maybe she wanted it for herself.'

And it was just about the loveliest photo of a father and his child that Saffron had ever seen.

'I've got a frame at home you could have,' she said. 'It's just the right size.'

Lewis blinked in surprise, as if he wasn't used to small kindnesses. But that wasn't quite true either, because then he told Saffron about going to stay in his nan's flat at the retirement home. By the time the current lease was up there, he'd be just about back on his feet. He flexed his fingers, said, 'So I'm going to up my jigsaw game. After that though, I dunno.'

Finances weren't going to be too much of a problem, because what was left of Maggie's money from the sale of her house was there waiting for him. But money was only one thing; purpose and confidence were something else. So, she pitched the café idea.

'Hang Ten?' he said. 'You sure that's not a capital punishment thing?' But his mouth was twitching with a grin.

Saffron had done it out of a favour to Maggie. But, oh man, wasn't it nice to realise that she actually liked Lewis Pascoe.

She told Lewis about her plan then, the one she'd started putting together with Broady – who, by the way, had been receptive in every sense; it'd been his suggestion to chat about it over dinner, which, Broady-style, had meant a grill on the beach, and quite a lot of rum; just her style too, apparently. And how, afterwards, they'd even roped Mullins in, to help spread the word in the community. She was sure Jayden would be up for it too, once his ankle was back to best. They hadn't got a name for it yet, but it was kind of like surf therapy, about getting people to enjoy the water who might not normally get a chance. Young people who were struggling with their mental health. Isolated older people. Anyone in between. As she described it, Lewis said it sounded pretty cool.

Saffron straightens up, saunters back behind the counter. The door opens – oh no, not customers, just as she's closing – but it's Gus. Keeping up his end-of-day tradition.

Gus and a woman.

'Saffron, hello!' says Gus.

Saffron waves, and watches the woman looking the place up and down.

'Skateboards on the wall?' she says, wrinkling her nose. 'Now I've seen everything.'

'Mona . . .' begins Gus.

'The colours are making my eyes hurt,' she says, 'I'll wait outside.' She spins back to the door; points to a sticker on the frame. 'Sex Wax? What is this place?'

'It's a surfing thing, Mona,' says Gus.

As the door swings closed behind her, he shrugs. Rolls his eyes. 'Emmet,' he says.

Saffron sets the machine going. Shakes the milk jug.

'Friend of yours?'

'Possibly,' he says. 'But not necessarily. We were married for nearly forty years.'

'Woah,' says Saffron.

'She's just broken up with the man she left me for.'

'Ah.'

'She invited herself down here and I thought, you know, out of kindness.'

'That was nice of you,' says Saffron.

'But the truth is, this is my happy place. And . . .' He appears to shiver. 'It doesn't so much feel like that now she's here.'

Saffron passes him two coffees.

'And so?' she says.

'So, she's leaving. This is one for the road.'

'Well, you've got things to be getting on with, haven't you?' she says.

Gus quickly looks up. She swears she sees a faint blush on his cheeks.

'I have?' he says.

'Your novel. What did you think I was talking about?'

As he leaves, she eyes the clock. Closing time. She glances towards the water. There's a scattering of people out there, lifting up and over the waves. Maybe one is Broady. Maybe not. The one thing she knows is that he's not going anywhere. Some people are made to stay in Porthpella forever. She's one of them, and so is he. Gus has potential; she wouldn't be surprised if he went and extended the lease on All Swell. Jayden and Cat, well, Jasmine was born here now: this is their home, at least for a bit. And Ally Bright, she isn't going anywhere. She might think she lives on the edge of things, head down, away from the crowds, but she's hewn from the rock and shaped by the sands. Bill said it once, when he came in the café not long after she opened. *This place saved Ally, years ago. And it's why we'll love it forever. It's why we'll never leave.*

Saffron unties her apron and hangs it on its hook. She reaches into the cupboard for her wetsuit. The water's waiting for her.

70

Ally stands watching the 'For Sale' sign go up, as behind her Fox darts in and out of the shallows. It will be someone else's dream now, no doubt bought as a second home or a luxury holiday let. All change again in the dunes. But maybe change is the only thing you can really count on.

She sees Helena shake hands with the estate agent, then watches him drive off, bumping slowly down the track. He'll no doubt be rubbing his hands: a place like Sea Dream won't stay on the market for long.

Helena waves and Ally waves back. She sees Fiona come out of the house and slip her arm around Helena's shoulders, kiss her cheek. So much has changed in so little time.

Whatever Helena's future, it looks a good deal brighter than it was with Roland Hunter.

Helena came over for a cup of tea yesterday. She explained that she'd offered Sea Dream to Lewis Pascoe first, for a rock-bottom price, but he hadn't wanted it. Not his style, he'd apparently said, and not his nan's either. *I'm starting again,* Helena told Ally. *I've never been brave enough to do that before. And I've got you to thank for that.*

And for the first time since Ally had met her, Helena sounded truly happy.

'Ally.'

Ally turns and it's Gus. Head shining like a pebble in the evening sun. That slow smile.

'Mind if I join you?'

They walk along together. The tide edges closer, its lacy edges dancing up to their shoes. Gus stoops suddenly and picks something up.

'Any good?' he says.

It's a purple top shell, a delicate mosaic of pattern. As she turns it in her hand, its pearlescent interior glints. She must have seen thousands on this beach.

'Beautiful,' she says, and slips it in her pocket.

On FaceTime with her grandsons yesterday they showed her an enormous conch shell that they'd found down on Bondi. The youngest, Sam, is a dedicated little beachcomber, and his hauls are frequently spectacular. They'll have fun together, pottering along the shore. And perhaps, on the other side of the world, she'll find her way with her art again too. She's finally spoken to Sunita about the upcoming season at the Bluebird and told her the truth: that she has nothing.

'When do you leave?' Gus says.

Fox drops a stick at his feet and Gus dutifully picks it up; hurls it with vigour.

'Next week,' she says.

There are so many things to organise by then.

'And remind me when you're back.'

'It's just for three weeks, so after Easter. By which time . . .'

By which time Porthpella would be in the fullness of spring. Clifftops exploding with flowers. The holiday crowds mostly been and gone – at least for a while. Been and gone, and Gus along with them.

'By which time I'll probably still be on the first draft of my novel,' he says. 'I told you that's why I came here, didn't I? To get it written?'

'You did,' says Ally. 'The detective novel.'

He rubs at his stubble. 'So, I think it's going to take longer than I thought. And, well, I can't leave until it's done.'

She stops. Smiles. The sea tickles her boots and she hardly notices.

'In fact,' he says, 'it might just turn out to be a life's work, this book.'

After a moment's thought, she says, 'I think that would be a life well spent, Gus.'

Bill's words, but she doesn't think he'd mind. He was always one for stopping and defining the moment; he'd be throwing a ball for Fox, or taking the froth off a pint of Doom Bar, or just standing out on the veranda in his bare feet, coffee in hand, hair sleep-mussed, saying, *This is a life well spent, Al.*

It was just about everything you could ask for, wasn't it?

'And what, the Shell House Detectives then opens for business?'

Ally shakes her head. 'We can't possibly be called that,' she says with a laugh. 'I like my privacy too much, apart from anything.'

'But unofficially,' says Gus, 'for those in the know.'

'Maybe unofficially,' she says.

She woke up this morning thinking it was absurd, this idea of Jayden's. She went downstairs and had to have a one-on-one with Bill in his BBQ apron.

I've been doing a bit of what you did, she said. *And the thing is, I think I'm quite good at it. I'm thinking of doing it some more. Is that lunacy?*

Bill smiled back. Like he always did.

And the thing is, they could call themselves anything, couldn't they, her and Jayden? They could declare one hundred intentions, but they still needed someone to come and ask for help. And the fact is, in Porthpella, most of the time life just ticked along. And when it didn't, the police were there to fix things. Weren't they?

But it was a fun thought. Life suddenly seemed bigger. Fuller. And it had Jayden fired up too.

'Glass of wine? To toast your travels?' says Gus.

'And your non-travels,' says Ally.

'All Swell or The Shell House?'

'What about just here?' says Ally. 'Best seat in the house.'

The sun's dipping, and soon the sky will be filled with pink light; the horizon about as wide and open as a horizon can be.

'The thing is,' Gus says, suddenly looking serious, 'if I left this place, all I'd be able to think was that it was going on without me. All the things I'd be missing. I'm too old for that kind of regret.'

Likewise, she thinks. He smiles at her then, as if he heard.

'I'll be back in five minutes,' he says, 'with a bottle of Sauvignon and two glasses.'

Ally holds her hand to her eyes. She can see Cat, Jayden and baby Jasmine on the approach. Fox catches their scent and is already off.

'Maybe make that four?' she says.

As Gus heads for his house, Ally watches him go. Then she settles down in the sand. She breathes deeply, taking it all in – the sea, the sky, the lot. No one ever knows what'll happen tomorrow, she thinks; all any of them can do is spend today as well as they can.

She waves, and Jayden lifts a crutch in the air in response.

The Shell House Detectives. She has to agree it's got a nice ring to it.

Author's Note

I began working on *The Shell House Detectives* in winter 2020, when we were locked down and homeschooling and I was longing for wide open sea and sky. The story grew from a simple but enchanting image: a weatherboard house in the dunes. While the setting of Porthpella is fictitious – as are all of the inhabitants – it's inspired by several different locations across West Cornwall: a patchwork of beloved places. As anyone who has spent time in that part of the world knows, the beauty and magic of the Penwith landscape is fact not fiction, and requires no embellishment.

Acknowledgements

I'm so grateful to everyone who has been part of this book's journey.

I'm particularly indebted to those who braved reading early drafts: Lucy Clarke, Emma Stonex, Jo Robaczynski, Kate Riordan, Louise Dean and my husband, Robin Etherington. Your generosity, enthusiasm and insightful notes made all the difference – as did the heartening chats, beach retreats and chocolate deliveries. Lucy, I wouldn't have the name 'The Shell House' without you, so I have to thank you twice (at least).

Susan Fletcher, Rosie Walsh, Patrick Neate, Nikesh Shukla, Veronica Henry, Lucy Diamond and Jacob Ross also offered wise words and kind encouragement during the writing process, for which I'm very thankful.

Thank you to Claire Miller for greatly valued advice on writing outside of my experience. To Megan Wilkinson-Tough for her marvellous hospitality in Padstow. And to the amazing gang at The Novelry: friends, colleagues and all of our writers – you inspire me every day.

Thank you to my editor Victoria Haslam at Thomas & Mercer, whose passion, vision and care have been a delight from day one. Together with the brilliant Laura Gerrard, you've made the editing process a total pleasure. I'm grateful to Deborah Balogun for the much-appreciated cultural read, Gemma Wain for a meticulous copy-edit, and Sadie Mayne for the proofread. Thank you to Marianna Tomaselli for the seriously beautiful cover illustration. Thanks also to Marketing Manager Dan Griffin and all of the wider Thomas & Mercer team. I'm so happy that *The Shell House Detectives* has found such a good home.

As ever, thank you to my wonderful agent, Rowan Lawton at The Soho Agency. We've been together for over a decade now and I hugely appreciate your continuing belief. Thanks also to the excellent Helen Mumby.

I'm so lucky to have such a loving and supportive family. Thank you to the Halls, the Green-Halls and the Etheringtons for all that you are and all that you do. Mum and Dad, this book is for you. As to my husband, Robin, and my son, Calvin, life with the pair of you is full of kindness, fun and adventure. I'll always remember us celebrating this novel on a blustery day out at Sand Point, Tunnock's teacakes in our backpacks, seashells in our pockets. Thank you for everything, always.

I first visited Cornwall when I was five years old, with my mum, dad, sister and Nibi the cat. We stayed on a farm outside Marazion, and the magic of the place has never left me. We've had many happy times there since – in St Ives and Gwithian especially. When my mum first read this book she said, 'It's full of the things you love, isn't it?' And it is. From strandline pottering to getting battered in the waves to soul-lifting clifftop walks, there's nowhere I'd rather be than on a beach out west. Ideally with a notebook close to hand, for plotting the next Shell House Detectives mystery . . .

My final thanks are to you, the reader, for taking a chance on this new series. I couldn't be more grateful, and I hope you join me on the adventures to come.

THE HARBOUR LIGHTS MYSTERY
BY EMYLIA HALL

If you enjoyed *The Shell House Detectives*, why not try the second book in the series, *The Harbour Lights Mystery?* Here's an exclusive look at the first chapter

Prologue

JP can hear the sea hurling itself furiously at the harbour wall and he pulls his coat closer around him in response; it's too big for him really but it's warm, and that's what he needs on a night like this. He shivers, feeling the ice wind licking at his middle. At this hour the harbour lights are long gone, and the tourist crowds along with them. A feeble streetlight shows the glistening black water, but the noise of the sea is everywhere. There's menace in the air tonight.

There were bad tempers at the Mermaid this evening too. Behind the scenes, anyway. Orders bellowed and knives hacked and oil hitting the pan with an extra hiss. That kind of energy always gets JP's blood up just the way he likes it: if you can't handle the heat and all that.

He pops on his heels as he walks.

JP's wired, like he's always wired after service. But in a place as dead as this he'll have to make do with a drink and a smoke on the sorry excuse that passes for a balcony, the view just silhouetted wedges of rooftop, the claustrophobic cluster of this village all around him. Back in London, this was when the party was just getting started but not round here: the flat-footed waitresses plod home and fall straight into their beds; that dullard Butt trails upstairs to his disinterested wife; and Dominic was never much of a fire-starter, even in the old days.

Nah, I won't be here long. Just long enough for JP to make his mark, get people talking, then move on to better things in better places.

The car park is full of boats pulled up out of the water and he weaves between their dark hulls as beyond the harbour wall the sea rages. He stops to get out his cigarettes, fumbling in the dark. He can't remember the pocket he stuck them in at first, then he lands on them; tugs the box free.

The blow comes out of nowhere. It lands, however, quite precisely – right in the middle of the back of his head. JP staggers forward, his palms skidding on the asphalt. When he hits the ground, everything seems to stop. Only his lip twitches, and he thinks, in that moment, how even the concrete tastes salty here. Then white-hot pain consumes him.

And his lights go out.

Chapter 1

THE NEXT NIGHT

Ally closes her hands around her cup of mulled wine, feeling its warmth through her knitted gloves. She takes a sip. It tastes like Christmas.

When Gus suggested going to Mousehole to see the lights she couldn't think of a good excuse not to. She's never been one for crowds, but his face was shining like a little boy's as he said *I've heard it's about as festive as it gets* and before she knew it, a plan was made. So here she is. Leaning against the harbour railing. The sweet voices of carol singers swirling through the cold night air, while wind rips at the strings of lanterns that swing high above their heads.

'It's a bit parky, isn't it?' says Gus, and whether it's intentional, or simply the jostle of other people around them, he moves a little closer to her. Then he raises his paper cup and bumps her own.

'Cheers, Ally. This is magic.'

His eyes twinkle, and she finds herself smiling. Then she looks quickly away.

Gus often ambles over the dunes from All Swell to The Shell House, sometimes bringing a bottle, sometimes just a slice of conversation. Gus: the holidaymaker who never went home. And it always feels easy. Just two neighbours sharing an appreciation for their corner of paradise, their conversation running as surely as the tide. But they don't do outings – the odd fish and chips at the Wreckers' hardly counts – and they don't present as any sort of pair to the outside world. Because they aren't a pair. Not at all.

And now it's Christmas.

Christmas is a time for family. But Bill is gone – although that hardly seems true, when his absence is as tangible as any presence. And Evie and the children are on the other side of the world; they won't be in Porthpella until the early days of the new year – cheaper flights from Sydney, her son-in-law said. Maybe Ally's over-thinking it but organising to do something with someone at Christmas just feels different. Maybe it's because of all the stage sets of decorations and twinkling lights: hope and expectation are everywhere. And is there anything worse than false hope? Or misjudged expectations.

'Is that an enormous fish pie I can see down there?' Gus's voice is easy with laughter. 'Not a classic Christmas prop, but okay.'

The pie is mounted against the harbour wall, perhaps six feet high. Three fish heads peep from the top. It crackles with blue and yellow lights, their reflections streaming like ribbons in the water below.

Gus's jollity is, as always, infectious. Although Porthpella has changed him in that way, she's sure. When he first arrived back in the spring, Gus was a hesitant sort of man. Amiable, but you'd likely miss him in a crowd.

But then again, Ally's never cared for crowds.

'Surely, you've heard of Tom Bawcock?' she says.

'Local lad?'

'Local legend.'

And so she tells him the story of the Mousehole fisherman who, hundreds of years ago, braved winter storms to make an epic catch that saved the village from famine. How he's celebrated to this day by the making of Stargazy Pie – so-named for the fish heads peeping from the crust – and a lantern procession through the village.

'23rd December is Tom Bawcock's Eve, Gus.'

'Now why didn't that spread to Oxfordshire? I'd have got behind a festive fish pie.' He nods towards the lights. 'Especially one that size.' He counts on his fingers. 'Where are we? Today's Monday, so the 23rd is Saturday. Shall we come here again?' As Ally hesitates, he takes a draught of his drink; flicks a glance at her over the rim. 'I mean, I might come here again. You don't want to spend all your time squiring about this old emmet.'

It's been some months since Gus has referred to himself as that. *You get to be an incomer now, mate,* Jayden told him back in the summer, *but the jury's out on whether that's actually an upgrade.*

'Though of course, if you did want to come,' he says, 'it'd make it all the better.'

Before Ally can reply, the choir strikes up a new carol, *I Saw Three Ships*, and a section of the crowd joins in with gusto. Gus lends his voice too. It's deep as a well – and surprisingly in tune. Ally smiles appreciatively, and the words dance a little in her mind too, even if she doesn't sing them out loud.

I saw three ships come sailing in
On Christmas day, on Christmas day
I saw three ships come sailing in
On Christmas day in the morning
And what was in those ships all three …

As the carol ends, Gus turns to her.

'I mean it, Ally,' he says. And his expression suddenly becomes so serious that she wants to look away – at the carollers, the lights, into the bottom of her cup of mulled wine. Anywhere but back at him. The choir starts up another number, *O Little Town of Bethlehem*, and Gus lays his hand gently on her arm. 'These last few months you've become very special to …'

373

But then his words are lost in a scream. It cuts through the smooth notes of the carollers. It cuts, too, through the more distant song of the sea.

It is, Ally thinks, a scream of pitch-perfect horror, and she instinctively grabs Gus's arm as the piercing note is held. His mulled wine tips in his cup and splatters his jacket.

As a wave of panic washes over the crowd the singing scatters to a stop, only a lone voice continuing unknowingly: *the hopes and fears of all the years are met in thee tonight.*

'What on earth …' begins Gus.

Ally realises she's still holding onto his arm and she drops it quickly. There's only one thing, surely, that provokes a scream like that.

About the Author

Photo © 2022 Victoria Walker

Emylia Hall lives with her husband and son in Bristol, where she writes from a hut in the garden and dreams of the sea. *The Shell House Detectives* is her first crime novel and is inspired by her love of Cornwall's wild landscape. Emylia has published four previous novels, including Richard and Judy Book Club pick *The Book of Summers* and *The Thousand Lights Hotel*. Her work has been translated into ten languages and broadcast on BBC Radio 6 Music. She is the founder of Mothership Writers and is a writing coach at The Novelry.

You can follow Emylia on Instagram at @emyliahall_author and on Twitter at @emyliahall.

Follow the Author on Amazon

If you enjoyed this book, follow Emylia Hall on Amazon to be notified when the author releases a new book!
To do this, please follow these instructions:

Desktop:

1) Search for the author's name on Amazon or in the Amazon App.
2) Click on the author's name to arrive on their Amazon page.
3) Click the 'Follow' button.

Mobile and Tablet:

1) Search for the author's name on Amazon or in the Amazon App.
2) Click on one of the author's books.
3) Click on the author's name to arrive on their Amazon page.
4) Click the 'Follow' button.

Kindle eReader and Kindle App:

If you enjoyed this book on a Kindle eReader or in the Kindle App, you will find the author 'Follow' button after the last page.